HANDLER

HANDLER

THE MARTENSEN CHRONICLES - BOOK I

John Gerts

John Streg Publishing

Acknowledgments

Cover art: John Gerts
Contributing Editor: Steve Gerts, Margretta Dumas
Research: Steve Gerts, John Gerts
Archive Collection, Copy Editing: Marda Gerts, Steve Gerts,

Thanks to Terry Gerts, my life mentor.

Thanks to my wife, Margretta, who is my inspiration, my love, my life.

Printed in the United States of America
First Printing, 2021
ISBN 978-1-7326034-6-2
John Streg Publishing
Ludington, Michigan 4943

CONTENTS

1

NAVIGATOR

The jobs of the Worker Ants are defending the anthill, collecting the food, cleaning around or inside the anthill, making more shelter if one is ruined, and working for the queen.

1798

The first day's winds puffed the sail on the jolly boat and wisped the fog starboard off the water in front of the boy. The boy could see clouds aligned in movement with the waves beyond the bow through the break in the mist. The boy pulled the tiller and gripped the sheet tighter, pointing the sailboat to sea. The steady breeze would allow him to reach Ketelswarf in two tacks. The boy sensed the wind in the sail, recalculated, and decided three shorter tacks would be faster, adjusting his course.

The boy glanced behind, marking a bead on one of the gray barns rising over the mudflats and the warft surrounding the hamlet on Oland Island. His home in the village of his birth stood with less than a dozen houses and outbuildings anchored magically above the sea. Fifty-three years ago, the last North Sea storm surge had forced the boy's grandfather and everyone in the settlement to abandon raising sheep to build up the hallig. Oxen teams hauled marl from the flats in two stages, first to drying fields, then to ring the village. The lad's father and friends completed the terp a generation later. Born in 1782, the homes and sheds, each in turn, had been raised one meter and under-filled with packed peat, solid as a rock. Sheep and cows grazed now on the field the boy had spent five years filling and leveling.

Sixteen now, the boy's strength in hand and back rivalled any man in the Frisian Islands, and he could steer passage among the isles. The boy's father had other sons old enough to help with the sheep, so Father arranged work for the boy with the owner of the kneipe at Ketelswarf on the larger Langeness hallig. Father's cousin, landlord of Gretsen House near the Ketelswarf Shipyard, would provide boarding.

The impending challenge at Ketelswarf excited the boy. Not afraid; not fearful of anything; work, stronger men, or storms. Girls might be another story. The adventure on the far side of the next island, bay, or horizon drove the boy. There were more than fifty islands in the Frisian chain. The boy had sailed to six, enough to appreciate the North Sea expanse and the possibilities of the islands and nations beyond. The boy spoke Frisian, a Germanic language that leaned somewhat towards English. Historically, however, the islands shifted between the declared territories of rulers or kings from Germany, Denmark, and the Netherlands, widening the islanders' vocabulary. Encouraged by the boy's mother to spend the night, all who stopped by his Oland Island home ate a hearty meal and discussed their travels with the children. Mother required her eldest boy to learn at least four words from each visitor and write them down with their meaning and language origin in the family bible.

The boy came about, nudging the jolly boat with a whisper touch into the pilings. He dropped sail, secured the lines, grabbed his sack of belongings, and stepped up to the dock. The seaside entrance to Ketelswarf Shipyard and Inn straight ahead attracted visitors, but the boy proceeded to Gretsen House up the path to his right,

On previous visits to the old seafarer's house, the boy had listened to tales of sea monsters and storm disasters, like the "dead trip" in 1777. Ice locked in dozens of ships on the ocean that year, costing the lives of 300 whalers.

The sailors told legends about beautiful native women and the weather, so hot men went naked to keep from sweating to death. Stories about food and drink so foreign and sweet a man could not move after a feast for the rest of the day. Narratives about the new land and the free peoples from all over Europe that fought the British army and navy and won independence just a few years before the boy's birthday.

Brigette Gretsen answered the door and hugged the boy once inside. The boy could not determine her age; all adults seemed old. A ribbon in a knot tied back her mottled blond hair. The boy thought her pleasant looking. She wore a fresh, clean apron over a skirt frazzled along the bottom seam at the floor. They settled on stools pulled up to a wooden cooking/preparation island near the cookery fireplace. After catching up on the family, Brigette explained the rules of the house.

"We have seven beds in two rooms here, for sailors mostly. We can hold twelve guests until one ship leaves and the next docks. Ketelswarf Inn can provide ten more cots. The crews sleep like lead weights. Great to have a solid floor underneath for a change, they say. Usually, the ships will stay no more than four days, unloading or loading cargo.

"Your bed is upstairs in the barn. You'll get used to the schedule. Expect you up at daybreak feeding the stock. Muck out the stalls. Breakfast is served next for the guests, but you'll be emptying chamber pots and eating afterward. You'll be washing dishes before you start over at Ketelswarf Shipyard. Same in the evening; muck, feed, and clean. Add in sweeping out the rooms and filling basins. Stack turf bricks for the morning fires.

"On Saturday, Ketelson will send you to the mainland for supplies, and I'll also have a list. Sundays are for church after chores, and the rest of the day is yours every other week."

The boy understood. It did not sound so different from home. Brigette took the boy to the barn, and he set his sack on the bed. The mud-chinked building stank of horse shit. He would be keeping the stalls clean for sure. The straw-filled mattress on the wooden framed bed looked more inviting than his corner upstairs back home. Wool blankets high piled on the foot of the bed. Sheepherders knew how to keep warm, at least. Next to the bed, a table with a cracked porcelain pitcher and wash basin completed his new home. A chamber pot under the table would get him through the night.

"That's all. You better get over to the Shipyard. Find Joyner; he'll boss you over there. If you see Sailor, tell him to get back over here. We need to work out a tax payment."

The boy walked back to the dock and approached Ketelswarf Shipyard and Inn. Vertical, salt-etched, barn wood siding, still dark under the eave, fronted the lower part of the manor on the south end. The north section, two stories high, trimmed out in weathered clapboard, indicated the mark of quality and wealth in the islands attributed to more prosperous times a generation ago.

Entering the hall, the boy noted the relocated bar, now in a more prominent position dead center. The dock office occupied the corner to his left. A stairway and passageway to his right led to the extra sailor rooms Brigette had mentioned. Sailor Gretsen sat at a table near the bar, his oak cradle crutch leaning against his chair. Stretched out next to the crutch, Sailor's leg matched the twists and gnarls of the stick. The boy nodded to Sailor and started toward the office, knocking on the door. No answer.

"He's out at the drydock. Never mind, boy, come and say hello. Been a while, right? Hardly recognize you. Shoulders, I guess. Sit!"

The boy shook his uncle's hand but did not pull out a chair.

"I better find Joyner Ketelson. Brigette said he'd tell me where to start."

"Yes, he'll keep you hopping, boy, but you are used to putting your back to it. You'll be fine."

"I know, Uncle Sailor, I don't mind. Brigette said to tell you she needs to show you some tax figures or invoices."

"In a minute, boy."

Sailor Gretsen unrolled a set of charts on the table, weighing down a corner with his empty mug.

"These are my maps, boy. I know you are a sailor. I hear a good one. I've been thinking you'd be the one to take over my collection someday. Njord, I won't be using them."

The boy circled the table to stand behind Sailor, helping to hold down a corner. He looked up and around the hall, then down at the table again, grinning. Sailor let the top paper curl up to reveal another one below. Whereas German identifying marks and locations covered the first sheet, the lands and water on the second looked similar, but with notations, the boy could not read. Sailor stopped briefly at each chart to allow the boy to study the similarities and differences. In the fourth plan, the English described the coast of Europe and America. Based on his limited sailing in the islands, the boy knew the distances indicated could not be accurate, but the words and terms fascinated him. His mother had given him the pages from the family bible with the phrases he had learned as a child when strangers stopped by.

"Words are smart," his mother had told him, "The more you know, the more you can use them. Let me feel your muscles."

The boy would hold up both arms, curled to show his growing biceps.

"Words pile up on top of those muscles and make you stronger."

The boy stared at the maps his mother would have called a gold mine. He could not wait. He shuddered, thanking Sailer Gretsen profusely. He asked if he could study the charts some night with Sailor's help; then, he headed back outside to find Joyner Ketelson.

After Ketelswarf Inn, the deck turned at ninety degrees along a channel dug and dredged each spring to allow larger ships to approach the wharf. Oak boards driven far into the mud lined the sides of an eight-meter canal leading to the drydock. The tides affected all the Frisian Islands in the North Sea. The mudflats surrounding the Hallig Isles, including Langeness and Oland, experienced the effects of the tidal changes daily. Joyner Ketelson stood next to the pier coiling rope as the boy approached.

"Halloo, boy, I heard you would be arriving today; glad to have another set of hands here. Sailor can only do so much with that leg of his, and it gets worse every year instead of better. Did you see him yet, or speak to Brigette?"

"Yes sir, all settled in. Brigette sent me over."

"Just cleaning the docks today. Give a hand with the ropes. Then we will fix the rail over at the end of the lock. A ship just pulled out of here yesterday, and they said a 15-meter schooner would head in after them for minor repairs. We'll assess the damage, make a list of supplies, and I'll send you to the mainland on Saturday to stock up."

The two worked the rest of the afternoon and dusk at the dock. Walking back to the hall, Joyner stopped and touched the boy's shoulder.

"Your father has helped me considerably in the past. I remember when the north wing burnt down. Middle of winter too. He speaks highly of you, boy; says I might take advantage of the skills in your head. First, you must know your way around the ships we work on."

"I'm ready, Mr. Ketelson. I'm ready to help and willing."

"I see that lad, and this is the place for it. You think about catching everything you can from Sailor. He may not be as handy with a sail these days, but I expect you to know the purpose of every part on every ship that anchors here within six months. Learn from the man."

The boy took off for the Ketelswarf Inn stables without being told. Once there, Joyner's wife, Abigail, reviewed the livestock chores with the boy. He set to, and when he finished her requirements, he asked to be excused for dinner and hurried over to Gretsen House. He completed the rest of the tasks outlined by Brigette that morning well after dark. Falling into his new bed, pulling two of the wool blankets up to his chin, the boy, exhausted, slept, satisfied he had done his best.

The boy had arrived at Langeness in the middle of September. All had been prepared for winter at his father's farm on Oland Island. Now he winterized Ketelswarf Shipyard and Gretsen House. The waters rarely froze around the Halligen islands; nevertheless, the boy helped with preparations. Shipping traffic dwindled to two or three ships from

January to March, so any removable docks needed pulling from the water. Logs tied to the sides of the drydock, withdrawn during extreme temperature drops, allowed for ice expansion between the oak boards.

Winds chilled the barn to freezing. The boy covered the window next to his bed with a blanket, then moved his bed out and piled straw bales between his bed and the wall. He added the weight of two additional wool blankets to his bed. The boy worked many days on the docks stowing ropes, oars, and sails, hauling jolly boats out of the water, and leaning them against the walls of the Inn. The warmth of his bed upstairs in the barn amidst the constant whistling winds provided sanctuary and comfort to strained muscles and frostbitten hands. No trouble sleeping.

At the end of January, Joyner and the boy started fashioning the two water wheel assemblies they planned to add to the drydock in the spring. The barn below the boy's bed doubled as a stable and Joyner's woodworking shop. The woodworkers planned to form two circles of oak tied together with V-buckets ringing the interior perimeter. Twenty such water-holding wooden cups swinging on cross-piece dowels needed carving. Catch gears on one end and release levers also required engineering.

Joyner Ketelson, an expert carpenter and sander, tutored the boy in ship repair techniques and honed his carpentry skills. The aroma of the oak and pine boards ripped from logs brought over in the jolly boat from the mainland warmed the chilling wind in the barn. The sawdust from the lathe covered and insulated the floor underfoot.

The boy turned seventeen in December and reveled in newly learned tasks at the Shipyard and Inn. Joyner showed the boy each new assignment, like turning the dowels, expecting the boy to pick up the idea in one demonstration. Joyner would leave the boy to complete the twenty pieces. As the boy mastered a sequence and boredom set in, he counted how many repetitions he had to finish before a new task would be assigned, eagerly starting the learning process and practicing all over.

The boy worked with Joyner as he had with his father from age eight all those years on the farm, lifting and jacking buildings up as they built up the Oland warft. He had driven the oxen dragging marl from the mudflats. When dry, he had helped pack the blocks on top of the layers his grandfather had spread. This kept their home, fields, and sheep from being overrun by the sea. The boy had used block-and-tackle to help lift each corner of a structure in small increments until the additional meter of rise in the building had been achieved. At age eleven, he suggested the addition of more pulleys. The men employed the lifting mechanism he developed to raise the rest of the buildings on the island.

The workings of the Ketelswarf Shipyard drydock interested the boy. After the first three or four ships had been brought into the locks and dry-docked for repairs, the boy suggested the waterwheels, drawing his idea out on the boardwalk. Joyner Ketelson perceived the concept, took up the charcoal, and recommended modifications to the gears and levers on the ends of the wooden water cups.

Sporadic work on the two wheels continued until the weather turned bitter, and the mudflats surrounding Langeness and Oland islands froze, forming a walkable isthmus between the two islands. A surprise visit to Gretsen House from the Martensen family of Oland reunited the boy with his mother, father, brothers, and sisters. The families took a three-day winter break to play games, carve puzzles, and tell outrageous stories.

Sailor Gretsen and the boy spent a whole day pouring over Sailor's maps with the boy's mother. Together, they compared labels and legends in the many languages indicated on the locations of similar ocean charts. The boy showed his mother the additional phrases he had learned from mariners whose ships had docked at the shipyard. He had carefully added these new expressions to the pages he had brought from his home on Oland Island. His mother beamed proudly at his progress on "muscle" words.

Joyner Ketelson took Mr. Martensen over to the barn. The water wheels impressed the boy's father when Joyner pointed out the parts of the design he attributed to the boy. The contraptions would be installed on the drydock when the weather broke. Meanwhile, the brothers and sisters played in the loft, building make-believe little houses and barns using the boy's bed, blankets, and straw.

It troubled the boy to say goodbye when it came time for the Martensens to leave. The boy's father took Joyner Ketelson and the boy aside, indicating a need for the boy's help on the farm for three weeks in the spring. Joyner agreed, reluctant to lose his apprentice's assistance even briefly. His mother made the boy promise to keep finding papers, books, charts, and anything to keep the "word" meaning moving forward. No need. The boy thought the maps to be puzzles. At first, he could not understand most of the words or symbols, but his mind would not let go of a language block. He slowly began to pick out locations he could interpret or translate by comparing similar diagrams. One discovery led to a nearby link about another term. Deciphered through questions to Sailor or a visiting mariner, one answer would lead him to the next question.

The family turned and waved goodbye just before they started back across the isthmus. The boy's youngest sister, only four years old, ran back crying to the boy. The boy knelt, caught the little girl in his arms, and cradled her for a time. When she calmed, he gave her a tickle under her chin until she laughed. With one hand under her armpit, the boy swung her up to sit on his shoulders, holding her hands partly over his eyes, making her believe he could not see. As he returned to where the family waited, he pretended to stagger, sway, and dip with the girl. He gave his sister to his father to carry, saying goodbye. He would see her soon in the spring. The Martensens set off.

Five weeks later, a break in the weather prompted the business to pick up at Ketelswarf Shipyards and Inn. The boy, Joyner, and Sailor reversed the winter storage process, preparing the docks and setting the boats back in the water. The boy reminded Joyner Ketelson about his promise to his father to help on the farm in the spring. He asked Joyner to wait for his return to install the water wheels; he wanted to be back to assist with the project. The boy set out for Oland in a jolly boat the third week in May.

Knocking on the door of his childhood home on Oland Island served two purposes. The knock announced to the Martensens that a guest had arrived and established his older independent status. His mother threw the door open for the family to see who had landed and hugged her son, swaying and turning both into the room, not wanting to let go of her eldest. The rest of the boy's brothers and sisters crowded around, each taking a turn embracing him. His father clasped his hand. He pulled the boy close for a hug, noting the power in the lad's grip and the firmness in his chest, amazed that their frames matched. All the lad's thoughts of independence evaporated.

The family had finished supper, so the mother offered the boy bread, cheese, and goat's milk. His brothers and sisters scattered to complete evening chores. His mother took the opportunity to give her son a stern look, squeezing his shoulder as he sat at the table.

"Son, you are in good health. Your strength and your color are good. Now tell me what you have learned since our visit last fall."

"Mother, I have a job at Ketelswarf, which is my concern."

"No excuses! I know you have time to yourself on Sundays. Tell me that head of yours hasn't been drained of the smarts we worked so hard to give you, replaced with idleness and the skirts of distraction."

"Mother, Joyner has made it a priority for me to learn everything Sailor Gretsen knows about sailing, all the parts of a ship, the responsibilities of sailors, quartermasters, navigators, and shipmasters. That's my spare time right there."

"Ok, what about those maps?"

"I'm not counting the maps. They're just fun to me."

The boy jumped up and ran into the other room, grabbing a pen and ink and ripping a precious blank page from the back of the family bible. Back at the table, the boy used light strokes to create an outline on the paper.

"This is the mainland coastline from the North Frisians north to the tip of Denmark and south to Hamburg. I can draw all the islands, see? Now on these lines between them, I'll mark the distance and compass reading from point to point."

After the initial sketch, the boy filled in more detail with heavier pen pressure. He labeled the isles and the villages along the coast. He lost himself in the task, and after forty-five minutes, he looked up at his mother in frustration, shaking his head.

"This last part is wrong. I'm still working on the area north of Aalborg. But the scale and the rest of it south is close."

The boy's mother sat at the table and took her son's hand, bringing it to her cheek, trying to absorb and reflect her feelings for such a one.

"You did that from memorizing a map? I think even I could find my way using this page."

"It's not hard, Mother; anyone could do it. I'm working on the English chart of the American coast. With help from the mariners that visit this summer, I should be able to translate the rest of the words I can't sound out now."

The boy's mother knew the exceptional nature of the page lying on the table, but she merely patted her son on the shoulder.

"So, do you think you want to be a sailor?"

"Not really, Mother, but I like working with those maps of Sailor Gretsen.

"I guess I want to see these places. I want to compare each place to what I imagine from studying the charts. I want to see what's out there. What's around the bend. The ocean, the water? It's like blank space between the lands I want to see."

Father and the rest of the family returned from the barn chores and readied for bed. The boy and mother headed for bed, and his father indicated that shearing would begin early in the morning.

Few families lived on the Oland Warften; most relatives of the boy bore the surname Martensen. All the islanders shared the tasks of wool production this time of year. The flocks of sheep had been herded into the corral the previous night and left unfed with no water. Early the following day, each ram and ewe, expecting to be fed, trotted to a shearing stand, one of ten at the end of the enclosure. Stations manned by two men or boys used shears to remove the fleece. First, the shearers clipped the tag from the back legs and butt and threw it into a separate pile, too dirty to attempt cleaning. Then they gathered and moved the fleece, shorn in one piece from neck to rump to the scouring troughs.

Constant turf fires burned underneath the scrubbing tub. A sluice transferred water to the washing trough, and workers stirred, sloshed, and kneaded the grease and shit out. The first of many cleaning rinses.

The boy worked this year with his younger brother Samuel, the fourth son born into the Martensen family. Samuel sheared every other sheep, alternating with the boy, learning the fine art of one-piece shearing. His younger brother impressed the boy. With a nod to Samuel and the boys on either side, the two brothers worked more rapidly to determine the fastest, most accurate shearer. One after another, the stations in the line joined in their neighboring station's increased frenzy. After each completed skinning, a toe mark in the dirt kept track. At the end of the day, jostling and attempts to erase a neighbor's marks made for good-natured arguing and laughing. It really did not matter; the effort exhausted the crew. The boy and Samuel never even declared themselves winners. Camaraderie exemplified the nature of the families of Oland Island.

Everyone in the community participated in the massive task of wool production. Even six-year-old youngsters received assigned tasks. They carried fleece from station to station, spreading rows of washed shearings to dry in the spring breeze and shade of the barns. Older children threw turf on the washing trough fire to keep the wash water at a proper temperature.

In two more days, pelts were divided into three piles; one to be bundled, one for spinning, and one heap for felting. The bundled fleeces served as the community bank to be further processed when needed at a future time. Men and women spread fleece for felting on slotted tables with water troughs steaming underneath from small turf fires. They beat the wool, then laid a second layer over the first at right angles, melding one layer to another. The combination remained weighted with heavy flat boards and stones, adding pressure to the newly formed felt.

Spinners worked on the third pile producing yarn of varying weight and thickness. The community also trained younger spinners. Spinning, regarded as a notable talent, generated hope among the young girls that might excel at the skill.

Seven days of sunup-to-sundown work completed the process. A day set aside for the *Festival of Wool* marked a raucous feast with fiddle dancing, drink, and food for all.

The next day the more muscular boys and men of the warften gathered, leading harnessed oxen pulled carts full of tools, marching out to the salt flats to collect turf blocks. The low tide exposed the mud to rise in the land where grasses could grow in saltwater. Further inland, the grassy marshes contained millions of years of grass growing/dying cycles, and the marl thus formed into the bricks used by the families for their cooking and dwelling fires. Only three standing trees remained on the entire Oland warften. No one touched them. To build the houses and barns on the warften, the islanders had hauled all the material from forests fifteen miles inland. Wood became as precious as gold here, but the salt flats produced abundant grass to feed the sheep. The marl could fuel the island for another million years.

The workers stepped on turf cutters, spades with two blades set at right angles, to cut a brick pattern in the marl. Another worker wedged an iron, a heart-shaped flat blade angled to the handle of a spade, to lift the block into the cart. Neatly stacked blocks hauled back to the drying barn remained for a year to dry. A second barn contained bricks from the previous year, all dried, dispersible as necessary to the Martensen families. Neighboring warftens and mainland communities exchanged goods and services for the slabs.

After seven days, the turf barn brimmed with turf blocks. Time for another community meal, complete with games for the toddlers, contests for the older children, and a tug of war across the muddy marl pit for the men.

The boy slipped back into the Oland routine, family, and the festivals on the island. In the back of his mind, however, he worried about his water wheel design; would it work? Would it help ease the workings of the drydock? He had responsibilities back at Ketelswarf Shipyard and Gretsen House. Considered a hired workman at Ketelswarf and not just one of the family doing his chores, he longed to return. His father had other plans.

The oldest barn needed shingle repairs, a two-man operation. The boy's father required his firstborn for this task, and the boy could see the importance of getting the two-story shed in shape. The boy awoke ready to work at dawn each day. They used a ladder to lay a second ladder up on the roof, attaching it temporarily. Father and son propped up another ladder on the other side of the ridge and encircled the two ladders at the peak with rope, binding them together. Now the two ladders could be moved laterally, providing footholds for the two workers as they repaired, replaced, or re-nailed shingles along the way. At the end of each day, the boy reminded his father he needed to get back to Ketelswarf Shipyard. Five days later, the father/son team completed the re-shingling.

"I hate to say it, son, but you must return. I thank you for your help these past three weeks."

"Glad you still need me sometimes, although, by the appearance of Jacob and Samuel, you won't need to call on me by next year. Samuel is already a better shearer than me, and Jacob's grown three centimeters since I arrived."

"I know, son. To tell the truth, I just needed one last moment with you. I am proud of you, boy. Always have been. I watch you work, doing the best you can. I will miss you, but I know you will be fine wherever you go, whatever you decide to do."

With that, the boy packed. He said goodbye to the family. His crying mother had replaced a framed picture in the living room with his map drawing. He pushed off in the jolly boat and headed for the mainland. He needed to gather some essential pieces of wood to finish the attachment of the water wheels to the drydock. He slept on the boat's bottom boards that night and the next. During the day, the boy trekked sixteen miles into the woods, felling small oak trees he could drag back to the shore. He spent a third day making three trips back and forth to the forest, hauling the logs he had cut before setting off for Langene Island.

Upon docking the jolly boat at the Ketelswarf Shipyard, the boy spent an hour unloading the logs he had brought and hauling them to the barn's woodshop. He strolled out to the drydock. The wheels lay on the deck near where they intended to be installed, but the installation had not begun. He decided to hunt down Joyner Ketelson.

Walking into the Ketelswarf Shipyard hall, a girl standing behind the bar holding a rag and wiping the surface looked up and smiled at him.

"What'll it be, sailor?"

The boy had never seen this girl or any girl in the bar except for Joyner's wife and Brigette Gretsen. From the doorway, she looked to have streaming brown hair and a white-as-snow smile. Joyner emerged from his office, noticing the boy staring, mouth open.

"Oh, that's Adela, daughter of a friend of mine over on Amrum. Worked as a barmaid the last two summers during our busy time. You must have met her on your visit a few years ago."

"If I did, I don't remember."

"She has grown some, a bit older than you. I think maybe by a year. Pretty smile, do you think?"

"Yes."

The boy walked over to the bar. The girl plunked down a pint of beer without waiting for the boy's reply.

"Are you the boy Joyner talks about? Invented those wheels out by the dock? The drydock is amazing, and your idea may make things even easier."

"We hope so."

"How did you come up with that design?"

"I, uh, drew it on the dock with chalk."

"Visited your family over on Oland Island, did ya? How they doin'. Haven't seen your people in a couple of years."

"Didn't recognize you when you walked in until you started talkin to Joyner. Then it came back to me who you must be. You must be a head taller than me now."

She grabbed the boy by the top of his arm.

"Got some beef on you too."

Adela kept talking as she moved down to the other end of the bar to refill the stein of another sailor. The boy did not hear most of what the girl rattled on about. Up close, he wondered in the blueness of her eyes, like the ocean calmed out at the horizon. Midnight navy: a considerable contrast to her snow-white smile, broad creases gracing the corners of her mouth. She wore a blue and white cotton scarf knotted at her throat. The boy concentrated on his beer, looking up occasionally, concentrating on eye contact but aware of her shoulder-to-shoulder ivory skin reaching down into the shadowed valley in her bodice. The boy had difficulty staying with Adela's ramblings, favoring a nod or a head shake when appropriate.

He finished his beer, trying to think of something to say in taking his leave, when a sailor approached Adela behind the bar, wrapping an arm around her, his hand resting on a portion of her bare shoulder. She shrugged him away. The man grabbed her again, shaking her a bit as he laughed near her ear. The boy objected.

"Let her go! Do not bother this lady. I'm sure she'll get you another beer in good time."

The mariner looked across the counter at the boy. The narrowed eyes and the ensuing frown and turned lip indicated trouble to the boy. The man rushed around the end of the bar to stand close to the boy, starting to say something. The boy did not wait, changing his stance, so his left foot inched behind the man's right foot. The boy swung his leg forward, catching the man's right calf with great force, enough to upend the man. The seafarer landed on his back, exhaling a woof of air.

The boy also dropped to the floor, his legs pinning the man's right arm, his hand holding the man's left wrist, and the boy's chest pinning the seaman. The man kept shaking his head; the wind knocked out of him. The sound of chairs scraping back from tables near the bar indicated others may now be siding with their boatmate.

Fingers jerked his shirt at the back of his neck. Twisting and choking, the boy turned to see that Adela had him by the scruff.

"That's my brother. He teases me all the time. Let him up."

The boy scrambled to attention in front of Adela. She still had a hold of his collar. Her heat in the closeness drove everything else out of his thoughts; he had no words. He grasped her forearm and persuaded her to let him go. She did. The boy gaped at her.

"Sorry!"

The boy turned and leaned down, offering to help the man stand.

"Pardon me, sir, I, I didn't know."

He turned, walked to the shipyard office, knocked, and entered. Joyner stood at the window, shaking his head.

"Yes, I saw the whole thing from the window."

"My brain melted. Embarrassing. Am I fired now? I don't know what happened out there."

"I do! Please do not make a habit of it. We will start tomorrow installing the water wheels. Werner is OK and protective of his sister. Do not blame him."

"I am sorry."

The boy did not promise that it would not happen again. A strange feeling suggested to the boy that he would not let anyone except himself tease that beautiful girl or hold her slim shoulders.

As soon as the boy had closed the door, leaving the office, Joyner smiled, rubbing his chin. He had witnessed the boy take on a man eight years the boy's elder, twenty pounds heavier, and half a head taller. He had laid him out in a blink. The boy demonstrated growth in all sorts of ways, perhaps outgrowing Ketelswarf. Joyner's smile shifted to a frown.

The boy stayed away from the Shipyard and Inn for the rest of the day. Instead, he caught up on chores at Gretsen House. He gave all the stalls a thorough mucking. He swept out the bedrooms, mopped the floor, re-piled turf bricks near the fires, filled the washbasins, and fed the livestock. He groomed the horses, checked his bed, added straw, repositioned the bales away from the bed, and removed the blanket hanging over the slits in the walls. Summer would arrive in a hurry, and he would relish any breeze through the barn.

At dinner, Sailor did not mention the incident at the bar. Brigette dominated the discussion with questions and comments about the news from Oland Island.

The boy arose well before daybreak to handle the morning chores at Gretsen House and Ketelswarf Inn. He then went to the woodworking shop where he had dropped off the logs he had brought from the mainland. He used a small hatchet to strip the bark. He separated each wood block into four lengthwise sections with a mallet and wedge. Then he planed the sections to flatness and size. At day's end, he piled the planks in the drying section of the workshop with stickers between levels. This provided adequate airflow around the boards, just as Joyner instructed. Now the boy could begin the yoke and mounting braces for the water wheels using lumber prepared nine months ago. Another of Joyner's rules. The amount of wood needed for a project must always first be replaced by an equal quantity from the mainland stacked to dry for the future.

The boy heard a swish of skirts at the barn door as he stacked wood. Assuming Brigette came to call him in for evening chores, he continued stacking his fresh-cut lumber. When he looked up, he saw Adela silhouetted in the setting sun.

"Ummm, the aroma of lumber shavings. Heavenly."

The boy, suddenly guarded, caught up a broom to sweep sawdust. Adela grabbed a second broom and joined in the shop clean-up. The boy relaxed.

"Thanks- for the help."

"So, what is next? When will you install your water wheels?"

"It may be three or four days. I will start on yokes and brackets to hold the wheels tomorrow. I'll use wood from this pile that's already dry. Here are the sketches of what they will look like."

"I see. Maybe I will stop by to see the progress."

"I enjoy your company Adela; I better get up to the house and back to work."

They left the shop, taking different paths. The boy could not tell if Adela was bored with his description and efforts or genuinely interested, probably fed up. Perhaps he should have walked her home. The boy booted a stone ahead of him; kicked it again harder, his mouth tightening. He did not know what to do.

At the table that night, Brigette said she saw the boy and someone else on the path from the barn.

The boy explained.

"That's Adela; she helped me clean up the shop."

Sailor Gretsen seized the opportunity he had hoped for to relate the incident in the bar with Adela's brother. Brigette kept her eyes on both until the end of the story. The boy spooned parsnips from his bowl and reached for more, avoiding Brigette's glance.

"Adela is two years older than you, my boy. She is a good worker. I know that girl. See that she doesn't interrupt your work."

"Ok, Brigette, but I don't believe she will be back. She was curious about the water wheels."

"I'm not so sure you'd be right about that."

Brigette turned to her husband and winked. Sailor laughed.

For four days, the boy spent every moment between chores working on the shaping and sanding of the yokes and brackets. He turned wooden dowels to fasten the collars and bracket pieces together. Joyner checked on his progress, showing the boy a technique for ensuring the proper connection using the table and vises. The boy dismantled the links, relocated a hole, and turned a new peg larger than his first attempt for a better fit.

Sure enough, Adela did return each day, noting the headway and sometimes assisting with a lift when the boy requested. After Joyner left the shop a second time, the boy asked Adela to hold the template on the last yoke while he scribed the outline on the board. Their hands became entangled at close range, and Adela started giggling.

The boy reminded the girl of the importance of the template remaining stationary. Still entwined, Adela ceased laughing and concentrated on holding the template still. The boy continued scribing but looked up for just a second, so near Adela, he kept his breath, leaned in a few more centimeters, and softly kissed Adela's neck.

Adela, struggling to keep both hands on the template, looked at the boy ardently and kissed him. The boy swept the template aside and pulled Adela around, and to him, an embrace so warm and wonderful the boy thought his heart might stop. He held her tightly but kissed her gently, not wanting to hurt her with his strength. His cheeks reddened, and he wished he had taken a breath to start, so damn clumsy and new to the experience.

Adela stepped back, smiling as she did the first time the boy had seen her in the Ketelswarf Shipyard hall.

"Maybe we should finish tracing the template."

The boy, nearly in a dream, kept staring at Adela.

"Yes."

The darkening sky approached, and they worked rapidly together to complete the scribe and clean up the shop. The boy anticipated the next time he would brave an embrace. Adela thought further into the future, pleased with the boy's gentle strength and the talents and directness he continually displayed.

Sailor and the boy carried the water wheel yokes and brackets to the drydock. They leaned against a bollard while Joyner reviewed the challenges the drydock posed to the operation of the shipyard.

The drydock involved two side walls spaced ten meters apart. Each consisted of thick oak boards driven far into the mud and reinforced with decking and outrigger posts hammered into the ground. The end wall of similar construction connected the two sides.

After settling fees for dry docking, room, and board for a crew in the Inn, hull repair, and cleaning, all cargo is hauled dockside, and any ballast that can be removed.

The vessel to be repaired is pulled forward at high tide until the bow nears the end wall. As the tide goes out, the ship lowers and rests on yokes five meters apart, stretching between the side walls.

At low tide, four posts are inserted into wells on the floor of the drydock in pairs. Each pair is separated so thick boards can be dropped horizontally into the side wall slots, and the tight space between the post sets forms the fourth wall of the drydock. Slotted horizontal planks continue to be inserted beyond the water level at high tide.

When the high tide returns, the ship is solidly stationary in the drydock, resting on the yokes. A maximum amount of the hull is exposed to dry out for repairs and to be cleaned of barnacles. Because these end boards are fashioned with a tongue and groove profile, they can withstand high tide pressure. The drydock can handle a vessel twenty-five meters long from bow to stern with up to an eight-meter beam.

All wooden ships seep water to some degree. The oak cross pieces making up the end wall of the drydock leaked, to be sure. Up to fifty percent of repair or cleaning time is spent bailing water.

That was the state of the Ketelswarf Shipyard drydock when the boy arrived the previous year. The boy had helped his father devise complicated pulley systems, scaffolding, and oxen-driven lever assists to help raise the buildings on Oland Island. Bucketing out drydock water had given the boy plenty of time to work out the water wheels in his head. The Ketelswarf Shipyard and Joyner Ketelson's reputation for hull repair had brought profit and commerce to the Hallig Islands. If the water wheels worked as the boy envisioned, Joyner stood to increase profits from their efficiency.

So, on the far side wall, Joyner directed Sailor and the boy to build a niche for one of the water wheels while Joyner started on the second niche on the opposite side of the drydock. At low tide, both teams cut into and then reinforced a portion of the side walls where the slot would be built. Then they began digging a one-meter by one-meter cutout, reaching the floor more than two meters down.

Eight aligned oak boards needed driving down vertically two meters into the mud and marl of the warft. A temporary iron cap set over a plank at the top permitted the pounding of the pylon into the sludge blow by blow with a heavy sledgehammer.

The boy caught Adela watching him from the corner of one of the sheds during her break. The hammer rang out against the metal, and after twenty blows, Sailor would trade-off, and the boy would go over to the other niche to spell Joyner. The boy dripped sweat, exhausted, remembered Adela, too embarrassed to go near her. By the end of the day, the boy could not tolerate his stink. He removed his shoes and jumped into the horse trough, washing his clothes while he bathed and then air drying as he finished his other Ketelswarf and Gretsen House chores.

With the niche walls driven and connected, the trio rebuilt the walkway dock skirting the niche and further staked it for added stability. Next, they put down an oak floor in the cavity to provide an immovable base to which the water wheel yoke could be rigidly attached.

Another two weeks of back strengthening work completed the preliminaries of both niches; ready now to install the water wheels.

That Sunday afternoon, on the boy's half day off, he pulled Sailor's roll of maps out and studied the map of the American coast on his bed up in the barn. The boy fell asleep in minutes, the chart forming a cover across his chest. Sometime later, in the fading light of the day, the brush of Adela's lips on his and her irresistible scent drifted into his unconscious. He attempted to sit up, but his aching shoulders, wrists, hands, and back resisted, and he voiced a groan instead of a hello.

Adela pushed him back down, kissed him again, and massaged the boy's arms. She used her thumbs and the heels of her hands to press on the boy with all her strength, but she could not dent the tight skin across his arm and shoulder muscles. In minutes, the boy relaxed and fell asleep again. Adela found room on the bed next to the boy and hugged him as he slept. The boy awoke in the pitch dark, the lass gone. Now rested, the boy shook his head at yet another missed opportunity to further his relationship with a woman. He slammed a fist on his thigh and again assumed she would be done with his inattention and ineptitude.

At low tide, Monday, Sailor, Joyner, and the boy fastened the water wheel yokes to the niche floors using the boy's brackets. The water wheels were installed and pinned into the axles. After months of planning and carpentry work, preparation of the drydock, and installation of the water wheels, the time had arrived to test the devices. On the next ebb tide, Sailor and the boy dropped plank after plank of the fourth wall into place. Then, as the leaking water began to fill the blockaded canal, the boy turned the crank of one of the water wheels.

The catches on the sides of the twenty buckets around the wheel's perimeter locked. Each cup dipped into the water at the bottom of the turn, scooping and carrying the water until it reached the top position. The catch tripped when a bucket hit its apex. The hatch dropped, releasing the captured water into the escape gutter that runs back along the deck, spilling into the sea beyond the drydock. Next, a gear engaged, swinging the end of the cup back to a closed position. A device released the bucket to hang free, creating less drag as the cup descended into the water.

But the trip latch at the top did not engage soon enough. Emptying the sluice trough missed the escape trough, dumping most of the water back into the drydock instead of the bypass chute. The diverting channels inhabited the optimum and only possible position in the niches. That meant the gears would have to be changed. The levers locking the troughs on the upward path and unlocking them after the water dumped worked as the boy had imagined. The boy found it difficult to turn the crank due to the heavy drag imposed by the rising water. He could rotate the handle all the way around but did not know how long he could keep it going.

Sailor and Joyner had a turn at the wheel. Joyner wheezed as he struggled. The boy let them catch their breath.

"I thought about what we need next, Joyner."

"Well, boy, what is the answer."

"We build a bigger gear to attach the crank to the axle. A set of gears and a slip engagement will allow the wheel to turn at various speeds depending on the strength of the person manning the wheel."

"Are you sure? Can you build it?"

"With your help on the carving, yes. And, of course, we need to adjust the position and size of the sluice trip lever."

After marking the wheels for the new placement of the top gears, they dismantled them and rolled them back to the workshop.

The boy worked on forming the new pieces and pins for both water wheels for another week before gathering all the new parts in the wheelbarrow. He spun each water wheel to its position and called on Joyner and Sailor to assist in the final assembly.

At the end of the day, the improved drydock and water wheels required testing. As the tide rose, the boy turned the crank of a water wheel, observing the sluice gates. Each hatch opened via the top gear precisely to spill the captured water into the escape trough to flow back into the sea outside the drydock. Joyner jumped from the deck and began working the handle on the second water wheel. Using the new lever, he could mesh into the primary gear as his turning gathered momentum. The larger cog eased the number of turns the operator needed for the wheel to complete a revolution, reducing the energy the water relief worker expended. Joyner and the boy could bring the water level in the drydock down half a meter with both water wheels operational in ten minutes. They could then rest for twenty before they found it necessary to operate the water wheel pumps again.

Before the water wheel installation, bailing required four men bucketing out the rising water continuously. Backbreaking work for grumbling sailors from the ships being repaired.

Joyner called everyone from the Ketelswarf Inn and Gretsen House to inaugurate the new engineering marvel of the water wheels. The crowd sat on the edge of the drydock as the boy, Sailor, and Joyner demonstrated their invention. Many men and even Brigette and Adela took turns at the crank, observing how the gear changes eased the effort to turn the apparatus and lift the water. Joyner wished to celebrate.

"Hear, hear, back to the bar; the first stein is on me."

Everyone jumped up and headed for Ketelswarf Inn except for the boy responsible for the invention. He again examined the parts, gears, and levers of both wheels. Standing back with arms crossed, he nodded his satisfaction with the world. From idea through construction to the installation; the hours of hauling felled trees, fashioning raw lumber; days of rework, adjustment, carving, and learning new techniques and skills; here it was, completed, and it worked. The boy smiled; his feelings and mood could not be topped in this world; until Adela's arms encircled him from behind, pressing against him, fitting her curves to his. The boy turned, embraced Adela, and kissed her long and sweet. Arm around her waist, they walked back to Ketelswarf Inn and entered the bar. The crowd stood.

"Three cheers for the boy! Hurrah! Hurrah! Hurrah!"

Many handshakes and back-slaps later, the boy sat with Joyner, Sailor, Brigette, and Adela. Over her second beer, Brigitte teased.

"Careful there, boy. I don't want you drunk during evening chores, sloshing pisspots down the halls."

Adela flared, "Perhaps he should be done with chamber pots. I would have thought a raise would be in order. The boy has a future to consider."

Brigette tensed. Sailor, who sat next to Adela, covered Brigette's hand with his own and looked hard at his wife. With eyes locked on Adela, the boy missed Brigette's exchange with Sailor.

The boy apologized to the table; smiled at Adela.

"Chores are chores Adela; I haven't minded chores since I was six.

Joyner, now that we know the wheels will work, I'm sure we can make an improvement that wouldn't take too much more time."

Joyner perked up.

"Oh? I am listening!"

"In looking at the layout of the niches we built, I believe we have room for windmills. At first, I thought about a single mill and a shaft connecting both waterwheels at the bottom of the drydock. I rejected that idea. The torque on the shaft across the canal may be too much for even a three-meter windmill. No, two smaller ones are the way we should go. If we..."

"By Njord, that would make a natural unmanned machine out of the whole gizmo. With the wind we get on the warft here, I doubt we'd ever have to jump down and crank. Boy, you keep coming up with ideas like that, and we will see about that raise."

Later that night, after the boy had retired to his bed in the barn, Sailor filled his pipe, lit, puffed, and sat near the cooking fire, pulling Brigette down on a second chair next to him.

"Ok, Brigette, stop stewing. Without a word, you've been rattling pots and pushing dirt and dust all evening."

"That girl has grappling hooks into my nephew, and we should have seen it coming."

"What's wrong with Adela and the boy planning a future."

"You know, from the last two summers she worked here, she trades men like marbles. Every one of them is shinier than the last one. And the boy is the best catch of them all."

"Between you, the boy's mother, and Adela, you plan the boy's life. What about letting him live a bit, find his own way."

"He's a boy, my dear. Look at him, a boy in a man's body. I want him to grow more, is all, and his mother hasn't pushed his mind over his muscle to settle as a sheep shearer on Oland island, that's for sure."

"Being a man that has never understood the schemes of your side of the species, I can't imagine how we're going to help the boy more than we have already. He'll make the same mistakes I, Joyner, and the boy's father made. It is the nature of our side of the species."

"Your maps are the key. The boy reads them as well as you do."

"Yes, he can rig and navigate and ship build too."

"He's smart about things, yes, but can he put them into practice?"

"When the time comes, he'll do fine."

"I'm going to discuss this with Joyner. The time is now!"

A week later, the boy knocked on the door to Joyner's office, entered, and sat across from his desk. He did not lean back or let his sweat-soaked shirt touch any blue velour cloth covering the chair's back, seat, and arms. The boy waited until Joyner looked up from his paperwork.

"What's next, Joyner? I finished reinforcing the shed wall. It should be fine for another thirty years."

"Boy, I have been trying to catch you all week. We both have been busy. Tomorrow, Saturday, instead of your usual run to the mainland for supplies, I have a more extended trip that I need you to undertake.

"I want you to sail up to Christiania, Norway, through the northern islands. I have been waiting a year for a ship to come through from there to bring me the dresser I bought for Abigail in England a long time back. Seems like forever ago. A cargo vessel carried it as far as Norway, but a freighter transfer mix-up left it stranded. They sent word down to me but could not be bothered with the dresser, for Njord's sake, and it's been stuck there ever since.

"I would like you to take the larger jolly boat and sail up through the islands and into the Oslofjorden to Christiania and bring back that dresser."

The boy, stunned, leaned back in the chair, forgetting his sweat. He brought up the map of the west coast in his head. Christiania, noted as Oslo in parenthesis on Sailor's chart, was over eight hundred kilometers north of Ketelswarf. The boy could not stay in his seat.

"Joyner, that trip will take six days one way with a decent wind."

"I am planning on two weeks or more. You can put into towns along the coast at night, but you will cross that stretch of the open sea. I want you to take Sailor for that reason. Keep him out of the bars. Learn as much as you can. I want you in charge as my representative. Take the rest of today to provision the boat. Ensure you take plenty of water just in case you are blown off course."

The sweat had gone cold on his skin against his shirt in the excitement of the trip. The boy's teeth chattered as he closed the door outside the office.

He could not wait to tell Adela. Sailor and Brigette needed to be informed as well. He remembered he had asked Adela to the first harvest festival scheduled the following Friday. Their first dance would have to be postponed yet again.

Sailor expressed no surprise over the trip. The two moved water jugs, food, bandages and emergency supplies, lanterns, plenty of kerosene, and even an extra sail into the jolly boat. Then they both went to Gretsen House to tell Brigette and collect a sack of clothes and blankets from the barn. She became as excited as the boy about the trip. She surreptitiously gave the boy money.

"The coin is for emergencies, but if you see an ivory pin in the shops in Christiania, try to buy it without Sailor seeing it and a pipe for Sailor befitting the look of his cane."

Brigette pawed through his sack when Sailor carried it back into the room.

"Isn't this a great opportunity for the boy?"

She winked at Sailor.

"Go back up and get your good wool sweater. Try and look as handsome as the boy here when you're walking the streets of Christiania."

The boy tried to keep his excitement tamped down.

"I know Joyner said I'm in charge, Sailor, but I never sailed more than thirty kilometers in the islands around Oland before."

Sailor stopped, turning back to the boy.

"Now's your chance, boy. I'll stay out of your way. This leg of mine has made me a landlubber. I'm just glad I get to come along. It'll feel good to get my nose full of the sea again."

The boy returned upstairs, took half his saved money, and laid it on the bed. Then he put half of that money in a small leather sack and the other half in a pocket in his pants. He ran to the Jolly boat and placed the money and his clothes bag in the stern hatch. Ready. He double-checked his provisions and then went over to Ketelswarf Inn. He reviewed the preparations he and Sailor had accomplished for the journey with Joyner. He asked Joyner for paperwork describing the dresser and a release letter for the warehouse personnel. He shook Joyner's hand and told him he and Sailor would be gone by first light in the morning.

Outside the office, the boy sauntered to the bar, where Adela washed dishes. He picked up a towel and helped dry the glasses.

"Adela, you will never believe where I'm off tomorrow."

"The mainland for wood for your windmills."

"No, I'm going much, much further. I'm sailing with Sailor to Christiania. I can hardly imagine it myself."

"What? Are you leaving me? Us?"

The boy noted tears welling and reached across the bar, grabbing Adela's upper arms and then lifting her chin.

"I'm not leaving, not for good. I'm going on a trip. I'll be gone for two weeks at the most. Maybe only ten days. I'll be back. I'm just picking up a piece of furniture for Joyner."

"But why now. Couldn't you wait until after the festival? I'm sewing a new dress to wear. Is it dangerous? What if a storm comes up? Sailor will be no help at all with his bad leg. I'm worried. That's a long way away if a problem should occur. Something could go wrong!"

"No, Adela, this is part of my job. I must go. But I will be back. You know I'm a good sailor. I'll be back before you know it."

"I have no idea if you are a good sailor. I've never been out in a boat with you. I'm worried and won't stop until you stand before me with your arms around me."

"Yes, Adela, I feel the same way, but I'll be back and thinking about getting back to you every moment."

He leaned forward across the bar and kissed Adela for all the patrons to see. Then he turned and walked away, returning to Gretsen House before his legs deserted him, and he crawled back to Joyner to tell him he could not go. He could not leave his sweet girl, Adela. In bed, he tossed and turned and did not sleep. Hour after hour, he thought about Adela and the trip. Maybe he should take Adela with him. If he did, perhaps they would not come back. Would she go with him? Leave her family? Could he leave Joyner, Brigette, Sailor, and his family? Yes, he knew he could if he had to. He could do it. But should he. Should he ask her?

In the middle of the night, he dressed and went to the jolly boat to recheck the supplies. He laid two blankets down and covered himself with a third to await the morning. In the gentle breeze and rocking, the boy drifted off to sleep.

The boy awoke, Sailor's hand on his shoulder.

"Ready to go, are you? Shake off the dew while I get the mooring lines, and we'll be off."

Dawn still had not reached the horizon. The boy mechanically shook out the blankets, folded them, and put them back under the forward hatch. The bow and stern lines stowed; Sailor pushed off with his good leg while he teetered on his lousy one.

Day one:

By three o'clock, the jolly boat had reached the last point of reference for the boy in his travels around Oland Island. They sailed adjacent to the island Fohr on the port side and far away to starboard the mainland meandered north and south. Fohr appeared many times larger than either Langeness or Oland. The boy's family had visited the town of Wyk on Fohr Island twice. He recalled trying to count the number of buildings and houses, losing track due to the distraction of horses, wagons, and people that kept grabbing his attention as they wandered the streets.

The boy studied the map he knew so well. Sylt, the next island, lies a little more to port than Fohr and miles ahead. In fact, the boy detected Sylt Island already because of the island's shape. He could see land wherever he looked. Yet he knew from the chart the form of the isle Sylt.

The boy concluded that the mainland was located to starboard; he would run into land whichever way he directed the jolly boat. He reckoned when he came to land, the sailors could run eastward along the coast until he reached open water between the island and the mainland. Then the boy worried that if he, in fact, came to the land comprising the landmass, they would need to turn westward and run up the coast until he found the opening between the mainland and Syk Island.

Time would be wasted if he made the wrong decision based on whether he had come upon the island coast or the mainland when he came to land on the other side of the bay. The boy decided to overcompensate and directed the jolly boat further to port to ensure he would meet Sylt Island.

Sailor, observing the boy, posed a question.

"Where are you going?"

The boy explained his logic to Sailor, who relaxed near the mast, laying back and resting his head on his hands, forming a pillow behind his head. In a few minutes, he sat up again, pulled his pipe from his breast pocket, stuffed it, and lit the tobacco, puffing.

"Look at the tree line over to your right, boy. See how high it is? But it slopes off as it nears the coast. That's natural. Now look left and tell me what you see."

"Well, it's not as lofty as it is to the right."

"Exactly. It is not as sizable a land area. Doesn't have time to get tall. That's the island. But it does dip down ahead of us. And the land to the right dips down as well out there. Sailing near shore is a matter of reading the land. Get to know how land dives into the sea. Look for the 'V' where two land areas come together. Maybe give that 'V' a nod and point us there. See if I'm right."

The boy took the advice to heart, relieved that Sailor was aboard and willing to teach rather than direct or take over. He wanted this to be his trip, but staring at never experienced open sea made him realize he still had much to learn. By dusk, they had reached the opening between the island and the mainland without a detour. They decided to spend the night in the boat. A gentle breeze vanquished the flies and mosquitoes, and sleep came again.

Day two:

In the morning, they ate hardtack and cheese. The boy stretched his legs by running up and down the beach. Sailor relaxed with his pipe and smoked. The map laid out between them; the boy indicated it would be wonderful if they could make Esbjerg on the mainland coast. Surely there would be an inn, a bed, and a warm meal.

The boy practiced reading the islands as they pushed on. Romo Island was next. Larger than Sylt, the boy could read the slope of the island and the relationship to the mainland. He close hauled back and forth, keeping the convergence of the land masses as his goal. A new wrinkle came into play as well. The map showed that the mainland bent around behind Roma Island, so the boy had to carefully note the distant mainland landmass behind the island. Island by island, the boy gained confidence. Sailor and the boy blew past Roma Island and approached Mande Island, a small island but nevertheless double the size of Oland Island.

Sailor mostly smoked his pipe and stayed away from the mainsail while the boy steered, referenced the map, and hauled the sail tight on each tack. As they neared Mande Island, Sailor sat up, peering far ahead toward the island. The boy became alert but saw nothing of note on the island.

Sailor gave the boy a second chance.

"What do you see out there? My eyes aren't what they used to be."

"I see trees and a beach. Doesn't look like much else. No buildings."

"No, to the right of the island. I think I see a bubble out from the shore and maybe a bird or two circling in that area."

"Alright, I see the birds."

"Does your chart have any notes about that spot between Mande Island and the mainland?"

"No."

"Just the same; let's pull the sail when we get up close and slow it through that straight."

As they approached, Sailor's fidgeting increased. The bubbling of the sea one hundred meters out from the island with birds flying overhead caught the boy's attention, and just now, a bird landed on the rock or boulder, peeking out of the water.

"You can bet that rock is just the tip of the iceberg, as they say. Sail close to that spot or between that outcropping and the island, and you'd be sure to rip the boat bottom and end our trip. Now we need to see if we can get through on the right of that rock or if we must head back to the left of Mande Island instead."

"But there is nothing on the map. No shallows indicated."

"Hey, this is your trip, boy; try it if you trust your map. I prefer to think of charts and maps as a starting point. Just as you must read the land to sail, you also must watch the sea, the birds, and the fish. Take note of the whales and the porpoises. Stay alive, boy, by considering every clue you can sense. I suspect you'll be correcting and drawing your own maps someday."

"Sailor, I'm learning. I'll pay attention, I promise. Any other lessons tucked away behind that pipe; I'll listen."

At sunset, the boy docked the jolly boat at the Esbjerg pier. Two bricked streets ran north and south across their path beyond the dock. Taking the second street a few blocks, they approached an intersection with another, wider avenue paved in brick, indicating the center of Esbjerg.

A few men and women headed into the pub. Smoke curled into a grey haze over the building, and three buildings down from the corner, Sailor and the boy found their way to The Hird's Inn. They decided to share one bed to save money and found a decent veal and potato stew for dinner downstairs in the dining hall.

The barmaid had just plunked down Sailor's third beer, and the boy nursed his second when two women invited themselves to sit at their table. Bending to climb over the bench, the low-cut bodice of the buxom woman revealed her taut nipples for the boy to admire. Luckily, Sailor still had his wits about him. Guessing their uninvited guests would not understand him, Sailor spoke in Frisian:

"Evening ladies, you gals look anxious for a beer."

The younger woman kept her eyes glued on the boy. Then touched his arm.

(In Danish) "I'm mighty thirsty, mister. Buy a girl a beer? How about it."

The boy laughed.

(In crude Danish) "We'll share the table. You are welcome to get your own beer."

Sailor joined in.

"That's right, boy, maybe they'll spot us a round" (In Danish). "You see, there's a pretty girl back home that this boy seems to be stuck on."

(In Danish) "True enough, Sailor, and Maam, my uncle here is married to my aunt, who is as gorgeous as my gal Adela. When we finish this beer, it's up to our bed and an early start in the morning."

The boy and Sailor stood, gulped the last beer steins, and headed to their room. Two men from the bar brought their glasses and a pitcher over and sat in the vacated seats.

Day three:

Sailor and the boy enjoyed hot oatmeal while they reviewed the map and decided on a goal for the day's sail. Sondervig, another small village on the coast, seemed attainable based on the distances they had traveled the first two days of the voyage.

Once in open water beyond Esbjerg, the wind and waves died down to a murmur. By ten o'clock, the boy became sullen as Sailor brought out his fishing rod and pipe and settled down in the hull, waiting for a bite. The boy studied the map and daydreamed about arriving home with the dresser and squeezing the life out of Adela, pressing her to him as he never had before. Then he thought of the opposite. Running up to her, touching her soft cheek, kissing and hugging her as she laughed and cried at his safe return.

Sailor watched the boy fidget.

"Studying that map won't make the wind pick up."

"I know, Sailor, but I didn't bring any other maps to study. I want to get to Christiania, load up the dresser, and return home."

"I know, but this is another thing to learn about an extended sail. Patience. We could go three days, a week, maybe three weeks without a breeze. On an ocean trip, when the wind dies, you start figuring out your supplies, your dwindling water rations; your food stores dropping to nothing. That can make you loopy. Many a man loses his mind before his hardtack and water run out. It's the stillness that never ends."

"How do you not go crazy?"

"You relax. Keep busy. If you're not alone, you tell stories. Go ahead, think of a story."

All the boy could think about was Adela.

"I can't think of one. Maybe after this sail. How about you, Sailor. How far have you traveled?"

"I signed up for a seal hunt in Iceland once. From Morocco, I helped move cargo over to Rio De Janeiro. Warm weather the whole time. We did run out of wind for a week in the middle of the Atlantic. I mostly captained between Amsterdam and Lisbon, Portugal, with many trips to Portsmouth, England, along the way."

So, the day passed. Sailor would take time from his storytelling to pack and light his pipe or grab his pole to pull in a fish. The boy listened with interest to Sailor's description of every destination. What did the people look like, and what did their language sound like? What sort of buildings did he see? What about the native people in South America, Friendly? Savage? What about his worst storm? Did he ever get lost?

Sailor described the sugarcane plantation he explored in Brazil. Larger by far than any island in the North Sea chain, stalks of sugar cane worked by bronzed-skinned Guaraní men and women stretched across a massive valley. Tobacco and coffee crates were loaded on the ships in Sailor's fleet. The bonus from that trip alone kept Sailor on land and living easily for an entire year.

In Morocco, Sailor learned of the powerful Muhammad III, who headed the first state in Africa to recognize the sovereignty of an independent United States.

Sailor portrayed Marrakesh as a stew of people of color, white, brown, black, yellow, and every shade in between. Religious rituals and ceremonies are as similar and yet unique as the leaves on trees, one neighborhood to the next: tolerance is the norm. The boy was fascinated by Sailor's talk of Sultans, flowing robes, hookahs, veils, and cities that moved across the desert.

The boy heard about the crimson-ice beach on the north shore of Iceland. The mile of seashore red from the blood of the seal hunt. Sailor only went on the one seal-kill and wished he had never signed up. He had no idea so many would be killed. Afterward, to this day, he refused to wear anything made from seal skin, preferring his wool overcoat instead.

The boy steered the discussion to women but did not know what to ask. Sailor spoke of several ports of call women he visited in his travels. The Moroccan woman, slight of build with beautiful breasts. The native woman in Brazil wished he would stay with her and rubbed his feet every night for half an hour.

But the accident ended his ability to captain and the visits to the women of his voyages.

This part of Sailor's story interested the boy. He could not imagine living the rest of his life on a crutch like Sailor.

"Can you tell me how it happened, Sailor? I know it happened at sea. There is a rumor regarding a shark attack. Someone told me a mariner cut you in a knife fight. Another sailor swore a storm tossed you hard."

"Really, boy, I never told you? Seems I left that one out all the times we've talked."

"You don't have to tell me."

"Important that I do now. With you being shipmaster of this here jolly boat. Remember what I said about sensing the signs of the sea. Live or die by that advice, boy."

Sailor, silent for a time, took a moment to relight his pipe.

"What happened to me occurred because of a dumb lapse in my sea sense. You better add another factor to what I mentioned the other day. Signs of the land. Signs of the sea. Signs of the birds and fish. In a boat this size, it's easy to become a part of the boat after a few days: a sort of second nature. Well, it may seem overwhelming on a ship, but you gotta have the same sense as you do on a smaller boat like this. Know every corner on the deck below the hold and up to the mainmast crow's nest. Important. Do you get that boy?"

"I am sure I know all the parts of a ship. Joyner tasked me with that when I arrived at Ketelswarf Shipyard."

"Not what I mean, boy. Sure, you know the terms. But I'm saying you must be mindful of all those components; the sounds they make, right and wrong; the shadows the sails and rigging make across the deck. Be aware that a pin is ten centimeters loose in a hole. Watch a tear in the jib eight meters up. That's what captaining is all about."

"It's impossible to know everything you have described."

"It is my boy, but the more you are in tune, the safer you'll be, and by extension, the people on your ship, from the crew to the customers of your cargo.

"In my case, the boys hauled up the second mainsail, making a heap of ropes on deck, so I started coiling one. I heard a weird sound up top, and a tug tightened the line. If I had been on my game that day, I would have told the men to hold for inspection.

"Instead, I allowed one more heave that broke the upper pulley, which snapped the other pulleys hauling the sail. The second sail crashed, and my leg got tangled in the coiled rope. Yanked me up twelve meters, upside down, and banged me unconscious against the mast and some broken pulleys, gouging my leg and apparently breaking it in three places.

"By the time they got me down, a bone stuck out, and blood poured on the deck. Langeness hallig and Ketelswarf Inn appeared closest, so we put in, and a surgeon from Wyk came over and tried to straighten the leg. On the fourth day, pus started coming out around the broken skin, so they bled me some for three more days, and the boils healed in five. Well, if you call this leg of mine mended.

"I recovered while lodging at Gretsen House, run by Brigette's father. When the fever left me, I opened my eyes to that woman and told myself to hell with sailing.

"Brigette has never said anything about my crooked leg, and that's the kind of woman you want to hold tight to."

The boy listened respectfully to Sailor extol his admiration for Brigette. He resisted interjecting the virtues of Adela, comparing and contrasting Brigette, his mother, and Adela. He attempted to steer the conversation back to the woman in Morocco. He could not inquire about the workings in bed between Sailor and Brigette. He could not even imagine. He ached for some clue of technique, mechanics, or steps to advance his cause and stoke his fire in Adela. When it came to the women in his life, he could only think of their softness and their forever primness. Blind to the strength, resolve, and intellect of these hard-working examples of Frisian womenfolk. His thoughts were dominated instead by their smells, hair, skirts, and bodices; his questions were again left unanswered.

The wind picked up at nightfall, and the jolly boat made the mainland shore, where the boy tied up to a tree. They both chewed jerky, and Sailor lit his pipe, and they laid out and slept in the boat. The boy was restless in his thoughts of Adela.

Day four:

The wind held steady the as the two sailors spread the map and ate their hardtack and cheese. The island chain behind them, the open sea to port, the jolly boat would cruise along the coast until they sighted Skagerrak Strait. As the boy cleaned up after breakfast, Sailor scrounged in the jolly boat and brought out an oilcloth-covered metal instrument. The boy could not figure out how it got on board and why he had not seen it when he double-checked their provisions before they sailed. Perhaps Sailor had stowed it the morning he found the boy sleeping.

Sailor handed the device to the boy.

"Other than memories, this is all I have left of my days as skipper of the Ardgowan. This here is a Hadley Quadrant. The former captain willed it to me as he lay dying. A flintlock backfire wounded him in the chest.

"I'll show you how to use this, and we'll take a reading each day at noon and after dark, so you can practice the rest of the trip getting from here to there and back again."

Although the boy wished to speed up their journey to get back to Adela, he listened intently to Sailor's explanation of the instrument. Soon the boy envisioned the possibility of achieving their destination quicker by navigating the open sea rather than sailing within eyesight of the coast.

They would use the sun's position at noon, find the North Star at night, and then calculate their latitude. By finding that same latitude line on the map, they would know whether they were ready to turn into the Skagerrak Straight and continue along the southern shore until they reached the fjord leading to Christiania.

The boy took several readings around noon to understand the instrument's precision, locate their latitude on the map and compare the land features with the same shapes on the map. That evening Sailor suggested finding an Inn in Ringobing. After supper and a second beer stein, the boy lined up on the North Star. Using their lantern, he pinpointed their location to the minute on their map.

Day five:

The sun creased the horizon over the woods of Ringobing while the Sailor and the boy repacked the jolly boat and set off by compass due north. If they could make Thyboron by nightfall, the boy's plan allowed for a day to cross the open sea of the Skagerrak Strait. Two additional days up the river through the fjord would see them docked at the port of Christiania.

The Ketelswarf Inn and the drydock work they had left dropped away from their thoughts. Both enjoyed the wind against the sail and the cloudless sky stretching over the mast. Adela caused a slow ache in the boy's heart. With the mainsheet wrapped around his wrist and the tiller under his arm, he concentrated on the compass. He kept his muscles warm and his focus on the signs of the sea. At noon, the boy took another reading with the Hadley quadrant.

He calculated their position as a little more than halfway to the 57th parallel of latitude, the mapped location of Thyboron, from where they began the day at Ringobing. Using Sailor's timepiece, the boy reckoned they should continue north for six more hours in the steady wind of the day. Then the boat would be turned due east, sailing into port, even though they would be out of sight of the mainland and unable to visually site the town.

Sailor neither confirmed nor denied the boy's calculations, smoking his pipe to avoid misrepresenting his thoughts to the boy. At seven o'clock, the boy turned east. Within another hour and a half, the boy jumped up and pointed to lights beyond the bow.

After docking the boat and retrieving their necessaries, Sailor spotted a sign with an arrow directing them to the Inn of Thyboron.

"I'd say the first beer is on me, navigator. Dead reckoning. Well done."

"The quadrant did the trick and steady wind. But it's still amazing."

"You're ahead of a lot of Sailing Masters already, lad. I've heard of a new instrument, a marine chronometer, that would allow you to calculate the longitude of your location in the open waters. Just think; you could plot a course from your current position in both latitude and longitude to your destination's latitude and longitude. With a compass reading of the plotted path, you could sail directly to a port."

The boy tried to understand how the chronometer worked over a generous herring, potatoes, bread, and beer supper at the Inn. Sailor's limited knowledge of the device helped little, but he described the complicated problem of longitudinal calculation based on his captaining experience. They spread their map on the table to discuss the open sea crossing planned for the next day. The boy noted the latitude and longitude markings, garnering another dimension to his chart explorations. In a sense, the geography of his map fascinated him more than the endless miles of saltwater between those same destinations. A reluctant sailor, not his passion: but a navigator? That was a challenge, an excitement, a muscle to flex.

Day six:

A stiff wind from the north/northwest caught the sail as they set out to cross the mouth of the Skagerrak Strait, approximately 200 kilometers northward. The boy checked Sailor's hourglass, comparing it to the ascendant sun. He noted the time and pulled a close-reach sail, keeping the boat aligned with his compass reading. Clouds crowded the sky at times as the waves and wind picked up. At noon Sailor called out and pointed to the rain and dark skies approaching from the northwest. The boy concentrated on taking readings during snatches of sunlight and made his calculations.

He bet he would need to allow for more drift from the storm. If by doing so, he missed the bay when he headed back east, the boy would still meet the coast, and he could hug the north shore of the strait on the morrow.

The tempest hit within the hour. Current and waves forced the boat west, and the skies grew darker. At times, the rains needled his face, and the mainsheet became nearly impossible to hold fast. Sailor wrapped the boy in extra blankets to prevent cold exhaustion, then he hunkered down in a blanket himself and baled water to keep moving.

The boy tied bandages around his hands to ward off frostbite. More than halfway across, as captain of the jolly boat, the boy figured going forward equaled the risk of turning back. The boy kept a picture of Adela in his mind as he scanned the horizon. Lightning flashed the sky and sea to their right. The eye of the storm passed them on the left twenty or thirty kilometers from their position, yet the clouds, rain, wind, and cold swirled as far as fifty kilometers to the west. Except for the lack of thunderbolts, they may as well have been in the middle of the maelstrom.

It came time, according to the boy, to turn east. Too exhausted to maximize the efficiency of his tack, he opted to hold on to his current compass direction and trust luck. They headed into the gale for a while, but Sailor and the boy could see a break on the dusk horizon as the tempest turned south. The boy thought they should be seeing the shore either to the east or to the north, but water still stretched in both directions.

After another hour, the rain ceased, but the pitch-black clouded sky made land sighting impossible. The boy slapped his face every few minutes to avoid falling over in sleep.

The air warmed, and the waves lessened. The water stopped breaching the gunnels. Suddenly the lantern lit trees and rocks in close. The boy let out the mainsail. He spotted a small opening in the boulders lining the shore and wedged the bow in the crevice. The boy dropped his hands to his sides, flexing his fingers, rubbing his arms, and slapping his legs to encourage circulation and warmth.

Sailor threw off his blanket and did a similar dance. He stepped out of the boat with his crinkled leg, using his crutch to steady. As he stood, Sailor's foot slipped off the wet rock purchase. The boy heard a double crack as Sailor turned his head and took a boulder to his cheek instead of his nose. The second crack sounded like a stick being broken for a fire as Sailor's boot wedged in a cranny, his weight causing a wicked bone break. A scream paralyzed the boy for seconds. *Had he screamed or Sailor?*

The boy skipped to the bow and jumped out. He scrambled across more boulders and secured the line around a tree. Returning to Sailor, screaming, the boy yanked his uncle out of the fissure and back into the boat. The boy hooked the lantern to the mast after gathering the sail and tying it down. He did not look at Sailor, opting to set conditions to maximize Sailor's comfort. He baled the rest of the water, sacrificed his wet blanket in the bottom, and laid the extra sail and two more blankets over the makeshift mattress. He dragged Sailor on top of the makeshift bed and, without asking, without hesitation, straightened the wretched leg, now broken in a fourth place above the knee. Pulling mercilessly until the limb looked as crooked-straight as the boy remembered. Sailor, delirious, did not object but screamed all the same.

Blood seeped from the cut on Sailor's cheek, but none soaked through Sailor's pants. The boy figured the broken leg had not breached the skin. He wrapped Sailor's head in a bandage around his ears, cheeks, and nose, tightening it to end the bleeding. It worked. He poured water into a cup.

"Try to drink this water, Sailor. I'll fix some food for us in the morning."

"Uh, Sorry! Damn fucking leg!"

"We'll both feel better in the morning."

The sky cleared. A half-moon hovered near the horizon. The boy unwrapped the quadrant and took a reading on the North Star. The latitude indicated the shore of the Skagerrak Strait, right where he intended. How far into the straight he had sailed, he would surmise on the morrow as he compared land features with Sailor's map.

He lay down next to Sailor and tried to sleep. He kept checking on Sailor, who continued to grimace in silence. The boy dropped off, exhausted.

Day seven:

Waking with a start, the boy threw off the blanket as he shivered in the morning chill. Sailor had never slept, so the boy prepared the boat to sail. The boy helped the injured man drink water from the freshwater jug and stowed the rest of the gear. The boy unwound the bandage. The left side of his friend's face looked swollen blue/purple, and the left eye was bruised shut. Otherwise, Sailor had good color. He declined food and asked for more water, insisting he remained comfortable, barely moving where he lay. The boy helped him pee in an empty jug.

"We'll have to tack up the river to Christiania, probably two days from here."

"I'm fine. Leave me there to heal and get on back with the goods."

"You old sea dog, perhaps I'll have to. I'll roust a surgeon and a doctor when we get there."

The boy set sail. He compared the bays and peninsulas he passed to determine his exact location on Sailor's map. They were both quiet as the boy continued sailing north. He kept calculating the time it would take for the remainder of the trip. Sailor's color began to pale, and sweat broke out on his brow. The boy helped Sailor drink water every half hour, yet the man's discomfort increased.

At ten o'clock, the boy sat back against the stern and stared at the sky overhead. He closed his eyes, relaxed, and let images of Adela, Bridgette, and Joyner feed his reasoning as he pushed on. He thought of his mother asking about his word muscles and his father not saying a thing but working by his side, forcing strength into his arms and shoulders.

Fifteen minutes later, the boy turned the boat around. He had calculated that he could get to the mouth of the straight by noon. He would take a reading of the latitude, allowing additional time for the current, which ran against him. The storm had left, but the wind had shifted. The vortex of the system, moving east now on land and dissipating, making a straight-line compass course with a broad reach sail on the outer side of the island chain possible. He would test his skill in the open sea rather than dodging the islands and the mainland shore on the bay side.

At six hours of sailing each day, it took him five days to get to the Skagerrak Straits, discounting the day they had lost in still waters. The boy calculated that he could return to Ketelswarf Inn by dusk tomorrow. He would sail all night, the wind would have to hold, and Sailor would have to hang on. The surgeon on Fohr island could be fetched, and Sailor would receive care.

He faced the failure of his assignment to bring home the chest of drawers and the bone pin jewelry for Brigette and Adela. After everything Sailor had done for the boy over all their years together, the boy knew Sailor had to be his priority. He resolved to return Sailor to Brigette and the capable surgeon who had fixed his leg many years ago. At noon, he took a reading with the Hadley Quadrant, aligned his map and compass, set the broad reach, and eliminated the sail luft.

To pass the time, he told Sailor about raising the buildings on Oland in his youth. The work was nearly impossible at first. Within a few years, thin muscles hardened to lift, turn, or pull any weight necessary. He described the block and tackle pulley system he had devised. The whittling, drilling, and assembly of parts eased some of the pulling the men needed to raise a barn or shed.

He admonished Sailor if he tried to speak, urging rest, stillness, and patience.

The boy soon ran out of stories and turned to song, sometimes singing as loud as he could, remembering the lullaby his mother sang to him before bed. He repeated each verse many, many times, his repertoire limited.

In the late afternoon, he grew quiet for a time. The islands to port became a faintly visible ripple on the horizon. The wind was steady, and the sky was vast and blue. He began to tire from the constant strain of holding the tiller and the mainsheet in a precise position. The compass had to be checked often.

The boy tried not to look down at Sailor. *Would he look worse?* He did not want to disturb him. When he did glance down, the boy hoped to find him in better color, on the mend, and not the withered man wrapped in wool Sailor had become.

Alas, when he did look down, he found Sailor's face half purple and yellowing and half white as a sheet. Sailor's forehead dripped sweat down his cheek, soaking the bandage surrounding his head. The boy knelt with a rag soaked in fresh water and mopped the sweat away from Sailor's brow. He asked Sailor if he needed anything while he helped the man pee in the jug again. Sailor lifted an unsteady hand and touched his leg at the point of the suspected fracture.

When the boy swept back the blanket, the contrast between Sailor's two ankles startled him. The swelling near the break pinched the cloth so tight the boy thought it a wonder the material had not burst. He brought his knife to the cuff and cut and ripped the pant leg above the bruising. Some tension left Sailor's mouth, and his body relaxed.

The boy offered Sailor more water, re-covered his legs with the blanket, wiped his brow, and returned to his station at the tiller.

As he readjusted his course and tightened the sail, five, no, six bottlenose whales swam thirty meters off starboard. Talking to the whales passed more time. He named each one as they swam along the jolly boat: Scruffy, Cutfin, Grey, Longnose, and Slowcoach (always bringing up the rear.) Then he played a game, trying to distinguish which led the pod. When they dove, the whales sometimes changed position, so the boy really had to concentrate not to be fooled. The whales veered away after forty-five minutes. The boy distracted himself for another thirty, searching and hoping they would return.

Sailor required another mop up and water break. He looked worse than the hour and a half prior, but there was nothing for it. The boy prepared for dusk and dark. He secured the Hadley Quadrant to the boat near at hand. He suspended the lantern just below the sail on the mast, to be lit later, and piled extra blankets for the temperature drop that accompanied the night.

The boy promised himself that the night would not be boring, long, and tiring. The importance of the push to Ketelswarf Shipyard became his sole focus. He ignored all negative possibilities and instead tended to Sailor. He thought about a hug from Adela, went over his somber report to Joyner, and steeled himself for his immediate return to the sea after delivering Sailor to fetch the surgeon from Wyk.

At about nine o'clock, he took a reading on the North Star and lit the lantern to read Sailor's map. He found the latitude on the chart. Judging that he could see only waves and water in every direction, the boy jabbed his index finger at the sheet, indicating his rough longitude. The boy calculated he would arrive by three o'clock the next day by measuring from his starting point that morning to his mark on the drawing and comparing that distance to the interval between his current location and Ketelswarf. He would be out of food and fresh water, near home, and medical help. With a steady wind and clear night, he would be home in eighteen more hours of nonstop sailing.

The boy had accomplished over one-third of the return trip. Sailor looked noticeably worse again when next examined. The hand sticking outside the blanket trembled visibly and did not stop. Sailor sipped more water and peed again into the jug, and still, the hand kept shaking. The boy had no idea what Sailor's trembling hand indicated. Bringing the lantern over to the injured man, the boy began to fear Sailor's condition.

What more could he do? What would the surgeon do? The surgeon would know if the break was straightened enough to optimize healing. The surgeon would watch Sailor's progress and bleed him if he showed no improvement.

The boy imagined having to perform a bloodletting procedure on Sailor's leg. The boy returned to sailing the jolly boat, working the helm, and observing the sea signs to get them home.

At around twelve midnight, the boy struggled to keep his eyes open, and his arm clasped around the tiller. He changed positions every fifteen minutes, splashing water on his cheeks and slapping his forehead. He leaned on the port side, the bow side gunwale, then the boy centered himself straight-backed.

Next, he stood, one foot forward to balance in the swales of the waves. Then he would switch his feet. At two o'clock, he started singing again. At three, he checked on Sailor, cleaned up Sailor's soiling, and shifted his position to port so he could bale the collected water.

By four, his eyes rubbed raw, his left wrist ached; the knuckles in his hands cracked when the boy straightened his fingers. His hand stung as much as his forehead when he slapped himself to stay awake.

His efforts agonized every muscle in his body. In the boy's state, staying the course seemed more difficult than moving, stacking, ox dragging, and placing turf in the fields of Oland Island for ten hours in the hot sun. His head weighed heavy on his sore shoulders. The middle of his back knifed him with pain. He looked down at Sailor to help him endure another hour of sleeplessness. He sang his songs again but did not seem to finish one before trying another.

Inevitably the sun cracked the horizon to port, and the warmth alerted the boy. He shook himself awake, the tiller still in the crook of his arm, the sail set. He knew he had lost the battle to stay awake, but for how long had he slept? Relieved that the shipshape jolly boat still seemed headed on the right course, he gathered enough strength to eat his bread and jerky and to drink water. Then he turned his attention to Sailor. With both hands shaking now, he responded with slow grunts and sighs to the boy's inquiries.

The boy uncovered Sailor's leg. Thankfully, Sailor kept his eyes closed and did not notice the boy's despair as he examined and prodded. The limb was snow-white from hip to break, purple/black and thick with swell from that point to two inches below the knee, and an unhealthy-looking reddish brown down to the ankle. The boy dug out a fillet knife, cleaned it in seawater, cut it across the bread, and rinsed it again in the sea. He finally washed the blade in freshwater, prepared bandages, and kneeled at Sailor's side.

He practiced a stroke from one side of the leg to the other just above the knee. Without a word to Sailor, the boy brought the razor-sharp edge to bear and cut the limb along the rehearsed arc. Not deep, but yellowish pus oozed out. Waiting until he could stand the sight no longer, the boy squeezed the thigh as Sailor gurgled in pain. He noted the blood flowed a bit redder, signaling the boy to stop and wrap the cut tightly in a bandage. He wrapped Sailor in the blanket, poured water over Sailor's lips and the cloth on Sailor's forehead, and took a drink himself. The boy took Sailor's trembling hand and told him they would be home in a few more hours. Sailor opened his eyes, looked at the boy, and squeezed his hand. The boy, encouraged by this small rally, smiled back, relieved.

The boy leaned back, stared at the infinite sky, and let the sea air clear his head.

In a few minutes, he sailed forth.

At noon, the boy struggled to hold the Hadley quadrant as he took a reading. He decided to sail one more hour on his current course, turning the hourglass as a reminder. No land visibly in sight, the boy struggled in the sun to keep burning eyes scanning the sea. Something caught his attention a few hundred meters off to port. Sure enough, six whales breached in turn and approached. When they got close enough to study, the boy believed they were the same whales he had seen the day before. The boy laughed.

"Hello, my friends. How about I throw you a line, and you can pull me along while I rest again? No? Why not! You certainly have more energy than me? Except for Slowcoach, last again, I see. Alright, be that way. Just keep me company. Sailor, this is the omen we've been looking for."

The whale pod dove in twenty minutes, breaching far off to starboard, then vanished for good. The hourglass ran out after that, so the boy turned the boat east for the final leg home.

Now each hour crawled as the boy strained at the horizon for any sign of a shoreline. At 2 o'clock, without doubt, he would see land?

Nothing. The same distant nothingness was evident at 3 o'clock, the boy's projected arrival time, and the boy's stomach began to tighten.

At 4:00pm, the boy alternated between standing and sitting in the jolly boat to stay alert, watching the top of the mast and sail instead of looking forward, holding his course, and striving to remain positive. Could he have drifted so far west? Did he know how to work the Hadley Quadrant, or did he get it all wrong?

He had not heard a murmur from Sailor in an hour, and the boy decided he could wait no longer to tend to him. Squinting again at the horizon ahead, unsure of what he thought he saw, the boy soaked his bandanna in the last of the freshwater, wiped his eyes, sucked on the cloth, and squinted again.

There it was. Langeness hallig.

With revived strength, the boy stretched and flexed his head, shoulders, arms, hands, and fingers. He shook his legs and feet and curled his toes. An hour and a half later, he reached the Ketelswarf dock. Dusk started to settle in. Unsurprised that no one came to meet him, he tied up and thought about Sailor for the first time in a couple of hours. His stomach tightened, and he hurried drunkenly into the bar with shaking legs.

Thankfully, Joyner huddled at the counter with Adela. The boy was suddenly speechless again at the sight of her startled look, her hair flipping back as she looked up. He sat down at a table to prevent falling over. He knew he looked and smelled a mess as he struggled to keep his wits and explain to Joyner.

"Sorry, Joyner. Had to come back. Sailor, accident. Got to get help for Sailor."

Instantly alert, Joyner came around the bar.

"What's happened? Where's Sailor?"

Adela went white.

"Are you OK? Are you hurt?"

The boy shook his head.

"Doctor, surgeon. Sailor needs help."

Joyner, charging out the door, "I'll see to Sailor. You two men, come with me."

The barmaid began to panic.

"What should I do?"

"Get Brigette. No, I'll do it. Go with Joyner. I need to see Brigette."

The boy stood, swayed, sorted his balance, and walked to Gretsen House. Brigette stirred stew on the stove.

"Brigette, come with me. Sailor had an accident and needs a doctor. I'll sail over to Wyk and bring him back. What's the name of the surgeon that fixed Sailor's leg before? It's broken again."

"Oh, no. Sailor has got to be careful. He's out by the boat?"

"Joyner and a couple of men will carry him here."

"Let us go. The surgeon's name is Gaaders. Here, take some of this mutton. You look exhausted."

When they approached the end of the dock, the boy pulled back a corner of the wool blanket still wrapped around Sailor. Joyner turned and took Brigette by both shoulders, preventing her from passing.

"I am sorry, Brigette, Sailor's gone. The boy did everything he could to get him back here for help, but that leg of his, in the end, bested him."

"What do you mean, Joyner?"

"He died, Brigette, Sailor's dead."

Bridgette gasped, then grew quiet as Joyner led her a short distance away. Suddenly, a low wail erupted from Brigette, her face still buried in Joyner's shoulder, growing in mournful intensity. The moan flew like a knife into the boy's heart. He bit on his lip so as not to begin moaning with her.

"How?"

"How is of no importance now, Brigette. The boy got back here as fast as possible to get help."

Brigette shook her head. She broke from Joyner, tugging her skirt straight, wiping a sleeve across her eyes. Her features turned hard, angry as a lioness.

"Most likely, he couldn't stop dreaming about that girl. Getting back to her."

The knife again. The boy knelt over the blanket, pulling it away from Sailor's face. He had never seen human death so close before. Staring for a full minute at the stillness of the man's face and shaking his head from side to side, the boy kept repeatedly whispering, *"No."* A crowd had formed from the inn, encircling the man in the blanket. No one spoke or moved. Brigette softened and began to cry softly. Adela arrived with an additional blanket and knelt beside the boy, putting her arm around his shoulder and urging him to get up and return to the house.

The boy shrugged her away. He could not think of anything but Sailor and what he should have done. He should have secured the boat himself. He had been so tired that night. No excuse. He tried to remember the last thing Sailor had said to him. He could not recall. They had worked so hard during the storm; Sailor bailed water, the boy holding the tiller firm, worried lightning would strike the mast.

Sailor was still. Someone had closed his eyes.

The boy, mechanical in his movements, went to the boat and brought out Sailor's clothing sack, the Hadley quadrant wrapped in the oilcloth, and the hourglass, setting everything neatly by Sailor. He returned, fished Sailor's pipe off the bottom boards, and added it to the rest of the belongings. He knelt over Sailor again.

Sailor was still. So still.

The boy began to shake, suddenly more tired than he had been on the entire sail. Adela came over, and again the boy waved her away. He listened to the crying of his aunt Brigette unable to look over toward her.

Joyner brought a blanket over, wrapped it around the boy's shoulder's and forcefully lifted the boy by the elbow, steering him toward Gretsen barn, handing him off to two men who led him up the stairs to bed. The bed was warm and quiet. He slipped into sleep in minutes.

In the afternoon of the next day, the boy awoke when shoulder-shaken. He turned and saw his mother sitting in the chair at the foot of the bed.

"How are you, my boy, rested?"

"Not sure, No."

"I'll go back to the house. Wash up and change and come in. We have a hot meal ready for you."

"I,,, you go ahead; I'm just not hungry."

"You will be when you see what we fixed for you."

"Mother, I,,, I can't go over there. Brigette, Sailor, please!"

"Sorry, son, the service and burial are at sundown today. The sea is calm, the day is beautiful, and Brigette requested you to speak for her."

"Me? Brigette wants me? How can I, Mom?"

"I don't know how you'll do it. But I know you will."

The boy looked at his mother, her mouth relaxed and soft as ever, eyes hard and demanding as ever, not to be denied. He swung his legs around off the bed, still dizzy.

"Alright, mother."

He stood, pulled his mother out of her chair, and hugged her, burying his head in her neck and hair, smelling her strength and muscle.

"Thank you, Mother, for coming."

"Of course, son. We'll be waiting."

After his mother left, the boy sat back on his bed, willing himself not to lie back down and drift to sleep again, shaking his head at the thought of facing Brigette. He slammed his fists against his knees. He poured water into the basin, stripped, and washed. He dressed in his best clothes, combed his hair, and soaped his teeth.

Every movement was challenging; he began to see how he could get through. A job. Work he had to finish, as he always had. His father had shown him how. As perspiration soaked his hat brim, sweat dripped off his chin, sometimes gasping for breath, he worked side by side ear his father into the night until completion. One foot forward, then the next.

The boy stayed focused even in the kitchen upon seeing Brigette and his mother. Brigette approached with open arms encircling the boy and hugging him close. He did not smile. Would the sadness ever be over? The boy suspected not, but the ache is his world now. The lamb chops were strengthening.

At sundown, everyone on Ketelswarf and Oland Islands gathered at the dock. As the boy, his mother, and Brigette approached the crowd, the boy's youngest sister jumped in his arms. Four boats made ready to sail, and Sailor, sewn into the extra sail the two had taken on their trip, lay in the first boat. The stitched decal of Ketelswarf Shipyard marked Sailor's head underneath the cloth. Adela had appeared at the boy's side and now held his hand tightly. In the absence of a clergyman, Joyner spoke:

"Thank you all for coming. Sailor will be buried at sea as he always talked about, but Brigette has asked the boy here to say a few words on her behalf. When we finish here, a pot of stew and beer will be up at the Inn. Everyone's welcome."

Joyner motioned to the boy to begin.

"I don't have much I can say, unlike Sailor, who never ran out of stories.

"Sailor wasn't from these islands. He just landed here. While sailing a few days ago, he told me about the accident that gave him that crooked leg.

"That's not important now except for the end of the story.

"He told me that when he woke up after the doctor from Wyk straightened him, bled him, leached him, and he could see straight, his eyes fell on this beautiful woman named Brigette. Sailor said that when he saw this woman, he knew he would stay and try to make her love him and be happy to be with him. I think we all knew and loved Sailor, my uncle. We loved his stories, laugh, and ability to drink more beer than any of us. Hell, I loved that damn crooked scraggly leg; I always knew when he was coming around the corner so I could outrun him.

"I'm sorry, Sailor, for what happened. You taught me well."

The boy withdrew his hand from Adela's and climbed into the lead boat with Joyner and one of Sailor's friends. The four jolly boats sailed out. They nosed the bows together when they reached deep water, far from the dock. The boy and the two men lifted the sail-wrapped body to the gunwale and tipped the body into the ocean. The occupants let their thoughts drift with the waves for a few minutes in silence. Then the sailors turned toward shore.

When they reached the crowd waiting on the dock, Joyner jumped ashore and signaled everyone to follow him to Ketelswarf Inn.

The boy, Adela, his family, and Brigette held back a time, watching the waves roll along the beach. Brigette pulled the boy aside:

"Thank you for your words. Sailor is so proud of you, as we all are. He told me before the trip that he would teach you how to use the Hadley Quadrant and then give it to you, along with the maps and the hourglass."

"I'm not sure I can take them, Brigette, after what happened, but if I do, I will honor Sailor and the charts by working with them and respecting the lessons he taught me."

The boy met up with Adela and, arm in arm, joined the food line at the inn.

Weeks passed. The boy preferred to work alone now as he prepared the shipyard for another winter. Lots to do, but he knew the routine and rarely needed to ask Joyner for help. He kept to himself in the evening as well. His stomach ached most of the time as he tried to stay focused on his job, trying not to think about Sailor, the trip, the accident, and the deadly stillness. He ate dinners with Brigette in a quiet Gretsen House. Brigette hid her pain and loss much better than the boy, and he admired her even more. On rare occasions, the boy caught her looking off, perhaps out the window toward Ketelswarf Shipyard, waiting for Sailor to clump along on his crutch.

One Saturday, the boy returned from picking up supplies on the mainland to report to Joyner in his office and found him conversing with another man sitting in the blue velour chair across from Joyner's desk.

"Here is the boy I've been telling you about."

Joyner turned to the boy.

"Meet Mr. Castell, the shipmaster of the *Creighton,* out in the dry-dock, twenty-five-meter double mast schooner."

"Pleasure to meet you, sir."

Captain Castell, straight-backed, shook the boy's hand.

"I'll get to it, boy. Lost a cabin boy to sharks a week ago. The fool threw a bucket of swab water over the side; simultaneously, a wave surge unbalanced him. Nothing we could do but watch the churn. Joyner tells me you desire to learn navigation. If I bring you on as an apprentice, that might be your future. Of course, cabin boy at the bottom to start.

"I'm off to bed in land luxury. Let me know what you decide. Joyner, look over my standard contract."

Captain Castell's stomach extended past the arms of the chair, and it took some effort for him to stand and leave the office.

"This contract is for an indentured servitude of three years. If you are interested, I can negotiate that down to two years and double the payout to you and your family. I would also write the stipulation for nautical navigation training."

"Why Joyner, why. Is my work here not good enough? We need to start on the windmills. I planned on building all the parts in the wood-shop this winter. Where does *Creighton* sail? I can't desert Brigette, who will help her now that Sailor... I can't leave Adela. She's, we..."

"I know, boy, I know. Slow down a second. The *Creighton* is a British cargo ship. Runs along the coast here from Christiania, Norway, to London, England, and down to Lisbon, Portugal. Shipmaster Castell's been coming through here for about five years. He is English but speaks Dutch and German; you understood him well enough. He is not my ideal captain, but he is not my least favorite. Knows his sea and has a marine chronometer. I never heard the end of it after Sailor spotted it two years ago. There would be an opportunity for you."

"Why, Joyner? I thought you approved of my work here at the shipyard. I'm learning here."

"Listen, son, I cannot in good conscience see a future for you here. One that matches mine and Brigette's, and your mother and father's idea of what we know you will achieve. Of course, we will miss you, your ideas, and your skills. You work hard. You follow through. You complete what you set out to do. This opportunity opens a hundred more doors for you. Your brother can take up your duties next year and help Brigette."

"Adela,,,"

"Adela will see a future with you while you open those portals. Talk to her."

The boy left the office in confusion. He finished his Ketelswarf and Gretsen House chores. He ate dinner with Brigette, not saying a word about sailing away for three years or two if Joyner worked it out. Up in the hayloft, he tried to think things through. Cabin boy. He knew he did not particularly want to be a sailor. Perhaps, though, this opportunity would allow him to learn navigation. Ultimately, he would have the skills to get a job on any ship sailing to any or all the destinations he wanted to see. Sailoring was a means to a dream he kept alive every time he rolled out one of Sailor's, now, one of his own maps.

The boy worried next about telling Adela. He would be gone for two, possibly three years. After three years, they could sail to England or America, where there might be more opportunities.

What if he refused. He would stay here with Adela, maybe take over the shipyard. It would be years before Joyner would be ready for him to take over. There is only so much ship traffic in the islands, only so much opportunity here. He did not want to tend sheep either. The boy had already conquered farming. He could shear sheep with the best men on Oland Island. He could move turf and build barns.

No, he would work with calculations, navigation, maps, and destinations. Brain muscles. He envisioned his future conditional on his decision.

The boy told Brigette about the Creighton schooner and Captain Castell during breakfast. Brigette exploded with excitement. She knew all about it and had kept quiet at dinner the night before to give the boy a chance to work things out.

"Joyner has been looking for a good ship for some time now. Your mother and father approve as long as sailing doesn't involve whaling, seal hunting, or fishing."

"Well, I'm not keen on being a sailor, but I want to see those places on Sailor's maps and learn how to navigate."

The boy thought about his life for the first time since Sailor's accident, not as punishment on a second-by-second journey through a barren desert. Instead, he contemplated the future, where he would be, and what experiences he might test. He thought about Adela.

Later in the day, during Adela's break, the boy asked her over to the workshop to talk. She listened as he relayed the conversation with Joyner and Captain Castell the day before. Adela remained silent while the boy outlined several scenarios for their future together; where they might live and what they might experience.

Adela's lips tightened.

"So, you would be gone for three years."

"I am sure I would stop here from time to time. The *Creighton* has a history of using Ketelswarf Shipyard for repair and barnacle removal. Ketelswarf is on the ship's cargo route between Lisbon and Christiania."

"I think you should stay here. Joyner has provided us both with such wonderful opportunities. Look at what you have done for this place. I can continue in the bar. Everything we could want, we can have right here. Our families and friends are close to visit. Couldn't you send for books and learn navigating right here?"

"Maybe. But haven't you ever thought of being someplace else, of seeing what's out there?"

"Brigette is behind this, isn't she, just like that foolish trip to Christiania!

"I guess I should think about it. It's new to me. I've always been here. My whole life is here. I love these beautiful islands. America. How would I understand what they say?"

Confusion choked the boy. He knew he had little time to give Joyner and Captain Castell his decision. Now he feared Adela might have trouble learning English. He had been working on his vocabulary for over ten years in his mother's house of invited strangers. Could he run away from the shame of losing Sailor on such a short, straightforward trip to Norway? Difficult to sit down at the table with Brigette opposite without contemplating a fresh start. Adela meant everything to him. The boy wanted both worlds. Adela and a new world. He wanted to journey with Adela.

In December, he would be eighteen. January would mark a new century; 1800. Where would he celebrate that fantastic day? What port of call would the boy be exploring? A knot twisted in his neck as he stared into the blue eyes of the girl he loved. He could never leave.

"Yes, Adela, think about the possibilities. I only know we should be together."

Adela returned to Ketelswarf Inn. The boy remembered the ditch Joyner had requested that he dig at the edge of the north barn. Perfect. After fifteen minutes of sweat and callus, the boy again buried his thoughts in work. The knot in his neck loosened.

His chores kept the boy busy that night until after midnight. He slept naked beneath a light sheet in the loft's August heat.

Startled awake sometime later in the night, the boy imagined Adela's fresh scent and a tangle of her hair tickling his ear. As he brushed at his hair, Adela stretched out next to him in the bed, her arm encircling his waist, her lips on the back of his neck.

The boy lay sandwiched, facing the wall. His back was pressed by Adela's curves, the back of his calves stroked by one of her legs. Adela, fully dressed, the boy not at all. Adela whispered.

"Quiet, Shh."

The boy had tried to imagine this night's closeness in his dreams. He bravely turned to Adela and kissed her, pulled back, touched her cheek, eyed the smile on her lips, and kissed her again harder, but not too hard. His hand stroked Adela from her bare neck to the bulging curves at her bodice, startled again at the undone laces. He continued down within Adela's blouse, amazed at the softness and fullness she presented and the tight tip standing out against the palm of his hand.

The boy decided to continue kissing Adela's lips and bare shoulders. She liked what he did, bending her neck to him as he tickled her with soft touches. She giggled, caught his face in her hands, and kissed him. He moved his hand softly over the mounds of her chest, delighted by the moan she murmured in his ear. He wanted to light the lantern to look at her beautiful softness, but he did not dare stop for fear Adela would be startled back to primness.

The boy's leg tangled in Adela's dress between her legs, constricting them both. The boy reached down and pulled up her skirt, feeling a moistness in Adela's bloomers.

At that point, Adela drew back.

"I love you!"

The boy swallowed the lump in his throat.

"I love you, Adela."

The boy tried to draw her back to him. Adela withdrew further, stood beside the bed, straightened her skirt and bodice, leaned over, kissed the boy, and danced down the loft ladder.

The boy reached up and touched his face, flushed with excitement. His legs were weak, his member stiff and burning. He cursed himself for not knowing what to do with a beautiful girl. He should have tried more. He should have gone slower, turned up the lantern, and caressed her more. Next time.

Impossible to sleep, the boy dressed in the mugginess of the loft and went out, walking in the direction of the docks searching for the coolness of a beach breeze. The Creighton was swaying majestically in the drydock, ready to sail away in the morning. Two masts, eighteen meters bow to stern with a three-meter prow board. Maybe a four-meter beam. In the moonlight, the ship commanded pride. Sleek of design and well buttoned. The boy went up and caressed the bow as it bobbed.

The vessel chomped at the bit in the drydock, mooring lines scratching and stretching with the strain. The boy connected with the rhythmically bobbing craft. He turned away, went to the Ketelswarf Inn, laid on the bench outside Joyner's door, and slept.

Joyner shook the boy awake and entered his office. The boy followed. Joyner handed him the document.

"Here is the contract. Like I promised, two years, apprentice for navigation. Read it over, and if it is OK, I'll sign, and you'll sign."

"I'll sign it, Joyner. I can't leave Adela. I'm in love with her. But I must do this. I want this. I'll make good for Adela. For us. When I return, she'll see how this can work for us."

"I think you are making the right decision, boy. You are almost eighteen. Your whole life with Adela is ahead of you. Your mother and Brigette will be proud of you. They will help Adela through your apprenticeship. Now go get your gear and get on that ship. I will go tell Captain Castell you are on your way."

The boy returned to the loft and packed his sack with his clothes, the Hadley Quadrant, the hourglass, his notebook of muscle words and notes, and his precious maps. Brigette stood at the door to Gretsen House and waved him to her. They embraced, and she kissed him on the cheek.

"That's from your mother. You make sure you write to us. Good sailing."

The boy met Joyner at the ramp leading up to the *Creighton*. They shook hands. Joyner hugged him, not letting go for a full minute. Carrying his sack over his shoulder, the boy walked up the gangplank. He heard a voice from the upper deck.

"Look sharp, boy, help with the plank. Now, Men, throw off the bowlines."

As the boy helped another sailor pull the gangplank aboard, he saw Adela run toward the ship from Ketelswarf Inn. She stopped as she saw that the *Creighton* had already pulled away. The boy waved to her, his eyes filling with tears. Adela did not wave back.

2 |

SHIPMASTER

Army ants of the subfamily Dorylinae are nomadic and notorious for destroying plant and animal life in their path.

1802

The mariner, carrying a canvas bag slung over his shoulder, spied an available table at the café across the street from the Marché Saint-Antoine in Pointe-à-Pitre. He had time to order a coffee and croissant. He spoke broken French to the garçon, untying the kerchief from his neck and dabbing his forehead. He adjusted the table and his chair to take advantage of the shade from the patio umbrellas. The garçon returned, setting down the small tray.

The booths in the market across from the café table held every fruit and spice imaginable, including maracudja, la mangue, la carambole, and la papaye. The women on the street wore bright blues, greens, yellow, and red-dyed blouses and skirts in every combination. The men preferred straw hats. Splashes of pastel colors adorned most of the buildings. The palm trees swayed in the offshore breeze.

The darkly tanned man enjoyed his coffee. Although only nineteen, crow's feet stretched from the corners of his eyes due to squinting in the Caribbean sun. Everywhere he looked, the men and women hawking or buying were either much browner or nearly black. The pale French soldiers bivouacked around Fort Saint Charles on the southwest shore, not yet obliged to venture on the island.

The man suffered withering stares from many strolling patrons. He heard the name Louis Delgrès floating in and out of the conversations of passersby and groups seated around other tables at the café. The Quartermaster of the *Friendship* out of Portsmouth had told him to be careful in port.

Four hundred mulatto and black insurgents had blown themselves to glory, killing several French soldiers surrounding them at a plantation east of the fort just two months prior. Napoleon's decree, in early May 1902, reinstating slavery on the island, had been met with disgust and resistance by Louis Delgrès and his followers. They had fought to their death. The mariner sympathized; he had endured two years as an indentured servant on the *Creighton* out of Liverpool.

Named by Christopher Columbus, Santa María de Guadalupe de Extremadura, or Guadalupe Island, had become a country in turmoil. Foreigners generally did not linger here during these tense days. The two-mast schooner *Friendship* would sail on the morrow.

The mariner signed on as the third mate of the *Caspia* for a solo cruise from Lisbon to Guadalupe. The *Caspia* landed in Pointe-à-Pitre just two days ago. As luck would have it, the *Caspia* moored next to the *Friendship*, sailing back to New England with a cargo of sugar and rum. The *Friendship* had stopped first in Martinique, where the second mate had contracted yellow fever on shore leave, forbidden to return to the ship. Thus, the opening for the mariner on the *Friendship* at Pointe-à-Pitre.

While in Lisbon, the mariner had relinquished his post on the *Creighton* at the end of his indentured servitude. The mariner, now a free man, master of his fate, possessed respected skills as a navigator. He wanted to escape the Creighton schooner for no reason other than he could. He kept his signed papers in his wallet, securely attached to his belt.

His last year of servitude had, in fact, given him the training and experience promised in the contract negotiated by Joyner Ketelson back on Langeness hallig. Captain Castell had been generous to a fault with his training. He shifted all his navigational duties from himself to his indentured servant. As a result, the mariner could work the marine chronometer and the math involved in point-to-point calculations. During his first year, he ran rigging, swabbed decks, hauled sails, and peeled potatoes as he learned deckhands' duties. The week after his two-year contract expired, the *Creighton* had pulled into port in Lisbon, and the mariner descended the gangplank for the last time.

Writing a letter home, at the time, the mariner explained his intentions to his parents:

> Agnes Lorentzdatter Martensen
>
> Oland Hallig, June 3rd, 1801
>
> To My Dear Mor,
>
> I have completed my indentured servitude and am now free to pursue my dream of sailing to the Americas. I must be careful not to be captured by a marauding British ship and pressed into service. Likewise, I will avoid French recruitment as well. Napoleon has ideas and ambitions that may be fatal to a lowly mariner. If the Royal Navy takes Napoleon on, we will surely see war somewhere in Europe.
>
> I dream of New England in the United States. I can't help but hope that the fledgling country will welcome my contributions and ambitions. A year ago, I heard Adele married a sheep farmer on Fohr. I cannot imagine trading my experiences of the last two years for the life I left. I often think of Adele and trust she is content.
>
> I will try to live in the quiet until I arrive in America. I do not want my history of working on a British merchant ship to follow me if questioned about sailing under a British flag. I trust Fader will know I mean no disrespect

in settling in America. Fader was my first teacher and will forever be dear to me. I will write from my destination, the United States of America.

Your son, **Martin Martensen.**

It took eight months for Martin to secure the position on the *Caspia*. In the meantime, he stayed close to the docks, working as a ship's joiner. He checked vessels heading to the Americas, avoiding British and French commercial lines. Martin turned down several positions for deckhands. He established his name on an account at the Banco de Lisboa in Lisbon. He lived miserly, drank socially to learn what ships might fulfill his needs, and picked up many Spanish and French words and phrases.

Finished with his coffee, Martin opened his bag, checking on the bulky Hadley Quadrant wrapped in his extra shirts. He opened a meter-long canister, extracted the map roll, and spread the English-labeled North American map on the table. Martin put a left-hand finger on Guadalupe and a right index finger on Portsmouth on the coast of America. He extracted his compass from his ditty bag and memorized the compass reading for the route. Would the Shipmaster head in the direction of Portsmouth in the open sea? If so, the navigation equipment on the ship probably included a marine chronometer. Or would the *Friendship* steer toward Florida and work up the coast to Portsmouth?

He would find out soon enough. Martin rerolled and stowed his maps and set off for the *Friendship*.

Captain Burgess required the first and second mates to stand on the bridge as they entered Portsmouth harbor, sailing up the Piscataqua River. On August fourteenth, 1802, Martin first glimpsed America. As the *Friendship* rounded the New Castle promontory, the first mate passed the ship's spyglass to him. He scanned the city of Portsmouth, New Hampshire. The many schooners, cranes, and frames evidenced the ship-building activity of the well-respected port. On the opposite shore, the village of Kittery stepped quaintly up the river banks. Homes and barns dotted the hill to the north.

As the ship tacked leeward, Martin sighted the signalman at the dock directing the *Friendship* to an empty berth between two three-mast schooners. Martin would be busy with docking, securing the ship, stowing lines, and instructing the deck hands on the care of the sails for several hours. The low sun backlit a church steeple in the west. Cargo unloading would begin in the morning, early. He took his leave ashore when his duties were complete.

As he walked the streets of Portsmouth, Martin could not dismiss the newness of everything, the fresh faces. He soon realized there would be no four-hundred-year-old buildings anchoring this city. Such structures, worn and dingy, were common in Lisbon and all the major cities he had seen in Europe. Slaves were everywhere here, working hard. The gentry walked tall, connecting with their ladies and the city. Workers rubbed shoulders on the streets with the elegantly dressed, and no one minded. A community feeling of moving forward draped the streets, satisfaction with what tomorrow would bring. All this in a city surrounded by the unimaginable vastness of land stretching west from the Atlantic shore.

To Martin, soon to be twenty years old, this anticipation of to-morrow's adventures fit him like broken-in boots that never made his feet sore, taking him comfortably around the next corner. This country would be his country. He could not be better matched. Ship repair, shipbuilding, sailing, engineering, navigating, and exploring. Options and opportunity wherever he glanced.

1805

James Danvers stepped up on the porch of the Waterbury Board-ing house of Kittery, Massachusetts, on a fine day in September 1805. Heeding the "Welcome" sign next to the door, he entered the foyer. Mrs. Waterbury, the proprietor, greeted him and directed him up the open staircase and railing to the third room at the top of the stairs. He knocked on the door. Martin Martensen invited him to enter.

Martin, hunched over a map pinned to a table positioned along the north wall of the room, did not look to the door. The windows in the dormer gave plenty of even light for his work. The ceiling slanted to four feet above the floor. Scattered on the table, Danvers noted a variety of pens, ink bottles of different shades, worn-down pencils, and rolled maps. A neatly made bed augmented another corner of the room with three Icelandic wool blankets folded smartly at the foot. Two easy chairs at a small side table piled with books completed the room layout. Framed dock scenes of Portsmouth and Kittery hung on either side of the entry door, painted by local artists.

The wall-mounted artifacts fascinated Danvers, and Martin's Hadley Quadrant was prominently displayed. A Guatemalan area rug in bright pink, greens, and oranges warmed the room.

"You can put the lunch tray over on the bed, Miss Marcia; thank you," said Martin, not looking up.

"I'm afraid I didn't bring up lunch. My name is James Danvers. By the look of your work, I presume you are Mr. Martensen. Martin Martensen?"

"Oh, I apologize, Mr. Danvers. My map carries me away."

The two men met and shook hands in the center of the sixteen-by-twenty-foot room. Martin directed James to one of the two easy chairs. Rather than take the other chair, Martin went to the door and called down the stairs to Mrs. Waterbury to add a sandwich to the lunch tray.

"What would you like to drink, Mr. Danvers, port, beer, coffee?"

"Coffee would be fine, thank you."

Martin yelled down to Mrs. Waterbury to add a cup of coffee.

"Now, how can I be of assistance?"

"Mr. Martensen, I represent an investment group contracted for designing and constructing a Portland-built, small, fast, two-topsail schooner. It will be ready to sail in three months, and we want you to Captain our ship."

"I am flattered, Mr. Danvers, and please call me Martin. But you see, I have turned down shipmaster positions in the past. Cartography and navigation are my specialties. I have a focus now. I have been correcting the maps of Portsmouth Bay and beyond for two years between my travels. I wish to continue in that vein. Besides, I Captained two years ago on a trip to Barbados. I have no stomach for meanly ordering men around under the guise of commanding respect. I wish to finish the revisions to the maps of the shipping lanes in this two-hundred-mile radius."

"Martin, your reputation as a navigator, as well as your map skills, precede you. That trip to Barbados was profitable for the cargo owners; we checked. You sell yourself short, sir. We know your passions and propose a joint Captainship for our enterprise. You would be Captain from September through February. Your counterpart would be Captain between March and August. That way, both captains could enjoy a home life and pursue other interests, such as completing maps, while not on duty.

"I must say, Mr. Danvers, your proposition sounds intriguing. A few questions, sir. You say the ship is small; what is the size, width, draft, and height of the masts? Is there any time for me to influence or approve the design? What cargo will you be carrying? I have personal reasons for not abiding by the slave trade."

"We'll be trading in New England lumber to sell to South America and the West Indies. We'll return with sugar, coffee, and rum, distributing those items along the Atlantic coast. I can arrange for you to view the progress of the ship build as early as the day after tomorrow."

Arrangements having been agreed upon, Martin closed his door on Mr. Danvers, sat back down in his easy chair, and relaxed in the room he called home these past three years. Martin lived in comfort here, remarkably busy. Opportunities kept knocking on his door in this new American world. Young, turning twenty-two in December 1805, Martin reflected on his good fortune. Yes, he is making his mark, he thought, but not ungratefully. He had worked hard to achieve status.

A big fish in the American pond? Indeed, he would not have been picked for such a prestigious assignment on a wood-fresh sailing ship in Europe, Asia, England, or France.

If the design of the new sailing schooner met with his approval, he would take the job.

Martin captained the topsail schooner *Sting* from November to February 1805, September 1805 to February 1806, and September 1806 to February 1807. The *Sting's* deck was fifty-two feet long. Sporting a twelve-foot beam and a hold depth of eight feet six inches, the ship profited by an eighty-seven-ton capacity.

A crew of twenty-eight manned the *Sting*. The swift ship had six, twelve-pounder carronades for protection.

Martin's quartermaster, a crusty man at least twice Martin's age, knew how to turn Martin's soft, sure orders into a bark. Captain and quartermaster Quintus Langland worked well together after the storm in January 1806 blew the *Sting* out to sea. Martin, at the wheel, kept the ship cutting the enormous waves of the gale without losing a sailor or breaking up any cargo.

He had a good crew, well paid by the owners' group. Samuel Good-all, the co-captain of the *Sting*, nearly as young as Martin, became good friends and comrades of Quintus and Martin. Over time, the investment group made a healthy profit. Clouds of war in Napoleon's stretching empire concerned the owners, thus the reason the *Sting* kept to the west coast of the Atlantic.

The typical run for the *Sting* consisted of a direct route from Portland or Freeport to a West Indies island such as Puerto Rico, Haiti, Martinique, or sometimes the Yucatan peninsula in Mexico. The men spent two days unloading the lumber the *Sting* carried in the hold. After one day of shore leave, the ship would sail to Puerto Rico to be loaded with sugar, rum, or coffee. Stops returning to Portland usually included Philadelphia, New York, and Boston; sometimes Washington and Portsmouth.

In the off months of his contract as a shipmaster, Martin sailed his twenty-four-foot sloop in and out of the coves and river outlets around Portsmouth and Portland. He used his own marine chronometer and sextant to accurately locate points on his shoreline sketches of the area. On rainy or cloudy days, Martin worked in his room at the comfort of his map table, formalizing his new map of the coast.

One such day in March of 1807, as a thunderstorm clapped the bay and rain pelted his dormer windows, Mrs. Waterbury brought in lunch, setting a tray on the bed.

"Sardines, sharp cheddar, hard roll, and strawberry jam for lunch, Martin. Milk to drink."

"Thanks, Mrs. Waterbury; I'll get to it soon."

"Martin, I have been asked to invite you to a cotillion in April."

"Really! Sounds a little formal for me, Mrs. Waterbury."

"Yes, perhaps, but you can't expect to stay cooped up in this room or on your ship forever. I'll see to you getting a formal invitation."

When the invitation came in the post, Martin looked it over once and dropped it on the side table holding his books. He picked it up, read it, and put it back down every few nights. In April, Mrs. Waterbury reminded Martin of the event that Saturday. He decided that it would please the widow Waterbury for him to attend. Martin considered her a friend, as well as his landlord.

That Saturday, Martin dressed in his finest pants, silk shirt, dark green six-button vest, and matching topcoat with tails. His black top hat added height to his five-foot-nine-inch frame. He kept the collar of his overcoat flipped up around the back of his neck. His Caribbean tan had faded, but his hair still appeared bleached from the tropical sun. He maintained the shoulders and muscular arms he had built up in the Halligen working alongside his crew. As such, he kept a fit stature, tight at the waist and slim at the hip. He never overindulged in food or drink. Downstairs he waited for Mrs. Waterbury to adjust her shawl. The buggy and driver were already waiting in front of the boarding house.

The debutante ball was slated to be held in Lady Pepperrell's house on Pepperrell Road, now owned by Mr. Jacob Sperling, across from the Congregational Church. It had been decorated by the mothers and sisters of the debutantes. Tables with fine linens lined one side of the hall, and caterers and servers swarmed over them, assuring fresh, filled serving dishes. Kittery was no match for Washington or Boston, yet all guests received the courtesy of being announced as they arrived just the same. Thankfully, Mrs. Waterbury steered Martin around the parlor, introducing him to people he would never remember but with whom he could display a modicum of politeness.

He took his leave to the veranda overlooking the bay, sipping port. He thought momentarily about the dance he had never attended with Adele on Langeness Hallig. A girl on the other side of the veranda, watching the moonlight sprinkle the water, caught his eye. Standing in shadow, Martin could not make out much of her features but enough to intrigue. A bell sounded. The girl turned, meeting Martin in the doorway, and they walked side by side back into the hall, running the length of the house. The girl stunned Martin in the soft candlelit glow of the massive chandeliers hanging about the room. Martin walked with her to the open staircase. The girl lifted the front of her dress, climbing the stairs. Martin took her left gloved hand in his, his right hand delicately taking her elbow, helping her up the first few steps, standing to the side of the stairs. She looked at him and smiled, mouthing a silent thank you before vanishing at the turn of the landing.

In a few minutes, four young women dressed in similar white gowns with hoop skirts aligned themselves on steps above the landing. They all stepped down one step, waved, and curtsied. The crowd applauded. When the applause ended, the first girl walked haltingly down to the landing and waited to be announced.

"Mr. and Mrs. Gerald Greiner present their daughter: Miss Emily Adeline Greiner."

Emily managed a crooked smile. Emily continued down the grand stairway and into the south parlor to be with her family. The second girl moved to the center of the landing.

"Mr. and Mrs. John Morrison present their daughter: Miss Sarah Ophelia Morrison."

Sarah curtsied and traipsed down the stairs, entering the north parlor. The third girl, the one Martin had almost met on the veranda, moved forward to the landing, head high: smiling. Looking at him?

"Mr. and Mrs. Richard Parsons present their daughter: Miss Rachel Parsons."

Rachel curtsied low as if she had practiced hundreds of times. Graceful to the point of seeming regal, at least to Martin, she curtsied a second time, then looked up at the last girl on the stairs, smiling encouragement. Rachel descended the staircase and moved into the west room, where her family awaited. The fourth girl came forward, but Martin did not see or hear anything in the hall after Rachel's second curtsy. He memorized Rachel's features, perhaps his last chance to see her among admirers.

Martin had spotted short heels, white stockings as she lifted her dress on the stairs, and slender legs. She had to be about five feet six. A single ostrich feather: fluffed with her movements, accessorizing her light brown pinned-up hair. She wore a delicate satin choker and carried her head upright and confident, not haughty, impressing Martin. Beautiful. The first girl in six years that Martin wished to hold close.

When Rachel moved into the west room, her parents congratulated her. Mrs. Parsons conversed with Mrs. Waterbury, who desperately scanned the room. When she spotted Martin, she gestured for him to come over. Mrs. Waterbury introduced him to the family; Rachel stood between her parents.

"Richard, Dorothy, I'd like you to meet Captain Martin Martensen. Martin, please meet Richard and Dorothy Parsons. Their daughter is Rachel, the third debutante introduced tonight."

Richard Parsons shook Martin's hand.

"Pleased to meet you, young man. What did you think of our fine young ladies tonight?"

"Mr. Parsons, Mrs. Parsons, pleased to meet you. Frankly, sir, your daughter has stolen the show tonight. Miss Parsons, I am pleased to make your acquaintance."

Rachel curtsied.

"My pleasure, as well, Captain Martensen. Would you care to take a dance on my card? I'd love to hear of your travels."

"I will take a slot, Miss Parsons; thank you. Although I am much more comfortable on a rocking ship's deck than I am dancing. Will you be patient with me?"

Rachel showed Martin where to fill in his name on her card, picking the fourth dance as a possible introduction to help Martin learn the steps. Other gentlemen were pulling Rachel into the center of a card-signing frenzy.

Mr. Parsons suggested he and Martin find another glass of port. They discussed Mr. Parsons' brick-laying business as well as the specifications of the *Sting*. Martin found the gentleman as easy to talk to as most Americans he had met. Mr. Parsons spoke about his successful business pursuits without hinting at the British snobbery that his former countrymen would have demanded. Martin made sure to give Richard Parsons one of his cards. Dorothy Parsons chatted with her good friend Mrs. Waterbury but kept an eye on the Captain.

When the string quartet began their introduction, the four girls greeted the gentlemen who had filled in their name for the first dance, meeting their partner in the grand hall and forming up for the dance. Although Martin did not know the first thing about the dance or the relatively easy steps. The dance consisted of a walk around and bow, coming together and nodding, backing away, and turning. Martin had developed a necessary and deft sense of balance on the rocking deck of his seafaring ships. Dancing incorporated the same light, balls of the feet approach. By the fourth dance, Martin relaxed, confident he could catch on with Rachel's help.

To his surprise, Rachel approached, greeted him, and showed him the hold for the fourth dance. She positioned his hand on the small of her back and took his left hand in her gloved right hand. Martin sensed the warmth of the last three dances in her back, virtually losing all concentration. In the fourth dance, a waltz invoked different steps from the step-together-bow movements of the last three dances. Rachel demonstrated the basic one, two, and three counts of the waltz just before the music began; then, they were off. Martin stepped out of sync with his partner the first two times around the room. He concentrated on his balance and the count in his head. Then he looked at hazel-eyed Rachel looking up at him. His shoulders relaxed. The music's repetitious three counts, Rachel's laughing smile, and the Captain's upright stature worked together, and the couple began to cruise around the room. Balance is the key to dancing, along with looking up ahead instead of at the floor and feet. By the end of the dance, Martin had accounted for himself appropriately.

"Thank you for the lesson. You are indeed a beautiful dancer."

"We did well together. We will dance again, I think."

As the last dance of the night began, many in the crowd started to sort hats and coats. Martin and Mrs. Waterbury thanked Mr. And Mrs. Parsons for invitations to the cotillion. Rachel broke away from the three boys capturing her attention and came to Martin to say goodnight. He bowed, kissed her gloved hand, and placed his other hand on top, holding her hand in both hands for a long moment, thanking her again for the dance.

On the carriage ride home, Mrs. Waterbury reviewed the events of the evening, the scrumptious food, wine, and decorations. Martin confessed it had been his first dance but enjoyable. Mrs. Waterbury shared more of Parsons' history, Richard's arrival from England, and their additional children. Martin's heart sank to hear that Rachel had just turned a sophisticated sixteen when he would be twenty-four in December. The captain shook his head. He was too old to be of interest to such a vibrant young lady as Rachel Parsons.

Richard Parsons, ready for bed, sitting on the side chair in the bedroom, considered the fate of Rachel, his youngest daughter. He had raised eight children, including Rachel. William, his youngest, had celebrated his tenth birthday two weeks ago. Two daughters had found husbands, but Nancy, twenty-three, and Mary, twenty, still lived at home. Richard pondered Rachel's prospects as he waited for Dorothy to finish dressing for bed. The young men close to Rachel's age were not serious about their futures yet; the party made that obvious.

"Nancy and Mary should be introduced to Captain Martensen.

"Perhaps we should have Captain Martensen over for dinner, my dear. He could meet Nancy and Mary and perhaps strike up a liking for one or the other."

Dorothy rushed back into the bedroom.

"Hush now, Richard; Rachel may have heard you. Didn't you see how they looked at each other during the waltz? Rachel put the man on her card for that dance, particularly to be close to him."

"But he is Nancy's age. He gave me his card. Perhaps he will present himself, and then we can have him to dinner. I do believe he is an excellent prospect for one of my daughters. I like him."

"Mildred Waterbury says he is the nicest, most respectful boarder ever renting one of her rooms."

"Yes, perhaps, but a shipmaster spends most of his time at sea. It is a dangerous occupation, especially in these times. I'm embarrassed by my countrymen raiding American ships, impressing American sailors. Then there is the weather."

"Perhaps you are right, dear. Snuff your candle. I'll take Rachel's temperature for the man tomorrow."

Dorothy already knew what Rachel would say.

Martin waited over a week before hiring a cab to take him to the address of Richard Parsons' house. He planned his arrival for seven o'clock, beyond the dinner hour, but early enough to catch the household in their parlor. Every day his conviction strengthened. He must see if Rachel might consider his friendship. If so, he must put the question of their age difference to a test.

In Martin's estimation, a ten-year-old answered the front door. Martin gave the boy his card and asked to meet with Mr. Parsons. The boy closed the door, and Martin heard a loud "Dad" through the door. In a minute, Richard Parsons, the boy at his side, opened the door and invited Martin into the foyer.

"William, this is Captain Martensen. He sails a ship named *Sting* between Portland and the West Indies. Why don't you go ask your mother to come out to greet Mr. Martensen?

"Now, Martin, may I ask the nature of your visit?"

"I wish permission to call on your daughter, Mr. Parsons. I arranged for Mrs. Waterbury to chaperone if you and Rachel grant permission."

Dorothy Parsons entered the front hall.

"Of course, you have our permission, Captain Martensen. Might I suggest that you join us for dinner Saturday night? You can meet the rest of the family. We'll fix a nice pot roast; how does that sound?"

"Why that would be fine, Mrs. Parsons, thank you."

"Certainly, we'll expect you at six o'clock this Saturday."

Martin arrived precisely at six o'clock on Saturday, offering a small loaf of apple bread, prepared by Mrs. Waterbury, to Mrs. Parsons when she opened the door. She led Martin into the parlor, offered him a chair, and suggested a small glass of port wine. Richard came into the parlor, followed closely by William. Richard shook Martin's hand and sat down on the chair next to Martin. Next, two women entered and were introduced as Mary and Nancy, sisters of Rachel. Martin stood, bowing to each. Rachel arrived in the parlor a minute later, followed by Mrs. Parsons. Pleasantries about the weather were exchanged, and, in the pause afterward, William sat down in front of Martin with his legs crossed.

"Have you ever seen any pirates, Captain Martensen? Have you ever had to fight a pirate ship?"

"So far, I have met up with three privateers on my run along the Atlantic coast. I have been able to outrun them or outmaneuver them without a cannon shot fired. Sorry to disappoint you, William."

"That would have to be some sailing to outsmart pirates."

"And a measure of luck."

Mrs. Parsons called everyone to dinner. Mary and Nancy sat on one side of the table, with Martin positioned awkwardly between them. Rachel and William were seated across from Martin. Dorothy and Richard were on the two ends of the table. When Richard or Dorothy made an amusing comment, Mary would touch Martin's hand while laughing. Rachel rarely smiled.

Martin, appalled, struggled to maintain civility. He felt he sat on the auction block at the county fair, being sold to the highest bidder for marriage. Mary outbid Nancy at the sale. As dinner progressed, Rachel became convinced of the outcome as well. Martin attempted to engage her in conversation across the table, but either Mary, Nancy, or Richard chimed in preemptively.

After dinner, Martin politely weathered dinner conversation in the parlor for an hour before taking his leave and thanking the family for an excellent dinner. Martin walked down the path to the street. Dorothy stepped out on the porch, closing the door behind her. She ran to catch up to Martin, hailing him softly.

"Captain Martensen, Captain Martensen."

"Yes, Mrs. Parsons."

"I wanted to apologize for your treatment this evening. What were we thinking? Mr. Parsons worries about all five of our daughters. It is his habit. Mine as well, if I can admit.

"Rachel told me of her excitement over your request to be chaperoned the other day. She may be upstairs writing in her journal as we speak. She is a strong girl and respects her older sisters. I hope you will not think unkindly of her."

"Rachel is a beautiful girl, Mrs. Parsons. I will admit to you that I have eyes only for her. Perhaps I have gotten ahead of myself. A shipmaster's life may necessitate a solitary life. Rachel will find an appropriate suitor. I am certain Mary and Nancy will as well. Thank you again for the excellent dinner."

Ten days later, Martin, working on his map's Portland area, heard a glass crash downstairs. When he went to the landing, he saw a vase with splintered glass all around Miss Rachel Parsons, standing still at the bottom of the stairs. Mrs. Waterbury picked up the significant shards and left to find a broom and dustpan. Martin leaned over the banister.

"Is everything alright, Miss Parsons? Do you need a plaster?"

"I am fine, Captain Martensen."

Mrs. Waterbury returned and began sweeping. She called up to Martin.

"Sorry to disturb you, Martin. Rachel brought over some quilt patterns Dorothy and I are patching, and I gave Rachel a vase of flowers to take back home. Unfortunately, the vase slipped out of my hand while I handed it to her. Quite a mess, but I think I have a handle on it."

Rachel agreed.

"Yes, I am fine, Captain."

"Rachel, before you go, would you like to see the map I am working on? That would be alright, would it not, Mrs. Waterbury?"

Mrs. Waterbury did not hesitate.

"I can't see the harm, Martin. Keep the door open, and let me know if you need anything?"

Rachel left Mrs. Waterbury for the cleanup and glided up the stairs. Martin held the door to his room for her as she brushed by.

"This room is amazing, Captain Martensen. This rug is so colorful. These are strange pieces on the wall. So worldly. You must think us insignificant here in Kittery."

"Not at all, Miss Rachel. I have learned that every part of the world and society has something to offer if you leave yourself open to explore it. This ornate spoon is from Lisbon, Portugal. The blankets on the bed are from Iceland."

He took Rachel by the elbow, leading her to the maps table. She recognized the ports of Portsmouth and Portland, Kittery, and Freeport. The intricate swirls and different ink colors struck her as a beautifully imagined painting. Much more than just a map.

Rachel took another moment to glance around the room and then back to the map Martin bent over. She appeared bewildered. This handsome, vital man who danced with a swan's grace seemed genuinely interested in her. His stature, obvious intelligence, broad shoulders, and shock of blond hair were incongruent with his gentle manner. Martin straightened, lost in the look of Rachel's eyes, the glow of her cheeks in the warm room, and the soft white of her neck. He kept a finger pointing to an unlabeled dot.

"That is the location of your house, Miss Rachel."

The Captain had marked her home on his map. Rachel's heart began beating so fast she almost fainted. Instead, she steeled herself, took him in her arms, and kissed him. Willing him to return her affections.

Martin thought her impossible to resist. He knew then that Rachel and he would sail and explore America together. He broke from her embrace for Mrs. Waterbury to set down a tray of sandwiches, acting as if she had not seen or heard a thing. She stayed while the three of them ate lunch.

Rachel said goodbye to Martin and Mildred Waterbury at the front door. As Martin turned away to the stairs, Mildred winked at Rachel. Rachel smiled broadly and nodded, already formulating her journal entry.

Martin asked Mr. Parsons for permission to request Rachel's hand in marriage on the afternoon of June 10th. He found Richard at the Parson's Bricklaying current building site on 8th Avenue in Kittery. Martin told Mr. Parsons that he intended to sail with Rachel in his sloop down to Newburyport for dinner at the Weatherton Restaurant and Tavern.

Rachel tested her sailing skills on a thrilling, windy trip down to Newburyport. She loved her Captain. Her family appeared to admire him as well. William could not get enough of Martin's stories of the Caribbean and his years on the Mediterranean. While wrapped in Martin's heavy wool coat, Rachel held the tiller until they passed Hampton Beach. The clouds moved out to sea, and the sun poured down on the sloop; the overcoat was discarded. At times Rachel stood at the tiller, her dress billowing in the breeze, her hair all a tangle, just the way Martin liked it. Martin kept one eye on the sea to assure their safety. A smile of anticipation never left him the whole trip.

That evening, as the candle burned down in the center of the small table, in the quiet of the Weatherton, in the middle of Rachel's forkful of cherry pie, Martin arose, kneeled, and offered her an engagement band. Rachel squealed, rising from her chair, jumping up and down like a little girl, turning around and around. She literally jumped into an embrace with her Captain.

"Yes, yes, yes, a thousand times, yes."

The couple sailed home and discussed the realities of getting married, where they would live, and what it might be like to be married to a sailor. The couple wrapped themselves in one of Martin's wool blankets for the trip back, arranging other blankets over the bottom boards as cushions. They were semi-prone on either side of the centerboard while Martin controlled the tiller. Their heads bent close together. Their kisses warmed them both. They imagined they could touch the stars, bright pinpricks against the black night sky. Behind their sail, the wind steadied for a run up the coast. They were far enough from the shore that Martin could follow the north star. Martin pointed out the Big Dipper, Cassiopeia, and the other constellations banding across the milky way. He kept one eye on the lights of the coast so as not to miss the Portsmouth harbors. They decided they would marry on the first Sunday in March 1808.

In late June, a messenger requested Martin to attend a conference at the Atlantic Import/Export and Shipping Co. offices headquartered in Portland. James Danvers gave nothing away in the message. Martin, called upon as it were, more than two months ahead of his regular schedule, anxiously proceeded to headquarters. Quintus Langland and Captain Goodall had already graced the office when Martin came in and sat in the remaining chair across James' desk. Greetings were exchanged; James began the meeting.

"Martin, to catch you up, the British ship *Ingot* overran the *Sting* east of Boston while returning from Barbados with a full load of sugar and rum."

Samuel picked up the narrative.

"The *Ingot* came out of the fog on our tail. When our crow's nest saw her, we had enough time to turn and show our guns on the port side. The *Ingot* fired a warning shot that missed our stern. I couldn't have put a dent in the frigate, so I capitulated."

Quintus continued, "They boarded us and confiscated as much rum as they had room for. They marched fourteen of our twenty-seven crew off to the Ingot. We hobbled home with what crew we had left, everyone working double shifts."

James had other news.

"Three other shipping companies have been attacked this month alone. The word is that the French have had some success against the Royal Navy. The British have so many ships they cannot keep them manned. We pay better, and our ships are supposed to remain neutral; it is no wonder British mariners wish to work for us instead."

Martin asked James if there had been any news from Washington?

"No, Martin, not a word."

"Jefferson has got to declare war on England if this keeps escalating. The British cannot be allowed to raid our ships. What recourse do we have, James? What about the *Sting*?"

"We have heard no reassurances from Washington. It seems Jefferson is reluctant to commit our forces. The United States Navy now has six frigates and eleven ships in the line. The British have over five hundred ships in the Royal Navy; most are overseas contesting Napoleon's navy."

James Danvers paused; he was responsible for dropping the other shoe.

"The owners have decided to cancel our winter runs and wait for developments from Washington. Who knows, we may all be impressed into the United States Navy by then and fighting the Revolutionary War again."

Martin had anticipated the owners' conclusions.

"I, for one, will use the time to establish a household. I'm getting married in the spring. James, I'd gladly help as a carpenter on that new ship you're building. I can stay busy. The crew, well, let's not rebuild the crew until we hear about Jefferson's next move."

Martin rushed home to tell Rachel he would remain in port for the winter. She had many questions about their March 6th wedding date next year. A week later, after many discussions between Rachel, Mrs. Parsons, and Rachel's sisters, the wedding date was moved to Sunday, November 1st, 1807.

1807

The Rev. William Briggs, the pastor of the First Congregational church across from Lady Pepperrell's house (where Martin and Rachel had first danced), conducted the ceremony. Martin socialized with the entire Parsons family for the first time. Richard's eldest two daughters had three children of their own. A confusing affair for Martin; he rarely took his eyes away from his bride. His euphoria and a rare sunny day in November made the day memorable for more than eighty-five citizens of Kittery. Martin secured the adjoining room to Martin's in Mrs. Waterbury's boarding house. The couple dined on Mrs. Waterbury's sandwiches and stews for over a week before venturing into the community as a married couple.

For one so young, Rachel felt an urgency to please her husband and establish independence from her family. Martin could not have been happier with Rachel's strength in learning the ways of married life. She took over several routine duties in Mrs. Waterbury's kitchen, assisting in the dusting, sweeping, and rug beating in tenants' rooms. She even prepared one meal per week for the household.

Mrs. Waterbury knocked politely on Martin and Rachel's door on Christmas day, 1807. The knock meant the New Hampshire Gazette had been dropped outside their door. Martin read the front-page headline with consternation. An embargo on all US commercial ships had been enacted by Congress at Thomas Jefferson's request. Martin read and reread the embargo conditions, trying to understand the implications for himself, the Atlantic Import/Export and Shipping Co., and New England interests.

Counterintuitive. Jefferson banned US ships from sailing to prevent the British impressment of sailors into the Royal Navy. No ships leaving port meant no impressment by marauding Royal Navy ships. The temporary hiatus from his trips to the West Indies had just become permanent. This action would economically hurt the British and French because they could not import US goods. Of course, the British could now garner the trade the *Sting* typically contracted with Caribbean countries. The only possible advantage might be a United States stall while Jefferson built up the navy in preparation for a fight with England. With no mention of naval conscription, Martin faced the loss of his job.

Martin informed James Danvers that he would seek work in Kittery to be near his home. When the embargo ended, he would return to Portland and continue as Captain of the *Sting*. Richard Parsons assisted Martin in securing employment as a carpenter. Richard and his masonry business worked hand-in-hand with a busy construction company. Martin worked steadily. Unlike most mariners stuck in New England ports, Martin and Rachel suffered little due to the economic downturn caused by the embargo. Working with his hands satisfied Martin as much as exploring the waterways of New England. When you are at it, work is work. The Hallig tasks from his youth came to mind as Martin whistled while he whittled.

1809

On February 28th, 1809, Rachel gave birth to Samuel. Baby and mother remained healthy and robust. Martin had spent much of the birthing pacing outside in an east coast snowstorm, walking one block and then another, checking in with Mary, Rachels' sister, on each circuit.

President James Madison lifted the embargo of 1807 on March 1, 1809. The fifteen-month ban had been disastrous for the economy of the United States and had not really stressed the British or French. James Danvers invited Martin to return to Portland and captain the *Sting* for his September regular run to the West Indies. His fall/winter runs to Guadalupe, Guatemala, and Haiti proceeded without incident, although he missed his son's first steps in late February 1810.

The Martensen family decided to build a house in Portland, Massachusetts, to be close to the offices of his employer. Shipbuilding in Portland and Freeport accelerated after the lifting of the embargo. Exciting ship designs, slimmer, longer, and faster, were launched from the two ports. Martin had prospered during the boycott. The Atlantic Import/Export and Shipping Company loaned him half the money to construct a home in Portland. Martin had saved the other half by adding part of his wages as a carpenter to his savings transferred from Lisbon.

Repairs to the hull of the *Sting* delayed the start of Martin's first run south in 1810. Martin spent the extra time gathering references and writing up his intentions to become a citizen of the United States. He appeared before a circuit court judge in Portsmouth with his documents. Eight years after his first sighting in America, Captain Martensen renounced his allegiance to the Danish monarchy and pledged allegiance to his newly adopted country. He became a damn proud Yankee. From that first week in Portsmouth and Kittery, he had known how well he would fit into this country, the United States.

As an indentured servant, Martin never turned bitter toward his British superiors on the *Creighton*. These days, he had no warm thoughts for the "Regulars." There were aspects of New England foreign to him, some even abhorrent. As a former indentured servant, Martin could not reconcile the institution of slavery. Work is work, but a modicum of freedom and worth should accompany a man's struggles. One by one, the countries of Europe banned the practice of slavery, including Britain, in 1807. Indians were like ghosts to Martin; rarely seen, but out there, sometimes raiding and killing, sometimes trading goods and cultures.

On balance, the people of New England wanted, no, demanded opportunities to improve themselves and the greater public. This entire country felt fresh and alive with promise.

He made seven round trips after the repairs to the *Sting* were completed, meeting up with only one British ship on his last return trip near Virginia Beach. Martin cut back to the bay at Hampton, Virginia. Before returning, the British chased the Sting to the Chesapeake Bay and the Potomac. Martin waited three days and then ventured back into the Atlantic on a night sail, continuing north to Portland without further incident. James Danvers read the account of the chase from the ship's log, always impressed with Martin's sailing skills on his escapades.

Mr. Danvers reported all such incidents to the commander at Fort Preble in South Portland. News of the British challenge to the *Sting* reached the command at the naval station in Portsmouth, and Mr. Danvers and Martin were called to the station for a meeting.

The naval station had doubled in size since 1800 when it opened. With the completion of a massive warehouse, Martin could not imagine the size of a ship that might be built in such a facility. Perhaps the largest ship on the line? President Madison seemed not as reluctant as Jefferson to test the might of the Royal Navy? Danvers and Martensen made their way to the conference room in the original building next to the construction sites. They met with the former naval station commander, Isaac Hull, now the commanding officer of the USS Constitution. A representative of the War Department, Mr. Paul Hamilton, also attended the meeting.

A chalkboard and a corkboard covered the entire wall in the front of the room. The other three partitions contained four-foot-high by three-foot-wide framed maps of three sections of the West Atlantic Coast. Introductions out of the way, Martin reviewed the chase of the *Sting* by the *HMS Shannon* up the Chesapeake Bay. Martin rose, approached the appropriate map, and pointed out the zigs and zags he had commanded to elude the British Frigate. Commodore Hull unbuttoned his dress uniform coat.

"That, right there, Mr. Secretary, is an act of aggression tantamount to an attack in the jurisdictional waters of the United States. When will Washington declare, Paul? When?"

"You know as well as I, Isaac, that if no shots were fired, we would be hard-pressed to call the British out on this run up the Chesapeake."

"Only because Captain Martensen outsailed the nincompoops on the *Shannon*, avoiding capture, impressment, or worse."

Secretary Hamilton interrupted the conjectures.

"Captain Martensen, your name has been called to our attention by Mr. Danvers on another matter we want to discuss. Commodore Hull has examined your ship's log. He supports Mr. Danvers's opinion of your sailing skills.

"We at the War Department are interested in another skill attested to by Mr. Danvers. We understand you have been revising the coastal map of the New England shoreline from the District of Maine down as far as Boston."

Martin replied with a modicum of pride.

"I would say I have concentrated on the area twenty miles north of Freeport down to approximately twenty miles north of Boston. Yes sir. Navigation and Cartography are my passions, along with attention to my loving wife and child. Another one is on the way, by and by. Of course, my responsibility to the crew and cargo of the *Sting* is paramount."

Congratulations circulated around the table. James steered the discussion back on track.

"Martin's maps are incredible, gentlemen. I have seen small boulders called out with tidal implications."

Secretary Hamilton rose from the table and addressed the others.

"Commodore Hull, what would be the value of these charts if war were to break out."

"Unquestionably, invaluable."

"That's what we thought. Captain Martensen, the War Department, would like to make a proposal. But first, a few details. We understand you have applied recently for United States citizenship. Why have you waited until now?"

The room quieted. Martin gathered his thoughts.

"As I understand the law, Secretary Hamilton, I must establish a permanent residence for several years before gaining citizenship. Spending as much time out to sea as I have makes that problematic. I have married and settled. I have experienced firsthand the promise this country presents to a man and have now adopted that promise for myself."

"And your father-in-law, Mr. Richard Parsons? Have you any reservations about the man? He is a British subject, I believe."

"Mr. Parsons has supported my family's endeavors throughout the Embargo. I have heard him extoll the benefits and aspirations for his new home over his embarrassment for his former involvement in England. He is an American entrepreneur, through and through, sir."

"And you, yourself are not British?" asked Commodore Hull.

"I am from a small Frisian Island off the west coast of Denmark, near the northern German border. My earliest memories are of work, hard, hard work, and hardship, but I hoped I may one day sail to America."

"We may well need your maps, Captain Martensen. Can you show us an example where our map is outdated?"

Martin stepped over to the wall map that included Freeport and Portland. He traced one of the bays with a wooden pointer, then moved to the chalkboards. Martin spent two minutes sketching an enlarged map of the bay he had traced on the board. The accuracy of the blown-up drawing was uncanny. Martin never looked back at the map on the wall to his right.

"The isthmus to the east of Atkins Bay is as shown, except there is a cove at this point. A hard-to-noise cove, not on the map, which you can't see unless you know it is there, jutting back toward the north shore. There is also one hundred feet of rock reef in the open water just south of that hidden cove. At low tide, the ridge of the reef is about two feet below the surface. On my map, the length and depth are noted."

"That's the level of detail on his maps that Martin has established and I have told you about," James interjected.

Commodore Hull knuckle wrapped the table.

"A large frigate in open water would be foolish to follow Captain Martensen into territorial waters he has mapped, gentlemen. Invaluable indeed."

Secretary Hamilton placed both hands on the table, leaning toward Martin.

"The government will supplement your pay in your off-sailing season to continue with your maps. However, you would inform your family and friends that the government has confiscated and concluded your work on the maps. If aggressions continue, President Madison will act, gentlemen. Be assured.

"British spies, however, may have interest in your endeavors. Please operate cautiously henceforth, Captain Martensen."

James, quiet for a few moments, offered an additional thought.

"If I may suggest, Mr. Secretary, we should avoid rumors of government involvement in this work. A bit of play-acting might be advantageous. Martin will publicly burn his maps and profess the discontinuance of his work in this area. He'll express frustration with his inability to be recognized by the government for his work."

Secretary Hamilton nodded and approached Martin hoping to shake his hand.

"What do you say, Captain Martensen? Willing?"

"Of course, sirs, with honor."

Martin continued his cartography of the eastern seaboard throughout the spring and summer of 1811. The bonfire of his maps on the lawn in front of his home occurred in early May. Martin's histrionics were recorded in an article for the New Hampshire Gazette. The burning maps (just blank sheets mixed in with existing rolled-up maps) did cause the Martensen family a bit of consternation. Neighbors and friends of Rachel suspected Martin of madness or despair. She assured her friends that she would weather his current mood. After all, she explained, their son, expected in October, would shake Martin out of his melancholy.

The *Sting* surreptitiously avoided a British cruiser on Martin's second trip out of Portland in September 1811. The deckhand in the crow's nest of the *Sting* could not make out the ship's name, only its colors. Martin dropped all sails, making his imprint on the seas indistinguishable from the horizon in the setting sun. The British ship never spotted the *Sting*.

Upon his return to Portland, Martin attended his son's christening, also named Martin, born in October, while he sailed back from Haiti.

In December, the New Hampshire Gazette carried an account of the Battle of Tippecanoe. Talk of impending war continued to mount. Rachel became fearful that their home would be overrun by the Shawnee.

"What if they invade while you are away, Martin? What should we do? The Gazette said that the British supplied Tecumseh with muskets and powder."

"The Gazette also said that the American force defeated the Shawnee at Tippecanoe. I am concerned, Rachel. You and the boys mean everything to me. From what I have heard, I believe we will be at war soon. Yet, I have a job, and the *Sting* needs to make as many trips as possible before the war starts. I've got to ship out."

That night in bed, Martin stroked his wife so softly and persistently that she relaxed and submitted to his need. Afterward, Rachel held Martin with arms wrapped tight, her legs encircling his.

On his last trip of the season in February 1812, Martin spied a British ship in his path to the south. He turned his vessel out to sea, taking the absolute swiftest tact in a good wind to distance the *Sting* from the British ship, heading northeast in the opposite direction. Martin sailed three days out before turning south, no longer afraid of being followed: navigating a direct course to Haiti and not crossing the path of British ships for the rest of the trip.

Upon Martin's return to Portland, James Danvers came down to the dock as Martin's crew tied off and began unloading the cargo.

"Martin, if you've got your land balance back, how about some beer to celebrate another successful trip."

"A quick one, sure, James. I want to get home soon, though. Rachel had a difficult time saying goodbye when I left this trip."

The two made their way to the Lobster Claw Tavern at the end of the dock. Sailors crowded every corner of the bar, but the owner knew James and Martin well, offering them a table in a back room, perfect for a quiet conversation over beers.

"I didn't take on as much as you would have liked, James. These days I think we should sacrifice cargo for speed. A frigate chased me again, this trip. That's why I'm late."

"If the war does come, when it comes, the Royal Navy will intensify their blockade, attempting to sink our ships."

"I agree. Perhaps we must put the business on hold again; stop shipping altogether."

"No, James, if it's another embargo, I think the Sting can continue to evade. But if war is declared, I say we must do our part. If the situation calls for it, I'll use the cannons."

"Don't you think they'll bring more ships to strangle us?"

"Yes, they will try, but my idea is to sail at night, hide in one of those four hidden coves I have sussed, continuing right past their blockade the second night. I must vary the coves we hide in enough that the British don't catch on."

"If you're willing, Martin. Of course, there'd be hazard pay incentives for the men if war is declared."

"When James, when there's war."

President Madison declared war on June 18, 1812. The citizens of Portland discussed their fears and bragged for days. Rachel, seven months pregnant, sat down at the table for breakfast. She was child hardy now, this being her third birthing. Martin brought her a cup of tea as well as one for himself.

"I don't know how long this war will last. The talk is that most of the fighting will occur along the Canadian border and the Great Lakes. Those waterways are too valuable for the British to concede."

"Are you thinking of volunteering for the Navy?"

"No, I think not unless I am conscripted. Besides, the Navy still doesn't have many ships to man. The merchant ships are just as important to keep supplies moving. I believe I can be more useful in the waters along the Atlantic coast. The waters I know well."

"That makes sense, Martin, but so dangerous."

"It's been dangerous. I keep quiet about it. I must do more now, so I'll have to be away. I'll still come home and see you and the children every chance I get."

The *Sting,* three-quarters loaded with lumber, readied to depart the first week in August: with Martin at the helm. Quintus came on board as quartermaster, and Samuel Goodall, normally Captain Goodall during the six months that Martin spent mapping the coast, acted as first mate. The three agreed that having two captains on board could strengthen the Sting's ability to withstand a British attack if one captain sustained an injury. Martin and Samuel would ship out year around until the war ended.

Beyond the range of the cannons at Fort Preble, scouts spotted three British warships between Great Diamond Island and Mackworth Island. Residents spotted a ship southeast of Cushing Island and a fifth ship anchored between the north side of the island and the south tip of Peaks Island. Other Royal Navy ships blockaded Freeport, eighteen miles away.

James Danvers directed three land crews positioned at intervals on the beaches in line with and beyond the two British ships near Diamond

Island. Each unit would flash a signal lantern intermittently to assist the *Sting's* escape. Picking a night of heavy rain, Martin sailed cautiously by compass past the two British ships, ducking into the first hidden cove detailed on his map.

After observing no other British ships the second night, Martin sailed the *Sting* halfway to Freeport, about eight miles, before turning east to the sea. On the third day, twenty miles east of Portland in open water, the *Sting* laid a course south to Martinique Island, their destination.

Martin navigated a dangerous direct route for the return. The *Sting* came in from the Atlantic to the windward side of Cushing Island, just out of sight of the British warship. Then, at twilight, the *Sting* sailed, bending to the wind, making a run up the straight, in plain view of the British, but soon coming under the protection of the cannons at Fort Preble.

Martin mounted the steps to his front door late that night, calling out to Rachel as he entered the house to ease her fear of home invasion. They were both so excited by the safe reunion that Martin's children slipped his mind until Henry, born on the twenty-second, woke up for another feeding. Martin's third son squirmed in Rachel's arms, calmer, perhaps quieter than he remembered of the first two babies she had nursed. Henry's soft cry brought Samuel, Martin's sheepish three-year-old, into the parlor and his father's arms.

The *Sting* made three more trips between September 1812 and July 1813. On each trip, Martin anchored in a different hidden cove he had outlined on his map. He varied his departure time, sometimes before daybreak, another time at midnight. One of the enemy ships had given chase, once, closing to within seven ship lengths, close enough to fire their forward cannons. Both shots fell short. As the enemy ship rounded the island, the *Sting* vanished. The British commodore knew that the *Sting* hid somewhere close, but to venture into the bay might mean a broadside by the *Sting* as they came within range.

Before *Sting's* trip in August, Martin, Samuel, Quintus, and James Danvers were called to a meeting with three other shipping company executives. They met in the back room of the Lobster Claw Tavern.

Mr. Magee of the North Cargo Shipping Company spoke for the group.

"We understand that you have made three successful runs through the British Blockade between the fall of last and February of this year.

"We have further heard that you use maps and secret coves to elude the British. On the other hand, we have collectively lost four ships, along with sixty sailors impressed by those bastards.

"We would prevail upon you as fellow Americans, rather than competitors, to help us in this time of war. Could we see your maps and discuss strategy together, Mr. Danvers?"

James turned to his friend.

"Martin, what do you say?"

"Some of my crew have loose tongues, dangerous to us all. I will correct that situation immediately.

"As to the maps, I have given my word. They will not be used or viewed by anyone other than the crew of the Sting."

"So, you would have us shut down all operations while your ship continues to use these maps to outwit our enemy."

"I must keep to my word, sirs. We are about to embark. I will contemplate your concerns. I will give you a final answer upon my return. Please have patience."

"We look forward to your safe return. Optimistically, we may all work together to thwart this disastrous blockade."

Martin conferred with James after the others left.

"If we make it through the blockade again, I propose we deliver our load of box shakes to Guatemala. On the return trip, I will sail up the Chesapeake Bay, branch off at the Potomac, and sail to Washington. I will meet Paul Hamilton and renegotiate our arrangement now that we are at war with Britain."

The *Sting* anchored on the Potomac at the Georgetown wharf on March 10th, 1813. Martin hired a cab to take him to the Secretary of the Navy's office at the United States Department of War building. Martin learned from the receptionist that Paul Hamilton no longer held the office of Secretary of the Navy. The receptionist for his replacement, Mr. William Jones, informed Martin that Mr. Jones could meet with Martin at three o'clock that afternoon. Having never been to Washington, Martin spent the time until his appointment walking the city streets. He entered many of the buildings open to the public, admiring the architecture and the engineering of the continuously growing city. The Capitol Building especially impressed Martin, as George Washington had described it in a newspaper article, for *"its grandeur, simplicity, and beauty."*

The receptionist ushered Martin into the office of William Jones promptly at three o'clock. Mr. Jones displayed a soft smile and an overall gentle appearance. Within five minutes, Martin knew that the softness belied an excellent grasp of the war's progress regarding the Great Lakes region and its strategic importance.

"Captain Martensen, I have reviewed your file and agree with Hamilton, the former Secretary's appraisal of the importance of your work. The British blockade of the New England coast has been on our minds as of late. Could you give me a broad update on the situation in Massachusetts, the District of Maine, and New Hampshire?"

Martin spread his map of the region out on the table across from Mr. Jones' desk. He pointed out the positions of the British warships blocking the Freeport and Portland ports. He gave the secretary second-hand accounts of the Portsmouth area.

"The situation is dire, sir, in terms of commerce. Yet our company, The Atlantic Import/Export & Shipping Company, has successfully pierced the blockade."

The two men again hunched over the table while Martin described and traced the movements of the *Sting* since the war began. Secretary

Jones, impressed, straightened when Martin finished, putting a finger to his lips, lost for a moment in thought.

"Captain Martensen, I am sure you have guessed that this war has caught the United States off guard regarding a Navy ready to defend a one-thousand-five-hundred-mile coast. This young nation is still building the rudiments of a government. Why this office has only existed for fifteen years. I don't have the ships, the men, or the money needed to man them.

"We have fresh ideas and strategies, such as yours, that match our will to survive and grow. That we have."

Secretary Jones, quiet for a moment, then seemed to decide.

"Captain Martensen, you may not have heard yet, but a new ship is about to be launched out of Freeport to be christened the *Dash*. The *Dash* is a topsail schooner built for speed by master builder James Brewer and the Porter brothers, Seward, Samuel, and William."

"I know Mr. Brewer but did not know of the *Dash*."

"As with our arrangement with you, Captain, we must work secretly with the few resources we can gather. The *Dash* has sixteen guns, although ten are wooden fakes. I would like you to work with the captain of the *Dash*. Allow the new captain access to your maps. I do not think you need to expand that knowledge unnecessarily to the other shipping companies. Too many eyes are still not favorable to your strategy. However, I can see where the *Dash* and the *Sting*, working as a team, could bedevil the British and allow more merchant ships to slip through. Do you think you might be able to expand your strategy regarding the other shipping companies out of Portland, Freeport, and Portsmouth?"

"Yes, sir, they are poised to contribute to the war effort."

"Well then, I will provide you and Captain William Cammett of the *Dash* a license for a private armed vessel. Each ship will receive a 'Letter of Marque and Reprisal' signed by the President. You will be authorized to subdue, seize, and take enemy vessels as prizes and to keep or sell the apparel, guns, and appurtenances.

"We may not have a sufficient Navy yet, but we probably have the most merchant ships. See what I mean? New strategies to fit our new country."

"Yes, sir, when will I receive this authorized letter."

"I'll sneak it under President Madison's nose early tomorrow morning and hand it to you in this office by one o'clock tomorrow. Captain Cammet's letter will be posted when I have evidence of the completion of the *Dash* and its seaworthiness."

On the way home from Georgetown, Captain Martensen and the *Sting* eluded the blockade with an audacious run right through the middle of the five British cruisers walling off the Portland entry points. Martin timed his approach for the dawn of a cloudless day. As the two closest British ships looked east, they saw only the sun's glare until the *Sting* reached the Fort Preble cannons. Two cannon blasts rang out from the British cruiser, falling short. The second cannonball splashed the stern of the *Sting* and wetted the deck. A return volley from Fort Preble kept the British at bay.

Martin, Quintus, and Samuel Goodall reviewed the latest trip and cargo manifest with James Danvers. An urgent knock on the door to the conference room drew the men's attention. Without waiting for an invitation, Rachel entered the conference room with Samuel, now four years old, hidden behind her skirt. Samuel leaped into Martin's arms, and Martin bounced the boy on his knees while the rest of the men greeted Rachel. Her hands were ice water cold and displaying a visible tremor. She arranged for Martin to join her for coffee after his meeting and discreetly left the conference room. Samuel would not part from Martin's lap. A four-year-old spy in the room.

The men decided that James and Martin should travel to Freeport to meet with the Porter brothers and see the *Dash*. James Danvers reviewed the 'Letter of Marque and Reprisal,' which declared the *Sting* a 'Privateer.' Profit would now be made by relieving British merchants and cruisers of their cargo while attempting to protect the interests of all the shipping companies of Portland, Freeport, and Portsmouth. James clarified that the crew's safety must be calculated in each endeavor. In other words, sink the enemy ship and lose the cargo, if necessary, to avoid injury to the *Sting* and its crew. James and Martin would leave on the morrow, meeting with the representatives of the rest of the Portland shipping companies upon their return from Freeport three days hence.

Martin and his son, Samuel, gathered Rachel, sitting patiently outside the conference room, and the trio turned the homecoming into lunch at the Lobster Claw Tavern. Martin switched from coffee to beer. Overjoyed at her husband's safe return, Rachel expressed concern over his new responsibilities. Martin consoled his wife.

"Rachel, I now have the ability and free reign to take effective and decisive action to preserve the ship and the men. You know me, Rachel. I will continue my defensive maneuver's unless I am certain that firing my cannons is the best solution."

Samuel perked up when he heard about cannon fire.

"Are you going to be a pirate now, father?"

Rachel corrected the boy.

"Your father will only be protecting our family and our home from the ships of the British Navy that are trying to hurt us."

Rachel turned to Martin for backing.

"That's right, Samuel. That is my job now, son. To protect the family from harm, as a privateer, not a pirate."

Samuel cocked his head, still confused but trusting his father.

"OK, Father, can I watch the cannons shoot?"

"Perhaps, someday, when the firing crew practices, you may get scared by the noise. Cannons are loud."

"I won't be scaret."

The following day Martin and James traveled the coast up to Freeport. They walked into the offices of the Porter Shipping Company unannounced and without an appointment. They glimpsed a ship through the window in the final stages of rigging for the sea. Seward Porter introduced himself. James requested a meeting with the rest of the owners and the new captain of the *Dash*. Captain Kelleran had replaced Captain Cammett. Seward Porter shook his head in disbelief at how much the two visitors knew of his operation. Martin produced the Letter of Marque and Reprisal, naming the *Sting* as a privateer for the United States. Seward showed Martin and James to the lunchroom containing tables and chairs for the construction crew and left to gather the others for the meeting.

He returned with Captain Kelleran, Mr. Brewer, and William Porter. Martin greeted James Brewer warmly, summarizing his meeting with Mr. William Jones, Secretary of the Navy in Washington a week earlier. Seward laid his cards on the table.

"Yes, we have been anticipating one of those letters, and we're working day and night to prepare the Dash for departure. The cannons arrived two weeks ago and are tied in.

"We have also been following the rumors of your successful runs through the blockade, Captain Martensen. Mr. Brewer is aware of your maps, suspecting the 'bonfire of the maps' article in the Gazette was meant to mislead. We would be honored to work with the Atlantic Import/Export and Shipping Company. I promise you, with the proper rigging, no ship in the Atlantic will catch the *Dash*.

"Enough talk. Mr. Brewer and Captain Kelleran will take us on a ship tour."

Mr. Brewer led the group down the dock along the ship's length. He described the *Dash* as a two-hundred-twenty-ton burden in a sleek, sculpted design. On the return trip of its secret maiden voyage to Port-au-Prince, a British ship chased them home. The speed and wind force sprung her mainmast, but the *Dash* still outran the enemy and returned to Freeport with most of the coffee cargo. The splintered mainmast was replaced with one more suited to a hermaphrodite brigantine. For James Danvers' sake, Mr. Brewer explained that a brigantine included two masts with a square-rigged foremast and at least two sails on the mainmast: a square topsail and a gaff sail mainsail. The taller mainmast stood second of the two masts.

The group entered the ship's hull, where Seward Porter pointed to the structure.

"We made a model from pieces of board shaped to represent halves of frames, which we attached to a board and connected with rib bands. The shape was made apparent, and the forms were cut and beveled. The speed record of our ship on its maiden voyage proved conclusively that Mr. Brewer, our designer knew what he was about.

"At the same time that we replaced the mainmast, we fitted a long sliding spar to the main boom, to which we attached a 'ringtail' to be hoisted to the gaff when needed, thus increasing the mainsail one-third. We also installed the gaff topsail on the longer main topmast."

Captain Kelleran ran his hand along a smooth board on the hull.

"We only wish we had access to the Cornish copper mines to sheath her bottom. As it is, we must cover the bottom with soap and tallow before setting sail from any port. A smooth bottom is not hard to achieve here on our wharf, but down in the West Indies, we'll have to careen the ship on its side for coating."

Hearing about soap and tallow and the need to careen the *Dash* reminded Martin of the more elegant drydock and water wheels system he had left on Langeness hallig years ago.

The group returned to the lunchroom and spent the next three hours poring over Martin's maps of the New England coast. Until the *Dash's* Letter of Marque and Reprisal arrived from Washington, the *Dash*, and the *Sting* would continue their blockade running in tandem. Martin and Captain Kelleran devised four simple flag sequences to indicate their intended chess moves on the waters of the Atlantic.

Martin and James Danvers returned to Portland and gathered the prominent shipping companies for a conference. Martin reiterated his determination to keep his maps a secret.

"Listen, our strategies and hidden coves must remain privy to as few people as possible. The Secretary of the Navy has commissioned the *Sting* and the *Dash* out of Freeport as New England privateers. For the safety of my ship, crew, and family, I will take my maps to the grave if necessary.

"However, we are a community, and you have offered your dedication to fighting this war. In our own way, we will do just that with continued commerce. The *Dash* and the *Sting* plan to cat and mouse the British blockade so that your ships, one by one, can sneak through after we clear the way."

That statement warranted a round of applause and table pounding by those present. The first ship, the *Algonquin*, appeared ready to ship out. The Dash and the Sting were also prepared a week after the meeting.

At the end of April, news of the Battle of York in the *New Hampshire Gazette* bolstered the spirits of New Englanders all along the coast. Now one of Portland's favorite sons, Lemuel Bryant, had distinguished himself on a ship of the flotilla in Lake Erie that had fired on the British. A sailor of nineteen years of age, he had advanced with a contingent of soldiers on shore to invade the city of York. In an interview with a reporter, Lemuel described the city's burning. He became an instant celebrity in the Lobster Claw Tavern.

The more Martin's son Samuel grew, the harder it became for Martin to say goodbye to his family. Samuel could not get enough of Martin's stories of the sea, already proclaiming he would also be a captain when he grew up.

Rachel clung to her husband the night before each trip, her affections growing as their relationship matured and their time apart lengthened due to the war.

The *Dash* had made its way from Freeport to Portland. The warship in its path, the *Caroline*, did not have enough time to turn around and then turn back to fire on the *Dash* as the ship flew by in a twenty-mile-an-hour gust.

Three ships set sail from Portland. The first ship, the *Dash*, steered toward one of the two warships anchored north of the city. Before entering cannon range, the *Dash* cut east, heading at the second warship.

As the *Caroline* had turned to chase the *Dash*, Martin, helming the *Sting*, emerged from the harbor running north, hugging the coast. The *Caroline* ended its chase of the *Dash*, leaving the second warship, the *Gallery*, to capture the Freeport ship.

The *Sting* had the surprise advantage on the *Caroline*, which needed to turn north to follow and attempt a capture. At that moment, the *Algonquin* appeared out of the mouth of the Fore River and shot through the middle of the two British warships: cutting through the channel between Long Island and Chebeague Island and away to sea.

The *Sting* had enough lead on the *Caroline* that Martin could turn his ship toward shore into the first hidden harbor, ready to broadside the *Caroline* if the British ship foolishly tried to search the bay for Martin's hideaway. The captain of the *Caroline* turned back instead to assist the *Gallery* in capturing the *Dash*. Captain Kelleran feinted his ship to the port of the *Gallery* and then came about to the starboard side of the British warship, leaving the *Gallery* flustered and floundering with sails luffing. The *Dash* flashed by, and neither the *Gallery* nor the *Caroline* had a chance to catch her. The *Dash*, the *Sting*, and the *Algonquin* had safely breached the British blockade. Fort Preble fired three cannons signaling the city of the safe escape.

The *Dash* and the *Sting* met again in Port-au-Prince, Haiti, on October 1, 1813. They discharged their cargo of lumber and careened the ships to be scraped clean and payed over with soap and tallow. Stevedores loaded the *Dash* with coffee, logwood, and five-hundred-fifty bags of coffee. The *Sting* took on rum and sugar cane for processing into molasses in New England. The *Dash* departed for Portland on the seventeenth, and Captain Martensen bid Captain Kelleran farewell. Two days later, the *Sting* sailed for home.

Martin never saw a ship the entire trip to Portland. He remained wary, coming toward the coast and crossing from near Freeport to Portland, but the British blockade ships did not appear. The captain spent two days with his family, attending church and worrying for Captain Kelleran and the *Dash*. He told only James Danvers about his concern.

Rachel sometimes caught Martin's furrowed brow, but she could not extract from Martin the reason. After church on Sunday, the congregation held a cake and coffee social. Martin enjoyed the event after being aboard the *Sting* for a month. He cautioned Rachel and young Samuel against mentioning where he had been.

Martin never talked about his exploits. His friends knew him as a shipmaster, but he never mentioned the ship's name. They assumed he shipped out on a merchant ship; hard going now with the war in full swing. Of course, most of the men at the social were members of the militia, ready to defend the city alongside the soldiers from Fort Preble. Martin protected his family and the shipping company by remaining silent. A British spy or sympathizer may be sitting in the next pew. He and Rachel took no chances. Still, the cakes were delicious, and the children ran around in the church basement with their friends, showing off somersaults to their father.

The British ships returned to their positions in the blockade of Portland. On November 5, 1813, the *Dash* ran by them, avoiding cannon shots by weaving an erratic and swift course down the channel. Martin and Danvers walked the dock daily to check for the *Dash's* arrival. Martin spied Captain Kelleran swilling beer in the Lobster Claw Tavern on the afternoon of the 5th. As the three men retired to the back room, Kelleran had a story to tell.

"As you know, Martin, we left Haiti heavy-laden on the seventeenth. On the thirty-first, we spied an English brig gaining on us from behind. I threw over four hundred bags of coffee, the spare spars, and two heavy guns. On November third, the bastards had gained on us, so I ordered one hundred twenty more bags of coffee sent to the deep. I offloaded twelve more guns, ten of those being the wooden decoys. At that point, I only had our thirty-two-pounder pivot gun and a cannon on either side of the ship left, but it did the trick. Trimmed out to design, we saw the last chasing brig two days later.

"Wouldn't you know it? The next day two more ships tried to intercept us. A seventy-four-gun enemy cruiser and a brig. No match for our speed, though, so here we sit.

"Josh, a beer for each of my fellows and another for me. If you please, gentlemen. I made it home with the owner's cargo and my skin, so we must celebrate."

The *Dash* and the *Sting* loaded up with lumber and readied to sail. The first week in December, the weather turned cold. Captain Kelleran and Martensen waited for better weather to ship out. The following week a heavy snowstorm blew through the city. The *Sting* took off, followed by the *Dash*. Better weather or not, both ships avoided the blockade under cover of the heavy snow at sea.

In Port-au-Prince, both ships unloaded and again careened to apply the soap and tallow. The ships were brought to shore at high tide and pulled over on their sides by ropes attached to the masts. The carpenter and Samuel Goodall oversaw the process for the *Sting*, with much of the crew helping to scrape & burn off algae and barnacles. They discovered and replaced one rotten plank. Samuel applied caulk to the gaps.

Caulking involves beating oakum into the seam between the new and old planks. The carpenter hits the oakum (old rope torn to pieces) with the caulking iron, wooden mallets, and iron chisels. Hot pitch is smeared over the seams to make it as watertight as possible.

The de-fouling process took eight days for the *Sting* and ten days for the larger *Dash*.

Both ships took on coffee cargo, and the *Dash* sailed out of the Port-au-Prince harbor on January 16, 1814, along with the schooner *Flash* out of New York. They encountered an English frigate at the mouth of the bay. Without a fort to protect them, the two ships returned to port. The *Dash* tied off to the *Sting*, and the *Flash* maneuvered to a position in between their bows. Protected by cannons and crews on all sides, most men were awake all night, awaiting a possible attack by boats from the brig. The tight little flotilla discouraged the British brig, which left the bay for easier pickings. The *Sting* and the *Dash* arrived in Portland on February fifteenth.

Captain Kelleran collected his bonus, resigned from the Porter Shipping Company, and retired to live in Boston. He had been an able partner and Martin's mentor. Martin expressed sorrow to see him leave. A month passed before Seward Porter met with Martin and James Danvers to introduce them to Mr. William Cammett, the returning captain of the *Dash*. Captain Cammett seemed reticent to work with Captain Martensen, ostensibly due to Cammett's inexperience with the *Dash* and how it maneuvered. Martin, put off by the man, let the new Captain sail on his own until Captain Cammett's confidence in trimming the *Dash* improved. The *Dash* sailed off for the West Indies the third week in May.

Rachel gave birth to the couple's fourth son on June 7th, 1814. Martin had stayed at home for an extended rest to await the delivery. William weighed eight pounds one ounce, noisy from his early moments on. On Sunday next, Rachel, holding baby William, lined up for William's baptism in front of the congregation of the First Congregational church. Martin stood next to Rachel, holding Henry, age two. Five-year-old Samuel stood next to Martin, and three-year-old Martin Jr. sat on a small chair before Martin. Somehow, even with all the fidgeting, the minister completed the baptism. Baby and family gathered again with the minister in the narthex. The congregation offered congratulations as the members exited the church.

Seward Porter informed James Danvers that the *Dash's* "Letter of Marque and Reprisal" arrived on June 18, 1814, having been delayed these many months due to administrative paper shuffling. On *Dash's* next trip, she would be a sanctioned privateer in the service of the United States.

The owners of another merchant ship, the *Alexander*, approached James Danvers, requesting the *Sting's* escort when the *Alexander* left Portland for New York. James and Martin agreed and worked out signals between the two captains for the run. When both ships were loaded and ready to sail, Martin waited for a fog blanket to cover the bay, which occurred on an early July day, just before sunrise. The *Sting* sailed unseen, dropping sails in one of Martin's hidden coves northeast of Portland. The fog lifted just after ten o'clock as the *Alexander* boldly ventured from the mouth of the Fore River. A British warship sped forward, challenging the *Alexander*. By arrangement, at that moment, the *Sting* swung out from the hidden cove and gave chase to the English ship, unnoticed for several minutes. The warship fired on *Alexander*. The captain of the *Alexander* anticipated the shots and turned into the path of the warship. The cannon fire landed beyond the merchant ship. Sailors on the British brig, helpless during reload, finally noticed the *Sting's* approach. Martin stayed at the helm, close enough to hear the brig's captain.

"Who's the son of a bitch supposed to be watching our rear. Come about, you worthless bastards, before that damn ship…"

With the Sting in a perfect strategic position, Martin gave the command.

"Fire at will. Hole her mates; we've got her."

Before Quintus could repeat the order down the chain of command, the cannon crews on the *Sting* blasted away, opening a fifteen-foot ragged hole in the brig at and below the waterline. Martin, hands tightening on the handles of the *Sting's* wheel, stared into the darkness of the rupture while he heard screams of "my leg, my leg," echoing from inside the hole. Martin, closing his eyes tight for a few seconds, wondered what he could do; could he help? The British blockade ship began sinking fast; the cries from below deck extinguished in the gurgle. Martin turned his attention back to his vessel, mariners efficiently going about their task as if they had not just sunk a ship twice the *Sting's* size.

The brig's crew scrambled into boats heading for the shore and the forest. Soldiers from Fort Preble would hunt down those mariners unable to make their way north to Canada. The *Alexander* sailed well to sea while another British blockade ship approached the *Sting*. Martin tacked back to the Fore River, where the Fort Preble cannons warded off the blockade ship. Late that afternoon, three American sailors from the sunken brig turned themselves in at the dock, claiming they had been impressed into service. They were hopeful to again serve on an American ship. They provided Martin and the Portland captains with helpful information about the British captains and ships remaining on blockade duty.

Rachel had heard all the cannons boom and had run down to the docks, struggling to carry baby William in her arms. When the plank of the *Sting* dropped on the pier, Rachel rushed on board, ignoring protocol, following her husband's voice issuing orders from the forward deck. When she saw him unscathed, she sat on a pile of coiled lines, struggling to compose her breathing. She heard Martin cry out her name. Sliding down the foredeck ladder to comfort her, he caught up with his wife and son, leading them down the plank to shore, where Mr. Danvers gathered her. Martin returned to his duties on the ship. Rachel witnessed the shudder in Martin's shoulders and the shake in his hands as he pointed to various sailors coiling lines, congratulating them on a job well done in the sinking of the brig.

A schooner named *The Constellation*, out of Boston, unfamiliar with the Portland strategy, heard about the success of the *Alexander* and proceeded to sail out from Portland the next day. A British brig picked it off in a "turkey shoot," sobering the dock sailors and captains.

On July 11th, Captain Cammett and the *Dash* returned to Portland for more cannon refitting; two more eighteen-pounders. The ship retained the long thirty-two-pivot gun. Captain Cammett was apprised of the letter from Washington, legitimizing the *Dash* as a privateer. Mr. George Bacon came aboard as lieutenant, having soldiering experience in the Battle of York.

In early September, word reached Portland of the burning of Washington City on August 24th and 25th. President Madison had fled the white house, which suffered severe damage. The fire swept over many of the buildings in the city. The Portland militia met with Fort Preble commanders in response to the Washington disaster. Security checkpoints and perimeter patrols were initiated as precautions against possible British troop movement. Citizens were at once terrified, galled, and boastful that this latest British affront would be answered in kind.

A month and a half later, Martin read an account of Captain Cammett's first trip as a privateer in the Gazette. Captain Cammett had sailed south of Bermuda, encountering a British man-of-war. The *Dash* out sailed the man-of-war and put into Wilmington, North Carolina. Here it became necessary to de-foul the hull.

While acquiring soap and tallow, Captain Cammett spotted a quantity of crude plumbago stocked by the merchant. The new ingredient added to the soap and tallow would increase the brig's speed. Due to the British blockade, Wilmington warehouses were overstocked. Prices were low for anyone wishing to attempt shipping out. Captain Cammett bought fifteen barrels of flour, twenty-four hogsheads of tobacco, one hundred forty barrels of tar, fifty tierces of rice, and four thousand Carolina reeds. Then, under cover of a cloudy, moonless night, the *Dash* sailed for Portland. The newspaper article in the Eastern Argus, written upon her arrival in Portland, indicated that the *Dash* repeatedly out-ran British cruisers and escaped only by superior sailing after throwing overboard part of her cargo. Captain Cammett used his new guns on one of the pursuers to beat them off. Still, it made for one of the most profitable trips of the year.

Martin read the article with some concern. He never wished to call attention to the exploits of the *Sting* for fear of full reprisal and danger to his family. Captain Cammett relished the *Dash's* ability to outrun the British. Compared to the *Sting*, the *Dash* had twice the sail, housed more cannons, and could outmaneuver or outrun earlier-conceived ships due to its design.

Rachel and her father were concerned with the change in Martin's disposition since the sinking of the British brig. He acted aloof at family gatherings. Martin, a quiet man by nature, now spoke even less. Rachel vowed to question James Danvers about the sinking at her earliest opportunity.

The Sting brought down two more ships during the first two weeks of October. The first; was a British schooner sailing too close to the District of Maine coast near Portland on its trip from Quebec to Natal, Brazil. The ship refused to surrender. Martin holed her with the rear cannon, causing no injuries. The schooner crew manned their boats and rowed the ten miles to Fort Preble under armed guards from the *Sting*. Martin transferred as much cargo as the *Sting* could carry, sinking the unexceptional craft. He returned the spoils to the Freeport dock, where stevedores unloaded the payload to a warehouse. The loot consisted of Hudson Bay wool spools, blankets, maple syrup, and other goods manufactured in Canada. Martin knew the goods would bring a nice bonus to his crew.

The second ship brought down by the *Sting* that week had been caught attacking a merchant ship out of Portland. Martin's strategy again baited the British warship into the bays of islands on the district's coast he knew so well. Since the burning of Washington and the British's sinking of three more merchant ships near Freeport, Martin was obsessed with finding additional targets for his cannons. He arrived too late to save the merchant ship being attacked that morning, but the *Sting* disabled the warship with a shot that hit the Mainmast three feet above the deck. The mainsail and mast crashed perpendicular to the ship, hanging into the water.

Martin swung the *Sting* around at an angle the disabled British ship could not match; their cannon banks could not aim toward the *Sting*. Martin ordered his cannons to continue firing. Sailors were jumping ship into the cold waters of the Atlantic to avoid being blasted. Martin heard cries from the injured. He stared with his jaw set, transfixed, at the empty crow's nest of the enemy ship. He continued to order his cannons to fire. Quintus touched his Captain's shoulder, breaking Martin's gruesome concentration. The enemy ship sunk, leaving only two lifeboats filled with sailors. Martin again singled out the impressed American sailors and accompanied the lifeboats to Fort Preble. Three days later, Martin and the crew of the *Sting* were ready to go on the hunt again.

Martin grimly determined he would see an end to this war.

Whether a self-destructive exasperation with the years of senseless destruction of ships and crews took hold of him or perhaps just exhaustion of luck, Martin's hunt in late October 1814 turned disastrous.

The *Sting* came about to turn into the bay that contained Martin's favorite hidden cove when Jim Oslan from the crow's nest yelled down.

"Enemy sloop astern, Captain. Six guns are showing on their starboard side. Top-sail schooner. Bearing down on us and gaining."

Martin responded, "Aye, sailor. Quintus, all hands to posts."

The crew of the *Sting*, well disciplined, hurried to their stations without looking aft. That is the Captain's job, and they depended on Martin as much as he relied on each crew member aboard. The British ship steadily closed the gap between them, using Martin's tactic of swinging out from Cousins Island to surprise the *Sting*. Not yet within cannon range, the warship closed too fast for Martin to turn into the bay and sail into his hidden cove.

Within seconds Martin decided to sail by the bay and head further into open waters. He would outsail the enemy, his only hope. He tacked back and forth to find the right combination of wind and wave to put additional distance between the two ships. This worked to a degree as the British ship tried to respond to Martin's misdirection, hesitating for seconds each time Martin came about. Still, the gap shortened. That day's wind blew unsteadily and too light to give Martin any advantage. For two hours, Martin played mouse to the warship cat. He repeatedly brought his spyglass to his eye, looking ahead at the wave crests on the horizon, the cloud movement high above, and a second cloud mass barely moving low at the horizon; Martin began to fear the worst. "Know the winds," Sailor Gretsen taught him many years ago.

Martin picked a route thirty degrees off the direction of the waves running toward the district's shore. The British ship followed him. Then, as Martin predicted, the wind settled into a near-dead calm, disastrous to sailing vessels. The *Sting's* sails luffed no matter which way the ship turned. Hopeless. Both ships faced the same predicament. The waves alone propelled the two ships toward shore. Martin instantly ordered the sails furled to reduce drag. Next, he ordered the boats dispatched and tied off to the ship. Half the crew boarded the boats to row, pulling the ship away from the enemy as the waves settled to calm.

After an hour and a half of rowing, Martin sent the other half of the crew into the rowboats to relieve the exhausted sailors. Five hours later, their row boats still pulled the two ships. The *Sting* continuously gained distance in the gap between the heavier British vessel.

But the British man-of-war did not give up. The *Sting's* reputation as a privateer must have shaken the British into a vendetta. The British ship appeared to have explicit orders to capture or sink Martin's.

The Sting had gained more distance from the British ship by nightfall. After switching the rowing crew, Martin told Quintus to gather the remaining mariners.

"Men, we can't predict how long we'll need to pull our ship in this dead sea. There's nothing for it. I say we show the invaders what we're made of. We'll gather in the stern and sing a rousing rendition of the sixpence song. The more boisterous, the better. Then I want Jim Oslan to play his piccolo until you mariners relieve the rowers. Then we'll go silent. With luck, we'll row away in the dark and find a cove to hide in. What do you say?"

Jim Oslan spoke for the crew, "Aye, Aye, Captain. We ain't licked, not by a long cannon shot."

The men assembled in the stern, singing as boisterously as they could muster, stomping their boots on the deck at each measure's downbeat.

> *I've got six-pence, jolly, jolly six-pence*
> *I've got six-pence to last me all my life*
> *I've got tup-pence to spend*
> *And tup-pence to lend*
> *And tup-pence to take home to my wife, poor wife.*
> *No cares have I to grieve, ----*

Perhaps it unnerved the enemy, but it relieved the tension of the day and bolstered the spirits of the crew of the *Sting*. The piccolo projected across the still waters for forty minutes afterward. At one point, an enemy cannon fired a shot that fell well short. The taunting splash was heard faintly by the *Sting's* crew.

The clouds dissipated, revealing the moon with a halo bright as a ghostly Halloween night.

Both ships rowed on.

By sunrise, both *Sting's* rowing crews were reaching their limits of endurance. Martin moved among the sailors resting aboard, striking up short conversations, asking about their families or their plans for when the war ended. At nine o'clock in the morning, a few flutters of a breeze caused Martin to return to the quarterdeck and begin to plan his next move. He looked through his spyglass at the British ship still on his heels. Martin examined the land to port and determined his relative location. He looked at the sea ahead, beginning to show movement, and far out, a ripple on the water's surface indicated wind. *Know the winds, know the land*. Sailor Gretsen's lessons continued to echo in his thoughts.

Martin again gathered the crew, giving his orders to Quintus but speaking indirectly to the men.

"Now we show our mettle, Quintus. When I give the command, the sails must be unfurled, and the lines tightened as fast as we've ever practiced. The towing crew will need to come aboard and leave the boats adrift. No time to secure them. Everyone will go to stations and be on the ready, alert for the next command. This crew is the best out of Portland, and today we will prove it."

Martin raised the eyeglass and calculated the distance to the squall up ahead and the remaining time before it reached the Sting.

"Now's the time Quintus. Raise the sails."

Quintus relayed the order, "Alright, mates, you heard the Captain, quick and steady, no mistakes, now."

The organized activity on board prevented any wasted steps or unsure pulls. Adrenaline drove the sailors beyond their exhaustion. The boat crews scampered up the rope ladders and were aboard and at their stations within two minutes. The rowboats pulling the enemy ship rowed back alongside and were hauled up and secured. That took time. The British warship had more sail to unfurl. Through Martin's spyglass, he noted that although the British crew consisted mainly of Royal Navy professionals, they appeared listless and undisciplined.

The *Sting* leaped ahead as the wind met sail, and Martin tacked against it, gaining even more distance from the British ship. Within several minutes, the enemy set sail.

The chase again afoot.

Martin had formulated a hope of a plan during the night, and as the wind picked up, his confidence increased. Martin checked his maps and concluded he might make it to another of his hidden coves. They may still have a chance if he could stay ahead, out of cannon range, until he reached the bay that led to the sheltered cove.

The enemy ship possessed more sail, slicing the sea faster than the *Sting* in a fair wind. Every time Martin looked back, the British warship was closer. He concentrated on his crew and their execution of his commands to reign in the sheet, turning the ship slightly to maximize his wind. Still, the enemy came closer.

Martin believed he was five minutes from the bay he sought when he heard cannon fire from behind. It splashed only twenty feet from the stern. The enemy would be in range momentarily. Still, rather than turn and fight, Martin continued. Quintus looked over at his steadfast Captain. Martin reassured him.

"Keep at it, Quintus. Trim the topsail if you please. Tighter on the port side, lads."

Martin figured thirty more seconds until the next cannon shot, but the *Sting* now cruised halfway across the bay he sought. He counted a fast twenty.

"Come about to port, ninety degrees, now, man."

Quintus barked the command to the crew, and the ship swung to port in seconds. Three cannons fired astern. The *Sting* canted over hard, cutting into the bay, only two hundred yards from the north beach. The *Sting* bent over and took the first cannonball high in the topsail, which broke the mast below the crow's nest. The crashing wood, sail, and rigging down to the deck of the *Sting* was deafening, even above the roar of the cannon explosions. Due to the turn Martin had ordered, as the cannons were firing, the second and third cannon shots splashed in the water behind the *Sting's* stern, harmlessly showering the deckhands.

Splinters from the blasted mast also showered down to the deck. Martin received a four-inch sliver in his back and a two-inch knife of wood to his neck, throwing him to the deck. He staggered upright to give Quintus the command to hold steady, ignoring the pain in his shoulder. He did not see his quartermaster, so he bellowed the order to the crew.

"Keep those lines tight. I don't care if the sails tip into the water. Stay this tack."

Martin grabbed his spyglass, splinters jutting out from him like a pincushion, catching sight of the British ship as it crossed to parallel Martin's, following the *Sting* for a final broadside. The faster topsail sloop would be two hundred feet distant from the *Sting* and in control of the battle in less than a minute, leaning over from the wind force much like the *Sting*. Martin swung his spyglass around to check the two ships' positions to his references on the shore. He swung the spyglass back, hearing a long and treacherous yawl noise turning into a screech as the warship careened over on the rock reef Martin had first mapped over two years prior. The tide, halfway low, effectively covered the reef, rendering it invisible on the surface, deadly to a ship and crew in this situation.

Martin ordered his crew to come about in a wide arc and station the *Sting* opposite the enemy man-of-war stuck on the reef. Cannons on the enemy's starboard side pointed at the clouds, angled in an impossible position to fire effectively. The British ship, aground and immovable, was now anchored at the mercy of the *Sting*. Martin ordered cannon shots across the bow and stern of the enemy, yelling across to their Captain that he had fifteen minutes to abandon ship and surrender.

After repeating his demands twice, Martin turned to his own ship. He rushed over to the fallen rigging, mast, and sail, gathering ten men and lifting with his good arm to clear the deck. The *Sting,* still maneuverable, needed the debris on the deck to be thrown over. Two sailors gathered the topsail, shredding in the wind, ripped beyond repair. Martin remembered he still needed to attend to the British prisoners.

Turning his attention back to the enemy, he noted a belligerent captain in the bow of one of the row boats, challenging his crew to make haste and attack the *Sting* by rifle force and saber. There was nothing for it. Martin sighed, shook his head from side to side once, and ordered his middle cannon crew to stop the boat with no quarter. Ten seconds later, the rowboat and twenty men were blown into the sky and water one hundred feet short of reaching the *Sting*. A crewmember of the Sting spotted a sailor with a white rag tied to a saber waving frantically on the canted deck of the warship: the fight over.

The men clearing the deck of the *Sting* found Quintus Langland and Tobias Slinman dead beneath the crush of the fallen mast. Martin kneeled over his quartermaster in prayer. The crew of the *Sting* gathered to pay tribute to the dead men. Jim Oslan came along and stood over his captain.

"Got to get that stick out of your back, Captain, your neck's bleeding as well. Quintus' friend Mark can doctor you until we get back to port."

"Go ahead, the two of you. Pull the fucking shards out now; they hurt like hell."

One of the men took hold of the big splinter and, on three, yanked back while another sailor facing Martin held his shoulders still. Martin hollered in pain. Jim stanched the shoulder with clean bandages, and Mark tightened the wounds from shoulder to armpit. Mark pulled the more minor splinter from Martin's neck. Wrapped in a collar of cloth, Martin returned to duty.

After the battle, work began. The *Sting* required cleaning up; prisoners restrained in the *Sting's* hold and guarded; food dispersed to the ravenous crew; the warship scouted for possible cargo and to assess the damage caused by the reef. Martin maintained his command. He waited for high tide, suspecting his prize ship would rock off the reef. The captain did not know positively if the water line would fall above or below the damage to the vessel. He ordered that all non-essentials be dumped overboard, and any cargo be transferred to the *Sting*.

That did the trick. When the ship buoyed off the rock reef, it became sailable. Both ships would progress under half sail to get back to Portland and, with some luck, not come under further attack. Quintus and Tobias were wrapped in portions of the ripped mainsail. After being underway for half an hour, the two ships were far enough out for an appropriate burial at sea for the two crew members. Martin, too weak to conduct the service, stayed on deck and sat silently with his men, tears dripping. He remembered his loyal quartermaster and the near disastrous sailing conditions they had at times encountered to-gether; the times Quintus had been invaluable. Jim Oslan read from the bible. Martin requested a reading for those of the enemy that had lost their lives. That done, Martin struggled to stand and led a salute to all those that had fallen.

Once within range of the Fort Preble cannons, Martin sat on the quarterdeck, holding a rigging line for support.

Martin and the few other injured sailors rode in carriages to the hos-pital. The surgeon cleared the wood bits from Martin's wounds, bled him clear, and applied clean bandages. The doctor likewise treated the minor injuries of the rest of the mariners. James Danvers arrived. Hear-ing a summary of the chase of the *Sting* and the Battle of Atkins Bay, James accompanied Martin to his home, determined to ease Rachel's anticipated stress.

Leading a heavily bandaged Martin into the house. Rachel cried out at the sight of him, then, when he looked up and smiled at her, color returned to her cheeks, and she rushed to her husband's side. The children were frightened of the ghostly man wrapped in white cloth and stayed back. Rachel led Martin to bed.

Martin spent six weeks at home recuperating. He tried not to think about the war; his ship, Quintus, or the battle at sea, exercises in utter futility. Whenever Martin closed his eyes, visions of water, wood, and pieces of men shooting into the air from his cannon shot crowded his sleep. He dreamed of white-wrapped mummies lying head to toe on the deck of the *Sting*, sliding the corpses in turn into the ocean. Martin remembered the crooked smile of his craggy quartermaster, how Quintus lifted his mug high before each swig of beer. And as he often did, he thought of Sailor Gretsen, his crooked leg, and matching cane.

Martin met with James Danvers over lunch at the Lobster Claw Tavern in late December. He turned over his updated ship's log and recounted the events of the chase. James related the progress of the repairs to the *Sting*. The war had slowed the production of new ships, which delayed the production of masts the size needed for the *Sting*. A proper mast was in the works and scheduled to be delivered the second week in January 1815. James asked Martin if he might be ready to travel to Freeport and meet with the Porters as soon as the *Sting* could ship out. Apparently, while Martin recuperated, John Porter, another brother of Seward, had returned from Europe and taken over the captaincy of the *Dash*.

James and Martin were about to travel to Freeport on the fourteenth of January when word of the *Dash's* return swept through the Portland docks. The bartender at the tavern identified John Porter. James and Martin introduced themselves. Captain Porter suggested a messenger might travel to Freeport and deliver word to Seward that the debriefing meeting with James and Martin should be held in Portland. John Porter, anxious to spend time with his new wife, had only been married and established in Portland since October. John and Seward Porter, James Danvers, and Martin Martensen met at the Lobster Claw two days later.

Captain Porter had taken to heart the *Dash's* new role as a privateer for the Americans. On November sixteenth, the *Dash* had captured a schooner named *Polly* en route to Martinique from Halifax. The schooner cargo consisted of lumber and fish. The next day the *Dash* captured a second schooner and sent it back to Portland. On December 12th, the *Dash* won the letter of the marquee schooner *Armistice* of New York. The *Armistice* had been a prized capture of the English frigate *Pactolus*. The following week the *Dash* captured a sloop bound for Bermuda and an English brig laden with rum and sugar the next day. The brig *Mary Ann* of St. John was intercepted on the same trip and surrendered shrub and lime juice casks before being allowed to continue its voyage.

The *Dash* had now captured nine prizes to the *Sting's* four. The *Dash* was known as the fastest ship out of New England. It had gained this reputation without the loss of a man or an injury from the enemy's shots. The *Sting* had lost two men but had bested much larger British ships and had always returned to Portland sailable.

Sailors considered the *Dash* and the *Sting* lucky ships. The best young sailors of Portland were anxious to serve on both. Martin and John conferred over Martin's maps. Both men were reluctant to leave their families, but Seward believed a load of lumber would be ready for the *Dash* to take to Martinique within two weeks. James, likewise, felt the *Sting* would be prepared to disembark about the middle of February. Port and Beer flowed freely by this point in the meeting, and the men celebrated their combined victories with mutual respect and admiration. Word of the American's decisive win in the Battle of New Orleans a week earlier launched a celebration loud with hope and relief at the Lobster Claw tavern.

John Porter and the crew of the *Dash* sailed the third day in February with sixty men aboard, accompanied by the *Champlain*, a private schooner out of Boston. A gale roared across the Atlantic two days later, and the captain of the *Champlain* altered course to a cove, but John

Porter and the *Dash* steered into the storm, never again to be heard of or any trace found.

On February seventeenth, two weeks after the *Dash* shipped out, the Congress of the United States ratified the treaty of Ghent, and the war ended.

Martin, relieved at the news of the war's end, took his family to church that night, asking Rachel to read her favorite passages to the family while Martin sat and silently thanked the Lord God Almighty.

There is something about ending a war, relieving shoulder tension, and providing one with a lighter step. No need to worry about looking suspiciously around for spies or sympathizers. Hope never to go to war again, ever. Rejoicing that the children will grow now worry-free. A new beginning.

The time came for Martin to readjust his ambitions, think creatively, and recall the lessons learned. Martin negotiated his prize ship as a bonus, leaving all the cargo bonuses to his crew members to split. Martin wanted that fast ship and started contracting the repair and re-fitting himself. The two masts and the rigging all came down. While carpenters re-planked the side that had caught the reef, Martin ordered a multi-mast mainmast, ten feet longer than the original. The new foremast would rise above the deck an additional eight feet. A flood of commerce opened between the United States and Britain as if the war had never happened. Martin waited two months for Cornish copper plates to arrive in Portland. Workers applied tarpaper to the hull, then bolted the copper plates over the paper. Tarpaper between the copper bolts and iron rivets holding the planks protected the hull bolts from disintegrating. Martin drew up the plans for the re-assembly of the new parts.

A Bermuda rig would now be incorporated. The two masts would be raked back from the vertical, allowing for a triangular mainsail, foresail, and jibs. Only the topsail on the mainmast would be square. Martin, the shipbuilders, carpenters, and sailmakers, finished the ship in five and a half months.

Martin examined the completed punch list, walking the dock from stem to stern, calling the project complete. The ship seemed dressed for speed:

Raked, streamlined masts.

Triangular sails: providing faster handling during changes in direction.

Bermuda rig: innovative but proven for faster sailing.

Copper-clad hull: No more time would be spent at port for soap and tallow application which meant faster cargo turns.

The Massachusetts Bank officer also inspected the ship and approved the project, confident that the three-year loan Martin had negotiated would be paid off early. He and Rachel had decided on the company name: The Portland Priority Shipping Company. Key selling points were the speed of the ship, the fast turnover of cargo, and the reputation and experience of the Captain. Due to the design refinements, the vessel could be managed with a twenty-man crew instead of the forty formerly needed. That meant less labor expense and more profit.

Know the Ship, know the crew. Martin, now thirty-two years old, still lived by the maxims of Sailor Gretsen, who died pounding life lessons into Martin's soul. Joiner Ketelson had opened the door of opportunity, beginning when seventeen-year-old Martin walked up the plank of the *Creighton* back at Ketelswarf Shipyard. It was time now to acknowledge that beginning. Martin commissioned a two-foot by four-foot, marine varnished, mahogany panel with arched, engraved white lettering outlined in red that read: *Creighton II*.

Rachel grew belly-large with child again and wished to have more children in the future. Perhaps her dream for a girl might be realized. The Parsons clan, James Danvers and the Porter families, Mrs. Waterbury, and a few friends from the church gathered on the dock at the stern of the *Creighton II* while the children ran around up on deck playing. It took Rachel only one big swing to break the bottle of champagne over the corner of the stern. The private christening amused a gentleman scanning the various ships along the dock. He approached Martin.

"This ship appears fast, young man."

"Portland Priority Shipping Company, sir, my name is Martin Martensen, owner and captain of the *Creighton II*. How may I help you, sir?"

"My name is Benjamin Henshaw. I trade in cotton goods and textiles from England. I want to discuss distribution along the Atlantic. This ship is a worthy candidate for my business."

"Certainly, sir, allow me to give you the grand tour. Rest assured, these rambunctious children and Rachel, my lovely wife, are my family, not my crew. The ship and crew will be ready to sail next Monday."

3 |

APPRENTICE

*The storm sent the ant hills on the patio into the wind,
gone. The next day the ants rebuilt their hills.*

1830

The boy turned twelve in July. His father sat in the dark on the edge of the boy's bed. The Captain of the clipper, *Creighton II,* shook the boy awake before dawn. He threw a potato sack on the foot of the bed, telling the boy to pack clothes for a birthday surprise two-week sail. The boy, awake in an instant, tossed pants, shirt, and his Sunday vest in the bag. He dressed and hurried downstairs to the kitchen table in less than five minutes, boots laced tight, hair combed, and presentable. The Captain and Mother sat next to each other in the banquette. Porridge steamed in a bowl in front of an empty seat. The boy sat down and began slurping his breakfast, hungry as always for food in the morning.

The Captain told the boy they would sail to Savannah, Georgia, with a stop in Washington on the Potomac. Various cargos had been arranged to be picked up and delivered between these ports. For over a year, the boy had anticipated his opportunity to go to sea like his brothers before him.

Samuel, his oldest brother, twenty-one this year, had worked up to quartermaster on the *Creighton II.*

Martin Jr., nineteen, the boy's second oldest brother, worked as a joiner down at the shipyard on Union Wharf. Both Henry and William, eighteen and sixteen and respectively, were apprenticing for the brush-making shop on Bramhall Street off Congress in downtown Portland. All his brothers had their turn on the Captain's ship when they were about the boy's age.

Mother stood in the doorway and waved. This she always did as the Captain left for a sail. He, in turn, looked back and waved to her before continuing down the dusty narrow street. The boy did the same. The Captain and the boy walked down the hill toward the docks. The Captain, forty-eight now, still had a strong back and a quick gait. The boy walked as fast as he could but still had to run a little after twenty steps to stay abreast of the Captain.

Mother viewed them until they turned the corner. Twenty-two years of waving goodbye. She was no longer worried about the Captain's return. He always did. Martin's reputation as one of the best navigators and ship's masters in Portland extended up and down the coast as far as Boston and Washington D.C. In fact, when Maine had become a state in 1820, breaking away from Massachusetts, the *Creighton II* had participated in the ship parade from Back Cove around Portland to Fore River in the lead position with the new governor, the cabinet, and their wives aboard, waving to the crowds lining the shore.

The walk to the docks took twenty minutes from their home on Payson St. Dawn broke from beneath the bay as they approached the *Creighton II*, a sixty-foot topsail schooner the Captain had commanded for over fifteen years. The ship sported double-raked masts and a square sail above the foresail. The sculpted prow and a combination of design elements contributed to the Captain's reputation for handling one of the fastest ships on the coast. Rumor had it that the Captain had been an engineer in his early years. He had invented many of the improvements incorporated into the ships of the day.

The boy had been aboard the ship in dock several times. He parted with the Captain's company, went to the ladder's base to the main deck, and waved up at the quartermaster, his brother Samuel, who called back.

"Find an empty bunk below and find Trent in the galley. He'll give you your orders. Glad to have you aboard."

The boy saluted his oldest brother.

"Glad to be aboard, sir."

By 9:00am, the *Creighton II* had weighed anchor and breezed out of port. The overcast day concealed a front moving in from the northwest. Upon reaching the open sea, the temperature dropped twelve degrees. The waves increased.

The boy, stationed in the galley below deck, helped the cooks prepare the afternoon meal. The boy's excitement over sailing with his brother and the Captain began to wear off as the rolling and pitching of the ship increased. He concentrated on the tasks assigned, but the cooking meat and soup stock began to sicken him. The more he focused on cleaning and plucking the birds, the more the soup stock, sloshing in the pot, unnerved him.

Trent noticed the boy's pallor and switched his assignment to table arrangement and dishwashing. It did not help. By noon, the boy realized what it meant to be seasick. The ship, crashing through each wave and the sideways roll back and forth as the vessel waddled in the wind, made the boy more ill. He washed a dish with one hand, holding on to anything solid within reach with the other hand. He willed himself not to be sick. He could not let his brother or the Captain down. He felt the cold sweat of death beading on his forehead. Still, the boy held on; his stomach swaying with the ship while his head bobbed in the opposite direction. He felt weary. Hard to stand. The boy shut out all the other sights and noises of the galley, trying desperately to concentrate on only two things: washing the dish in his hand and holding his breakfast porridge down.

The boy had to shift his feet back and forth to balance as the ship rolled. Suddenly, he spotted the slop bucket in the corner of the galley, and his morning porridge rose. He rushed to the bucket and spilled his guts on the feathers and rotten ruffage, half-filling the bucket. He felt some relief and, in a minute, lifted his head only to find the small room spinning around him. No one paid him any attention. Trent and the galley crew went about their business as if nothing had occurred. The boy, on the other hand, embarrassed, could hardly speak.

"I'm sorry, sir, I,,,"

"Take a breather, lad. Go up on deck and look to the horizon off the port side. See if the breeze revives you. Don't get tossed over, boy. The captain would throw me to the sharks."

The boy sheepishly climbed the ladder to the deck, grabbing the rail tightly and staring at the low-hanging clouds on the horizon. In five minutes, he felt sick again. He ran to starboard, hurtling more from his guts with the wind over the rail into the sea below.

At least he had not made a mess on the ship. He went back to port and stared more intently at the far horizon. It did not work. The waves in his peripheral vision kept interrupting his concentration on the earth's edge far away. In addition, his legs began to give out, and he had to hang on the rail with an ever-tightening grip to prevent himself from falling in a heap to the deck. He just wanted to curl into a ball, close his eyes and be suddenly well. When he did close his eyes, his head started spinning inside his skull. He kept both eyes open, but they hurt from the effort and concentration.

Samuel appeared at his side and put an arm around his shoulder.

"Rough day. We've all gone through it. You just happened to pick an awfully rough introduction. It doesn't seem like it now, but you will get your sea legs."

"But the Captain; what will he think. I've got to get back to the galley."

"Don't mind about him, boy. As far as I know, he never has been seasick. Rumor is he was born at sea. Besides, I'm the quartermaster, and you follow my orders. My bed is the best on board, dead center of the ship. I'll take you down, and you can sleep it off. You'll most likely feel better tomorrow."

The boy did not argue. His legs wobbled like rubber. He crawled into his brother's pullman while Samuel found a clean bucket, placing it conveniently next to the head of the bed. Samuel left.

The boy vomited three more times. Beyond that, he dry-heaved well into the night and finally slept. Samuel checked on him later that night and returned with the Captain. The Captain noted the boy's whiteness and cracked lips but did not wake the boy. Back on deck, the Captain took Samuel aside.

"Give him light duty in the morning polishing brass."

"Aye, Captain, remember both Henry and William were seasick at first. They were fine the next day. Of course, the sea was calm in comparison."

"They didn't look as sick as the boy. Keep me apprised."

The boy awoke thirsty. Samuel had left a stein of water in a hollow carved in the floor beside the bed. A chunk of bread on a plate was next to the stein. The boy, determined to have a better day, sat on the edge of the bunk, holding the mug of water between his knees.

A faint repugnant odor of leftover beer hit the boy like a brick, and he set the stein back into the hollow. He could not even look at the bread. Plugging his nose, the boy picked up the stein, swallowed two gulps, and set the mug back down. Even in the ship's center, each roll and toss brought dizziness to the boy. He stood, and in a few seconds, his knees buckled, and he sat and rolled back to the curled ball on the bunk that offered partial stillness in his head.

He tried again to stand, fighting the sickness that returned whenever he ventured beyond the bunk. He could not, would not succumb to the illness gripping him. Staggering up the ladder, he looked up to find Samuel on the upper deck. The boy waved and attempted a smile.

"Reporting for duty, sir."

"Come on up, boy."

The boy forced each step up the ladder to look like his normal gait, pounding the ladder one foot after the other, quickening his pace for the top two steps to stand before the Quartermaster, smiling.

"Today, you will be polishing brass. Take this cloth and fiber, and make any metal you find shine until you can see your reflection. Start on this deck so I can check your progress."

"Aye, aye, sir."

The boy took up the fiber, cloth, and soap bar and wandered to a far corner of the deck near the rail, somewhat out of Samuel's sight. He began polishing a brass sconce with his eyes and head still in the ship's sway. Twice he swallowed bile before he could hold it in no longer, projecting over the rail and spraying into the sea. There was not much left in his stomach to churn up. The boy wiped his sleeve across his forehead to eliminate the cold sweat dripping into his eyes and continued polishing. Samuel stayed on deck discussing duties with two sailors, paying no heed to the boy.

The quartermaster knew of the lad's distress. The boy spent a half hour polishing the sconce, a task Samuel knew the boy would complete on a good day in about five minutes. From the corner of his eye, he caught the boy retching again over the rail. After another hour, Samuel went over to the boy and, on one knee, took the boy by the shoulders and forced the boy to look at him. He could feel the weakness in the boy's arms, and his cheeks looked hollow. His color was even paler than the day before.

"You need to get some water down, boy; you're drying up. I'm sending you back to bed, but you've got to drink as much water as possible. Can I depend on you to do that?"

The boy nodded with a furrowed brow, holding back tears. He felt good for nothing, now to be labeled the worst sailor in the family of sailors. But the thought of the bed below relieved the spin, and he made his way off the upper deck to Samuel's cabin. His rubber legs gave way when he reached the bed, and he rolled in.

Later in the afternoon, Samuel regularly walked the passage near the boy's bed. He heard the soft moaning of the boy and the echo of hurling in the bucket. He left the boy be.

In the cabin's dark that night, the shivering boy felt a hand on his shoulder and turned to face the Captain. He attempted to sit up and salute.

"I'm sure I'll be better in the morning. I haven't thrown up lately. I have been drinking the water, see?"

"Don't try to get up. The sea isn't doing you any favors on your first big trip, lad. Hell, I've got three other sailors in the same shape as you. This isn't the roughest sea Samuel, and I have dealt with, but it's sure, as Aegir, not the smoothest. Keep sipping your water and try to rest. I'll check in on you tomorrow morning."

The boy laid back down, fighting tears and shivers and feeling despair in disappointing the two men he admired most. He turned away from the Captain, who signaled Samuel, leaving the boy to the cabin's quiet.

"Tomorrow, we'll put in at the port of New York. How close are we, Samuel?"

"We're close, Captain, not more than three hours north by northeast. We'll backtrack. But Captain, it will kill the boy to know he caused any delay. How many times has he heard you say, 'Sail till you're there, no matter what?'"

"We'll put into New York. I'll take the boy to a doctor, give him a day of rest on land, and take him by stagecoach back to Portland. You'll take the *Creighton II* on to Washington and Savannah."

"Captain. Father, are you sure? The boy will be fine in another day or two."

"The only thing I know is that neither you nor I are doctors, and I will not delay care for the boy, no matter what it costs me. I once watched a man die by my doctoring, and I'll not take a chance with the boy.

"I also know you can command this crew for the rest of the trip.

"The boy will get over his disappointment. None of you boys have ever let me down in any manner. Hearing from you how the boy fought to work through his sickness is good enough for me."

The *Creighton II* anchored in New York Harbor early afternoon the next day. Samuel lowered the listless boy into the arms of the Captain, balancing in a skiff. He and a crewman rowed to the docks, where the Captain transferred the boy to a carriage. The boat returned to the ship. The *Creighton II* sailed in two tacks out of the harbor under Samuel's guidance and continued back on course to Washington and Savannah. Satisfied, the Captain inquired at the office for the nearest, most capable doctor or surgeon. The harbor master drew directions to a doctor's office at Five Points in lower Manhattan.

Though still weak, the city beyond the carriage window fascinated the boy. People everywhere. Carriages were near to crashing into one another, the horses rearing. Ditch diggers along the road for a mile, laying pipes five feet below street level. One carriage had tipped into the ditch, breaking two wheels into splinters. Men, women, and children of all colors were bustling about. At every other crossroad, posted signs pointed the way to the Erie Canal. Many of the people in the streets headed in that direction. The Captain's carriage driver needed to inquire three times for suggestions amid many projects and detours. He stopped in front of a two-story brownstone, the only non-wooden structure. The Captain knocked, and the whitewashed front door opened. The Captain helped the boy inside.

The swivel chair behind the reception desk sat empty. The Captain rang the bell. An exquisitely dressed man with a gold lamé vest stepped out of an adjoining room. Something about the man looked strange to the boy, but it wasn't until he led him into the examination room and held his wrist gently that the boy realized his skin was incredibly dark compared to his sickly white wrist.

The Captain described the boy's symptoms, and the doctor asked relevant questions about the length of the voyage, the temperature and humidity of the weather, and the boy's eating habits before, during, and after the trip. Then the doctor gave his appraisal.

"I believe you were right to bring the boy to see me. His strength is depleted, and the coldness of his forehead with no sweat on such a warm day indicates a further depletion of liquids in the body, putting him at extreme risk."

"What would you suggest, Doctor?"

"I have a bed in the back room beyond the office. We'll see if the boy can keep water down now that he is off the ship. A small cup of water every half hour to start. We'll try some sugar water and a slight salt solution later today. I will observe his progress over the next six hours, and I am sure nothing more will need to be prescribed. Sleep boy. It should be easier to sleep now that you're on solid ground.

"Sir, you may wait in the library. Plenty of reading material there. Or you can explore the city and return for a progress report."

"I would like to stay, Doctor; thank you."

The boy looked at the bed in the darkened back room with relief. Though his stomach continued to churn, the water refreshed him. Asleep in minutes, the Captain followed suit in a chair in the library.

By the next day, the Doctor felt the boy capable of travel. He and the Captain ate breakfast at the Doctor's table; scrambled eggs, biscuits with honey, and grits. The Captain and the doctor cautioned the boy to take small portions. Dr. James Ogjobi looked older than the Captain. His curly hair, on top, was entirely gray and slicked back behind his ears. He struggled to rise from the table to retrieve more coffee while he related his history of becoming a doctor to his two visitors.

He had lived his whole life in Five Points and could remember good times living among his family and bad times fighting the squalor of this area of New York. The doctor had seen malaria, yellow fever, and even an isolated smallpox epidemic among unvaccinated slum neighborhoods. At seventeen, he had nursed several in his family through these diseases; some had died. He traveled to work as a footman, seeing less illness and death in the city's affluent, cleaner areas. He reasoned a correspondence between the conditions in the streets with the death toll. He had taken it upon himself to gather his family and assign a rotating schedule for everyone each morning before work to clean their block of sewer waste. Another family member would fetch clean water from a spring in the hills. Others would haul garbage and kill as many rats as they could discover.

James Ogjobi had volunteered in 1811 at West Battery to hold off the British. There he trained as an army surgeon based on his enlistment interview and professed success with the sicknesses of the city. The fort never saw action but did house troops, and the injured rotated from battles in Detroit and Ontario. He mostly continued to care for the city of New York's less fortunate. His reputation grew, and the affluent found his expertise valuable and paid well. He established the practice, bought the building where they sat eating breakfast, and continued his study of medicine.

The Captain spoke briefly about his travels to Constantinople, Ireland, and the West Indies. The boy listened, amazed at how comfortably the two men conversed: sharing experiences of their youth. These two men could not have looked more different to the boy, sitting across from each other at the breakfast table, yet the Captain and Dr. Ogjobi enjoyed coffee like old friends. The boy, politely entranced with the conversation, learned things about the Captain he had never heard. He discovered from Dr. Ogjobi that a hard life existed beyond the boy's home in Portland, Maine.

The Captain settled their account and hailed a carriage to take them to the stagecoach station. The Captain planned their return trip to Portland with the station master. They would take the 2:00pm stagecoach to Stamford, Connecticut, a six-hour journey. That same evening, they would transfer to a hired carriage and ride to New Haven, Connecticut, arriving at 2:00 am the next day.

The stagecoach from New Haven to Springfield, Massachusets, would leave at 8:00am arriving by 5:00pm. They would continue to Boston from Springfield, a long day's ride. Another day would be spent traveling from Boston to Portsmouth. After that, they would spend over half a day traveling from Portsmouth to Portland and home.

The Captain cautioned the boy to let him know if he started feeling any relapse as they traveled or if the trip proved too strenuous. The boy felt confident he could withstand the jostling stagecoach but assured the Captain he would be honest about his condition.

The countryside in between the towns looked raw, rugged, and beautiful. Farms intermittently lined the turnpike, and beyond the farms, the forests stretched up into the foothills to the southwest. Despite the constant rattle of the stagecoach, the boy still felt weak from his ordeal on the Creighton II and slept, leaning against the Captain for most of the journey's arduous first day and night. A young couple and a businessman with a satchel full of tonic samples joined them on the stagecoach on the second day. Although the Captain remained quiet, the other passengers kept a running commentary on the state of the union and news from the capital in New York.

Both travelers were up at dawn in Springfield. They were ready to board the stagecoach that pulled up to the station at 8:00 am. By midday, the stagecoach had turned east on the Worcester Turnpike, heading to Boston. Late that night, the stagecoach pulled into the station. Since the next stagecoach to Portsmouth would leave at 9:00am the next day, the Captain and the boy stretched out in the corner of the station house. The boy used his potato sack of Sunday clothes as a pillow, and the station master found a blanket that covered them both. The wood floor felt soft and smooth. They had no trouble sleeping.

The Portsmouth stagecoach spent an hour navigating the streets of Boston, and the boy looked at the myriad shops along the city streets. The stagecoach passed general stores, a millinery, three shoe stores, blacksmiths, tack shops, hardware stores, cafes, hotels, and many taverns; too many to count. On the outskirts of town, the boy noted multiple city block buildings with connected smokestacks spewing ash into the surrounding neighborhoods. The Captain explained that these buildings marked the bustle of the manufacturing plants, mills, and factories, spurring the city's growth.

The Captain decided to spend that night in a hotel in Portsmouth. In the lobby, a businessman named Mr. Henshaw recognized the Captain. The gentleman freighted cotton goods imported from England on the *Creighton II* to be distributed to ports along the east coast down as far as Florida. The boy noted mutual respect exhibited between the two men. Mr. Henshaw invited them both to dinner and encouraged the boy to order the toffee pudding on the menu for dessert. The boy politely refused, still aware of his recent sickness and the Captain's cautionary advice on food portions, but his curiosity grew.

"How did you come to hire the *Creighton II* for your cotton, Mr. Henshaw?"

"Well, boy, the first time, I admit I picked the first ship that looked good at the docks. The Captain sailed out that week from Portland during a winter storm that numbed my face and hands. The news came about two other ships that foundered in the blinding snow twenty miles south of Portland, but the *Creighton II* made it through with my cargo safely and on time. I haven't used any other ship since."

The Captain rocked back in his chair.

"Arthur, I never mentioned it before, but I rode out that storm in a protected cove fifteen miles south of Portland. Of course, I had to make up the time lost with a direct route we navigated further out to sea than I usually care to venture, but we made up the time. Probably shouldn't have brought that up."

"Amazing! Well, it doesn't change my mind. This man, lad, I would trust with a load of diamonds navigating through the icebergs of Iceland."

The boy just shook his head in despair. He had not even finished his first voyage on a moderately rough sea.

The Captain put his hand over the boys and gave him a silent but reassuring look.

They rolled into Portland around 4:00pm. The boy seemed comforted seeing familiar streets. His strength had returned, and he felt ready to face Mother. The Captain and boy remained silent during the thirty-minute walk to their home until the Captain stopped the boy with a hand on his shoulder and, kneeling, turned the boy to face him.

"That was quite a trip, boy. Time well spent. Sometimes children get a little lost in a family, being in the middle between four older brothers and your younger sister and brother. And sailor or not, which you may or may not be someday, we have made this journey together, and I think we are both the better for it."

The Captain knelt and hugged the boy. The boy put everything he had into reciprocating that hug, determined never to get on board a ship again. Equally determined to find another way to someday accomplish something that would warrant the Captain's hug.

Four years later, the boy sat back straight on a bench outside Harrasey's General Store. He waited for twenty minutes across Union Street. The door of Jasper Hattery across the street opened; the bell fastened to the top rail tinkled. Mr. Jasper checked for debris and horse droppings along his frontage. Satisfied, the man closed the door, turned the sign in the window to read 'Open' instead of 'Closed,' and vanished into the shadow of the store.

The boy stood, smoothing his pants and tugging his vest. His boots were polished and still clean after the walk from home. The slick-backed hair contained just a bit of axle grease near his ears. His reflection in the hattery window represented his best foot forward; he opened the door and stepped inside. The time: 8:30am: the street, still deserted, too early for Portland shoppers.

"Välkommen lad. Are you here to pick up a repair or re-blocking forz your fäter? Do you have hisshticket? Well, never mind, tell me wish of sheese two hats is your fäzzers, and I will box it for you. Everysing is paid for, is it not?"

"I'm sorry, sir, I am not here to pick up a hat. I am here to apply for an apprenticeship. I have studied your shop, and I know how busy you are. You have a brisk business here, and I want to help you and learn the trade."

"What?"

"I want to be your apprentice. I sat on that bench across the street this past week and counted thirty-four customers carrying hat boxes as they left your store. In town, more and more gentlemen wear their top hats and caps whenever they are out."

Mr. Jasper stared at the boy, perplexed. The business had been picking up this year. He did not know what to say.

"Nonsense."

The boy's legs weakened at the proprietor's exclamation. So far, he had managed to explain himself quite well.

"Mr. Jasper, I would expect no pay for twelve months. I have references from the Captain of the *Creighton II*, the joiner Martin, and my brothers Henry and William of the brush shop on 16th street as to my diligence. I have not missed a day of school or work since I turned twelve. I am sure you would find me useful and a quick study."

Now the wheels were turning for Mr. Jasper. He picked up the fine silk hat displayed in the corner window.

"What makes youshink you would be any goot as a hatter. Do you know anysing about it? How long it taysto get it right? The deadlines to get a hasdone on time? Let me shee your hands. Ok, you've been working, I give you zat."

"Mr. Jasper, I know that this hat is fine. I think it is one of the finest hats I have seen. The black ribbon here around the base shines with quality. The Captain says you are the best hatter north of Boston. I do not know how you do it yet, but I'm certain I can learn."

"Boy, I'll shink on it. No promishes. Now let me get to work. I am busy."

Outside, the boy quickly stepped toward home and turned the corner. He had not been turned down like the other three places he had tried this month. The butcher had even raised a cleaver at him to get him out of his shop.

At sixteen, the boy knew how to work. Now he wanted to find work right for him. Wherever he had worked since the sail on the *Creighton II*, he had been determined to find a passion that would drive an entire career. A job had to be more than bearable. A job is a day-in, day-out grind. To learn how to navigate a ship like Samuel, craft the prow like

Martin (piece by fitted piece,) or proudly sell brushes initialed on the handle, these passions sustained his brothers. The boy knew he must find a path for himself.

He returned to school after his disastrous sail, finishing his studies when he turned thirteen. His mother and Captain approved of his choosing to work with Martin in the carpentry shop. For two years, he learned to work with his hands and the 'carpenter's' tools while fetching material and fastening boards with clamps so Martin could smooth hulls. The trouble began when the boy determined he did not like Martin. His older brother was abrupt to the point of seeming angry with the boy most of the time. Never encouraging, continually finding yet another fault with the boy's work even as others in the shipbuilders' crew expressed satisfaction with his skills' progress.

The boy loved the aroma of wood freshly planed. The softness of wood shavings piles as he shoveled and cleaned the shop floor. Wood's sheer fluidity could be sculpted to whatever shape a master imagined.

His brother Samuel was always attentive and patient as the boy grew older. Martin, at work, seemed, at times, hostile to the boy. Did he resent the boy's rising skill level on advanced joining tasks? The boy had good hands, a firm grip when necessary, and a light touch on the planer. When a section looked good to the boy, Martin would tell him he spent too much time, causing the crew to fall behind in the schedule. The boy knew he worked no slower nor faster than others on the dock.

Did Martin browbeat the boy to ensure he would become a better joiner than himself? The boy sweated under this assumption, striving to please his brother and winning the praise of the crew. But the atmosphere became intolerable. After a year and a half, the boy began to look around for a way out.

After two years, he approached Henry about switching to brushmaking. Henry spoke to William, and they agreed to talk to their foreman about taking the boy on. It would mean starting over at the bottom for the boy and working his way up. It implies the boy must win approval from the Captain and explain the switch to his brother Martin.

Henry and William returned in a week with qualified approval by the foreman. The expanding demand for brush manufacturing by the growing cities along the coast would allow for another apprentice if he could live up to his brothers' capabilities. The Captain approved on the spot. He reasoned that the more skills the boy acquired at a young age, the more options he would have in the countless years of wage-earning. The Captain and the Mrs. believed in the power of knowledge and the importance of diversified skills. Schooling and excellent grades had been expected of all their children. Rachel assisted in the children's studies. Upon returning from an extended trip, the Captain consistently inquired about his children's progress, and it had better have put each child at the top of the class.

When the boy told his brother, Martin, of his decision, he never saw a flicker of emotion in his brother's features. The stroke of his arms never showed a moment's hesitation as he pulled his drawknife across the clamped board. Perhaps one of the other brothers had spoken to Martin, preparing him for the boy's wish to depart. Martin told the boy to clean his workspace, put away any tools and wood he had been preparing, and be gone; now.

The boy knew then he had made the right decision. Work is work, but it must be satisfying in its sense of accomplishment, and there should be ease among the surrounding workers. Work can be challenging, perhaps nearly unbearable. Without success and comradery within unimaginable sweat, men are animals with yokes.

At sixteen, the boy finished his one-year apprenticeship at the Canfiss Brush Company, where William and Henry worked. The company made four styles of brushes, all for whitewashing or barn painting. They made hundreds of these four styles a year and sold them in general and hardware stores all along the east coast. The making of a brush required little machinery. Twenty-two employees delicately bound the bristles by hand. Within four months, the boy developed expertise in making each brush style. The workers at the plant showed great pride in their skills. The quality of a Canfiss brush rested on the delicate handwork of twenty-two employees. The boy gained confidence and more skills at Canfiss, so much so that he wondered if other possibilities might be even more fulfilling. The busy Portland city shops and factories offered opportunities in multiple directions.

He selected and approached ten enterprises that might increase his social standing, earnings, and interest. Some businesses, like the butcher, rejected him outright. Once inside the depths of the butcher's shop, the boy heartily thanked the butcher's rejection. The boy's investigations included candlemakers, coopers, and a brewery.

The hatter's shop interested the boy for several reasons. The small shop had plenty of contact with the residents of Portland and tourists passing through. The proprietor currently worked without an apprentice; the shop could take on more help. The hats in the window varied in design, and a few were unique to the boy's experience. The boy sat across from the shop on several half days off from the brush company. He studied the designs and the customers that patronized the store.

The boy informed the Canfiss owners of his decision not to continue at the company. They already had two other apprentices training and would not feel the loss. William and Henry had understood his decision as an attempt to strike out on his own. A mark of maturity in the family. Martin had scoffed during the Sunday family meal, but the boy considered the source. Samuel and the Captain were away in the west indies, but Mother asked several questions. If the employer provided a future and was interested, she would approve and convey the boy's decision to the Captain. His younger brother George asked Henry if he could become an apprentice at the Canfiss company. William laughed at his seven-year-old youngest brother but assured him that he would be more than welcome to learn the trade when the time came after his schooling.

The next day the boy sat on the bench across the street from the Jasper Hattery for an hour. The sign in the window never changed, despite two passersby peering into the window and knocking on the door. The following day the door did open, and a woman, presumably Mrs. Jasper, turned the sign to 'Open,' and the boy entered the shop.

"Good morning. Is Mr. Jasper available this morning? Last week, I spoke to Mr. Jasper about a possible apprenticeship here in the shop."

"My name is Cora Jasper. Silas spoke to me about your visit. He is under the weather today. He is asleep. We won't bother him. He could hardly get moving this morning. His hands hurt so much yesterday that he couldn't hold his tack hammer, but he is better now. He will be back at work on the hat orders tomorrow."

"I can return tomorrow. Mr. Jasper said he might consider taking me on. I have reference letters and believe I would be a capable assistant."

"Oh, my boy, Mr. Jasper will take you on at my insistence. Please give me your letters of reference. I'll review them. Assuming they are in order, let's have you start the day after tomorrow. That will allow my discussions with my husband to percolate.

"You will find my husband a skilled craftsman."

"From the look of these two hats in the window, Mrs. Jasper, I agree."

"Yes, an expert hatter, but I want you to know he can be a bit forthright in his approach to people. At times, customers, associates, and even family find him overbearing. I blame it on his headaches. They are sometimes unbearable, and you must not take affront during those episodes.

"We can use assistance during times such as today when his headache incapacitates him. He would never admit this, but his coordination can sometimes be problematic. You probably noticed he can be difficult to understand at times."

"He's from Scandinavia, isn't he, Mrs. Jasper? He sounds a little like the Captain to me? "

"He is indeed, but he also has a bit of slur mixed in. Patience will be a prerequisite. Do you still think you can handle this work? Good. Day after tomorrow, 7:30 am! The door in the alley!"

On August 15th, the boy started work at Jasper Hattery. He knocked on the alley door at the proper time, lunch bucket in hand. Mr. Jasper opened the door himself and offered a broad smile and handshake.

"Glad to see you, lad. Come on in. You may address me as Mr. Jasper, always. Refer all customers to me. Mrs. Jasper has concluded that you will get a small wage during your apprenticeship. However, I must determine if you have a possible future as a hatter. So, pay attention."

For the first hour, Mr. Jasper showed the boy the small workroom where he made his hats. Two people turning around in the space would prove to be complicated. The work counter held a maple turntable, three inches thick and two feet in diameter, with a hole in the center. Behind Mr. Jasper, a stove vent piped heat into the room. The eight-foot-long counter and a clutter of tools around the turntable indicated Mr. Jasper's workspace. A space had been cleared next to the propped open window at the counter's far end. The boy pictured room in that corner for a second turn table, but he decided not to get ahead of himself.

The wall to the left of the stove displayed the tools of the trade. Several sizes of foot tollikers, heart tollikers, rounding jacks, puller-downs, and two runner-downs hung on the wall or sat on small shelves. Every tool had a place. Mr. Jasper named each device without explaining its use: Rounding jacks, slip sticks, shackles. The boy tried to commit all the terms to memory, succeeding with about half of what Mr. Jasper fired off.

Two-dimensional wooden blocks, each in the shape of a finished hat, only flat, graced a whole section of the wall to the left of the tools; the hat size it represented was engraved on each block. A wall-mounted open shelf unit to the right of the stove held various irons. Mr. Jasper called these hatter's shells. The box irons incorporated a heated slug; curved edge irons filled the next shelf. The boy noted that some curved to the right if held in the right hand and some curved left.

To the right of the irons shelf, a narrow door led to a hidden pantry, wide enough to step inside, deep enough to extend into the room behind the workshop. Shelves, floor to ceiling along one wall, held all the supplies and materials for the hats. Mr. Jasper cautioned the boy about always keeping the door closed. The small room stayed sealed and caulked so no rodents could wander in and feast on the expensive beaver furs. Only Mr. Jasper handled the beaver furs hanging independently of the walls of the pantry. Mr. Jasper made felt from the cheaper rabbit furs, brushing quicksilver salt on the coat to roughen the fibers and make the fur mat down. Beaver fur was costly and had natural serrated edges, making this step unnecessary.

All in all, the tour of the workshop and the explanation of the tools and materials fascinated the boy. Unlike his experience at the brush company, he believed it would take more than four months to master making even one hat style. He knew, however, that he could learn the complicated process of constructing hats. The young boy had mastered carpentry and brush making, skills requiring strength, patience, and fine dexterity. He could not wait to tackle this new craft.

Mr. Jasper emphasized the placement importance of each tool. He caressed the pantry's ribbons, feathers, and furs with a light touch and clean hands. The hatter spoke proudly and deliberately to the boy of the elements of his trade.

Mr. Jasper's mood seemed the opposite of his brusque demeanor when the boy first approached him. He made small jokes about the description of specific tools, like the foot tollikers, which reminded him of little-elf's feet. The morning passed in a blink. Mr. Jasper, expecting a customer to pick up a finished hat that afternoon, needed to turn his attention to the final cleaning and presentation. He gave the boy the task of cleaning the shop inside and out from top to bottom. The boy looked around, spotting a small cobweb in the corner of the room at the ceiling. Otherwise, the room seemed spotless already. Determined to impress the Jaspers, he dusted, swept, and mopped inside and outside the shop. He tackled the windows, straightened the tools on the counter, and aligned them on the wall so that they pointed in one direction and were sized from small to large.

He finished at around 6:00pm. Mrs. Jasper appeared and nodded approval, releasing the boy for the day.

The boy worked at the hattery for three months before Mr. Jasper decided he showed promise as a reliable, observant worker and spent a whole day showing the boy in detail the process of making a hat. Until that day, the boy had kept the shop spotless, the stove stoked with coal, the tools organized, and the felt prepared and inventoried. He had delivered hats to customers, picked up hats for repair, and visited vendors to pick up supplies. These duties allowed Mr. Jasper to concentrate on producing more hats in less time. On some days, the boy fetched tools and irons for the master as he sat on his stool and worked the turntable. The boy began to see a pattern to Mr. Jasper's headaches, and on those days, the boy would keep tools within a foot of Mr. Jasper's reach.

This day, Mr. Jasper's demeanor seemed lighthearted. He asked the boy to stand shoulder to shoulder as he worked, describing each step. The material for a hat, including rags, cloth, and string, was soaked in a pot of water. The water turned a shade of blue as the excess dye rinsed out of the material. Then Mr. Jasper racked the formless hat above the steam pan on the stove so that the steam billowed the cloth a bit. When Mr. Jasper thought the time right, he moved the pliable material to the turntable, draped over a wooden template. The master hatter formed a slip knot in the commander string and tightened it around the crown as tight as possible. He used the runner-down tool to work the commander string down to the band line where the crown meets the brim, squeezing excess water from the felt.

Then Mr. Jasper picked up the hatters' shell iron and forced the air pocket out of the top. Next, he rewetted the brim and used the foot tolliker to smooth the rim, pushing out water from the band line to the brim edge. Using hatters' shell irons in both hands, Mr. Jasper ironed the brim flat, steam clouding their faces. Mr. Jasper allowed the boy to unfasten the commander and use the heart tolliker to smooth out the line on the hat made by the commander string.

The boy fetched the puller-down tool from its place on the wall, and Mr. Jasper used it to force water from the crown with each down stroke. A lighter touch on the upstroke raised the nap on the hat. Mr. Jasper continued by showing and explaining to the boy the use of the rounding jack to cut off the excess felt. The duckbill tolliker and the curved edge iron were employed to dress the edge of the brim.

A slip-stick removed the hat from the block, carefully popping it off from the form as Mr. Jasper worked the tool around. He moved the hat to the flange stand that had a brim previously affixed. He placed the crown of the rewetted felt upside down on the flange and covered it with a cloth. Mr. Jasper then put a stretcher inside the hat and ironed the underside of the brim. He tied the fabric over the flange and hat to set the rim's shape. This hat would need to dry overnight. The lesson was done for the day; the boy returned to his regular duties. Mr. Jasper worked on preening three other hats for customers due to pick up their hats later in the day.

The boy, eager to continue his lesson the next day, met Mrs. Jasper as he walked into the shop.

"Not today, my boy, perhaps tomorrow. Please keep busy by yourself today cleaning the stove out and setting the tender and coal up for to-morrow. I am hoping Mr. Jasper will be back a pace on the morrow."

"I could also deliver Mr. Linderman's hat this afternoon. The address is on the sales slip."

"Thank you. That will be fine. If the customer of the hat you were working on yesterday stops by, you may refer him to me. Just cover the work in process with a muslin sheet."

After covering the two hats Mr. Jasper had begun over the last two days, the boy spent most of the day cleaning the used-up cinders and ash from the stove. He scraped all the inside compartments and then cleaned the top of burnt-on residue drippings from steaming felt or fur. When the stove was clean, the boy polished all the metal handles and nameplates till they shined bright. He filled the chamber with coal and prepared the starting tender. In the afternoon, he wrapped twine through the cloth handle of the hatbox and around the base, connecting another piece of string around the box at ninety degrees. He tied two loose loops in the twine where he could stick his arms through, allowing him to carry the pack on his back, his hands thus free.

The boy experienced another quiet and varied work day despite the disappointment of not finishing the hat-making lesson. At least no brush or other tool had been thrown at him by Mr. Jasper in a rampage state of headache-induced pain. Portland looked alive that afternoon with children hooping, visitors strolling, and couples sitting close on benches in the park. The clouds overhead caused alternating sun and shadow to cross the boy's path. Between the clouds, the blue sky looked freshly washed and clean compared to the heat of the packed-down, dry dirt streets.

The boy studied and rated each building and storefront he passed. The architecture or style of store embellishment fit the commodity displayed in the window, or the boy marked the enterprise as a Portland disappointment. The speedy growth of the city could be garnered by viewing some of the blocks the boy walked where multiple buildings were afterthoughts, glued to the building next door. But the boy felt comfortable here. He may not have wanted to see the world on a pitching ship, but he wanted to know and experience every corner of his city. Portland, Maine, still possessed a quaintness amongst prosperity that garnered the boy's respect. Opportunity and challenges tumbled endlessly in the boy's thoughts on the streets of his city.

The next day the boy entered the shop and found Mr. Jasper scurrying around his turntable laying out tools and waving the boy over, apparently ready to resume the hatter's lesson.

Mr. Jasper took up the hinged shackle to form the rolled edge of the brim. The hat required minimal drying time and needed little steam. He painted it inside and out with shellac, stiffening and waterproofing the finished product. This hat required a block creaser to be placed inside. Mr. Jasper fastened together a spring dent clamp on the outside.

The spring dent clamp would be removed before the store closed, and the hat could be boxed and delivered the next day.

The transfer of knowledge to his apprentice so excited Mr. Jasper that he continued explaining the special blocks and brim flanges and their use on different hats for the rest of the day. Of course, Mr. Jasper owned a hat block for every head size. The boy learned the proper measuring technique to ensure the fit of the finished hat. Any measuring or hat production error could be costly because Mr. Jasper guaranteed an ordered hat's acceptable fit. Lettering on the storefront window described this guarantee. The boy witnessed Mr. Jasper grabbing a custom hat off a gentleman's head, trying it on, and shouting at the customer about the unacceptable fit. Eventually, Mr. Jasper calmed.

"Please return to the store in two days for your replacement."

Another time the boy returned from a vendor pickup and found Mr. Jasper arguing in a high tone with a customer who disparaged the fit of his new hat, demanding a replacement. The boy could not tell if it might be a headache day or pride that made Mr. Jasper raise his voice. Mrs. Jasper overheard the argument as she entered the shop from her kitchen. The hatter's wife walked over to the customer, took the hat, turned to her husband, and sent him to the workshop. She calmed the customer, smiling, shook the man's hand, and asked him to return for his replacement.

After the customer exited the store, Mr. Jasper returned from the shop, took his wife by both hands, sighed, and embraced her.

"If it veren't for you, I vould have no cushtomers at all, Mrs. Jasper. Mind boy, the cushomer is always right. The argument is pointless, even when the man has absholutely no idea ashto proper and perfect hat fitting."

Mrs. Jasper only smiled at her husband, turned away from him to the boy, winked, then returned to her kitchen.

Months passed, and Mr. Jasper gave the boy more opportunities to work on the hats. He would give his apprentice a singular task for the whole month, such as tight-tying the commander string. Mr. Jasper hovered. Not tight enough? The boy did it over. The boy tried a record nine times on a weird-shaped hat he found difficult. His index finger became numb after the seventh retie. He daydreamed of soaking it in a tub of cool water. He continued, however, until that ninth time, and the small task met with Mr. Jasper's approval.

The following month the boy used the slip-stick to pop the hats from the forms. That task seemed simple enough until one day, the boy hurried, and the stick pierced the felt, ruining the hat. Luckily, it happened on one of the owner's 'good mood' days. Mr. Jasper pulled it from the form, stuck his finger in the hole, and waved it at the boy. Without a word, Mr. Jasper shrugged, tossed the hat in the scrap bin, and started over. The boy redoubled his vigilance and made no more mistakes. He spent a second month with the slip-stick to ensure his technique.

A nearly ideal apprenticeship. The long hours of hard work and patience with Mr. Jasper's headaches paid off. Most nights, the boy returned home pleased and not at all restless. He learned and earned his keep. Mother appreciated his coins on the table, and his little brother and sister listened to stories of the customers that graced the shop.

SHIPMASTER
1838

San Juan, Puerto Rico, January 20, 1838. *The Creighton II* arrived in port. Captain Martin Martensen ordered the offload of approximately half of the board lumber in the hold. Jorge Arias, the buyer's representative, and plantation owner, Carlos Diego Valdez, counted out the lumber.

Jorge's stevedores had finished unloading cargo from the ship anchored next to the *Creighton II*, *The Cocodrilo,* the week before. Martin stayed as a guest for three days at the Hacienda of Señor Valdez. Word came by a rider that morning that dysentery had broken out on *The Cocodrilo.*

Martin returned to the *Creighton II* and set sail for the town of Ponce on the southern side of the island to unload the rest of his lumber cargo. He desired to load rum and sugar there for the return trip to Portland.

Halfway through loading his ship, the port authorities were notified of the dysentery outbreak in San Juan. They quarantined Martin's ship and confined the Stevedores who packed the vessel to the dock office. Three men of *The Creighton II* contracted dysentery, and one man died. Fifty-five-year-old Martin Martensen passed on February 7th, 1838. He and Rachel had produced eleven children. The Captain had most likely contracted the disease from a water jug Jorge Arias had filled aboard *The Cocodrilo*.

Rachel agonized over the delayed return of Martin from the Caribbean until April, when the news of Martin's death and the quarantined ship reached Portland.

Samuel and Martin Jr. traveled by steamer to Ponce, Puerto Rico, at which point Samuel captained the *Creighton II* back along the east coast, delivering the freight his father had collected on board. Martin Jr. returned to Portland on the brig *Henry*, guarding his father's remains. Captain Martin Martensen was buried with a prominent headstone in the Evergreen Cemetery in Portland, Maine.

Friends, Captains, and Portland dignitaries memorialized Martin at the service for the guiding way he raised his children and the love he had expressed for Rachel whenever he returned to port.

.

APPRENTICE
1840

Three years slid through the boy's fingers, mastering the hatters' craft before the passing of his father, the Captain. Two more years blinked by, but by the spring of 1840, the boy, now twenty-two, considered himself a hatter, no longer the apprentice. Mr. Jasper still single-handedly converted furs to felt with the quicksilver (mercury) back in the pantry.

The boy contemplated opening his own shop. He was confident he could buy converted fur manufactured elsewhere in the city, avoiding quicksilver altogether. For three years, he worked a second turntable at the end of the counter next to the window. The window offered fresh air for the workshop and remained open for ventilation from the quicksilver vapors during the winter and summer. The boy did not mind. His vest kept him warm enough through the winter, and a cool breeze reached him from the sea during the summer. When Mr. Jasper suggested acquiring a second station, the boy volunteered to fashion the turntable down at Martin's woodworking shop.

He used one of Martin's lathes to turn a circular track in the base and table, which floated on iron ball bearings; by waxing the grooved channels now and then, the table rotated with a touch of a finger. A spring-loaded wooden peg could be pushed down through the turn-table into one of sixty holes in the stationary base permanently attached to the counter. The mechanism thus allowed the hat to be perfectly positioned for ironing and ribbon attachment.

The boy had grown taller than Mr. Jasper. He still looked some-what slight with delicate hands. After contributing most of his wages for room and board at his mother's home, he spent the remainder of his money in various high-end shops along the main streets of Portland. He appreciated a tailored suit. He paid to have his shirts pressed, and his dress boots were of the softest calfskin, which he kept polished to a glisten. In the winter, he wore one of the city's most expensive-looking beaver top hats, which he made himself. In the summer, he wore a uniquely styled straw top hat, a bit wider in circumference at the top than the current standard, a design he had influenced. The hat made him look like the young man in charge at gatherings. He sometimes even ventured south to Boston on the stagecoach to explore the city and purchase the latest men's fashion.

In truth, he reveled in the energy of the city. Portland's sights and sounds, the growth of changing neighborhoods, and the history that had culminated in the state of Maine fascinated the boy.

As Portland grew, a constant flow of people walked by or stopped to peer into the front windows of the hattery. The boy always focused on his turntable and the shaping of the mounted hat. He could hear the clatter of boots outside, the exclamations as people stopped and gawked at him, or the display of hat styles.

At ten o'clock each day, the boy would be sure to have finished any of the many steps in his hat-making process, and for five or ten minutes, he would rearrange his tools or clean and sweep the scraps around his workstation. This effort allowed him to keep an eye on the front window instead of focusing intensely on his turntable.

At that time, every day without heavy rain, a gentleman of the age his father would have been, walking with a cane in his right hand, passed slowly by the front of the store. His left arm would be held tightly by a girl the boy hoped would be about his age. She did not help the older man exactly but assured him no missteps would send both slipping to the street.

The man appeared gaunt but immaculately dressed except for his top hat, which the boy's trained eye gathered to be a bit worn through at the front of the brim. The hat, probably a comfortable favorite of the man, hid his bald head until he doffed it. The girl alternated between three dresses, green, blue, and brown. Each dress had a complimentary collar, sleeves puffed from shoulder to elbow, and lace and ribbon trim at the bottom of the skirts. The girl clutched her skirt in her left hand, raising it a few inches to protect the material from debris that might obstruct their path. Her waist, loosely corseted, allowed her dress to flow more as she walked. The boy determined her to be strong-willed due to her departure from the impossibly tight fashion restrictions of the day. His own mother dressed similarly.

The girl's bonnet covered most of her face, exasperating the boy. Most days, he would only be able to note the blush of her cheek and turned-up nose as the couple strolled by. Occasionally, they stopped and studied the hats displayed in the shop window. From that day forward, he willed her to interrupt their stroll and look in the hattery's window, which the couple often did. The boy shifted the hats in the display each morning so the girl might stop again to show the gentleman.

After a few weeks, the boy schemed to go a step further. He prepared a free-standing hat display. He suggested to Mr. Jasper the idea of placing it outside the front door. In good weather, the collection might be a further enticement for possible customers to come into the store. Thus, a little before ten o'clock, the boy brought the hatrack outside and fussed with the two hats he wanted to display. He brushed the hat on the higher peg, tilting it first one way and then the other, stepping back to admire the effect, and then leaning the hat the other way. He did the same with his second hat choice, becoming so absorbed in the display that the girl and her presumed father suddenly stood beside him on the walkway, waiting for him to finish.

"I beg your pardon, Miss, and sir, I am trying a new display technique for my hats. I apologize for being in your way."

The dapper gentleman pointed to a top hat in the window.

"We have noticed your hats many times, young man. My daughter has an eye for good workmanship, and she has mentioned the exceptional quality of the hats in your store."

"If I am not being too presumptuous, sir, we strive to produce the best hats in Maine. We have customers from as far away as Boston that buy a custom-fitted hat at Jasper's Hattery."

The girl, still holding the gentleman's arm, grabbed the hat stand with her free hand. It swayed a bit.

"It would be a shame if someone accidentally tipped over this outdoor display, dirtying these beautiful hats. Why not just keep your front door open during good weather? The hats, I believe, will sell themselves if you can entice people into the store. Perhaps with an offer of a cup of coffee, a pot, ready next to the front door. The aroma of coffee in the air always makes me smile."

"Your daughter has a friendly smile and an excellent idea.

"The next time you stroll in the neighborhood, I hope to have that cup of coffee ready for you."

The older man tugged the girl along.

"Thank you, young man. Looking forward to it."

The boy could not quickly think of a way to keep them from strolling away.

"Yes, sir, I wish you both a good day."

When they were gone, the boy twirled, ecstatic. The girl seemed bright and of a height just a bit shorter than himself. Her soft alto voice sounded gentle yet sure. It had been all he could do not to take her gloved hand during their exchange and lead her into the store. *"Why didn't he ask them to step inside? Perhaps they found him too forward and will take an alternative route in the future."* Momentarily saddened, he could recall no indication that the strolling couple would return for a cup of coffee.

He went to Mrs. Jasper to promote the girl's idea. Mrs. Jasper, looking up at the boy these days, caught him by the sleeve as he entered the kitchen, and they sat down at the table.

"Mr. Jasper will not be much help this week, I am afraid. The hand tremors are worse, to the point of dropping tools. You can't imagine his state of mind these days. We are always thankful to the lord for your efforts here and your kindness to Mr. Jasper. You have kept your composure even on days that he rants endlessly."

"I understand, Mrs. Jasper. I have learned the trade thanks to Mr. Jasper. Perhaps now I might try to learn the business side of a hattery. I have a suggestion for welcoming even more customers into the shop. As these are the warm weather days, we could keep the front door to the shop propped open and have a coffee pot steaming just inside the door. It has been suggested to me by a potential client that the whiff of coffee reaching the walkway would entice browsers into the store where we might better sell them our hats."

"We're not a café, my boy; we don't sell coffee."

"No, we wouldn't sell them coffee, but give the customer a small cup they could sip while looking around the store."

"We can try it. I can make a pot of coffee easy enough."

"Great, we'll put the coffee pot out at a five to ten. People are ready for another cup of coffee mid-morning."

After meeting the hatter in the shop, the gentleman and his daughter continued their stroll. The Father leaned toward his daughter.

"Well, Cordelia Bryant, the lad took notice of you. He indeed seems personable."

"Father, you're impossible. But he was genuinely nice and smart, wouldn't you agree?"

Lemuel smiled at his daughter, cocking his head.

"After five minutes of conversation, I believe he is brilliant beyond compare."

Cordelia squeezed her father's arm, not minding his tease. They would stop for coffee the day after tomorrow, and she would learn the boy's name. She contemplated the possibilities a young, well-dressed, successful store owner might offer her.

The boy felt crushed when the girl did not walk by with her father the next day. He kept seeing her in profile, walking by the shop in his imagination. At ten minutes after ten, he saw someone in a bonnet and darted for the open door, but the girl was not his girl. *His girl, whatever put that idea in his head.* His stomach roiled the rest of the day miserably.

But the next day, the father/daughter strollers came into the shop at ten, just after Mrs. Jasper had set out the coffee pot. Mr. Jasper's headache incapacitated him again this day, so the boy had the shop to himself again. The boy poured two cups of coffee. Coffee on the house, sir, madam. Enjoy our shop for as long as you wish. If you find you have a question, I will be more than happy to attempt an answer. My name is **Daniel Martensen**."

"My name is Lemuel Bryant, Daniel, and this is my persistent daughter, Cordelia. If I'm not careful, I will have three new hats today."

Cordelia poked her father in the chest.

"Father, you know it's your birthday in two weeks, and I've been looking at these wonderful hats as a gift for you. Mother and I want you to give that old thing you've been wearing to the church charity. What say you, Mr. Hatter."

Daniel looked into Cordelia's eyes to respond.

"You can't top the feeling of a well-broken-in top hat, Madam. I appreciate that your father may be accustomed to his hat and reluctant to start the breaking-in process of a new hat.

"On the other hand, Mr. Bryant, I believe the custom hat I could make for you would fit so well I would guarantee a comfortable fit within a day of wearing it.

"On my best hats, I have used a calfskin sweatband stretched and supple as those gloves you are wearing."

Cordelia rubbed her father's shoulder blade.

"You see, Father, I told you. The hats in this store are the absolute best."

"I'll consider it, my dear; now, we must be pushing on."

Daniel felt he had successfully set the stage for a hat sale and more meetings with Cordelia.

"That's fine, sir, and thank you, Miss, for your endorsement."

That afternoon three men came in off the street and, while sipping coffee, decided to be measured for a hat. One gentleman placed an order. Mrs. Jasper considered the coffee pot a success. It would be part of the daily routine in the shop from then on.

Three days later, the Bryants were back in the store. Daniel measured Mr. Bryant for a hat while Cordelia retained hold of his arm. This made movement around the couple awkward for Daniel, but as it put him within inches of Cordelia, he did not object. He discovered a small mole on the back of the girl's neck at the nape and lost concentration, wishing he could be measuring Cordelia, touching her auburn curls.

Another three days passed. Mr. Bryant had been measured, but no order had been taken.

As Daniel set out the pot of coffee on the fourth day after Mr. Bryant's measurement visit, he turned and almost ran into Cordelia coming through the doorway.

"I am sorry, Miss Cordelia; I was working on setting the coffee pot. Is that a new outfit?"

Daniel had not seen Cordelia in this dress, a deep purple that made the white of her skin at the neck and her hair even brighter in contrast. Cordelia picked at the lace around her wrist.

"I just finished adding trim this morning. How could you possibly know this is a new dress? It is, but how could you know?"

"Oh, well, it seems new, crisp, and of a new clothes scent."

Cordelia was a bit taken aback by the hatter's presumption but also pleased he had taken note of her new dress. After all, she had been hoping the outfit would impress. Apparently, it had. Daniel almost ran behind the counter to cover his embarrassment. "*Totally unprofessional conduct, speaking of her dress.*" His comment had erupted out of him in his excitement at seeing her. Today she exemplified royalty in that purple dress. Should he come back in front of the counter and bow slightly? He gathered his thoughts.

"How can I help you today, Miss Cordelia?"

"I'm going to order a hat, of course. I came alone because my mother and I wanted to surprise my father. His birthday is in three days. Does that allow you enough time?"

"I am certain I can meet that deadline. I will deliver your father's hat in the morning on Monday. Is that acceptable? Now let's select a style, shall we?"

The boy spent the next hour and a half describing the features of each hat he felt appropriate for a tall thin man such as Mr. Bryant. He left no detail out of his remarks. Cordelia inquired about at least one of the aspects of each hat to keep the conversation two-sided.

Cordelia chose a beaver tophat. Daniel completed his measurements worksheet and nodded his approval.

"Your choice and your father's measurements will provide a fine hat. The order will be placed if you add your signature to the measuring sheet. That will be $9.45 payable now or upon delivery."

Cordelia did not quibble. To Daniel's surprise, Cordelia brought out a checkbook from her reticule and wrote a check against the Bangor Savings Bank. She made the check out for ten dollars.

"You have given me an excellent price, and I insist you keep the whole ten dollars."

Daniel modestly accepted the payment. He had half-priced the hat just for her. With the drying time and Cordelia's color choice, a soft grey, the project would take over two days to complete. He had only three days, and two orders should be filled first. But he had made many wellingtons, his most practiced style, perhaps his favorite hat to make.

"By the way, on Saturday night, our youth group at First Parish Church on Congress St. has scheduled a speaker you might be interested in. Of course, I don't know your leanings on subjects other than hats, but there will be strawberry shortcake and many of my friends."

"I'll be there. Strawberry shortcake. My favorite. Until then, thank you for the invite and the order."

Cordelia left the store, turned the corner, and pounded her forehead with her gloved fist. What possessed her to be so forward. She should have let Daniel ask her to a function. On the other hand, a church meeting is hardly a governor's ball. Hopefully, it would be a meeting of interest to them both.

For his part, Daniel put both hands on the counter and sighed. Now he had even less time to finish the hat. To meet the deadline and attend the social at Cordelia's church, he would have to ask Mrs. Jasper if he could work late into the night both nights.

That afternoon Daniel never looked up from the counter as he worked rapidly but carefully on the two hat orders scheduled for presentation in the afternoon on the morrow, Saturday. One mistake on either of these hats would make Cordelia's deadline impossible to maintain. At ten o'clock that night, he had finished both. Exhausted, Daniel walked home. His mother had already gone to bed. Daniel retired as well. The grey Wellington appeared in his restless dream, first with more and more design ideas and then as mistakes or missteps that prevented the delivery of the hat on Monday.

He awoke again at 5:30am. He dressed and made his way to the hattery. He worked efficiently, stoking the stove, filling the steaming pan, laying out the necessary tools and irons, and checking his measuring sheet.

Luckily, the pantry held an adequate supply of the grey felt he had brought out and sold to Cordelia. Daniel concentrated and performed best in the morning. He set about what he believed to be his most crucial assignment with confidence.

At eight o'clock, Mrs. Jasper swung the door open from the adjoining kitchen and perused the shop.

"Ah, the light grey. The beaver that grew that fur wouldn't recognize himself in it. Mr. Jasper won't be down again today, I'm afraid. If I can help with customers, ring the bell. Still, Silas can make beautiful felt. That is the softest piece in the pantry. What style are you building?"

"A wellington, Mrs. Jasper, and the material cost will be deducted from my salary. I have written the receipt and put it in your cash drawer."

"What? Whatever are you, oh, is that elegant coffee girl responsible for this endeavor? Be aware, Daniel, and don't go too far out on a limb with her or her father."

"Do you know the Bryants, Mrs. Jasper?"

"I know of the family, Daniel. There are now a few families in Portland in a circle above the others. Lemuel Bryant was a war hero who survived the 'Battle of York.' He has been favored by patriots ever since, which has provided considerable wealth to the family. He now owns many of the docks and warehouses in South Portland. His crowd includes the new factory owners, fishery processors, and government officials.

"Having said too much about his crowd, I have heard many charitable remarks about Lemuel Bryant's good works. Word to the wise, Daniel, word to the wise."

Daniel kept an eye on the clock, estimating the time to complete each process on the hat, not wanting to start a process that would make him late to meet Cordelia. Still, when it became time for him to clean up and walk to the church, the incomplete hatter shell forced him to continue ironing for several precious minutes. For once, Daniel left his tools and irons cast about the shop in haste to change into his other shirt and Sunday vest. He glanced around to ensure the irons and stove could be left, then hurried off to the church.

Luckily, the church stood only ten blocks away. First Parish Church, impressively built of grey granite, had an eight-foot door that opened without creaking. The speaker had begun, so Daniel stood in the back of the church, searching out Cordelia. She sat in the fifth pew on the right, her purple dress and auburn hair recognizable. A tall gentleman sitting beside her bent close, and the pair conversed quietly while the speaker presented.

Surprisingly, the topic advocated a call to action for the nationwide abolition of slavery, drawing Daniel's attention away from Cordelia and her gentleman friend. Maine had joined the Union twenty years ago as a free state. Slavery was such a contentious topic across the land that States were accepted into the Union in pairs; one slave state, the other a slave-free state. The speaker referenced the speech given by Prince Albert, husband of Queen Victoria, last month to the more than 4500 attendees of the Anti-Slavery meeting in London. The speaker proclaimed that American standards must exceed the example set by England. The Abolition of Slavery Act of 1833 abolished slavery in the British Empire. Suddenly a gentleman stood from his pew twenty feet from Daniel, raising his voice to the crowd.

"You cannot compare the backward colonies of the United Kingdom with the economic powerhouse of America. The human resource represented by the negro in our southern territories and states is why you here in the north can afford the goods and materials you need to grow your own economy. Stop this nonsense. You use horses and oxen to help plow your fields. Would you give the animals a choice in the matter?

"The negro is uneducable, godless, and simple-minded. Put on this earth to serve their intended purpose; to work for us.

"We will keep our slaves, thank you."

At that, ten others in various pews about the sanctuary stood and attempted to shout down the speaker at the pulpit. Men at the rear of Daniel gathered and approached the man standing in the pew who initially interrupted the meeting, encouraging him to leave. Other men rose and began manhandling the disrupters, showing them to the exits. The crowd, more interested in the civil discourse presented by the speaker at the pulpit, ignored the disruption, and the speaker continued.

Daniel sought out Cordelia as she turned to watch the near chaos in the pews. She appeared calm but defiant, and Daniel thought she might try to tackle a protester herself. Her gentleman friend took her by the elbow as Cordelia stood to counter the protesters and coaxed her into sitting down again. She had seen Daniel standing behind the last pew.

The fifty people attending the meeting filtered into the adjoining parsonage, where small plates of strawberry shortcake were set out for the taking. Four young friends surrounded Cordelia. She held two plates and broke with the group to offer Daniel dessert. She drew him back to her friends for introductions. Her gentleman friend, James, moved to Cordelia's right side and never strayed. Cordelia's best friend Emma looked athletic and had a good laugh. Black hair, blue-eyed; Emma's square jaw kept her south of beautiful in Daniel's eye. Mary and Samuel both shook Daniel's hand. Cordelia asked him how he liked the speech by William Trumbull, a founding member of the Portland Anti-Slavery Society.

"I'm interested in what Mr. Trumbull said about Prince Albert's speech in London. Prince Albert reflects the sympathies of Queen Victoria. Quite a royal statement from a country where Americans continue to hold residual animosity. Cordelia, I thought you might take your parasol to one of the protesters."

James shrugged.

"I don't know how Cordelia can get so upset. Slavery is not going anywhere. The fifty sympathizers attending this meeting are so few within the political mindset in America it seems pointless to pursue. Daniel, Cordelia says you are a hatter. What other passions do you have, horse riding, quoits? Do you play chess by any chance? I'm looking for a challenge. Samuel here is getting tired of losing to me all the time."

Cordelia gathered plates, handing them to James.

"James, stop grilling, Daniel, and return our plates to the kitchen. Give him a chance to get to know us before you poison his opinion. Emma is dying to meet you, Daniel, after I told her how we met and how elegant your hats are."

James left for the kitchen. Daniel smiled at Cordelia and her friends.

"I assure you I will return and get to know you and your friends better, Cordelia. How did you become acquainted with these four? What are the connections?"

"Emma and I went all through school sitting next to each other. Mary happens to be a member of First Parish Church, like my family. Samuel is a cousin of Emma's from South Portland. James is, well, James is James. He's attending Westbrook Seminary with a scientific emphasis. I'm attending next year to study ladies' classical after I talk my father into it."

James returned from the kitchen carrying three more plates of strawberry shortcakes, handing one to Samuel and one to Daniel.

"Put a little weight on you, Daniel; it can't hurt. Cordelia, do you and Emma and Mary want more? There is plenty left out there."

The girls all shook their heads. Daniel finished his shortcake.

"I'm sorry, but I must be going. Thank you, Cordelia, for this interesting evening. I am anxious to get to know you all better. Mary, James, Samuel, and Emma, nice to meet you. Cordelia, I will perhaps see you Monday morning. Good night everyone."

On the walk home, Daniel could not shake James out of his head. James apparently wished to pursue Cordelia as much as Daniel. And

Cordelia, understandably, did not hide her interest in James. Daniel foresaw disappointment ahead if he continued to pine for Cordelia. There was nothing for it. He could not stop thinking about Cordelia and that beautiful purple dress.

Daniel awoke at first light on Sunday and walked rapidly to the shop. By eight o'clock that evening, the hat sat on its stand, ready and perfect. He spent another twenty minutes wrapping the hat box in gift paper. He tied the package with a black silk ribbon Cordelia could salvage from the wrapping to pull her hair back if she wished.

On Monday morning at 10:00am, Daniel knocked on the front door of the Bryant home. The butler opened the door and led Daniel to the parlor, too nervous to sit. Cordelia and her mother swept into the room, Cordelia smiling broadly. She introduced him to Mrs. Bryant, who commented on the wrapped hat box as extra trouble, unnecessary, but beautifully accomplished. After ten minutes of polite conversation, Mrs. Bryant left and returned with Mr. Bryant on her right arm, just as Cordelia supported her father on their city strolls. Upon entering the room, Mr. Bryant shook Daniel's hand.

"I suppose I should look surprised, young man, but that would be playing false. Good to see you again, Daniel, right? Now let me have it. You have a guarantee, as I recall".

Cordelia took the wrapped present from Daniel and presented it to her father. He sat in a straight-back chair and proceeded to unwrap the hat box. Daniel relieved Mr. Bryant of the wrapping, subtly handing the ribbon to Cordelia and whispering, "For your hair Miss Cordelia."

Mr. Bryant lifted the hat from the box and admired it, turning it round and flipping and twirling it to show his dexterity. He liked the look of the Wellington. A darker grey ribbon at the brim set off the light grey felt hat. On the left side of the wellington, in the center of the dark grey ribbon, an off-white ribbon gathered in the shape of a fan resided, tucked into the ribbon. The curve of the brim on the sides looked like the wings of a swan floating in a lake.

Cordelia and Mrs. Bryant ran to Mr. Bryant, taking the hat and passing it back and forth between them to examine it up close.

"Come, come. It's a masterful hat, but let's see if it fits."

Mr. Bryant stood and took the hat back, cocking it in both hands and placing it on his head, tugging the brim to lower it to just above his brow.

"You win, Daniel, we'll see on our walk tomorrow, daughter, but it is certainly comfortable now. That calfskin lining has the right amount of give to feel comfortable and secure."

"Thank you, sir. How about you, Mrs. Bryant. Does the hat pass your inspection?"

Mrs. Bryant stroked the soft top of the hat.

"It does, young man. The most beautiful top hat I've seen. Mr. Bryant will be the envy of his men's club. My friends will think it came from Paris. I'll just let them go on thinking that way."

Mr. and Mrs. Bryant left the parlor to Cordelia and Daniel. Both struggled with how the conversation might progress. Cordelia spoke of a fox hunt her friends would participate in on Saturday next, but Daniel said he would have to work. He confessed, red-faced that he did not know the first thing about horses, having lived near the center of Portland within walking distance to most everything the family needed. The Captain had never seen the necessity of owning horses, being a man of the sea his entire life. Daniel promised his willingness to learn, perhaps on another day, and Cordelia suggested James or Samuel would be excellent instructors for a beginning rider.

Daniel suggested a picnic in the park near the Battledore & Shuttle-cock court and perhaps a game or two. Cordelia retrieved her social calendar. She had promised to be at the fox hunt and planned a trip to her aunt's home in Bangor. Daniel began to feel that James had captured Cordelia's time, and, in the end, they could not agree on the next chance to be together. He thanked her again for the business. She thanked him for providing a perfect hat for her father, and he left for the shop.

A month passed before Daniel spied Cordelia and her father walking along the shop window. Probably on their first city stroll since he had presented the wellington to Cordelia's father. Daniel's legs became anchors, resisting an urge to run after the couple. He could not seem so anxious and obvious and forced his eyes back down to his turntable.

Every few days, he would see Cordelia walk by the shop and mentally plead for her to enter, if for no other reason but to enjoy a cup of coffee. When she and her father did stop in for coffee one day, Daniel, surprised and flustered, spoke of the beautiful weather and the need for rain. A customer entered the store, and Daniel excused himself to take the customer's hat measurements. Cordelia left. Nothing accomplished. Three days later, Cordelia and her father passed by again, and Daniel could stand it no further as they passed the front door without entering. He dropped his iron back on the stove and rushed after them, walking with quick but measured steps to appear happenstance.

"Hello, Miss Cordelia, Mr. Bryant. I am on my way to the ribbon factory. So nice to see you. Perhaps I could walk with you awhile? You seem to be going in my general direction."

Mr. Bryant nodded.

"Of course, you are welcome, my boy. By the way, I do not believe I have expressed my delight with the excellent fit of this hat. It's like it was made for me, oh, ha, ha, it was. It is the most comfortable hat I have ever acquired. Thank you."

"You are most welcome, Mr. Bryant. Miss Cordelia, you seem to have a spring in your step this morning. Are you off to your Aunt's in the country, or is this a shopping trip?"

"Well, I am excited, I guess. Father has agreed a year at Westbrook Seminary studying ladies' classics will make me more tolerable. I can't wait till September to start."

"And your other friends, are they attending as well?"

"James received his acceptance letter yesterday. Samuel is attending, and I think I have Emma talked into applying."

Daniel changed subjects.

"Perhaps I could accompany you to First Parish this Sunday. Would that be permissible, Mr. Bryant?"

"Of course, Daniel; what do you say, Cordelia?"

Cordelia looked eager.

"I would like that, yes."

That Sunday, Daniel waited outside the Bryant house. Cordelia stepped out in her light green dress, matching shoes, and bonnet. A pink parasol and reticule completed the ensemble. As they walked arm in arm, the swish of her skirt and petticoats thrilled the boy.

Daniel found himself entranced by the Unitarian minister's sermon at First Parish. He had not expected the minister to touch on things scientific and social. Cordelia and Daniel stayed for tea after the service. Daniel met Isabel, another friend of Cordelia's.

All in all, Daniel delighted in the three hours he spent with Cordelia. He asked her on the walk home if he could accompany her the following Sunday, and she agreed.

Daniel walked Cordelia to church the next three Sundays in a row, chatting on the way there and back. They spoke at length on the topic of abolition. Neither shied away from the issue. Daniel related his experience with the negro doctor so long ago and his amazement with his father's and the doctor's conversation.

Cordelia spoke briefly about her father and his dealings with Indians during and after the war. Daniel appreciated Cordelia's thoughts about the world around her. He realized as she spoke of injustice that she would not be a woman to be silenced. Daniel's father, the Captain, had taught all his children the tolerance he had gained through his travels to foreign lands and with people he had met. Cordelia fascinated Daniel.

Cordelia enjoyed Daniel's willingness to listen and not judge her ideas and forthrightness. She knew she spoke out more than ladies were taught to in sewing circles. Daniel put her at ease and never laughed or rebuked her. A handsome man, she thought.

The next time Daniel arrived at Cordelia's house on Sunday morning to walk her to church, Cordelia and James emerged from her house.

The three walked together to First Parish. The discussion centered on the weather and then turned to what experiences Cordelia and James could expect when they attended Westbrook Seminary in the fall. James cordially invited Daniel to ride with his friends that afternoon. The spell between Cordelia and Daniel could not be sustained with James in the mix, but Daniel found he liked James, thankful to be included as one of the boys.

In fact, Daniel had a great time that afternoon with James, Samuel, and George, another friend of Samuel's that could not ride worth a lick. James brought forth a seventeen-hand black mare for Daniel to ride. James directed Daniel to spend time with the horse before mounting, putting the horse and Daniel at ease. The horse, indifferent to Daniel when he mounted up, never caused trouble on the ride. Daniel held his own, learning, watching James' posture and handling of the reins. All four boys enjoyed the day together as James, the apparent leader, comfortable with the trails on his estate, led the way.

In the back of his mind, Daniel grappled with how and why the others had so much leisure time. It appeared that none of them were tradesmen. When they asked Daniel about his father, Daniel proudly spoke of a couple of the exploits the Captain experienced on the *Creighton II*. He found out from Samuel that his father, a state senator, traveled to the capital in Augusta each week. James' grandfather had been one of the original landowners in Portland. James's father sold bits and pieces of their remaining estate to provide for James, his mother, three sisters, and two brothers: all much younger than himself. Still, none of the three new friends worked at anything: unheard of in Daniel's experience.

The summer progressed with various invitations from Daniel's new friends, many of which he had to turn down due to his six-days-a-week, ten-hours-per-day work schedule. But he attended every event that he could. A Quoits tournament and a late evening of billiards on a table in the home office of Samuel's father were highlights. The boys begrudgingly gathered with the girls at social events and church gatherings.

Daniel tried not to act too enamored with Cordelia unless they were alone on a walk. He bolstered his courage to speak with her forthrightly about his feelings and desires when, on a Thursday morning, she and her father entered the hattery. Taking up a cup of coffee, they looked over the hats on display. Cordelia's cousin apparently enquired about Mr. Bryant's top hat, and Cordelia wanted to assist in selecting a suitable style.

Daniel waited on her, capturing her attention.

"Miss Cordelia, Cordelia, I would like to call upon you to discuss something that I... I need to express...."

Mr. Jasper, furious, entered through the swing doors of the shop.

"Daniel, I have shpoken to you before about leavink irons laying aboot. I vill handshell these cushtomersh myself, thankshu."

Of all days for Mr. Jasper to be acting drunk. He had not even been in the shop for two weeks. Daniel's neck and ears burned.

"I'm sorry, Mr. Jasper, but these are long-standing customers of mine. You will find that my iron is safe on its hot plate."

Cordelia stepped back, away from Mr. Jasper.

"Who is that man, Daniel, and why is he drunk in your establishment?"

Daniel pulled Cordelia and her father to the corner of the room.

"He's Mr. Jasper, and he is not drunk Cordelia, but he is ill. Mrs. Jasper will appear any moment to lead him back into the house. I'm sorry you had to see that. He is, at times, a gentleman. Today is apparently not one of his better days."

"What do you mean? This is your establishment. You should not let him speak to you like that."

Cordelia had not yet connected Mr. Jasper to the store's name, Jasper's Hattery.

"My establishment? He's the owner of the hattery. I work for the Jaspers. He is ill now, but Mr. Jasper has trained me over the years, and I am grateful to both Mr. and Mrs. Jasper."

"But I thought you owned the store. I told Mother! You have misled me, Daniel."

Mr. Bryant tried to support Daniel.

"Cordelia, I have never heard Daniel...."

Daniel wanted to start the day over.

"I don't know how you got the wrong impression, Cordelia, but we can discuss it on Sunday. If I could call on you, I could explain and speak to you about another matter."

"No, I'm sorry, Daniel. James and I will be working on school preparations for Westbrook. I will be leaving next week."

"Perhaps I could stop by tomorrow after work."

"I have too much to do now, Daniel. We'll speak again over Christmas break. Alright? Father, we must be on our way. Thank you, Daniel, for everything."

Crushed, Daniel's eyes welled up as Cordelia hurried from the store. Her father, for once not on her arm, trailed doggedly with the help of his cane behind her.

For the next two weeks, Daniel could think of nothing else; no one else but Cordelia. He pictured her arm in arm with James exploring the Westbrook Seminary campus, attending classes, and meeting new friends. At first, Daniel schemed to unexpectedly call on her at home to plead his case. After all, he had met all obligations to his family, contributing more than his share to help support his mother and four younger brothers and sisters. Given half a chance, Daniel would explain his plans to own the Jasper Hattery one day or start his own hat shop. He had a small savings account earmarked for just such a venture.

In the second week, he considered hiring a cab and seeking Cordelia out at the Seminary. He still wanted to speak with her and profess his feelings. His intentions were of the highest caliber. He would work toward owning his own hattery within the next two years. They could wait to be together until that time if Cordelia required or, if her feelings were more ardent, Mother's large house could accommodate them.

Daniel began letter after letter explaining himself. None were posted. He could not take the chance on a letter. He needed a face-to-face meeting to judge Cordelia's reactions.

At the end of the second week, Daniel thought of quitting his job and traveling away from Portland. He needed to escape the reminder of Cordelia and his walks to church and the social events their friends attended. His stomach ached. His work suffered.

Some days he would resolve to forget Cordelia. The next day he would see her image in every shop window on his way to work. Cordelia in each of her outfits. The loose string of her corset trailed from her vest. The mole on the back of her neck near her right ear, sometimes hidden by her collar but occasionally exposed.

Three weeks after Daniel's disastrous exchange with Mr. Jasper in Cordelia's presence, Daniel resolved to proceed with his ambitions and become the entrepreneur Cordelia expected. He looked back on his progress as a joiner, a brush maker, and a hatter. Each experience provided a solid learning experience and built his confidence.

The Captain had been his own man. Each of his older brothers was a respected family man and tradesman. Samuel: now a shipmaster in his own right on the *Creighton II*.

Daniel focused his efforts on the hattery. Mr. Jasper scarcely appeared for work now except to process furs to felt. He could still handle this task with his shaking hands without sacrificing the quality of the hats Daniel produced. Mr. Jasper could also mix up new batches of quicksilver salt solution used in the fur scraping stage.

Mrs. Jasper took over all the bookkeeping and accounts payable and balanced the cash drawer. With each passing day, she relied more and more on Daniel. She guarded Silas; protected him from curious potential customers and former clients.

In late October, in the Jaspers' warm kitchen, over coffee at the end of an exceptionally prosperous day at the shop, Mrs. Jasper dabbed at her brow with her embroidered handkerchief. Daniel withdrew a folded paper from his vest and unfolded it on the table.

"Mrs. Jasper, please don't consider me impertinent, but I wish to discuss the possibility of buying the hattery from you and Silas."

"Daniel, you have been a godsend since the day you first walked into the shop, scrawny and short. I have fretted these past two years over our course of action. Mr. Jasper's condition is so...

"Do you know he married me despite the objections of his mother? Silas worked so hard after his own apprenticeship. We started in our former house on Grimmel St., hardly a thoroughfare for customers. But Silas made it work. Every hat he produced had to be perfect. He would say that. 'This is the best hat I have ever made, Cora, don't you think?' And it was. He worked day and night to make a go of our little business."

"Yes, Mrs. Jasper, I have taken that lesson to heart. Every hat must be guaranteed to be the best."

"I know you have, Daniel. These last few years have been challenging for Silas. I have often caught him crying as he tries to tie his shoes. Most days, he struggles, but sometimes I see him crying. And you know he has his great days as well.

"For two years now, I have put more savings away. We will struggle with the care and medicine required for Silas, but there you have it. Even on his worst days, Silas still rubs my shoulders before dinner. It is a little thing, but it means the world to me.

"Here now, let's look at your figures."

"As you see, I estimated the store's expenses and revenue. Out of the profit, I propose a pension for you and Silas to continue for ten years. The amount on this line will continue to be my contribution to my family's care. With what remains, I can save for whatever the future holds for me. Of course, I would expect to pay rent for that portion of your home used for the storefront and workshop. That amount is on this line."

"In concept, Daniel, I couldn't have imagined a better solution. I will study and review the figures with Silas in the next few days. Your expense estimate is close, probably low, and the revenue is ambitious, but with your young spirit, maybe. You should think more about Silas and me hanging on in this house in the middle of your new enterprise."

"I have cogitated on this, Mrs. Jasper and I think this could work for us. The important note would be that I would be considered the owner and proprietor of the establishment."

"I understand, Daniel. Perhaps this has something to do with a certain girl and an expensive silk ribbon?"

"Perhaps, Mrs. Jasper. Perhaps."

In early December, Daniel received a letter from Cordelia. In it, she noted she would spend the Christmas holidays with her Aunt in Bangor. She could not join Daniel and their friends until the summer when she returned from school.

The tone of the letter encouraged Daniel. The scene in the hatter's shop before she left for school seemed forgotten and never mentioned. He began writing to Cordelia in earnest. He remained circumspect in tone, again waiting to take her hand in his. He wanted to talk to her eye to eye and present his plan for their future.

Cordelia responded to all his letters. She wrote of her advanced courses, and Daniel was fascinated, wrote back with questions, and offered polite analysis. Agreeing or disagreeing with Cordelia at times. Every few days, when a letter would arrive, Daniels' outlook soared as he breathed the slight scent of Cordelia on the envelope.

Daniel and Cora Jasper met weekly, noting adjustments to the figures Daniel had assumed. He practiced all the processes of running the business, an education that indebted him to Cora. These sessions excluded Silas Jasper, but Cora assured Daniel that Mr. Jasper supported the transition of the hatter shop to Daniel.

In late spring, just two weeks before the end of the semester at Westbrook Seminary and Cordelia's return, Daniel prepared for the ownership transition of the hattery. Daniel, his brother Samuel, Mr. and Mrs. Jasper, and the Jaspers' lawyer had drawn up and reviewed all the necessary papers. Daniel called for a meeting at the law offices of Roberts, Tillotsen, and Grant for the signing.

Mr. Grant placed copies of the agreement on the table in front of Mr. Jasper and Daniel, along with a signing pen.

"What isshdis Cora, why am I signing thesh papers? What is this about? I have been feelink quite well for the lastwo weekshand. I'm ready to get back in the shop. I've decided there is no need to sell the hattery. Sheemy hands are not shaking. I am as clear-headed as ever; thank you, let's go home. Daniel, you are velcome to stay on or leave if that is your wish. You have been of considerable asshistence to Cora and me, and we certainly hope you will continue."

Daniel noted Mr. Jasper's held-out hands, shaking as much as ever. His stomach tightened as he glanced at Samuel and Mrs. Jasper while trying to maintain a calm appearance. *How is this happening?* Mrs. Jasper had assured Daniel that Mr. Jasper knew his intentions and the progress of the transition at every turn. He could not believe what he had just heard.

"Sir, this plan assures your wife's and your future should a turn for the worse yet occur. Today you may feel fine, but what of tomorrow?"

Mr. Grant spoke to Silas.

"Silas, we have often been through this arrangement and these documents. This is absolutely the best possible arrangement for Cora and the legacy of the hattery."

"Nothing needs to change regarding your involvement with the shop, Silas. Please, you would be welcome back in the shop whenever and as often as you feel up to it."

Cora pleaded with her husband.

"Silas, you old husband of mine, make sense. Sign the agreement now!"

"Cora, if shis is your plan to get rid of me, I schwear to God I will never forgive you. Now let's go home. You know lawyersh make me nervous. Shee, I'm shaking."

Mr. Jasper stormed from the office. Cora Jasper noted the surprise in everyone's eyes, made an exasperated shrug, squeezed Daniel's arm, and followed her husband.

Daniel gestured to the rest of the group.

"I apologize. You must understand that Mr. Silas will likely wake up tomorrow or the next day and not act like the man we saw today. I will sort this out with Mrs. Jasper and schedule a new time to sign the sales agreement.

"Thank you."

Outside, Daniel and Samuel walked together in the direction of their homes. Daniel shook his head slowly, staring at the dirt and mumbling. Samuel put an arm around his brother.

"At least he didn't tear up the contract. That would have cost you even more lawyer money."

"But Samuel, if he doesn't change his mind, I will have no prospects. I will have nothing to say to Cordelia. Nothing to offer. Samuel, I am in despair."

"Come, come now, man. Stop such talk. Think of what you can offer the girl. You proposed a fair and gentle buyout to the Jaspers. The captain would have admired the integrity, hard work, business acumen, and management you demonstrate daily at the hattery. Your girl will see that, or she won't, but brother, you will be fine either way."

"She'll be back from school in less than a week. Mr. Jasper has just got to get better soon. He's got to snap out of this latest delusion about Cora. You saw how shaky he was, even as he denied it."

"We all witnessed the episode, Daniel. Mrs. Jasper seemed equally frustrated and sympathetic. Do not lose hope."

Mr. Jasper made no appearance in the shop the next day nor any day following. Daniel knew Cordelia had returned from the Seminary, but with no signed documents, how could he proceed when he did see her? Mrs. Jasper continually promised a resolution to the situation the minute Mr. Jasper awoke to a morning without headaches and shakes. Daniel feared that day might never again occur.

As Daniel put out the ten o-clock coffee pot on a rainy day in July, Cordelia came sashaying through the front door held open by James, who followed. She bounced up to Daniel, kissing him on the cheek.

"Daniel, it is so good to see you. It seems forever. Why haven't you called on me? I really enjoyed your letters. Sometimes school seems stuffy, and your thoughts are always greatly appreciated."

James shook Daniel's hand and squeezed Daniel's arm with his left hand.

"Daniel, when are we going riding? I have to get the boys together. What do you say? Are you willing to lose a little poker money? How about Friday night. I'll get some of the fellas, and we can meet late after you get done here at the shop."

"I would like that, James. It has been a while since I lost money to your group of card sharps. I've been studying the game, though, so I may not be the same pigeon as the first two times we played."

Cordelia clasped both her hands on her chest, prayer-like.

"Can you step outside a moment, Daniel? I'm bursting with excitement."

"I should think so. There are no customers currently. I can stand by the front door."

The trio went out in the rain and stood together under Cordelia's parasol. Daniel, beside himself at seeing Cordelia again for the first time in many months, put his hands in his pockets to keep them warm. Her fragrance mingled with the rain, causing his throat to tighten. He anticipated encircling her in his arms, kissing her. Yes, kiss her.

"I have something to show you, Daniel," Cordelia began.

Cordelia extended her hand toward Daniel, and as he reached for hers, he noticed the gold ring, wet from the rain, featuring a large opal surrounded by a set of diamonds. Daniel gawked, almost choked, and then took Cordelia's hand to examine the ring closer, covering his panic while Cordelia continued.

"We're getting married. James McMasters and I are getting married. Can you believe it? James asked me last week, and I said yes, yes, yes. Well, we're thinking not right away, we both want to finish at the Seminary next year, but we're thinking a June wedding would be perfect in Portland. June 8th, 1843, that's a good date, don't you think?"

James grabbed Daniel's hand again.

"What do you think, Daniel? Crazy, right? But I'm crazy about her."

Daniel, struggling to recover, stammered.

"Why, that's, well, congratulations, James, I'm happy for you both."

The rain sweat on the back of Daniel's neck turned cold, and his cheeks, flushed with excitement upon seeing Cordelia, paled. He turned his back to the couple; closed his eyes to concentrate.

"Let's move inside out of the rain; we'll soak out here."

Daniel fumbled with the door, taking three deep breaths, and by the time they were all inside shaking off the morning drizzle, he could face Cordelia and James, his demeanor calmer. A wry, closed smile turned up the corner of his mouth as he winked at them.

"You two! So, this is what you learned at school. I should ask about your grades to see if any studying went on."

Cordelia was smiling and nearly crying. With joy?

"Oh, Daniel, I'm so thankful you approve and can be happy for us."

James already sounded like an old married man.

"Yes, my friend, there will be plenty of time for us to ride together and play a little whist. A man must have his chums along to enjoy life, right?"

Daniel felt like *The Man in the Iron Mask* as he looked from his friend to his heartache.

Did I say I was happy??? But of course, I am. Now run along, show that expensive ring to all our friends, and share your news.

Cordelia turned back as she passed through the doorway, tilting her head and mouthing silently. *Thank you!*

Daniel smiled and nodded as she closed the door. With fogged eyes, he somehow stumbled to a chair in the back of the shop, sitting hard enough to break it. He buried his head in his arms on the counter, trying to darken his world. Trying not to lose himself in sorrow.

Why had he waited? Where did he go wrong? How could he have been so naïve as to think she enjoyed his company.

She did enjoy their discussions; she said that. Daniel returned to Mr. Jasper's delay in signing over the shop. Perhaps he was destined by fate to exist in this small corner of a hat-making shop; alone.

A customer entered the shop, and Daniel grabbed his handkerchief, wiped his eyes, blew his nose, and went out to face the new world he now lived in. A world without Cordelia at his side.

For the rest of the summer, Daniel joined in on many of the activities of James and Cordelia's group of friends. Cordelia paired Daniel with Emma for two social events, asking him to accompany her to her baby nephew's baptism and an ice cream social at First Parish Church. Daniel behaved politely on both occasions, but Emma's hands sweat whenever they meet. She did not have Cordelia's scent about her. He still furtively glanced at Cordelia, looking beyond her at times to not be seen staring at her dress, neck, or ankles.

The happy couple went to Westbrook Seminary for their final year of study. Daniel concentrated on each hat on his workstation, carefully upholding the precision of his stitched bands and perfectly curved brims. Gentlemen were coming from Boston, occasionally, for his hats. But when he finished working on a hat; when he tried to sleep; when he sat down to dinner; an image of Cordelia holding his arm as they walked to First Parish Church penetrated his resolve.

January 1843 ended with a snowstorm that blanketed Portland with an unusual ten inches of snow. All the schools and many of the businesses closed, including Westbrook Seminary. The quiet of the city hovered over the snow, noticeable. Daniel trudged to work, but no customers ventured out to shop for hats. The next day, he again saw no customers, but in the afternoon, James' friend George stopped in and practically forced Daniel to close the shop and join a gathering at First Parish Church for what turned out to be a snowman-building contest and snowball fight.

Samuel, James, George, Daniel, Emma, Cordelia, and three others Daniel did not know made up one team. They attacked a gang of ten from another neighborhood, racing and chasing the other team to the edge of a frozen bay of the Fore River. The group in front of them skidded across the ice, James, Daniel, George, and Samuel pummeling them with snowballs, the girls screeching behind them. James led with Daniel at his heels.

"Come on!"

"Right with you, James."

James took off at an angle to head off the lead boy in the rival group. He ran ten yards and vanished through the ice. A sickening crackle of ice broke the muffled silence of the bay as Daniel skidded to a stop just at the edge of the break.

"George, grab my feet; I'll get to James. Samuel, lie down and make a chain, grab George's feet. Spread eagle and hope the ice holds us. Girls, run. Get help!"

Daniel lay down on the ice, and when he felt George's firm grip on both his ankles crawled forward. When his stomach hung over open water, he reached down with his arms, fishing for James, hoping to grab his coat. Nothing but water swirled within his range of motion.

As the gathering crowd gasped, Daniel bent down into the water. His face, hands, arms, and chest were now engulfed in the freezing river, and Daniel could feel the current's pull. Still, he could not feel or see James at all. He came back out of the water, gulping air and spitting water. A rope had been brought by one of the men. Daniel tied it around his waist tightly, glanced at a horrified and screaming Cordelia on the shore, and slid into the hole. Men strung out on the ice playing the rope out little by little. Daniel, underwater, could not make out anything, so he just let the current carry him, flailing with his arms, hoping to come across James.

As his lungs were about to burst, he felt the rope tug drawing him back. He tried to swim to help the men on the rope fight the current. Out of breath, chest burning, eyes widening in panic, blacking out, Daniel's head buoyed up into open water, and the men pulled him out. He lay on his back, shivering uncontrollably, the men throwing blanket after blanket on him and carrying him to shore.

Cordelia bent down over him, and Daniel could only shake his head, crying over his failure to save James.

Samuel bent close to Daniel, whispering, "You did everything you could. He's gone."

The men carried Daniel on a makeshift stretcher the many blocks back to the church. Samuel and George helped him out of his wet clothes, and weak-kneed Daniel asked for a bucket. Nauseous from the horror of watching James vanish from their lives knotted Daniel's stomach as he heaved bile repeatedly into the bucket.

George made Daniel lie down before the fire and covered him with dry wool blankets. A doctor entered the room, closing the door behind him as dozens waited with guarded concern. Daniel, white as the snow covering Portland, could not stop shivering or open his eyes. The doctor directed Samuel and George to rub and twist Daniel's extremities to assist the fire and blankets in warming him. He noted no frostbite. The men had pulled him out in time.

Three days later, Daniel, fully recovered, went back to work.

James' body had been snagged on a branch at the shore where the river opened to the sea. At the funeral for James McMaster, Cordelia, in a black dress with a black lace veil, sat with her mother and father in the front row with James' parents and siblings. Daniel sat respectably, ten pews back. Afterward, when people began shaking Daniel's hand, he discreetly left the church without speaking to Cordelia.

Eight sad months passed before Daniel heard from Cordelia in the form of a letter delivered to the hattery.

> September 18, 1843
>
> Dear Daniel,
>
> I trust this letter finds you well. The maples in Maine make Portland such a beautiful place to live. From my window, I watch the ships pass by on the horizon, their billowed sails like low clouds, white against such a blue sky.

The pain of that frozen day and my frozen heart has weakened me. You are my hope now.

Will you write back to me? The letters you wrote while I was away at school, were always anticipated, even though they took four or five days to reach me. You could have arrived by horseback in a day and hand-delivered them. I would have liked that.

I never had the opportunity or strength to express my amazement at what you did that day to save a life. I believed I might have lost you both when the men dragged you back to the surface. I must not lose you. Please write.

Your close friend,

Cordelia Bryant

The letter had taken three days to arrive from across town. Daniel kept rereading the letter and sat down to reply. He retrieved a pen and inkwell, but the only paper in the shop showcased *Jasper Hattery* on the letterhead. Too impersonal.

His excitement overcame him. His decision made, he threw on his scarf and best top hat, looked one last time in the mirror to straighten his tie, locked the shop, turned the sign to 'Closed,' and took off in the direction of the Bryants home.

Fifteen blocks later, Daniel stood in the street across from the steps to Cordelia's front door. A passerby might have thought him a lost puppy, wagging his tail, hoping someone would open the door and invite him in. All the way there, he considered his approach, throwing out one after another starting points or explanations of his absence in the Bryants' lives.

Since February, so much has happened. On a dark night in July, Silas Jasper had broken his neck and died falling down the stone stairs in the park near the tavern two blocks from his home. Passersby testified at the inquest that he seemed drunk and disoriented; his speech slurred as he sang. For Cora Jasper's sake, Daniel stopped such testimony by volunteering to take the stand and describe Mr. Jasper's illness, sure that he had fallen due to such a flare-up in his condition. Daniel testified that the onset of Mr. Jasper's disease had affected his equilibrium on many occasions.

Last month Mrs. Jasper, her younger sister, Daniel, and his brother Samuel had met with the lawyers, and the transaction for the sale of the hattery had finally been accomplished. Cora decided to move out of the hattery and in with her sister in Dover. Daniel moved into the quarters above the shop. His younger brother George and two younger sisters, Sophia and Julia, remained with Daniel's mother.

The business experienced a downturn right when Daniel took over, and he worked day and night to keep on top of it. During the day, he built hats and kept the books up at night.

Daniel joined the Order of Odd Fellows to occupy his time and mind. Samuel, a member of the Free Masons like the Captain before him, attended that group's meetings when in port. Daniel felt the Odd Fellows fit his social conscience better and enjoyed the discussions and fellowship. The business contacts did not hurt.

The front door of Cordelia's house opened as if by Daniel's will. The butler stepped out with a broom to sweep the steps. Daniel stepped forward as the butler recognized him. The man said he would announce Daniel's presence and directed him to wait in the parlor. Daniel stepped through to the parlor but did not sit, removing his hat and undoing his scarf.

Mrs. Bryant swooped into the room, smiling broadly.

"So nice to see you, Daniel. You have surprised Cordelia, but you must give her time to prepare. I hope you can wait. Please have a seat. These past months have made a difference, Daniel; you are filling out that suit. I used to think your mother didn't feed you."

"You look well, Mrs. Bryant. The weather this fall has indeed been pleasant."

"Yes, now Daniel, before Cordelia comes down, I must tell you how... how ashamed I am at how I may have influenced Cordelia in her reactions to your friendship. Mr. Bryant scolded me the day Cordelia returned and told me you had misled her into thinking you owned the business where you work. Sometimes my station and background get in the way of my common sense. Mr. Bryant, bless him, can straighten me out most of the time. Cordelia talked of you daily and in her letters to me from school. I came to realize how much she appreciated your friendship. I interfered inappropriately. I apologize. What you did that day at the river. It was…"

"What I did, Mrs. Bryant, what I failed to do still haunts me daily. I can't…."

Mrs. Bryant's glance to the doorway made Daniel turn to see Cordelia, a bit thinner, radiant in her purple dress, standing in the hall-way. She went straight to Daniel, taking his hand and sitting beside him on the settee.

"Oh, Daniel, this is an unexpected and pleasant surprise."

"I just received your letter. It is such a fine day! I thought you should be out and about, brightening the city of Portland in your purple dress and wonderful smile. What do you say to a nice walk and a Sarsaparilla?"

Mrs. Bryant took Daniel's left hand, grabbed Cordelia's right hand, and pulled them both off the settee.

"Cordelia, that sounds like a perfect way to spend the afternoon."

"You don't have to convince me, mother. I already decided we would go for a walk. Come on, Daniel, I can't wait to get to the park."

Over the next several weeks, Cordelia and Daniel strolled through the city together. They would walk or sit in the park, window shop, or walk to and from church. At first, passersby stared at the girl once engaged to the boy who drowned. They would nod at the boy who jumped into the icy water to attempt a rescue. But they were ultimately ignorable, off the front page of local gossip. They were now just a part of the cityscape, recognizable but not stared at. Daniel no longer accosted for handshakes; Cordelia no longer eyed with pity. The two, arm in arm, dared the city to smile and laugh with them, and the city responded with acceptance.

Cordelia returned to walking with her father, stopping into the hattery every morning they were out for a sip of coffee. While Cordelia attended a church function one evening, Daniel went to the Bryants' home and requested an audience with Mr. Bryant. Daniel, invited into Mr. Bryant's office, sat opposite the desk while Mr. Bryant stoked his pipe. Mr. Bryant's white hair sifted to a darker grey around his collar and ears. The swoop in his hair imitated the Andrew Jackson style of the day. Mr. Bryant crossed his ankles with his feet on the desk, leaning back in his leather-covered armchair.

"What can I do for you, Daniel? The hat you made for me is still in perfect shape. I doubt I will be needing a new one for years."

"I am asking your permission to propose marriage to your daughter, Cordelia. I am now the owner of *Jasper Hattery*. The name will soon be changed to *Martensen's Fine Hats and Accessories*. I consider myself a good provider as I have cared for my mother, younger sisters, and brother since the Captain died. I may not be as well off as some in Portland, but I promise to provide for Cordelia and her comfort."

"I have no doubts you will, my boy. I have favored you from the start. I noted your drive and your honesty when we first met. Odd Fellow friends have spoken of your kindness, honesty, and business acumen.

"Entrepreneurship is tricky. There is usually a little luck involved in each successful business venture. I also know that Cordelia will be your first concern when it comes down to it. I saw that when we first met as well. You have my permission to court Cordelia.

"As you know, she is strong-willed and independent. She'll have her own ideas about the world and may act more like a man than a woman sometimes, but if you accept that in her, you will have an exciting life together."

"I know I will, sir. If I hurry, I will walk her home."

Daniel met Cordelia at First Parish Church just as her meeting concluded. He took her arm and led her into the sanctuary and up to the altar. The sunset streamed through the rose window in the rear of the church. Daniel dropped to a knee and proposed marriage.

"Of course, I will, Daniel. Now stand and kiss me in front of God and the world." Cordelia's smile said it all.

Daniel did just that.

The couple was married one year from the day Daniel proposed. The Bryants hosted over a hundred friends and relatives at the big joyous wedding in November 1844 at First Parish Church. Cordelia made her elaborate white lace dress, and Daniel made two new exquisite grey beaver top hats for himself and his new father-in-law, both with white satin ribbon bands. Daniel wished Cordelia would honor James by wearing the opal engagement ring James had given her. When they were married, Cordelia left the opal ring on her right hand and accepted Daniel's simple gold band as a symbol of their union. Daniel received a similar simple band, a bit wider than Cordelia's.

The couple was celebrities again for a few days, but it did not faze them. They were together in the city they loved. Together, and in love.

Nine months after the wedding, Cordelia informed Daniel that she was pregnant. Daniel gathered his extended family on a Sunday afternoon, announcing the news. Samuel, Martin, William, and their families joined Daniel's mother, his younger brother George, and sisters along with Cordelia's family at an August picnic along the Eastern Promenade. Business at the hattery had picked up enough for Daniel to hire an apprentice, Joshua Colter, who worked out very well. Daniel held Cordelia's hand throughout the afternoon, convinced she had somehow become more fragile and needed additional care. The families participated in foot races and played battledore and shuttlecock until dark. Martin had long since acknowledged Daniel's success as a respected hatter, married to one of the prettiest women in Portland.

The group lit torches and moved to the river Fore for a bonfire and singalong. Lemuel Bryant called for a toast to the new President, James K. Polk. The families politely acknowledged Mr. Bryant's toast, although some glasses were raised higher than others. Cordelia, never a woman to back away from controversy, moved closer to the fire, the glow highlighting her face.

"You men and your president's. With all due respect, father, this *'Manifest Destiny'* theme of O'Sullivan's in the *Democratic Review* this month is trying to justify imperialism. It seems we should hearken to our founding father's reaction to the colonialism imposed by England."

Daniel was not so sure.

"The men who fought at the Alamo, dear, were Americans, true-blooded. Crocket and Bowie died protecting families establishing farms and ranches in Mexico. Would you have Americans trying to put down roots in this great land abandon their dreams? Shouldn't they be accepted as pioneers with a right to establish themselves on this continent, just as our forefathers did? There is enough room for everyone."

Lemuel, speaking as a veteran, had more to say.

"Excellent point, Daniel, and you as well, Cordelia. The Republic of Texas fought hard for its independence and sovereignty, and it might be a welcome addition to the United States. Texas provides natural protection against invasion from the south."

Cordelia would have none of these arguments.

"Father, an additional slave state in the South is not admirable protection. You all know I am an advocate for the abolition of slavery. This nation can only be great if we follow the principle of freedom for all its peoples."

"But darling, let's be practical," Daniel said, trying to calm his wife. "Take the long view. If we strive to make slavery impractical and uneconomical, it will cease. But I don't see how we can stand by while Americans die for choosing the hard life of homesteading in the West."

Daniel's brother Samuel added, "I can imagine when I might carry cargo from here around to the Pacific coast. Now that is an exciting prospect. Wouldn't that be something?

"All right, enough of this talk. The kids and I need to get to bed. Raise your glass for one last toast to Cordelia and Daniel. May their new addition to our family enjoy good health and prosper, and they accomplish good works for the betterment of all."

After separating from the others on their walk home, Daniel stopped Cordelia and turned to her, heart thumping, the moonglow beauty reflected in her eyes, her nose, and the smile creasing her lips. His embrace and kiss reminded them both of their togetherness. Happy to discuss and engage. Happy to kiss and cuddle.

Daniel and Cordelia prepared a nursery during the following months. Daniel trained his apprentice. Talk around the men's clubs and taverns and even at the church social events around town seemed to gravitate to news of the West. Polk's offer to purchase California and New Mexico had been rejected. American troops had been moved to disputed territories in anticipation of a conflict with Mexico. At the end of April 1846, Mexican cavalry attacked a group of U.S. soldiers in the disputed zone. On May 13th, Congress declared war despite opposition from some northern states. The nation, torn apart politically until that day, came together to defend America.

Cordelia gave birth on May 15th to a son, suitably named Lemuel. Born into a nation at war. Not since the war of 1812 had the citizens of Maine had to deal with their sons heading off to war.

The States were asked to provide militias of enlisted men for one year. Daniel felt strongly enough to bring the matter up over dinner while Cordelia kept one hand on the cradle, rocking their son, who remained asleep.

"Cordelia, I must do this. I will be in the 1st Regiment, Wendell P. Smith's 'G' Company. I will be one year away. I want my son Lemuel to grow up in an America that protects the values I stand for, opportunity, and freedom of religion, without fear of reprisal for how he thinks. I know you are against this war. All I can say is that I respect your views with all my heart, but in this case, it is not my view."

"Daniel, you have responsibilities. It would be best if you considered your job, our livelihood. Can you really think of leaving this sweet baby? If you don't come back, he will never know you. I couldn't bear losing you. Please reconsider. I have never known you to hunt or even own a gun. You live in the city. Regardless of my position on this conflict, there are many reasons you should not enlist."

"I have considered all those reasons for not enlisting. There is only one reason that trumps those. It is that in my heart I feel I must. I love my son, and I love you. I will go to the end of the earth and return to you, but I must stand for America, as the Captain did when he first came to this country. Once he became a citizen of this country, he fought and would have died for his friends, community, and adopted country. He determined this to be the best place in his travels to live, work, and raise eleven children. A proud American. Perhaps it is a legacy he has built into me as well."

Cordelia let the cradle come to rest. She arose and stood behind Daniel, encircling him in her arms and laying her head on his shoulder. For many moments, Cordelia remained silent. At last, she spoke in a soft tense voice.

"I know how strong you are, Daniel. I've seen it firsthand. You live and love hard, and I must believe this is right for you and us. Please, please be safe and come back to me."

"I'll do my best, darling."

Daniel visited his father-in-law the next day. Lemuel Bryant listened solemnly to the news. He expressed no excitement, but neither did he object. He accepted the news as fact and an everyday thing, like needing to tie one's boots while dressing. By the set of Lemuel's jaw, Daniel could tell that at some point in the past, Lemuel had been where Daniel now found himself.

"Daniel, we should allow you to see how you shoot before you go in. It would be best if you were as prepared as possible. You will be trained, but survival depends on being the best. You've got three weeks before you meet with your company. I'll help as much as this game leg will allow. I don't talk much about my time in the service, and I won't start now. I will only say this once. It is hell. A hell you can't even imagine until you are in it, so it is no use trying to describe it.

"There is a shooting range west of Portland up in the hills. We'll go tomorrow. It would help if you practiced every day that you could afford to be away from your shop. Now I must break the news to Mrs. Bryant. Cordelia and little Lemuel will stay with us while you are away."

Lemuel arrived at Daniel's home on Wilmot Street at eight o'clock. When they arrived at the shooting range an hour later, Daniel helped Lemuel down from the buggy. Lemuel reached back under the seat and picked up a rifle wrapped in canvas.

"This is an M1841 rifle. I bought it for my collection last year from a foreman at the Springfield Armory. This uses a percussion lock system to fire. They are much more reliable than flintlock muskets. You'll be trained on those when you enlist. We'll ensure you can fire this rifle thrice a minute when you enlist. Guard this rifle. Don't worry about the fairness of this advantage. War is war. The object is to survive."

Daniel trained with the war veteran Lemuel Bryant for the next three weeks. Lemuel advised Daniel on clothing to take, boots to break in, and incidentals such as medicinal salves and a small tool set. Powder, patches, and .54 balls would be supplied by the army. Caps were exclusive to the M1841, so Daniel packed as many as he thought he could carry in a small leather pouch.

Lemuel taught Daniel as much about the woods and survival as time allowed. Daniel bivouacked alone for two days and two nights at the end of Lemuel's training. In the end, Daniel had begun to understand what lay ahead. Lemuel reiterated that Daniel still had no clue.

On June 26th, 1846, racked by an intense stomachache and dry throat at the thought of leaving Cordelia and baby Lemuel, Daniel presented a calm front as he said goodbye to his mother, brothers, and sisters.

Turning to Cordelia, who held the baby, he tickled little Lemuel under the chin and unwrapped his little feet from the blanket. He gently squeezed each toe and then bent down and kissed the bottom of each foot, imprinting on his cheek and in his mind the feel, the size, and the weight of his son. He took Lemuel in his arms, hugged and kissed him, and passed him to Mrs. Bryant. Daniel took Cordelia into his arms, lifting her off the ground and squeezing the breath from her. Setting her down, he kissed her on both cheeks and soft mouth, again to memorize the feel and scent of his beloved wife.

Daniel, twenty-seven, picked up his pack and canvas-wrapped rifle and walked away.

4 |

SCOUT

Ants are social insects of the family Formicidae. They live and work together in organized colonies.

1846

Daniel passed through the South Portland, Fort Preble gate in the early afternoon of June 26th, 1846. A freestanding, makeshift sign across the courtyard, neatly painted with 'Registration,' and an arrow pointing to an office door along the porch. Daniel headed across, noticing a group of twenty or thirty men aligned in rows of eight in the middle of the courtyard. An officer standing to one side shouted drill commands at the group while they tried, somewhat in vain, to follow his step orders. Once inside the office, the desk sergeant welcomed Daniel. Within ten minutes, he had enlisted, repeating the oath of allegiance and promising to obey all ensuing commands.

Daniel concentrated on the group march outside, attempting to decipher and learn the movements. The sergeant glanced in his direction.

"Soldier, you didn't sign up to watch. Get over here. Double time. Next to the last man, there, in the last line."

"Yes, sir!"

For the next three hours, Daniel learned how to salute, present arms, march in formation, and stand at attention. The group also practiced how fast the company could assemble. As it turned out, the extent of Daniel's formal army training ended that afternoon.

Upon the company's dismissal, Daniel found the quartermaster's office. The sergeant behind the counter issued Daniel's uniform and equipment.

1 Blue Dress Cap 2 Flannel Shirts
1 Forage Cap (glazed silk) 2 Pair drawers
1 Blue Uniform Coat 4 Pairs of Bootees
1 Grey Woolen Jacket 4 Pairs of socks
3 Pr. Blue Woolen Overalls 1 Leather stock.
1 Cotton Jacket 1 Fatigue Frock (Lin.)
1 Pr. White Cotton Overalls 1 Blanket

The sergeant directed Daniel to a group of six-man tents arranged in one corner of the courtyard where the recruits were lounging: waiting for the dinner calls. One of the soldiers approached Daniel.

"Daniel, right? Remember me from grammar school? Lorenzo Brennan. I recognized you. It's been a long time since school, but I was there when McMaster fell through the ice.

"That's right. Brought the rope, as I recall."

"That's true, but I would never have done what you…

"Hey, you might remember some of these other fellows. Let me introduce you.

"This is John Adams, lawyer type. Nate Bartlett, a painter. John Tukesbury, trader, and Ed Wedgewood, he's another lawyer we don't need. Fellows, this is Daniel Martensen, a hatter."

Nate was the last to shake Daniel's hand.

"Bought a hat from you about a month or two months ago.

"We were all in the same class, a year behind you."

"Long time ago," Daniel noted, then he recognized one of the other soldiers.

"John Tukesbury, didn't you slice up an arm chasing a girl in the seventh year?"

"Healed up OK, I guess. I can almost straighten it out normally. Our tent has room if you're looking for a place."

"Sure, thanks. I'll have to catch up with you all. How about the man in charge, Sheriff Smith? How's he to work with?"

The group looked to Lorenzo.

"He's old, must be forty or so. Mean, if you cross him. But he's been around some bad people over the years. He can handle himself. I guess Captain Smith is as good a leader as any of us would be. Most likely better.

"With you here, there are over thirty of us. More comin' in every day. He addresses us at dinner with a list of duties."

Lorenzo and Daniel exchanged histories as they walked the perimeter of the Fort, each relating news of their families, careers, and in Daniel's case, his son, Lemuel. The fort's walls had undergone several changes and additions over the years. An anonymous soldier had spent his free time making clear signs explaining its history. Daniel hesitated and read them, fascinated. A portion of the fort was built between 1808 and 1816. President Jefferson anticipated British aggression before the War of 1812. Jefferson replaced the British engineers with American engineers to design all the New England forts. Fort Preble, a modified star-shaped, second-system fort, encased the original fourteen cannons in prongs of stone and earthworks. Previous fort design allowed a single cannon shop fired along the straight-line length of cannon placements to destroy an entire battery and incapacitate a fort. This was not the case with Fort Preble and this star design.

Fort Preble received a third system design enhancement and added twelve cannons north and ten south, built into thick masonry walls in 1845. Daniel's senses alternated between total security and claustrophobia as he walked within the fort's walls with Lorenzo.

Called to dinner, Daniel stored his clothes and possibles in an unoccupied corner of the tent and accompanied the group to supper, scanning all the men headed for the mess hall. At least eight of the group looked to be under twenty years old. A few looked older than Daniel but fit. The ages of the rest were somewhere in the middle.

The oldest at dinner, Wendell P. Smith, addressed the group after everyone cleared their plates.

"We'll keep this discussion informal. You'll understand why after I have relayed the news from Augusta.

"First, I want to welcome any newcomers who have joined us since my last address. You have volunteered for a challenging twelve months. Up until now, militia men only served three months. Twelve months will be hard on your businesses, jobs, and family.

"Truth of the matter is, as militia, we haven't seen more than a skirmish since the war of 1812, before my time. So, we're lost in training, organization, and purpose now.

"You all have volunteered to fight, and I admire every one of you. But remember that you, we, are at the bottom of the totem pole.

"A directive has arrived from Augusta. The legislature has decided that the militia volunteers of the great state of Maine will not be activated or participate in this war. The militia will be used as reserves or to defend Maine from attack."

The grumbling amongst the tables reflected relief, stubbornness, and anger. Someone shouted.

"We ain't here to sit around. We're here to fight and get this here war over."

Wendell let the table discussions rise and fall for several minutes as each man absorbed the news.

"Alright, let's come to order. I've more to say.

"I guess I went through the same emotions you have displayed in this room when I read the orders. We've all signed legal documents, and we're stuck. I thought about this situation the whole day and decided on a course of action to offer.

"I reviewed enough of the general strategy of the war with the Fort Preble officers to have a general idea of how these first few months of the war will be prosecuted.

"There will be two actions. Remember, we declared war last month, and moving men and equipment thousands of miles to the front takes time.

"Soldiers are being gathered in the disputed territory of Texas to push back the Mexicans and beat them down. Mexico is a large territory, and battalions will also be gathered at the west edge of Missouri. This army will drive west along the new Santa Fe trail and take territory to the Pacific. As President Polk would have it, our destiny will someday mean Americans walking on American soil from sea to sea."

Smith paused to make sure he still had the soldier's attention.

"So here is my proposal. With all haste, I will lead the present company, volunteers only, with no obligation, west to St. Louis. We will join the Missouri volunteers and do our part to secure our border in the west. I'm interpreting the State mandate to defend Maine's border there instead of waiting for an invasion here.

"Future volunteers and all who do not wish to accompany my company will stay and train here under the capable command of Lieutenant Charles Little for the duration of their obligation or until the end of the war, whichever comes first.

"I want you all to think this mission through, and those that believe I have not lost my sanity will muster at o seven hundred tomorrow morning in the northwest corner of the courtyard, gear ready for the trip to Missouri. Questions this evening should be directed to Harold Goddard, my second in command.

"Dismissed."

Daniel, Lorenzo, John Tukesbury, and Ed gathered with fourteen other volunteers, nervously awaiting the approach of Wendell P. Smith and Harold Goddard. John Adams had decided to stay in Portland and not lose his chance at marrying his girl. Daniel had not thought much about traveling to Missouri. He had already made up his mind to go to war weeks ago. He purposely did not second guess his resolve.

Captain Smith came out of the office in a dark blue dress coat with gold epaulets and gleaming black boots. He carried his hat tucked under his armpit.

"Boys, here's the plan. We have little funds from the state, but I have a war chest for supplies funded by the Bryants, McMasters, and several other prominent Portlanders. We'll draw on that account at the Massachusetts Bank only when necessary.

"We'll start by taking the B&M train down to New York and then the B&O train to Baltimore. Let's see, there are twenty of us, all told. We'll buy three wagons and twelve horses in Baltimore and drive to Cumberland, Maryland. Nathan Barker, our resident stable keeper, will oversee the livestock and be looking for assistance. See him if you have any riding or caretaking experience with horses. I know most of us are city dwellers.

"From Cumberland, we'll take the National Road to Vandalia, Illinois. Then we'll make our way to St. Louis. In St. Louis, we'll find a steamboat to commandeer to take us, horses, wagons, and all, up the Missouri River to Fort Leavenworth, where we'll present to Colonel Kearny.

"So, we'll travel long and hard till we get there. Drills will begin at daybreak for an hour before we get on the road. This company doesn't look so good now, but discipline in the face of the enemy may save your butts, so take everything I say and teach to heart. Work hard at soldiering. Respect yourselves and the man next to you. He may save your ass someday.

"Let's go! Form up!"

At two o'clock on June 30th, the company drilled on the outskirts of Baltimore while Nathan Barker negotiated the purchase of horses and wagons. The trains and transfers took three days.

Daniel had never worked horse chores. The stable boys handled those tasks when he rode with James and Cordelia's friends on the

McMaster estate. But from those long-ago outings, Daniel proved a decent rider, and Nathan requested his assistance. Lorenzo stuck close to Daniel and volunteered for horse-handling duty as well. Lorenzo had only ridden a horse twice in his life. Nathan recruited Charles Gardener, nineteen years old but harboring a love of horses and having plenty of experience.

On the second of July, the company headed down the thirty-foot-wide National Road into the Allegany mountains. Captain Smith ordered the company to march alongside the wagons as the horses pulled up the incline. For two ten-hour days, Daniel marched and sweat. Exhausted, some of his companions groused late into the night. Daniel recalled the advice of his father-in-law. "*War is hell*," Daniel thought, "*this is just the beginning.*" He kept his mouth shut.

Without passengers, the wagons rolled over the hard-packed macadam stone paving without a problem. Since the refurbishment of the Road in 1830, the thirty-foot highway has carried a surprising amount of traffic. A steady stream of Conestoga wagons brought settlers west while freight wagons headed east for more supplies. The company tents were erected each night behind one of the accommodating taverns peppering the side of the road along its six-hundred-and-thirty-mile length. Edwin Bowes, a confectioner by trade, became the chief cook with three rotating assistants for each meal. Every third day the company ate at the tavern where they bivouacked. Captain Smith sprinkled in four more days of burning, double-time marching to test the men. The grumbling stopped.

Two soldiers went missing along the Road, reducing the company to eighteen men. No one could remember who the two were that turned back, although Lieutenant Goddard had a record of their names. The two men melted into the wilderness.

The mile markers along the road begged the company-wide question, "Are we there yet?" On July fourteenth, the end of the National Road turned into a smaller tollway leading into St. Louis.

Steamboats were abundant in St. Louis, loading up supplies for the troops at Fort Leavenworth. Captain Smith finagled pay for the company, horses, and wagons, in exchange for loading and unloading the ships carrying the supplies for the army at Fort Leavenworth.

Government agents wandered the streets of St. Louis and neighboring towns, buying mules, horses, wagons, and provisions. They contracted the manufacture of wagons, knapsacks, and other articles necessary for the army. Thousands of pork barrels at $10 per barrel and thousands of pounds of "clear bacon sides" at five cents per pound were purchased in St. Louis and sent by way of a steamer to Fort Leavenworth. The mules became increasingly valuable, going for $100 apiece. The army needed thousands of them, along with hundreds of horses and perhaps ten thousand oxen, to pull the supply wagons to Mexico and California. The Maine Company loaded pack saddles on two steamers for three days. Daniel figured his fellow soldiers had hauled over four hundred aboard.

The bustle in St. Louis never stopped day or night. No one questioned the members of Wendell P. Smith's Company 'G' of the 1st Infantry. Soldiers were everywhere, coming and going, marching or maneuvering, gathering, and stepping aboard steamboats for passage to Fort Leavenworth. Captain Smith never needed to present papers or orders. He approached the busiest Lieutenants directing pier activity and offered his men to assist. No one turned him down. The supply lines of the war machine needed to gear up and move with all haste.

On July twenty-fourth, Company 'G' finished loading Bacon and Pork on the steamship *Misery* by two o'clock in the afternoon. The steamboat captain started complaining to anyone on the dock that he intended to leave with what he had on board if no other supplies showed up within the hour. Of course, it was all bluster. The army, desperate for supplies, did not tolerate empty space in the cargo bay of the steamboat. Further, unused cargo space did not contribute to the accumulating wealth of the steamboat captain. Wendell P. Smith recognized an opportunity and approached Mr. Gurney, the vessel's Captain.

"Our wagons, horses, and my men would fill your space. We could be ready to leave within the half-hour.

"Passage to Independence is eight dollars a soldier. The wagons full of supplies will cost you twenty-four dollars apiece, and the twelve horses will cost you one hundred twenty dollars."

"We'll pay you one hundred dollars to carry the horses. The wagons we'll sell to the army Quartermaster in Independence and pay you for their passage when we arrive. We'll give you four dollars each for our soldiers' passage, but we'll unload the supplies at the dock in Independence."

"One hundred ten dollars for the horses' passage. I must put up with the stink of horse shit the whole way."

"Deal! Let's go. Say, why Independence? Isn't Kearny's army at Fort Leavenworth?"

"You've got some catching up to do, Smith. Kearny left Fort Leavenworth with his force in the first part of July. I wouldn't worry too much. A two-thousand-five-hundred-man army moves slowly. You can take the Santa Fe trail to Bent's Fort. You will probably catch him there. That's another five hundred miles on the Independence trail."

Daniel and the rest of the company brought the wagons and tied the horses to iron rings and rails attached to the deck. Captain Gurney and his crew shoved off midafternoon.

The trip up the Missouri River proved to be long and tedious. Captain Gurney pulled to dock before twilight each night. The river, famous for gashing the sides and bottom of steamboats, Captain Gurney, took no unnecessary risks with the *Misery*. True to his word, Captain Smith awoke the company daily at daybreak to discuss and practice combat and troop movement and signals.

Though Captain Smith had no war experience, he had commanded the police force. He had also led a posse in capturing a band of outlaws and criminals around Rattlesnake Mountain northeast of Portland. Daniel appreciated the Captain's approach, which included keeping under cover when available, avoiding unnecessary risks, and waiting for a sure shot instead of taking a quick one. Daniel could see that the drills might sustain him when and if the Company ever entered the battle.

On the night of the full moon, the fifth night on the river, the steamboat docked at Council Spring. The small community had a general store and four homes next to the dock. Edwin and the supper crew had prepared some pork and beans, the smell of which wafted through the little village. A group of men approached the boat. The frontman held a torch and appeared to be in charge. Six men were in the group. The torchman hailed Captain Gurney on the steamboat.

"Halloo there, the name's Slim Timmer; permission to come aboard?"

"Reckon not, though I'll be right over."

Captain Gurney jumped to the dock.

"Now, what can I do for you?"

The company had gathered for supper at a table on the starboard deck. The crates and wagons tied to the deck created a barrier to the activity on the dock. The after-dusk darkness allowed the soldiers at the table to look over the supply boxes without being noticed. As Daniel's eyes adjusted to the torchlight, he saw the men on the dock dressed in buckskins. Three of them wore coonskin hats. All looked to have muskets held with one hand behind their backs. The leader reached out, and Captain Gurney shook his hand.

"We're from the First Regiment Mounted Missouri Volunteers. We're trying to get to Fort Leavenworth to join Colonel Alexander W. Doniphan, our commanding officer."

On the boat, Captain Smith signaled Daniel in a whisper.

"Something's not right with those men. They look skittish. Be ready!"

Captain Smith jumped ashore.

"Captain Wendell Smith here, 1st Infantry, Maine, Company 'G' We're assisting Captain Gurney with this shipment of supplies to Kearny's army at Bent's fort. What's your business tonight."

"To be honest, we want to relieve you of some of them supplies you're talking about. We haven't been paid. Believe it or not, we've been starving for three days and haven't eaten in five."

"I'm sorry to disappoint, but these supplies must remain sealed until we arrive at Bent's Fort. Orders, you understand."

"You know, at this point, I'm not too understandin. My boys here have handled bears tougher than you blue-and-whites, and we are hungry as bears. If I give this torch a heave, those supplies won't do none of us any good, but I'm hungry enough to risk it. Now, out of the way.

Daniel signaled Lorenzo and the men around him to follow his lead and spread out along the deck. In seconds they were ready. Daniel stood on a box, aiming his rifle at the man with the torch. The rest of the company stood, weapons at the ready.

"Sir, I'd consider it neighborly if you wouldn't throw that torch. Captain Smith, may I offer an alternative."

Captain Smith nodded approval.

"Now we are all on the same side in this war, and I say we all sit down to a pork and beans dinner together and work this out. We'll keep the supplies sealed and prepare the meal from our Company's food stores.

"Perhaps we can coax the general store owner over there to provide more food for these brave Missourians in the morning. Surely our Company supplies could be refreshed. What do you say, Captain, Mr. Timmer? Do we fight or eat?"

Captain Smith reached out to shake hands with Slim.

"An excellent alternative, private; what do you say, Timmer?"

Slim Timmer looked around at his men and acquiesced with a smile.

"I say, let's eat."

The Missourians propped their rifles against the railing on the dock and clambered aboard; the mood lightened. Everyone shook hands and found seats at the table or nearby crates. Edwin Bowes broke out lots more beans and pork slabs and cooked them up.

Daniel swore under his breath that the buckskins the strangers wore stunk twice as much as his own dirty sweat and vowed to bathe and wash his outfit at the next opportunity. He could imagine the forest game sniffing these men out and scampering away before they could creep into rifle range. The opposite might be the case. The group stunk like deer and perhaps could get close before they fired at the deer. Regardless they ate supper as if they had never seen food before, devouring everything on the table.

Their beards were lengthy for the most part, but Daniel could not fault them for that; his own beard did not adhere to the regulation, at least not the Fort Preble regulation.

To assist with congeniality, Captain Gurney broke out two bottles of rye whiskey (marking them down on his list of army expenses.) The two companies attained a jovial comradery. Still, Captain Smith posted a guard to stand over the sleeping bodies sprawled out wherever they could find space between the crates.

In the morning, a happy general store owner replenished the supplies of Company 'G.' He also filled the saddlebags of the Missourians. The store owner wrote everything down on the lucrative army account ledger already signed by the Quartermaster out of Fort Leavenworth.

At midmorning, the Missouri Volunteers rode off, and the crew of the *Misery* pulled anchor and continued upriver.

Daniel washed his personals twice in the seventeen additional days of the river trip to Independence. He let his beard grow. After two days of unloading the supplies on the overflowing Independence dock, Captain Smith ordered shore leave, and Daniel headed into the first barbershop he found. Over two thousand residents considered the thriving town of Independence their home. Taverns, restaurants, and stores were abundant. Captain Smith, conscious of the Company's need to join Kearny's forces, limited the leave to one day. Daniel and Lorenzo Brennan took great advantage of the time off. They ate heartily, paying out of their own purse. They drank some, meeting up with more soldiers in one of the bars. Daniel played a few hands of cards and sauntered up to his room. Lorenzo invited him along to the whore house the soldiers talked up, but Daniel declined, deciding to write a letter to Cordelia with the hope it may reach back to Portland.

Captain Smith cleared his account with Captain Gurney and negotiated army teamster pay for the Company at twenty-five dollars per month with the Quartermaster out of Fort Leavenworth. When the company gathered at their assigned five wagons for the trip to Bent's Fort, another soldier, William Plummer, could not be located.

Plummer, well-liked in the Company, one of the oldest soldiers, and overweight, struggled to keep up in the marches but seemed dedicated. Captain Smith fumed, vowing that further desertions would be treated as criminal and local authorities notified. The Quartermaster's office provided four additional saddle horses for Nathan, Daniel, Lorenzo, and Charles Gardener. Six single-shot, percussion pistols were issued to the horse riders, Captain Smith and Lieutenant Goddard.

On August sixteenth, Company 'G' set out in five wagons heading for Bent's Fort. Two (or in one case, three) soldiers rode on the bench back of the buckboard in each of the five wagons loaded high with Company 'G' personals and army supplies. Tarps covered the supplies tied through grommets to each of the wagons. Four riders, including Daniel, rode alongside the wagons. Six additional wagons driven by army teamsters also began the journey with the Company wagons. The Company 'G' wagons outdistanced the teamster wagons, who had no incentive to push forth. With the weight of the chock-full loads, Company 'G' would hope to make fifteen miles a day. The Santa Fe trail did not compare favorably with the smooth, paved National Road. The path proved challenging to follow, rough, and bumpy. The rain made the wheels tough to turn in the muddy ruts.

By the third day out, Daniel could hardly mount after lunch. The insides of his ankles rubbed raw; the right one bled and required a plaster. His inner thighs and legs burned red, as did his butt. After the second day, Lorenzo cajoled another soldier into taking his place in the saddle. Nathan already seemed comfortable in the saddle, and Charles, younger, lighter, and smaller, did not seem to be experiencing any pain.

Daniel persevered. After ten days, his saddle sores toughened, and his saddle softened from the constant riding and heat of the August sun. Lorenzo, keeping with his two days on, two days off technique, experienced constant pain; in the end, giving up his horse to another soldier. From then on, Lorenzo merely assisted with the horse chores in the morning and night under Nathan's direction.

Daniel, setting his horse to a walk each day, listening to the creaking wheels of the wagons, tried not to think of the agonizingly slow progress they were making along the trail. He imagined holding Cordelia, the beautiful woman he had left in his arms. He tried to imagine little Lemuel beginning to crawl.

Trying not to seem too obvious, Daniel asked Captain Smith permission to scout ahead mid-morning and again midafternoon. These excursions allowed Daniel to gallop ahead for a few miles and explore some of the hills and canyons, careful not to venture too far beyond the sight of the trail. Then he would find a tree, dismount, water Sandy, his dark brown horse with the lighter brown mane, tie the reins off to a branch, and lie down on the tree's opposite side for a quick nap. The absolute quiet of these times somehow helped Daniel feel connected to the land and his family, despite the fifteen hundred miles that now separated them.

Even though he had neither seen a Mexican enemy nor fired a shot, the supplies the company transported would sustain the men that needed them to continue the war effort. It was enough for now. Relatively safe and learning new skills, his mother and the Captain would approve. He had nine months of service remaining before returning to Portland, his city.

Heading back to the wagon train, Daniel practiced quick mounts and dismounts. Sandy and Daniel were becoming partners. With the constant heavy physical activity, Daniel kept gaining weight and muscle in his arms and shoulders.

On the afternoon of August 28th, as Daniel distanced himself from the wagons, he spied an outcropping towering near the trail some distance away. The wagons now traveled across flat as a pancake prairie land. When Daniel squinted, the view in all directions seemed like a greenish-brown ocean; the prairie grass waves undulating and hypnotic. When he reached the rock, he estimated it to be over one hundred feet tall. It proved an easy climb to about fifteen feet from the top. Looking back down the trail, he spotted the wagons and the puff of dust dissipating in the wind.

Daniel turned to look forward down the trail, noticing another plume of dust far into the distance. He could not determine what caused it, suspecting a herd of buffalo moving south. Before scouting further, Daniel carved his name, Cordelia's, and Lemuel's into the rock with his hunting knife. Names and initials of Santa Fe trail travelers covered the rock. Perhaps Lemuel would pass by on some future adventure and find this record of his father's passage.

Daniel rode for another twenty minutes before determining that buffalo did not cause the great swath of dust. A caravan of Indians, pulling travois full of teepees and belongings, stirred the sand cloud. Daniel guessed they might be Comanches heading south to winter hunting grounds. Daniel kept his distance. He could make out a count of twenty in a group at this distance, calculating that there may be two hundred to three hundred Indians fronting the dust plumes. Herds of horses were being steered along by men on horseback. Dogs ran back and forth, chasing animals and playing with children as they walked.

Upon returning to the wagon train, Daniel reported what he had seen to Captain Smith. The Captain, relinquishing the reins of his mule team to the soldier sitting next to him, pulled out his pocket map and unfolded it in his lap. After just a bit of study, he turned back to Daniel.

"The quartermaster back in Independence marked this spot here on the map as Pawnee Rock. We'll want to keep our eyes peeled tomorrow for the Cimarron Trail cutoff. We'll head to the right and continue to Bent's Fort."

Daniel had a question, "What about the Indians?"

"We'll give them a wide berth. In fact, let's camp at Pawnee Rock. If there is any trouble, it may provide us some protection. We'll give the Indians a day for stragglers to cross the trail."

The Company camped by the Rock. Nathan made yet another Pork and Beans meal, and a sentry remained on watch on the rock throughout the night. In the morning, a trickle of dust could be fathomed far to their south. Captain Smith decided to push on.

Daniel did not cross the fork in the trail for two more days, but when he did, there was a sign with the words "Bent's Fort" pointing to the right. The Company had not seen any more Indians for two days, but Daniel spied another, much larger dust cloud on the horizon that did turn out to be Buffalo. Edwin Bowes, beside himself with the prospect of Buffalo steaks, suggested a calf be killed and dressed before continuing.

"Buffalo hides are great for wearing, but the meat on those big ole bastards will pull out your teeth trying to chew it.

Go after them, baby cows, and I'll cook you up seventeen slices of heaven."

Nathan, Charles, and Daniel rode out to the herd. When they pulled up their horses, the buffalo still moseyed south. Looking south, the pack appeared to stretch over the horizon. To the north, Nathan surmised an end to the herd about half a mile out.

"From what I know, we should shoot a calf as the stragglers of the bunch go by. Let's be patient and enjoy the afternoon till we see the last of 'em."

Daniel, bored, spoke up.

"Sounds right to me. The day's dry and warm. Wake me if they get too close."

The buffalo did get closer. As the perceived end of the herd aligned with the men lying in wait, the pack widened. Charles had lost count of a thousand buffalo from the time they approached. The men decided to back off the herd, still not seeing the last of the big beasts.

The wait paid off, for the herd thinned to a trickle, and several calves followed the cows at the back of the pack. The three hunters moved to within one hundred feet of the cows, who sensed danger. Daniel had never hunted before, and none of the three knew to approach their prey from downwind. It did not look that hard to Daniel, though. He knew from his practice with his father-in-law that he could hit one of the calves. Signaling the others, Daniel picked out a calf and fired. Nothing happened. Daniel thought he saw the calf stagger a bit, but it continued. Daniel reloaded his percussion M1841 rifle as he practiced, taking his eyes off the calf for a few seconds. When Daniel looked up at the herd again, he had no idea which calf he had shot. Undoubtedly, the calf had been wounded.

Frantically scanning the cows and calves, Charles thought he spied the wounded calf and fired. The three soldiers heard bellowing from the herd, but a couple of cows were now between the soldiers and the calf they were trying to bring down. Daniel stood and scanned the end of the herd again. Seeing a calf stumbling, he raised the rifle to his shoulder and fired at the calf again.

The calf dropped, but the herd spooked at the cracks of the gunshots and started running, running every which way. A giant moving wave took hold as each section of buffalo felt compelled to run. The men were witnessing their first stampede. Daniel sprinted to his horse.

"Time to skedaddle! Let's go!"

Charles was hungry for steak.

"What about the calf?"

"Later, maybe."

The three mounted hastily as the pounding hooves shook the earth beneath their horses. Daniel urged the slowest.

"Hurry, Nathan."

Daniel, galloping, headed back along the trail. Nathan had not responded; he probably did not hear Daniel's cry over the din, but his horse, in full gallop, moved as fast as possible. On Daniel's left, Charles' horse's right front hoof stepped into a prairie dog hole, and the horse, ass-over-head, dove at the prairie. With God's grace, Young Charles flew to the ground beyond and rolled to a stop, shaken but able to stand.

Daniel pulled up short. The buffalo were gaining on the men fast. Daniel spurred Sandy over to Charles, grabbed his arm, indicating the right stirrup Daniel had vacated, and Charles swung up shakily.

"What about my horse?"

"No time!"

The three men on two horses fled back along the trail while portions of the herd turned in different directions. They sighted the tail end as the buffalo straightened out and headed south again, gradually slowing. As Company ' G ' wagons approached, a vast thundercloud of dust washed over the riders. The three hunters looked like ghosts, covered from head to toe in dust and blood from the scrapes of Charles' fall.

Charles put down his horse due to a broken ankle, and another soldier found the calf amazingly untrampled. The Company moved on, Daniel, nearly asleep in the saddle from exhaustion.

The buffalo steaks were scrumptious that evening, although Daniel mused that any fresh meat would have been welcomed as delicious. After supper, Daniel reported to Captain Smith. Behind one of the wagons, Wendell offered Daniel a cigar.

"Charles told me how you went back for him during that stampede. Saved his life, he said."

"Not sure about that, Captain; those buffalo were turning this way and that. They would have missed him, most likely. I'll say one thing, if I may, sir. We seem ill-equipped and uneducated about how we do things out here. I still feel like a city slicker, and today proved it. I'm sure we went about hunting that calf wrong, and someone could have been killed."

"I agree with you to a degree. We must do the best we can. Learn as fast as we can.

"Private Martensen, Daniel, you have shown initiative on more than one occasion. You're a natural leader, and I want you to know that I appreciate it and the Company is better for it. I can count on you to stand tall for Portland and the State of Maine if we ever get into this war."

Daniel did enjoy the cigar. With a light head and sitting by the campfire, he thought again of Cordelia. Acting rashly and foolish would not get him back to Portland. Buffalo did not shoot back like Indians and Mexicans. Daniel still did not know how he would react under that kind of pressure. *"Remember your training,"* he repeated to himself, over and over. *"Remember your training."*

On September 20th, 1846, Company 'G' passed through Bent's Fort gate with five wagons of supplies intact. Captain Smith went straight to William Bent's office in the back of the two-story adobe brick building in the corner of the plaza. Fifteen-foot-high adobe brick walls surround the square plaza; the heavy wooden gate is opposite Bent's living quarters and office on the north wall. The wagon house and inner corral were built against the fort's walls behind the offices.

Daniel passed a small group of Indians negotiating the trade of buffalo hides with a short, gentle-looking man in the plaza's center. Two Indians sat on the porch. Each Indian had a feather flapping in the breeze attached to the knot in the back of their hair. A soldier from the fort volunteered that Cheyenne Indians mode up the first group, and the two on the porch were warriors of the Arapahoe tribe. Supplies were stacked everywhere, sometimes higher than the walls of the fort.

Twenty minutes later, the Captain emerged to address the Company.

"Too late again, soldiers. We keep trying to catch up to Kearny. He left here on August 14th. We're gaining on him. As far as anyone here knows, he's still in Santa Fe dealing with the Navaho. The word that Kearny's forces were on the move hadn't reached Independence yet when we were there. Sending us to Bent's Fort was a mistake. We should have taken the trail southwest at the Cimarron cutoff instead of following the sign to Bent's Fort eighteen days ago.

"Most of the supplies here must be hauled to Santa Fe. We'll be on our way two days from now when the horses and mules are rested. All the companies composing Kearny's western forces are rendezvousing in

Santa Fe for the push to head west to California and south to take Mexico. We should make it there in twenty more days or so. That puts us joining close to two thousand soldiers on October 10th. Moving our wagons to Santa Fe should still be important to the war effort. Rest up for this final push. We'll start at daybreak, the day after tomorrow. We'll have the blacksmith work with Nathan to ensure our horses, mules, and equipment are in top shape to head out."

That afternoon Daniel found a cot with a thin straw mattress in the regular soldier's quarters; devoid of bedding, he covered himself with his blanket and slept like a thirteen-year-old dog. Lorenzo and Ed shook him awake after dark for a six-man poker game up in the community room of the fort. Daniel, beaten out of all his matchstick chips early in the game, returned to the soldier's quarters to write another letter to Cordelia. He imagined her receiving the letter and perhaps sharing it with her father, Lemuel Bryant.

Company 'G' prepared to ride out of the fort on the Santa Fe Trail. Before leaving, Mr. Samuel Jones, the fort's quartermaster, hurried out of his office carrying a box full of pistols.

"Give me fifteen minutes to show you how to clean and operate these Patterson Colt repeaters. I'll take your single-shot pistols in trade. Out here, a better weapon may mean you'll keep your scalp. I've got five guns here to issue.

"To shoot, thumb the hammer back. That rotates a chamber in line with the barrel and locks the cylinder into place. The folding trigger drops down from the frame into position. See that? You sight through this here notch to the blade at the end. Accurate to fifty feet unless you're mounted. On a horse, I would want to be within a few feet. You've got five shots before reloading, but be smart and leave one chamber empty, so you don't shoot your foot off."

The quartermaster proceeded with the cleaning demonstration and went through the procedure twice. The weapon impressed Daniel: it weighed little more than his single-shot percussion pistol. The quartermaster issued Daniel, as the scout, one of the new pistols.

Ten days out on the trail southwest of the fort, the soldiers of Company 'G' began singing *Vive La Compagnie,* under Lorenzo's direction, as they drove their wagons: John Tukesbury squawking on his harmonica in accompaniment. Captain Smith encouraged any activity that kept his men's minds from dwelling on the thousands of miles the Company had journeyed and the day-in-day-out repetition of their fifteen miles per-day progress. Daniel had resumed his morning and afternoon scouting ventures.

September 30th, 1846; that afternoon, Daniel, a few miles ahead of the wagons, began to hear shots fired forward on the trail. He galloped ahead until he came over a rise and discovered a Conestoga wagon pointed in his direction on the side of the path, backed up to a small copse of trees. Pulling up short, Daniel saw that the horses were nervous and still harnessed to the wagon. A man, still as death, lay sprawled on his stomach near the stamping horses, and another still man leaned against the rear wheel, head lolling on his chest. Daniel could make out at least three arrows in the man. Occasionally a rifle shot sounded, which Daniel traced to the area behind the wagon where someone fired from cover. Four Indians on horseback tore back and forth in front of the wagon, shooting arrows at whoever had ducked behind the wagon. The Indian whoops sounded like a man's screams clenched by a bear trap's jaws.

The whole foreign scene scared Daniel shitless. If an Indian came from behind the copse of trees, the shooter behind the wagon would be done for. There was nothing for it. Daniel spurred Sandy, reaching the rear of the wagon in seconds. Dismounting and tying off his horse to the rear wheel opposite the dead man, he glanced at a grey-bearded man, who, thankfully, had not shot him as he approached.

Daniel pulled his rifle from its horn loop and affixed his bayonet; only God knew why while he assessed the situation. Over the hollering, Daniel leaned close to make out what the older man said.

"Stranger, you're a welcome sight. Probably the most foolish man I've ever met in a tight spot."

"I figure you need help looking to your rear. Help should be along."

Of a sudden, a high-pitched, yodeling scream commanded Daniel's attention. Looking up and turning, an Indian rushed him, a heavy club raised high over his head. The sight of the screaming burnt umber skinned man, his primarily bald head painted bright red, a red line across his nose, scared piss out of Daniel as he reeled his rifle around, firing and missing the screaming red man entirely. Daniel jerked his rifle around as the Indian swung down atop him. Daniel's bayonet drove into the man's chest at his breast bones. The butt end of Daniel's rifle dug into the dirt, and the war screams turned to agonizing howls as the Indian flailed, flopping like a Sunday meal chicken with its head chopped off. Daniel shrugged the Indian and rifle away and pulled his pistol. With renewed calm, he began to fire at the riders in front of the wagon through the spokes. The Indians did not expect him to fire in such little time between shots, and Daniel shot one warrior off his horse: dead.

Company 'G's wagons came over the rise, stopped, and the soldiers began to fire on the Indians. Captain Smith called a cease-fire. The excited soldiers had continued firing even though all the Indians had long since been shot dead.

Daniel still shook as Lorenzo came forward and clapped him on the back. Thankfully, Daniel's soiled pants were drying.

Captain Smith decided the copse of trees and the stranger's wagon could assist in cover if another attack occurred. He ordered the Company to set up camp. He set up a three-man perimeter picket. The rest of the soldiers buried the five raiders; Pawnee, the stranger reckoned. He and Daniel worked on the graves for the older man's companions. Introducing himself, Daniel shook the stranger's hand. Jeremiah Capshaw dug into the entangled root prairie as if his occupation were ditch digging. Daniel, at least thirty years the man's junior, attempted to hold his own as dirt, sod, and roots flew into a pile. Capshaw's companions were buried, and the graves mounded and smoothed before one of the Indian graves had been completed. Captain Smith introduced himself, inspecting the completed graves and offering sympathy.

"Sorry, stranger, for your loss. Were those two fellas kin?"

"No, they were hired hands to see me back to Missouri. Good men too, but they stayed out front of the wagon. Mistake! Paid for it!"

Daniel, curious, joined the two men.

"Where did you start from, Mr. Capshaw? Looks like you came a long way."

"I have Daniel. Don't mind if I call you Daniel, do ya? I reckon to be on a first-name basis with a fella that saves my life."

"You picked a good spot to defend but exposed your backside."

"Right, you are, young man. Captain, if your private had hung back twenty more seconds, I doubt I'd be talkin to you now."

"Daniel seems to have a knack for intervening in a disaster."

"I'm from Las Californias, Santa Clarita Valley, to be sure. My Señora, Sophia, passed last March, so I followed my son to Philadelphia, where his family has settled. Went to Thomas Jefferson College to be a doctor."

Captain Smith looked over Jeremiah's rig, certainly the worse for wear.

"You certainly have traveled a fair distance. We should know we're from Portland, Maine, high up on the eastern coast of the Atlantic. Got a long way to go as well."

'No matter. Got the time and means to get there. That is if trouble would stay away. There seems to be a lot of trouble brewing back in Santa Fe. Never seen that many men with rifles by their side. Buckskin soldiers, most of them. Spittin Missourians, they said.

"That's where we're heading; to join up with them. Join us for supper?"

Daniel's stomach churned well beyond dinner. He wandered the camp's perimeter, checking with each sentry, keeping his feet moving and mind off red paint. He could not imagine putting red dye, made of who knows what, all over his face and head. Frightening, which he now understood to be the reason for it. Terrify your enemy until their hands shake and they cannot pull a trigger. Luckily, that initial club swing had gone limp. The way the Indian thrashed would not leave the space behind Daniel's eyes. He saw red everywhere he looked. Even the sunset that evening cast a red glow shadow. Daniel seemed lost. *Had he killed a man, two men, or hideous creatures, as people called them? No, he had seen the sweat on the Indian and the muscles in his arm swinging down. The reflection on killing a man is awful; the action just happens.*

Daniel sat late by the fire, staring into it until his eyes watered, feeling the heat on his eyelids and forehead. He lost himself in the red glow of the pulsing embers, fire licking up and down the burning wood.

Jeremiah appeared from behind him. With an effort, he sat down next to Daniel, huffing as his bones and balance belied his age. Daniel examined his new acquaintance in the firelight. His face was craggy as eroded sandstone; his beard was rough cut at a couple of inches leading up to dark gray sideburns before turning back into a wave of white hair. His hands and nails looked permanently mangled. Slight at the shoulder, Jeremiah showed his age in the stoop of his back. Daniel knew from digging in concert with the man the massive muscle of his arms.

"Can't sleep either, son. Close call today. At my age, I don't feel lucky; I feel like tomorrow's another day."

"That's a good way to look at it, Jeremiah. The first stream or lake I see, I'm going to take a long bath and wash all my clothes. I will dress up after that like I'm going to when I see my son back home next year. I can't wait to put on a big smile for my wife, Cordelia, as she looks up from mending, sees I'm home, and smiles back."

Daniel looked at the mountains in the distance.

"What is California like? The Pacific Ocean must be like the Atlantic Ocean I'm familiar with."

"It is beautiful. The beaches and the balmy breeze. The heat ain't as bad as in the desert territory in Mexico. The Sierras are beautiful. I've seen trees with trunks so thick around my wagon could drive through one of them. Sequoias, they're called. Guardians of the forest to the Indians.

"My valley is thirty miles northeast of Los Angelos. Santa Clarita Valley is the name of it. My home since 1842 when I joined up with Jose Francisco de Gracia Lopez, a family friend of my wife. Lopez leased land from his uncle and discovered gold in the Cañon de Los Encinos (Live Oak Canyon). I panned gold there for three years until it got too hard. I had found enough to keep me lazy in Philadelphia. Paid for my son to go to college.

Jeremiah dug into a pocket on his vest. Fetching a small tobacco pouch, he pulled the cinch apart and fished in the bag, bringing forth a shiny object the size of a black bean in the palm of his hand to the firelight.

"This pouch of gold is yours, Daniel, for saving my life. I keep quiet about my past 'cause I'm carrying my wealth in that wagon, thirty pounds worth."

"No need for that, Jeremiah, just a matter of the right time and place."

"Take it, Daniel; I won't miss it. This ain't much, probably enough to make a ring to remember the occasion, but I'd be honored. Only if you would; let's keep it between us?"

"Alright, Jeremiah. I doubt I'll ever forget this day, ring or no ring."

In the morning, after breakfast clean up, the Captain approached Jeremiah.

"Jeremiah, you can come to Santa Fe with us."

"Thank you, Captain Smith. I'll continue. The horses and wagon are in good shape."

"Traveling alone out here does not seem the wisest course, Jeremiah. Will you reconsider?"

The prospector paused momentarily from packing his wagon and addressed the Captain.

"Could you spare two of your soldiers to accompany me to Independence? I could pay each man one hundred dollars for their troubles. Of course, I'd pay the Company one hundred dollars for the inconvenience."

"Let me talk it over with Lieutenant Goddard and Daniel."

The three men gathered a short distance away from Jeremiah's wagon. The captain explained the situation and asked for comments.

Lieutenant Goddard looked over the soldiers left in company 'G.'

"I don't know about you two, but the more these boys are together, it seems the ornerier we all get."

"That's what I'm considering. Besides, we're going to be a drop in the war machine bucket when we meet up with the troops. It's a matter of time before the next three men desert."

"Who's it going to be then, Captain. Ask for volunteers?"

"Volunteers seem fine other than you, Nathan (our blacksmith,) Edwin (our cook,) and Daniel here (our scout)."

Daniel surmised from the Captain's last comment the reason for his inclusion in the discussion. Samuel Bragdon and Charles Appleton, one of the nineteen-year-old youngsters, volunteered. The two soldiers sorted their personals and loaded them into Jeremiah's wagon. Jeremiah shook hands all around. He had Daniel's Portland address in his notebook and promised to write to Cordelia when he arrived in Philadelphia. The Company (down to fifteen soldiers) departed toward Santa Fe. Jeremiah's wagon and the two soldiers, riding the dead men's horses, plodded out of sight in the opposite direction.

Daniel transformed from a daydreamer into a cautious scout. Scouting ahead meant the company's survival, but now he never ventured out alone. Either Charles or Nathan or sometimes Lorenzo always went along. Daniel figured if they saw trouble, one rider could hightail back to encourage the wagon train to advance on the run. The second soldier could give aid if a silent arrow struck one army scout. Daniel bluntly explained his reasoning to the Company.

"Let's face the facts, fellas. We're still greenhorns out here. The Missourians would be laughing their asses off at our blundering forth. We've got to smarten up. We will not want to look like fools when we meet the Mexican force. Think about our path through this Indian territory every step of the way. Jeremiah told me if a Pawnee party attacks, and we can spare a few horses, let 'em have them. They may leave off. Am I way off, Captain Smith?"

"Not a thing wrong with your thinking, Daniel. Let's remember what we have learned. We're good at living off the land and sheltering from storms when necessary. We've avoided illness. You can load, shoot, and reload as fast as any Missourian, and you're all pretty good shots. Remember not to think when it gets tight in Mexican territory; just do."

The Company now headed south; the Sangre de Cristo Mountain peaks looming high to the west. The temperature at night eased off to forty degrees or lower. The gradual assent through the foothills slowed the wagon's progress. On October 18th, the trail turned sharply back in a northwest direction. The wagons, horses, and riders continued to climb through the mountain pass, waking to snow or ice-covered tents and steaming coffee.

The company found the valley of Santa Fe on the morning of October 21st when they crested a hill overlooking the town. The wagons rolled down into the dirty dry village. The brown, flat-topped, adobe houses were indistinguishable from one to the next. The road leads to a plaza in the center of the mud huts. A fraying American flag drooped on a twenty-foot wooden pole next to the largest building in the square.

The soldiers' disappointment grew as the wagons drew closer to the thirty white tents neatly picketed in rows on the plaza's edge. The army of the west had clearly moved elsewhere. A sentry leaned on his rifle on the top step leading to what looked like the army headquarters. Captain Smith dismounted from his perch on the lead wagon.

"Afternoon, soldier. Could you direct us to General Kearney's headquarters?"

"You're here, Captain, although General Kearny is not. At the end of September, he set off for California with three hundred soldiers."

"I see. How about Colonel Doniphan of the 1st Regiment of Missouri Mounted Volunteers. We met a few of his recruits along the Missouri River. Could I be directed to his headquarters?"

"He and the 1st regiment are on their way south to Passo del Norte with soldiers from General Sterling Price's 2nd Regiment of Missouri Mounted Volunteers."

"So, who is in charge, soldier?"

"That would be Charles Bent, appointed by General Kearny as governor of this here territory, and General Price, in command of the garrison here. But Charles Bent resides in Taos, so that would be a trek for you, about seventy miles north of here."

Frustration overcame Captain Smith. He avoided looking at his men. Dismounted, they were waiting expectantly for news. He looked around at the empty plaza, glanced at the clear sky above the dirty pueblo setting he stood in and turned back to the sentry with a sigh.

"When did Doniphan's troops start south?"

"Now there, you may be in luck, Captain, 'cause the troops moved out just twelve days ago."

"But we have just come from the south and saw no troop movement."

"Different trail. The troops moved south through the pass between the Sandia Mountains and the Manzano Mountains to the east. Captain, it takes time to move five hundred troops; I bet you could catch him in no time."

"Ok, thank you, soldier. Do you have a quartermaster here? Fresh mules for the wagons would be beneficial."

"Right through the door here. The first room is on the right. Colonel Price's office is further down the hall if you need more information. If you head south through the pass, keep the San Andres mountains on your left, the Rio Grande to your right."

The Quartermaster in Santa Fe located twenty fresh mules for exchange, but it took three days. Nathan spent the time checking axles and horseshoes. Daniel and Lorenzo hobnobbed with some regular soldiers stationed in Santa Fe.

Daniel wrote yet another letter to Cordelia. Apparently, mail traveled along the Santa Fe trail from California. Daniel did not mention the Pawnee attack on Jeremiah's wagon. He did describe the sharply peaked mountains surrounding Santa Fe. The Appalachian Mountains, he noted, were molehills in comparison. In fact, Daniel surmised Santa Fe probably existed at a higher elevation than the highest peak in the Appalachians.

Daniel wrote a few words in his letter to Lemuel, his son, attempting to maintain a connection to the little tyke two thousand miles and four remaining months away.

Two days from Santa Fe, Daniel, scouting ahead with Lorenzo came to the Rio Grande. The trail south followed the river and provided ready water for cooking and cleaning. The days were still warm and the nights cold. The wagons seemed to be generally heading down in elevation. The trail was less traveled than the Santa Fe trail but passable without the need for block-and-tackle to cross canyons.

On the morning of the tenth day, November 12th, Company 'G' approached posted sentries and a meadow where forty tents had been erected in four groups of ten tents. Wagons were lined up at the far end of the field. Lots and lots of wagons. Daniel counted eight rows of thirty wagons each. Each group of tents surrounded a clearing and campfire. Sitting and standing near two campfires, soldiers dressed in buckskins with rifles close at hand were passing the time. Two other groups of sixty men drilled in the field beyond the tents. One group worked on the command for a charge. A second group belly crawled, keeping to cover in a practice skirmish. Another part of the meadow contained roped-off corrals for the horses, oxen, and mules.

A soldier directed Captain Smith to the regimental headquarters tent near the river. He brought Lieutenant Goddard and Daniel along for support. Inside the tent, two desks faced the tent flap, and two soldiers, one in buckskin, the other wearing a blue jacket and white cross belt, were reviewing papers, presumably orders for the day. The three Company 'G' soldiers came to attention and waited. The soldier dressed in blue looked up.

"At ease, soldiers, First Sergeant Sanderset and Lieutenant Benton. State your business; we must get these orders to the field."

"Captain Wendell P. Smith at your service, gentlemen, of the 1st Infantry of Maine, Company 'G' This is my lieutenant, Mr. Harold Goddard, and Private Daniel Martensen, our scout. Our purpose is to meet with Colonel Doniphan or his representative and offer the services of our company of fifteen soldiers to the war effort."

"Wait, did I hear you say you're from Maine? All the men here are of the 1st or 2nd Regiments of the Missouri Mounted Volunteers."

"You did indeed hear correctly, sir. We have traveled from Maine to offer our service in this fight. We recently drove five wagons of supplies from Independence through Fort Bent and Santa Fe to join the troops under Colonel Doniphan."

"That would seem to put the two of us in a quandary. I'm not even sure how we can proceed. Are you equipped? What munitions can you handle? How would you fit into the command scheme?"

When First Sergeant Sanderset ran out of sputter, he looked at Lieutenant Benton and shrugged.

"I can only suggest we take the matter up with Colonel Doniphan upon his return."

"Yes, sir, that is most agreeable. When do you expect his return?"

"The Colonel is leading a contingent of three hundred and fifty soldiers west to Ojo del Oso (Bear Springs), near the headwaters of the Rio Puerco. He is to meet with Narbona, leader of the Navajo, Zarilla (Long Earrings,) and José Largo to sign a treaty. That meeting is taking place some two hundred miles west of Santa Fe. We hope he'll arrive by November 20th and return to our rendezvous point here by December 4th or 5th."

"Thank you, First Sergeant, that brings us up to date. May I ask what the general plan is going forward?"

"So far, we have met little resistance from the Mexican residents and towns we have encountered. Santa Fe surrendered without a shot fired. It takes time to move so many troops south. We hope to continue following the Rio Grande and be at Passo del Norte by New Year's, about two hundred fifty miles south. Beyond that, we have orders to join General Wool and take Chihuahua deep into Mexico territory."

"Thanks again, Sergeant. Now, as to our quandary, may I suggest we add our wagons in with yours and work under the direction of your supply specialist until Colonel Doniphan returns. We could camp by the wagons if that meets your approval."

"I doubt the Colonel will turn down additional volunteers who have traveled so far. You stand out like toy soldiers, but that will be your concern. Go ahead and bivouac by the wagons and stay out of trouble with our Missouri boys."

"Yes, sir."

Company 'G' staked their tents twenty feet from the river near the rows of wagons, two hundred eighty-five of them. Beyond the wagons were the horses. Daniel helped Charles and Lorenzo tie bows in their mules' manes, Sandy's mane, and the rest of their company's horses. They arranged a secondary rope corral around their company's livestock. Nathan followed suit with the other livestock and equipment managers. Late in the morning, Edwin gathered with the other company cooks to start work on supper. The rest of the company 'G' soldiers stayed out of the way of the Missourians. Captain Smith allowed the company passes for the rest of the day if no one curried trouble.

The soldiers of Company 'G' spent days waiting in the meadow for the return of the troops from the west, observing the customs of the Missourians, a different breed. Tobacco jawing and tall tales ruled the campfires, accompanied by much farting of the buckskinned soldiers. The stench of the buckskins kept Daniel many an arm's length away. He looked for Slim Timmer, the Missourian he had met on the Missouri River. He did not find him even after two days of scouting the camp. Daniel assumed Slim to be west with Colonel Doniphan.

The few adobe huts across the river belonged to the village of Los Lunas. The troops were forbidden to cross the river. Three men had broken that command in the early days of settling in the meadow. Each had gone under the lash. Where there are women, there will be rules broken. After two days, one of the Company 'G' soldiers tried it. Luther Pingree, thirty-three years of age, paid for his transgression when he did not report for parade until mid-morning. Seen swimming the river, a Missourian reported the sighting to First Sergeant Sanderset, who, in turn, informed Captain Smith.

Captain Smith could not afford to let the breach slide. Two men trussed Pingree to the lash post, and Captain Smith offered the ten lashes personally. Luther stayed in the hospital tent for two days and mysteriously vanished from the camp. Company 'G' now consisted of only fourteen men.

One night three companies from Missouri and Company 'G' from Maine joined for a hoedown. Two fiddlers, a washboard, and an upside-down tub drum offered music. John Tukesbury joined in on the harmonica while two boys sang duets. An exciting, peaceful event. The faces around the fire were either absorbed with the dancing and comradery or, like Daniel, lost in unobserved reminiscing of family and loved ones far away.

By Thanksgiving, the Missourians were restless, and fear of desertion became an issue. Lieutenant Benton issued drill orders that were too often ignored. The fourteen soldiers of Company 'G' were just as restless. 1st Sergeant Sanderset sent hunting parties out from camp in three directions with orders to bring back elk or deer for the feast. He also sent an official contingent across the river to Los Lunas to purchase as much claret punch as possible. The Thanksgiving meal eased the tensions in the camp for as long as the venison and elk stakes lasted. The claret ran out within the first half hour, with companies at the front of the serving line tossing down a mug and taking another cup further down the line. Thirty drunken frontier soldiers amongst two hundred thirsty bastards set tensions off like cannons. Fights broke out around camp as the hoarders captured some sweet jugs of wine and tried to carry them to seclusion to drink. The day ended in disaster, with eight soldiers held to the lash.

On the thirteenth of December, the sound of the pounding hooves of the Doniphan brigade preceded the sight of the three hundred or so mounted volunteers raising dust through the village and splashing across the Rio Grande into camp. Daniel, carrying the day's orders for Company 'G,' gawked at the lathered horses. Colonel Alexander Doniphan pulled up fast for a quick dismount. First Sergeant Sanderset and Lieutenant Benton emerged from the command tent, coming to attention and saluting the Colonel.

Daniel saw the commander he had chased across the United States for six months. The man was impressive. He dismounted smoothly, and his movements were quick. He seemed eager to begin his next task, the trip south. Yet his face embodied concentrated calmness. Daniel mused that women would most likely depict the man as handsome. He looked nearly forty years old with some signs of wear around his neck, but the softness of his countenance belied a younger man. Doniphan dressed in army-regulation white pants and gleaming calf-length black boots dusty from heel to toe from the ride. In keeping with his Missourian roots, he favored a buckskin jacket. He gave a suggestion of a salute back to his two subordinates.

"I'll want to see the daily log to catch up on the conduct of the camp. In the meantime, gather the company captains and lieutenants here for orders. I want the regiments ready to move south by tomorrow at day-break. Nothing more should stand in our way to drive the Mexicans out of the territory."

Lieutenant Benton, relieved, smiled.

"So, you were successful! The Navaho chief signed the treaty."

"I still can't figure out how much of a chief the man was. He signed the damn paper, and we had a good pow-wow. He seemed sincere. We'll have to see. Lieutenant Benton prepared a five-man team to carry and guard the treaty back to Independence, St. Louis, and Washington. You'll be responsible for getting it there safely, so pick good men you can trust."

"Yes, sir."

Decisive, tolerant, thinking, and planning while moving ahead. Daniel felt he could follow this Missouri lawyer-turned-soldier.

Captain Smith, Lieutenant Goddard, and Daniel attended the short officers meeting outside Doniphan's tent a half hour later. The thirty-three men were excited about leaving the meadow camp behind. The Colonel retrieved an empty wooden crate from the side of the tent, turned it over, and stood on it to address the officers.

"First off, you've undoubtedly heard about our successful mission to the West. We have a signed treaty with the Navaho Indians. If we stick to our obligations stipulated in the treaty, both sides will benefit. Let me note a couple of the particulars of the treaty.

"Article I: Firm and lasting peace and amity shall henceforth exist between the American people and the Navajo tribe of Indians.

"Article 2 notes that the treaty includes New Mexicans and Pueblo peoples as Americans.

"Article 3 guarantees free trade between both sides, with the protection of any molestation.

"Articles 4 & 5 allow the prisoners and property taken by both sides to be restored.

"I expect you and your men to respect the conditions of this treaty and abide by its rules. You, men, members of the Mormon battalion of volunteers, can appreciate what it means to live with the respect all men are rightfully due."

A Mormon Captain behind the officers offered a hardy, "Here, Here!"

Doniphan looked at the man, nodded, and continued.

"We must remain vigilant and our scouts mindful of any transgressions against the terms of this treaty by any Navaho party we meet or hear about.

"For the next twenty to twenty-four days, we will follow the Rio Grande to Passo del Norte before we break from the river and head to Chihuahua, deep in Mexican territory. The three supply wagons I took to Bear Springs must catch up with us. I want to move. We rode hard from the treaty signing, but now there are over five hundred of us to move south. I want to make all haste. So be it if the Mexicans continue to fold without a fight in our path. If they stand up to us, every Missourian and Mormon here will cut through them like a knife to butter. I can see it in your eyes. Get ready to move out at daybreak."

The Colonel nodded to the sergeant at arms, who came to attention. "Dismissed."

That night, after supper, Company 'G's three leaders approached the regimental headquarters tent requesting an audience with the Colonel. They were allowed five minutes. Once inside, the three came to attention in front of Colonel Doniphan. The Colonel remained seated but put down his pen, folding his hands before him.

"What is it, gentlemen?"

"Captain Wendell Smith of the 1st Regiment of Maine, Company 'G' at your service Colonel Doniphan. This is Lieutenant Goddard and our scout, Daniel Martensen.

"Yes, I have read about your circumstances in the daily log and discussed your situation with 1st Sergeant Sanderset. He spoke of your conduct in camp, the discipline of your small contingent, and your wish to accompany us south.

"It would be difficult for us to consider such a small unit as anything more than reserves in the chain of command. I would be most grateful if you could drive your wagons and the three hundred teamsters on our supply train at our rear. Is that acceptable? We do not know what will occur when we face the Mexican army in battle, and every man that will move forward with us is welcome."

"Perfectly acceptable, Colonel Doniphan. I would recommend Daniel here as an asset to your scouting unit. He's an excellent rider and has proven his worth in an Indian skirmish between Bent's Fort and Santa Fe."

"Very well, have him see Lieutenant Harrison. Give him this note."

Doniphan finished scribbling a one-sentence note and signed it before handing it to Captain Smith, who passed it on to Daniel as they left the tent.

Two days later, as the troops and caravan of wagons drove south, several soldiers in Narbona's Navaho camp came down with the Grippe. The eighty-year-old Narbona had been suffering from the symptoms at the treaty signing. Six days later, perhaps twenty-five percent of the troops had chills, fever, a cough, or a combination of these symptoms. Three men from Company 'G' caught the disease, and in another week, pneumonia had overtaken two of Daniel's friends. They soon died, reducing the company to twelve men.

The regiments pushed on further south. Orders were to meet General Wool in Chihuahua. Colonel Doniphan would not allow his troops to miss that rendezvous. Added to the difficulties caused by so many incapacitated men and the care they demanded, the caravan came upon a blinding white desert flat that seemed to stretch to the ends of the earth. The so-named Jornada del Muerto trail presented a new challenge to Colonel Doniphan as they became cut off from the Rio Grande. He ordered all casks and jugs topped off with water, not knowing when the next river might be crossed. By the third day in the drifting sands, devoid of plant life, soldiers (even soldiers not sick with the Grippe) began dropping from their horses in the sun's heat. Dehydration caused more deaths. Water rationing became necessary and harshly enforced. Armies lost many men from diseases. In this case, sixty-five men (twenty-two soldiers and forty-five teamsters) died on the trail before the Grippe ran its course. Daniel and the scouts came to the end of the white sands desert five days later.

On the day before Christmas, Lieutenant Harrison sent Daniel and Timothy, a Missourian scout, back into the desert to determine how long it would take the caravan of soldiers and wagons stretched out along the march to catch up to the main body of soldiers. In the late afternoon, Daniel found his way back to the front and reported to his superior, which in turn, relayed the news that the tail end of the caravan, fifteen miles to the rear, had begun to double-time march to catch up. A full day (a hard day's ride for wagons and men) would be required to gather the regiments once all the wagons were finished with the desert sands. The Colonel's entourage emerged from the desert at El Brazito ("Little Arm") on the east bank of the Rio Grande. The soldiers began to picket their tents. Doniphan told his lieutenants and captains that Christmas would be a layover day. He, for one, would be sleeping in while the tail end of the caravan caught up to their position at El Brazito, a favorable spot east of the Rio Grande.

On Christmas morning, Daniel dressed early after a restless night. He had spent the night reminiscing last year's Christmas dinner of roast duck and scalloped oysters. Cordelia had prepared the family meal with her mother, Eliza. Cordelia had just begun to show her pregnancy. Still, Daniel, Cordelia, Eliza, Lemuel Bryant, and Daniel's mother, Rachel, enjoyed every bite, down to the mincemeat pie and parsnips. A bit of rum added to the eggnog spurred the lively after-dinner discussion.

Daniel could never have imagined the events that brought him to this Brazito Christmas. Instead of waking Lieutenant Harrison, Daniel broke out Sandy from the corral, saddled his companion, and headed south to escape all things army. Daniel and Sandy forded the Rio Grande and climbed the foothills west of camp. For a while, Daniel wandered, lost in imaginings of his son, Lemuel, bouncing on Cordelia's knee back in Portland.

Out of habit, Daniel looked up from his reverie to scan the valley of Brazito and the way south toward Passo del Norte, thirty miles away. Daniel headed in that direction, staying high above the plain. After five miles, Daniel dismounted and walked Sandy for a few minutes. He tied his horse to a tree and fed her a handful of oats from the sack he carried in his saddlebags. Looking across the valley to the mountains east of the Rio Grande, Daniel noted movement, too far away to distinguish shapes. He pulled out his spyglass for a better look. Apaches; a party of twenty.

Since joining Lieutenant Harrison's scouting unit, Daniel learned to recognize many Western Indian tribes. Most Missourian scouts were frontiersmen, having traded with or fought raiding parties in Missouri, throughout the Indian Territory, and even further west in the mountains. The scouts knew and respected the characteristics of the various tribes. Navaho, Apache, Comanche, Cheyenne; each tribe identifiable. Daniel now knew which tribes farmed, which were plains hunters, and which sent raiding parties to steal horses. The Apache party on the distant mountain was all mounted and observing something further south. They did not appear to be restless or preparing for a raid, but rather, they seemed to be enjoying the Christmas morning, much like Daniel.

But as Daniel peered south through his spyglass down on the plain, he picked up a distant cloud of smoke or dust low to the ground. He swung up on Sandy, picked his way along the ridge for two more miles, and pulled out his spyglass again. The cloud of dust, obvious now, could only mean one thing, Mexican troops. For a moment, Daniel's hands turned cold. He looked once more at the enormous cloud, ever closer. He turned back, hastily reaching the valley floor, cutting down the foothills at an angle to not cripple his horse. Once on level terrain, he spurred Sandy to a fast gallop. It would take him a good hour to return to camp.

Late morning, Daniel skidded to a stop in front of Colonel Doniphan's tent. First Sergeant Sanderset bent over a wash tub, a mirror propped in a branch, shaving. His suspenders were drooping around his knees; half of his face was still lathered with soap when Daniel reported.

"Army double time marching in our direction, Sergeant."

"What? Where have you been, soldier?"

"Up on the ridge west of the Rio Grande, at least seven miles south of camp. The advancing army another two miles south of me."

"The size of the force, could you tell?"

"The dust from the march stretched across the entire valley. It's a major force, larger than ours, I can tell you that much."

"Wait here."

The Sergeant entered Colonel Doniphan's tent. The Colonel stepped out within two minutes, dressed and alert.

"Scout, you were one of the men that traveled back along our stragglers yesterday. Looks like we'll need them now. Sergeant, sound assembly.

"We need those stragglers, soldier. Head back north for five miles and sound the alarm to the caravan. At full speed, those troops should reach us as reinforcement as the Mexicans meet us. Hurry!"

Daniel had been rubbing down Sandy while waiting for the Colonel to issue orders. Sandy snorted nervously, ready for the ride north. Outside the camp, as he paralleled the wagon train and troops heading into camp, he shouted to every group of soldiers that Doniphan needed them on the front to battle the Mexican army. After forty-five minutes, Daniel turned Sandy back. He relayed his mission to a mounted soldier and asked him to turn north and alert the rest of the caravan of the impending battle.

Daniel arrived back at Doniphan's tent to report but found the area abandoned. In another two minutes, he found the center of Doniphan's army running helter-skelter but with the apparent purpose of forming a line perpendicular to the trail from Santa Fe to El Paso del Norte. The Rio Grande gurgled in a rush, perhaps two hundred yards behind the troops. Any Mexican rush from that direction would need to noisily splash across the river. Doniphan's troops could therefore concentrate on the Mexican attack before their line.

Daniel found Doniphan's command position and reported to First Sergeant Sanderset. Sanderset caught Doniphan's attention, pointing to Daniel and then back to Doniphan with thumbs up. Daniel mounted Sandy, about to leave to find Company 'G,' when another scout rode up to Sanderset from the south on a lathered horse. Colonel Doniphan sidled over to Sanderset to receive direct information about the enemy.

"What news, soldier? How much more time do we have before they're upon us? What's their troop strength. News, man, news."

The Scout rubbed his beard with a fisted hand.

"I estimate at least five hundred cavalry, sir, and seven hundred infantrymen, including at least two hundred ragtag militia. They've formed in front of the last of the sand buttes in front of us. They could attack at any time, Colonel."

Disturbing news, although Colonel Doniphan never twitched. Daniel knew their own army consisted of five hundred soldiers with an additional two hundred teamsters who primarily drove wagons. The rest of the caravan troops were essential for survival.

Another scout rushed into camp and dismounted. Daniel recognized Mark Stanton, a friend from his scouting unit.

"Sir, a single man waving a black flag is approaching. He'll be in rifle range within a minute or two. Our sharpshooters can take him down at any time, sir, on your order."

"No scout, Sergeant Sanderset, pass along the line that the black flag can come forward without molestation."

Sanderset snapped to attention and saluted.

"Yes, sir!"

"Time! Ten more soldiers from the Santa Fe trail will come to our line every minute they wait."

Fascinated by Doniphan's strategies, Daniel stayed to listen to the parlay. Eight more minutes passed before the Mexican soldier, in full dress and spotless uniform, approached within forty feet of the American front line. Missourians were pouring in from the desert and taking positions along the front.

The soldier holding the black flag came to attention.

"Major Antonio Ponce de Leon, commander of the Mexican regulars of Providence of Chihuahua, demands your immediate surrender."

Colonel Doniphan came forward through the line stopping about twenty feet away from the soldier with the black flag.

"Now, perhaps I can understand you better. Once more, if you would, sir."

"Major Antonio Ponce de Leon, commander of the Mexican regulars of Providence of Chihuahua, demands your immediate surrender. Our forces are far superior. You will suffer greatly from our charge."

"Ah, yes, now I have heard you, sir."

Daniel watched the Colonel take three more deliberate steps forward before snarling at Black Flag.

"Charge and be damned."

Doniphan turned on his heel and slowly walked back and through his front line. He addressed the gathered officers.

"Sergeants pass the word. Let the bastard take my message back to this Ponce de Leon. Every minute of delay gives us time to prepare our line."

Daniel led Sandy along the front line at a gallop until he spotted Company 'G' uniforms mid-way on the line to the left. Wagons formed a backdrop to the line on this side, and Daniel led Sandy behind a wagon and tethered her. Affixing his bayonet, he nudged into a spot between Lorenzo on his right and Tukesbury on his left, assuming a prone position, ready to fire.

Captain Smith knelt behind the front wheel of a wagon to Daniel's left. The rest of the Company 'G' soldiers were stationed around two of their wagons or lying tight together on the front line.

Themen's chatter revolved around the clouds, rare in the desert, blowing in off the mountains from the east. Soldiers up and down the line checked their bayonets, laid out ammunition for second and third shots, and continuously aimed downfield at some small cactus or bush, hopeful for the range and accuracy of their weapons.

A roar rose from the sand butte in the distance, and the Mexican infantry marched into view, yelling and yodeling in Spanish as if at a Mexican festival. A drum beat from behind the Mexican line was keeping the advance measured.

Just behind Daniel, a captain on horseback flew past. Every fifty feet, he pulled up and relayed the command strategy from Colonel Doniphan.

"The grizzly bears are comin boys. Like in the mountains, you better hold that shot until you can make out the hair whiskers around their snouts. Shoot them down close before they can swipe you with their claws. Remember, fifty feet away, shoot."

The captain rode off, repeating his analogy to the next group of cool and calm Missourians.

The enemy line stopped four hundred feet away. The Mexican soldiers knelt and fired on command. A second line standing behind the kneelers fired as well. Both lines reloaded as they advanced in a slow march toward the American line. The boom from a howitzer shook the wagon behind Daniel, but the cast iron shell fell well in front of the Americans, and gunpowder sprayed sand in a harmless cloud. Daniel still could not make out individual soldiers across the divide. He wanted to shoot before they came close enough for him to see their faces. He could not look at them as men. They were uniforms.

The Mexican line advanced another seventy-five feet, kneeling again, for two rounds fired. Daniel could see them clearly now, his trigger finger shaking. Lorenzo, on his right, rose to one knee and turned away from the advance.

"I'm going back by the wagons; a wheel should steady my aim."

Daniel reached out and grabbed Lorenzo by the ankle, tripping him down. At that moment, the Mexican line fired a third round.

"Get down, fool, you're here now, and there is nothing for it. Remember what Captain Smith taught us. Keep your fucking head down. Take a good shot, not a quick shot. Reload."

The howitzer roared again, and this time when the shell hit, sand sprayed over the soldiers to Daniel's right, still harmless. Lorenzo scurried back down, elbow to elbow, with Daniel as if Daniel might give him protection with his closeness.

Ten seconds later, the Mexican line charged, sprinting, bayonets gleaming. Now they were fifty feet away, and the American line fired at will, cutting the enemy down in their tracks. Daniel picked out the white crosshatch belts of a soldier, aimed, and fired. He never saw the man's face as he went down.

Lorenzo fired wildly, sat up with his back to the enemy, and reloaded. Again, Daniel grabbed him by the back of his collar and dragged him down.

"Stay down to reload."

Daniel reloaded his own percussion M1841 Rifle in half the time of the soldiers with muskets around him. To his right, out of the corner of his eye, Daniel caught site of twenty mounted Missourians leaping over the American line and charging toward the howitzer, visible now in the distance. To Daniel's far left Mexican lancers had snuck around the wing of the American line, attacking the soldiers protecting the wagons.

Following the mounted charge to Daniel's right, seventy Missourians charged on foot to capture the howitzer. The Mexican line, so close, scattered in disarray. Many Mexican soldiers remained, sprawled in the sand, lifeless. Scores more limped or clutched wounded arms, heading back toward the sand butte.

The Mexican Lieutenants called for another charge, but only half of the Mexican line responded. Daniel fired again in concert with the rest of the Americans. The Mexican line turned and ran, vanishing over the sand butte in the distance. All gunfire quieted.

Daniel nodded to Captain Smith, retrieved Sandy, and galloped off to find Lieutenant Harrison for scouting orders. At Colonel Doniphan's command post, Daniel found the Lieutenant. He had sent scouts east into the mountains to spy on the Mexican army's next move. Harrison ordered Daniel to return to the foothills west of the Rio Grande for reconnaissance.

When Daniel reached the scrub line west of Brazito, he dismounted and pulled out his spyglass. He could not hold it steady, even sitting on a rock. He set the spyglass on a nearby boulder. Daniel clasped his hands together between his knees, bowed his head, and closed his eyes. Yes, they were there, in the back of his eyes, Mexican soldiers charging and falling in front of him. Daniel breathed deeply, again and again. His shaking subsided. Looking up at the mountain, the clouds of the battle had evaporated in the desert heat; the mountain tops were brown, contrasting with a clear blue, peaceful sky. Sandy neighed. Daniel fed her oats from his bag. He leaned his head against her mane, the horse's softness, warmth, and calm a substitute for the love of his life so far away. Two minutes later, he took up the spyglass and held it to his eye.

He saw the Mexican army moving south with haste. Daniel counted groups of ten and twenty men heading in many directions from the main body of the march. Militia (farmers probably,) who had enough of American soldiers, deserted by the scores to return to their homelands.

Another curious sight caught Daniel's eye. The Apache party he had seen the day before was charging down on stragglers and creating havoc for the retreating Mexicans. Against the demoralized soldiers, the Apache raiding party acquired many horses. The fight had gone out of the Mexican regiment.

Charge and be damned had been just that.

Two days later, Doniphan's army entered the undefended settlement of El Paso del Norte. The troops doubled the population and extended the outskirts of the settlement with their white picketed tents and wagons. Doniphan's army awaited the arrival of General Wool's forces from San Antonio. With the combined strength of Wool's and Doniphan's men, they were to take Chihuahua, the capital of the Mexican providence. Captain Smith passed on to his Company all the information discussed at Doniphan's command headquarters at the edge of town.

After the Battle of Brazito, Company 'G' soldiers, now field tested, were anxious to get on with the war. A week went by. Then a second week. Many Missourians spent time in the El Paso jail sleeping off Cactus Wine distilled in the back of the Sombrero, a local saloon.

Thus, the Americans occupied the town, the saloons, and the women and grew increasingly restless for another fight. More American-mounted volunteers streamed in from Santa Fe. On January twenty-first, word came that Wool's force had turned back. His heavy artillery proved unworkable in the desert landscape, continuously mired in the shifting sand.

Upon entering the Sombrero Saloon on that Friday evening, January 22nd, Daniel and Lorenzo spotted a card game at a corner table and approached. Lorenzo elbowed Daniel and tipped his head in the direction of the dealer. Daniel recognized Slim Timmer, one of the Missourians they had invited to a meal of beans and bacon on the steamboat Misery. Lorenzo waited for a break in the play.

"How are you doin, Slim? Giving or taking pots on this balmy Friday evening?"

The gambler looked up from his cards, feigning recognition of Lorenzo and focusing on Daniel.

"Why, Hello. Can't keep names in my head that well. I remember you, though. Still own that percussion M1841? Were you in it at Brazito?"

Lorenzo answered, "We were in it, that's sure. Daniel yanked me down just before a bullet whizzed over my ear. How'd you make out."

"Killed my share of them fancy uniforms. That's right, your name's Daniel."

"It is, Slim; good to see you're still kicking."

"Tell you what, Daniel, if you come across my bleached bones in Chihuahua, you're welcome to my new buckskin coat. If I come across your sorry ass bleeding to death in the sun, I'll requisition that rifle of yours."

"Fair enough, Slim, but I must tell you, I'm keeping my chin pinned to the sand from now on. I'm determined to get home and see my son take his first steps."

Slim spit on his hand, extending it to Daniel, who hesitated a second, spit, and shook on the deal.

"Don't blame you, Daniel. Now, you two want to join the game?"

Everyone at the table laughed. The table was quiet during the card play, except for Lorenzo. Never subtle, Lorenzo expounded on his gruesome burial duty at the Brazito battle site. Forty-three graves were dug for the Mexican soldiers who died there. Officials counted one hundred fifty wounded Mexicans. On the American side, no one died, and only seven Missourians were injured. If the Americans continued to control the battlefields as they did at Brazito, neither Slim nor Daniel would win their bet.

Daniel played a few hands, cashed in, and left Lorenzo losing money while he tossed a last drink at the bar and returned to his tent.

Doniphan's army occupied El Paso for the entire month of January. Daniel and Lorenzo caroused with Slim Timmer and his small unit of Missourians to pass the time. The days were filled with listless drills, rides up into the mountains, card games, and rotgut whiskey. Daniel drew the line at dalliances with the whores of El Passo del Norte. In only five more months, he would return to his young bride.

An alliance emerged between Mexican and American merchants of the city. They needed to move their goods south, to Chihuahua, for sale and safety, and they wanted army protection from the Apaches to ensure they would get there.

On February seventh, 1847, the bugler sounded assembly. Orders to move out on the eighth were passed to all companies. Colonel Doniphan had received permission to attack and occupy Chihuahua, over two hundred miles south of El Paso del Norte, without the aid of General Wool's forces. During the month's stay, Doniphan had gathered nine hundred twenty-four soldiers, three hundred twelve wagons, and the three hundred civilians and merchants, formed into a battalion by Major Samuel Owens. Doniphan had added the captured Mexican artillery to his arsenal. The horses, oxen, and mules were rested and ready for travel.

The caravan stretched along the trail over a mile on the first day of the trip, proceeding slowly in the mild February heat. Doniphan did not want a repeat of a battle employing a straggling force.

The trail now led into the heart of the formidable Chihuahua desert from the lifeless White Sands flats. Blowing and drifting sand slowed progress on the windy days, and torrential rain on the fourteenth washed out the trail, spreading rivers across the landscape. The day after the downpour, there were cacti of all shapes and heights blooming from the rain. On either side of the lush, colorful trail, shades of red and yellow blossoms complimented the Mexican serapes some teamsters wore. Anyone venturing off the track found themselves surrounded by deadly beauty. Fields of cactus, sometimes only a few inches tall, growing so close together as to form carpets of needles, were impossible to navigate without puncturing a boot or moccasin. A spine through a boot to the skin to bone was a frequent, bloody cactus occurrence.

In the afternoon of February 25th, Colonel Doniphan ordered his troops to camp on the north bank of the Laguna de Encinillas, approximately sixty miles north of Chihuahua, according to his crude map. Four of Harrison's scouts, including Daniel, pushed ahead to locate the Mexican troop movements. Twenty-five miles south of Doniphan's army, the scouts found fifteen hundred Mexican soldiers holding a village purported to be the county seat of the Governor of Chihuahua. Two scouts were sent back to report to Lieutenant Harrison while Daniel and Mark took positions out of sight on either side of the village to watch the Mexican army.

The Mexican troops broke camp, and all fifteen hundred soldiers headed south away from Doniphan's army. This baffled Daniel because the Mexican army had more soldiers than the Missourian force. Daniel agreed to continue watching the retreat of the Mexican soldiers while Mark rode north to inform Lieutenant Harrison.

Daniel soon discovered the Mexican strategy. Staying well out of range and out of sight, Daniel spied the battalion crossing the Rio de Sacramento and meeting an even larger contingent of their army, busy fortifying the pass.

Daniel surreptitiously took up several hiding places along the river. With the aid of the spyglass, Daniel made a note of as many as twelve hundred soldiers, fourteen hundred militia, and twelve hundred cavalrymen on horseback. The soldiers were finishing several redoubts to protect their troops and artillery. Daniel counted sixteen cannons and culverin pieces among their defenses. Daniel scurried back to Sandy and set off to inform his superior officer. Daniel did not have to wait long to report. The U.S. forces continued their march five miles from Rio de Sacramento.

Locating Lieutenant Harrison, Daniel pulled out a sketch he had made of the pass and the positions of the Mexican cavalry and infantry. Harrison took one look.

"Come with me, Daniel; you can explain these markings to Colonel Doniphan without a middleman."

The Lieutenant and Daniel approached Doniphan and Sanderset. The Colonel used his own spyglass to scan the desert. The enemy line now littered the horizon. Harrison saluted and requested to speak to the Colonel.

"Colonel Doniphan, sir, Private Martensen, here, has just returned from observing the enemy, and I suggest he report to you."

Doniphan interrupted Sanderset's report to concentrate on Lieutenant Harrison.

"Good Lieutenant. What have you got for me, Scout?"

Daniel reported his estimates of the Mexican troop strength. Doniphan asked Daniel if he could think of anything to add?

"My general impression, sir, is that the Mexicans learned a lesson at Brazito and will not be foolish enough to attempt a head-on charge against our artillery and seasoned soldiers."

Daniel pulled out his sketch of the Mexican army positions.

"They're protecting their cannons with redoubts on the left and right sides of the pass. They've dug them in deep. They seem to be preparing a contingent of lancers behind the redoubts on the left side of the field."

"Anything else, private?"

"No sir, except maybe it will help that there is some cover from sand mounds on the right here, and the cactus is sparse over there as well; treacherous most everywhere else."

"Good! This drawing... good work. If your numbers are accurate, the enemy has a four-to-one advantage. We need to even things out. This map may do just that. When a Missourian knows where the game is, nine times out of ten, he'll bring home supper.

"A couple of questions. What would you estimate the distance between the left and right redoubts?"

"At least fifteen hundred, maybe eighteen hundred feet."

"Good, and they're probably all pointing center battlefield to stop our charge?"

"That's correct, sir, and they're dug in deep. Hard to swing them."

Doniphan asked Daniel to stay while the bugler called the Company Captains together for a war council. The Colonel stepped into his tent alone. Thirty minutes later, he emerged and addressed the thirty Lieutenants and Captains.

"You Infantry Captains will divide into four columns with a quarter of the wagons each for cover when we attack. In between each column, I want artillery crews to move and fire until our infantry can engage. Ok, the cavalry units will now be in front. They will screen our artillery and harass the enemy on the gallop.

"When the artillery and infantry reach the top of this plateau, we'll be able to lob shots into the belly of their force."

The Captains nodded their approval. Doniphan then focused on the individual officers he would give special assignments.

"Now, just before we advance, Captain Reid and three cavalry units will swing around the right side of the Mexican redoubt and approach on that side. We know their cannon will be aimed at the center of our four columns, so let's hope you catch them off guard.

Captain Weightman, you'll be ready to move up your twin howitzers to keep the enemy busy while Captain Reid and Major Owens lead the charge on their right flank. The cannon dug in on their left side will be out of range of our army on the right.

Captain Reid, you'll need a scout who knows the cover on the right flank. That will be you, Private Martensen.

"Dawn, we move forward close enough to fire our cannons.

"Any questions? No? We won't stop now till we take Chihuahua.

Daniel's stomach flopped when he heard his name connected to the all-important first charge with Captain Reid. Instead of keeping his chin pinned to the sand, he would ride Sandy into the Mexican thicket.

Daniel stayed up late writing a letter to Cordelia and his son. He did not write about his duty on the morrow, the strategy of the Missourians, or the situation they were in, outnumbered four to one. He wrote about three things he would like to do with them when he returns home. *"A picnic with just the three of them came to mind. He would make a little hat for Lemuel. He would buy Cordelia a store-bought new dress with his army earnings."* His obligation to the 1st Regiment of Maine, Company 'G,' would expire in four months. After finishing the letter, Daniel snuffed his light and spread his blanket outside the tent by his saddle, watching a million stars move across the sky, trying to drift off to sleep. Way before dawn, he roused himself and shook Lorenzo awake. Daniel gave his friend the letter. He did not bother to ask him to send it. Instructions were unnecessary. Then he saddled Sandy and rode off to join Captain Reid's unit.

The American force moved forward an hour before dawn on February 28th, 1847. The four columns behind the galloping cavalry stopped, giving the artillery crews time to adjust cannons. On the bugle call, all carronades fired, the boom echoing off the mountains north of the Mexican blockade. The Mexican guns responded a minute later. The salvos from both sides fell short. Doniphan's force feinted a charge as all four columns moved forward to a point just shy of where the initial Mexican barrage landed: out of range, out of deadly danger.

In the meantime, Daniel, urging Sandy to a run, led Captain Reid and one hundred fifty mounted Missourians. The riders swung to the right and spread out behind the mounds of sand Daniel had pinpointed the day before. They dismounted well within the range of the Mexican cannon Daniel knew to be out of sight behind the redoubts, but no cannon fire came from the enemy.

From behind, Daniel heard Captain Weightman's howitzer crews approaching noisily to two of the sand mounds. At the same time, another salvo from the central columns masked Weightman's approach. Captain Reid pointed to the redoubts where flashes and smoke from the last enemy salvo had landed, and the howitzers began a swift bombardment. The twin howitzers fired in syncopation every forty-five seconds, keeping the redoubt under constant fire.

Daniel ripped off two frayed ends from the bottom of his pants and busied himself stuffing his ears to fend off the tremendous noise of the cannon from both sides and the howitzers yards to his right. He kept waiting and dreading the whistle of a cannon shot from the redoubts.

The howitzer crews adjusted their trajectory and aimed before each salvo. After fifteen minutes of howitzer bombardment, Daniel heard a massive explosion that vibrated his chest. When he looked over the sand mound, smoke and fire rose from the first redoubt. A howitzer canister must have hit a Mexican ammunition dump stored deep in the redoubt.

Captain Reid rose and shouted down the line to Major Owen, who also stood. The two men led charges from the two mounds toward the Mexican's right flank and the subdued redoubt. Daniel jumped up and scrambled over the sand mound, running forward as fast as possible, waving Reid and his men further right to avoid a cactus field that could cause more casualties than the enemy fire. At three hundred feet from the redoubt, a musket ball zinged the cactus he had just avoided on his left. Another shot spit sand between his feet as Daniel ran. He tried zigzagging, varying his pivots to prevent a pattern, and finally came close enough to shoot with accuracy.

Daniel kneeled, steady, fired, and the Mexican white cross belt in his sights flopped backward. To his left and right, the rest of the company kneeled, fired, and reloaded on the run. Now at the redoubt, Daniel pulled his pistol. Captain Reid and Daniel led the men swarming over the Mexican earthworks. Most of the artillery crew were running away. The enemy stalwarts were surrounded, having waited too long to escape. Some threw down their weapons to surrender, and others fought and died.

Major Owens' troops were struggling to take the second redoubt. Daniel, glancing over, saw the Major fall dead from a bloody shot to his head. Nodding at Captain Reid, he and twenty other Missourians rushed over to reinforce the unit about to overrun the second mound. Daniel knelt again and fired his M1841 at a Mexican soldier aiming at one of his fellow advancing Americans. The Mexican soldier pitched forward. Daniel reloaded in twenty-four seconds, taking off on the run, closing on the enemy enough to fire his pistol. The combined American units overran the Mexican position, capturing or killing the artillery crew.

Daniel and Reid's rangers formed again at the redoubts, reloading, preparing for the next charge, and awaiting orders from the Captain. He and Daniel stood atop the second redoubt. The four columns of the American line had successfully reached the plateau; the American artillery in between the columns fired at will into the middle of the Mexican forces. The scene in front of Daniel could only be described as Mexican chaos. Shells from the plateau were devastating the enemy. Mexican infantry left unprotected on this side of the battle, panicked due to the loss of their artillery captured by Reid's companies. The Missouri infantry charged down the plateau ridge, swinging toward the right, out of reach of the Mexican cannons still intact in redoubts far to their left. Using Daniel's spyglass, Captain Reid pointed far afield at the body of Mexican Lancers charging the U.S. position on that side of the battle. The steady Missourians were dropping the lancers leading their charge. The lancers left alive turned and galloped back among their own force. Reid stood, ready to move forward.

"Let's finish this, men. We'll meet the main force and head for the redoubts on the other side."

Daniel and nearly all of Captain Reid's one hundred and fifty soldiers took off to join the four columns moving forward: chasing, killing, or gathering surrendering enemy soldiers on the way. Daniel incredibly met up with Lorenzo and Company 'G' midfield. The U.S. Artillery on the plateau continued to blast the redoubts on the far side of the battle and any Mexican units nearby.

As they approached the Mexican force near the left redoubts, Daniel heard the whine of a canister whistling ever closer. He could not locate the damn sound and just kept running. Suddenly, Lorenzo, who had spotted the incoming cannon shot, tackled Daniel with a knockdown at his shoulders. Daniel, unwilling to drop his rifle in his left hand or his revolver in his right, hit the ground chin first, a cactus needle piercing his thigh, Lorenzo all over his back. Then the explosion, fifty feet away. Shot, rusty nails, and flack sprayed the area. Daniel shoved Lorenzo aside. Blood and metal peppered his friend's back and legs. His head bled; something had knocked him out. Daniel had a couple of minor wounds on one leg.

No time to deal with Lorenzo; a medic would hopefully find him and take him to the field hospital. A determined Mexican unit continued fighting close to Lorenzo. Daniel's best help for Lorenzo would be to destroy the enemy, all four thousand, so that Mexican soldiers could not finish off his friend.

For the first time as a soldier, Daniel boiled, mad. Furious at his own stupidity for leaving his wife and son. He was crazy mad at Lorenzo for his sacrifice. He was angry at Mexico and any Mexican soldier that crossed his path. Daniel, enraged, ruthlessly killed, reloaded, and moved forward; killed, reloaded, and moved forward; killed again. With each fallen Mexican, he stuck full force with satisfaction, stepping on their chest to pull his bayonet out. *Get it over with*, he thought, *finish it*. The last redoubts fell to the Americans, and the Mexican army fled south. At around five o'clock, Daniel, exhausted, dirt-covered, spitting sand, bloodied from flack and a severe cactus wound, sat down in the sand to breathe, spent. The battle of the Rio de Sacramento finished.

The American army organized their position at the Mexican camp for the next three hours. Field hospitals were moved forward for the six hundred wounded Mexican and American soldiers. The seventy-two

Mexican prisoners were disarmed of knives and pistols, their hands tied behind them for a rough night's sleep. Graves were dug for the five hundred sixty Mexican soldiers killed during the battle. In front of the rows of Mexican graves, on a mound rising from the desert, two notable graves were dug; one for Major Owens and another for a Missourian infantryman, literally the only Americans killed during the battle.

Daniel spent the first hour and a half locating Sandy. He first went to the sand mound where he had left her but did not see her. Then the scout went to each of the three corrals holding the livestock. He, at last, picked her out, still saddled, and brought her over to where Company 'G' pitched their tents. Captain Smith had located Lorenzo in the field hospital, alive, awake, and dealing with his injuries. Unless an infection developed, Captain Smith felt Lorenzo would survive and, in time, rejoin the company.

Daniel walked to the hospital, waited another hour for a plaster for his lower leg and one for his thigh, and then sought out Lorenzo. He found his friend asleep on his stomach. Daniel stayed with Lorenzo for another two hours without disturbing him before returning to his tent and bedroll. Exhausted, he slept till Reveille woke him one and a half hours before dawn. He wolfed breakfast and assisted with the camp breakdown. Captain Smith suggested that Daniel report to Captain Harrison.

Harrison's orders for his scouting unit were simple. The scouts were to stay far ahead of Doniphan's troops and report back on the double if the Mexican army stopped their retreat and dug in for another battle. Two scouts headed to the east of the trail: Daniel and Mark to the west.

Two days later, the American troops entered Chihuahua without resistance. Daniel spent a week tracking the Mexican army retreating south. Stragglers regularly exited the body of the force in all directions, returning to their farms. The rest of the listless troops marched south. Daniel and Mark decided no threat of re-engagement existed and returned to Chihuahua.

Upon his return, Daniel tried to locate Lorenzo, only to find out that Lorenzo still occupied a bed at the field hospital at the Sacramento River. Many Mexican and American wounded were too injured to survive the trip to Chihuahua. In a month or so, the field hospital would move to Chihuahua.

Three of Slim's friends approached Daniel in the saloon the day he discovered where Lorenzo was recuperating. Eric, Slim's best friend, placed a wrapped package on the table before Daniel.

"Daniel, you may not have heard, but Slim died two days ago from a lance wound he received at the river battle."

Daniel, shocked, stood, shaking his head.

"That's a cryin shame, fellas. Slim was a good man, a good friend!"

"True Daniel, he led us well and charged those Lancers. Ahead of us all, he bayonetted two of those Mexicalles before a third lancer poked him good. Even with that wound, it took till now to kill him."

"Still, hard to take. You know Lorenzo is in the hospital up there. He covered me and took the shrapnel from a canister explosion. Saved my life for sure."

"Really," said Tim, another friend of Slim's, "from what he told us about Brazito, we figured he would stay buried under a wagon somewhere."

"He came through when it counted. They say he'll be OK."

"Daniel, that package is for you."

Daniel cut the string and unwrapped the paper to find Slim's buckskin coat.

"Eric, one of you Missourians should have this coat. I couldn't...."

"Slim told us to look you up, Daniel, while he could still talk. He really wanted you to have it. The deepest respect for you is what he said. Said you could have shot him on the Missouri River when you had the drop on him. Thought your moxie got us all out of a tricky situation."

"This coat means the world to me, fellas. A city slicker like me is damn lucky to have made it this far in a land as foreign to me as an African jungle. Damn, lucky. You boys and Slim. Yup, it means a lot.

"To the bar, boys, first one's on Slim and me."

Daniel removed his uniform jacket and tried the buckskin coat, which was stiff but a good fit. He got the bartender's attention and ordered shots.

Over six thousand Mexicans and Americans thrived in the city of Chihuahua. The city forms an oasis in the dry, hot region because of the intersection of the Chuviscar and Sacramento rivers. It is also the midpoint layover between the Río Bravo del Norte (Rio Grande) and the silver mining city of Hidalgo del Parral. Unlike New Mexico, the Mexican natives were not enthusiastic about the American army occupation. The American businessmen, on the other hand, demanded from Colonel Doniphan. Protection for their business interests, wagon shipments, and their families.

Colonel Doniphan's orders from his superiors seemed contradictory from one week to the next. News of Major General Zachary Taylor's and General Wool's success at the Battle of Buena Vista, four hundred fifty miles south near Saltillo, reached Doniphan and the troops in Chihuahua two weeks after their arrival. The rumor swirled in the camp that the Missourians would join the assembly of soldiers from Kentucky and Indiana and the Arkansas horsemen in Saltillo for the final march on Mexico City. A dispatch arrived two weeks later, dismissing Taylor's push further south. Doniphan's troops waited for further orders.

During March and most of April, Daniel made four and five-day scouting forays in several directions to assure Captain Harrison that the Mexican Army kept its distance. Daniel enjoyed the light duty. The farmers and Indians he met paid him little attention. Sandy and Daniel palled around in the mountains and plains, counting the days until Daniel's release from the army and his return to Portland.

The field hospital relocated from the Sacramento River battlefield to Chihuahua in April. Daniel visited Lorenzo whenever he returned from his scouting assignments. Lorenzo continued to fight an infection in his left leg and remained in the hospital. Dysentery and yellow fever struck many of the troops stationed in Chihuahua. Many died, including two soldiers from Company 'G' Incredibly, hundreds of soldiers perished from disease, whereas only a handful had been killed in battle. Daniel, thankful for the duty that kept him away from Chihuahua for the most part, remained healthy. There were now ten soldiers left in Company 'G.'

Then, in late April, Taylor ordered the First Missouri Mounted Volunteers to leave Chihuahua and join him at Saltillo. The American merchants could choose to follow or return to Santa Fe. Both options were chosen.

When Colonel Doniphan and his caravan arrived in Saltillo, they picketed their tents, set up corrals, and grouped their wagons near but not intermingled with the troops already encamped at the edge of the town.

Major-General Taylor's war council met daily for the next week, working out the strategy for prosecuting the war to its conclusion. Captain Smith attended all the meetings and reported to the remaining nine soldiers left in Company 'G.' Lorenzo Brennan had rejoined the Company but with a slight hitch in his step. Captain Smith indicated that the drift of the superiors at the war council shifted daily.

"There seems to be an impasse as to how to proceed. The Major General seems hesitant to advance on Mexico City. I respect Old Rough and Ready Taylor for common sense. He's right in a conflict with the rest of us. He's lost a lot of men and won a lot of battles. Hard to argue with him.

"The rest of the commanders want to push on to Mexico City and end the war. The problem is that all the American victories thus far have sent the Mexican battalions in full retreat to Mexico City. The last desperate stand for Mexico could be in that city, and we've experienced how desperate men fight when cornered."

"Tell them about Colonel Doniphan; what he said in the meeting today, Lieutenant Goddard reminded Captain Smith.

"That's the interesting piece. Colonel Doniphan pointed out that the twelve-month service of the men of the 1st Regiment of Missouri

Mounted Volunteers would end in June. He is legally bound to return his men to Missouri then."

The stable keeper, Nathan Barker, said, "That's the same for us, isn't it, Captain? I, for one, think it's time to head back to Portland."

"I'm in complete agreement, Nathan. We've done our duty. The new volunteers are being shipped in by steamship from the states and dropped off at Fort Brown, two hundred fifty miles east of Saltillo. I have permission from Colonel Doniphan for our Company to start for the coast tomorrow. We should be there in about two weeks, ahead of the Missourians. We'll travel light; two wagons, four mules, and four horses."

Lorenzo slapped Daniel on the back.

"Looks like you're right around the bend from seeing that pretty wife of yours, Daniel."

"I can't let myself believe it till I see her. I'm more than ready, that's sure."

Preparations were made, goodbyes were toasted at the saloon with Slim's Missourian friends, Captain Harrison, and Daniel's scouting friends, and the next day at dawn, Company 'G' left on the long trek home.

Daniel had purposely geared his thoughts to his duties as a soldier for twelve months. Now, each day, every day, he thought about home. He pictured his house, the hattery, and his church. His life in the West differed from life in the city. Before enlisting, he never would have imagined himself a scout for the army. He had grown up a city man and loved Portland. Of all the cities in New England, he considered Portland the prettiest, the busiest, and the best place to raise his family.

He would never have thought of himself as an expert horseman. The things he had done, the Mexicans and Indians that he had killed. Every dull day of the march to Fort Brown put more questions in his head and more fear in his heart. Looking at the sky and the beautiful horizons didn't keep the remembrances from resurfacing. He tried to focus on Cordelia and the feel of her. Then he would toss those dreams aside, looking down at the ground and Sandy's bobbing head and blowing mane.

The closer they got to the Fort, the more Daniel wanted to ride away alone with Sandy, build or find a cabin to live in and maybe hire out as a ranch hand somewhere. Forward momentum kept him a member of the Company. He wondered if others in the company had similar thoughts. As Daniel looked around on the trail, most men were sullen and lost in their histories.

Even Sandy weighed Daniel down. The horse was the best friend he had ever had. Never questioning, judging, yelling, or commanding; never a danger to him. *Should he ask Captain Smith if funds could be had to take him on the great steamship? Would that be allowed?*

A day or two before they reached the fort, Company 'G' camped at a farm owned by John Tarkinson, a Scottish immigrant. His voice boomed. He had red hair, as did his two sons, James, fourteen, and Jeremy, twelve. Tarkinson's wife wore a black blouse and skirt that must have been hotter than Hades in the plains sun. She worked on the meal, the laundry, or the garden, while Tarkinson jawed with Captain Smith. Captain Smith offered to provide the supper meal in exchange for water for the livestock and a place to picket the tents for the night.

Jeremy made no bones about his admiration for Daniel's horse. The family had two work horses and a saddle horse that James or John rode, depending on the chore required. After forty-five minutes of introductions and negotiations between Tarkinson and Captain Smith, Jeremy approached Daniel.

"Be glad to water and brush your horse, Mister."

"You're welcome to, lad. What's your name?"

"Jeremy."

"Give her a good brushing. You'll find oats in my saddlebag. My name's Daniel. If you have an extra handful of hay, she'd also appreciate that. No horse for yourself yet, eh?"

"Trying to save up for my own someday. I'm up to twenty dollars. We have plenty of grass and oats to feed another horse."

"Good luck to you, then. I've learned a lot from this gentle beast."

While Jeremy cared for Sandy, Daniel, and Lorenzo fed and watered the rest of the Company's livestock. From time to time, Daniel glanced over to watch Jeremy continuing to groom Sandy above and beyond what she required. With the camp settled in, Daniel went over to Jeremy.

"After supper, how about taking Sandy for a ride. She's used to eight hours daily, and we stopped here early."

"Sure, Mister. I have my dad's old saddle in the barn strapped to my size. If that would be OK?"

"That will be fine, Jeremy. It looks like supper is ready."

After supper, Daniel supervised Jeremy while he saddled Sandy. The boy knew horses, and Daniel remained quiet while Jeremy mounted and took off down the road to Fort Brown. Jeremy obviously cared for Sandy. The boy's excitement in riding a horse with the get-up and go that Sandy displayed seemed to thrill the boy. Daniel walked over to Captain Smith, smoking on the porch swing. The Tarkinsons were off working on additional nightly chores.

"That boy sure loves horses don't you think, Captain?"

"That's sure, Daniel. He hasn't taken his hands off Sandy since we got here."

"I'm thinking we should sell that horse to Jeremy. I'm not too fond of Sandy returning to battle with another soldier on her. Hate to see her come up lame or dead from a lance."

"What would you expect to get for her? That's one of the finest horses I saw on this trip. Steady as a rock and fast when you needed her."

"I'm thinking we could get at least twenty dollars for her out here on the range."

"She's worth a hundred dollars back in Independence or at Fort Leavenworth."

"Out here, I know where we can make a fast twenty dollars for her."

"Sounds right to me, Daniel. Check with Mr. Tarkinson."

Daniel led Sandy over to Jeremy in the morning after breaking camp.

"Jeremy, I've decided I could use twenty dollars a lot more than I could use a horse back in Portland, the city I'm from. I would consider selling her to you if you promise to care for her daily like you did yesterday."

"This horse, twenty dollars? I've got twenty dollars, but this is a champion horse. I can tell; worth five times that at least."

"Only to you and me, Jeremy. I want her to have a new best friend, and you measure up.

"Sandy, my friend, you take care. I'm going home."

Daniel climbed into the back of a wagon for the final ride to the fort. He handed the twenty dollars from Jeremy over to Captain Smith for the kitty.

Company 'G' at Fort Brown turned in their wagons, livestock, and pistols to the quartermaster. As Company 'G' headed for the dock to board the gunboat USS Vixen (returning to New Orleans for supplies and troops after the Siege of Vera Cruz,) Lorenzo told Daniel he wished to leave the company.

"I'm done with Portland, Daniel. I keep thinking about returning, and there just isn't enough to interest me. My parents are gone. My brother's family is there, but he's a son of a bitch that always thought me worth less than two cents.

"I'm a soldier now. I'm thinking of heading west to California for a while. I may sign up for the regular army if this war runs down. I don't know for sure. I hear parts of California are prettier and a lot warmer than Portland. The whores are better out here as well."

"My friend, you saved my life. I can't imagine you not being around. But you know, I sympathize with your thoughts."

Daniel coughed to settle the catch in his throat as he started to walk away. He turned back and hugged Lorenzo tight. Turning to go once more, Daniel waited until he felt he could speak plainly, but what else to say?

"Adios, Amigo."

"Goodbye, Daniel. Say hello and give a hug to Cordelia for me. I thought the same as you that she was the prettiest girl in Portland."

Company 'G' gathered on the dock in New Orleans at the end of the seven-day voyage on the USS Vixen. Having spent the first three days of the trip miserably seasick, Daniel got his sea legs. He could not wait to relay that fact to Samuel, his older brother, a shipmaster on the family sailing ship *Creighton II*. Captain Smith returned from the steamboat terminal with some news.

"The Big Missouri steamboat leaves the day after tomorrow for St. Louis. We'll transfer to a smaller steamboat at the Ohio River and continue to Louisville. On foot, we'll go around Louisville Falls and pick up a packet ship to Wheeling, Virginia. From Wheeling, we'll travel back on the National Road to Cumberland by stagecoach and then to Baltimore. Then we'll take the train back to Portland."

One of the Company 'G' soldiers eyed some of his friends, then took off his hat in deference to Captain Smith.

"Hold on a bit, Captain. Some of us have been talking. We'd like to see the sights in New Orleans for a while. This is a big city, the biggest we've seen since Baltimore, and we sure didn't take in the sights there. Since we're no longer in the army, we were thinking that you could give us our passage in cash, and we could work out getting home on our own."

"Alright," the Captain responded, "who's for continuing together or taking the travel fare in cash and pissing it away in the gambling saloons here in New Orleans. It's no one's business but your own."

Only four of the original Company 'G' decided to push on. Nathan, Lieutenant Goddard, Captain Smith, and Daniel. Hearing how excited the five other soldiers felt about New Orleans gave Daniel a turn. He wanted desperately to get home with all speed. Yet the ache in his stomach, not the fault of sea sickness, kept nagging him to stay west.

Captain Smith acquiesced to the group's demands to stay in New Orleans. He extracted funds from his money belt and paid off the five men. Then just the four headed for the dock. The Captain acquired the tickets for the *Big Missouri* paddleboat. The sidewheel wooden hulled packet at over three hundred feet could hold two hundred passengers. The purser working the dock directed the four remaining travelers to their two assigned staterooms. The Captain and Lieutenant headed to the onboard saloon. Nathan wanted to rest in the room he shared with Daniel. Daniel left the boat to explore the city, at least for one night.

Daniel preferred to be on his own. In truth, he felt almost afraid to go home. Besides the issued army trousers, clean but nearly brown from wear and washing instead of white, no one could tell the scout had recently soldiered in the war. He had scrapped his forage cap and now wore the hip-length, buckskin coat Slim had willed him. With his hair swept back behind his ears and reaching long past his collar, Daniel looked more like a mountain man than a skilled hatter. His beard was fair colored like his hair.

His eyes, somehow sunken in a too-thin, darkly tanned face, gave him away as a man who had seen killings.

But there it was. Daniel felt hollow since being away from the war, in the boat, and now in New Orleans. He had never looked into the eyes of the Mexicans he had shot. There were times a glance, in passing, at a face lying in the sand at Rio Sacramento reappeared in the back of his vision. He had seen the red Pawnee inches from his nose as he stuck him. Some would call the Indian an animal, but Daniel had smelled sweat and rancid tooth decay while the bulging muscles of his enemy twitched until still. Why did it bother him now?

After wandering in and out of saloons and gambling houses along the great river, Daniel happened on a small establishment serving crawfish and andouille grits. He sat in a dark corner of the bar. Four negro couples danced and cavorted to music produced by two Creoles pounding out syncopated beats on waste-high, hollow, skin-covered drums. A washboard scraper, a banjo strummer, and a piano player hammered dark hypnotizing chords in rhythm with the drums. The gyration of the women moving with actions far from the staid steps of Portland. The men dancing close with the women were ruffling their skirts, moving their hands over their partners' arms, necks, and butt cheeks.

Daniel drank another whiskey, losing himself in the atmosphere of the saloon, so foreign to both Portland and Mexico. Lost to both the dead men in his nightmares and Cordelia in his dreams, he tossed back another shot. In the pre-dawn, Daniel's wandering brought him back to the massive steamboat, *Big Missouri*, and his stateroom. Daniel visited the Creole saloon the next night, returning to the sidewheel steamboat just in time for it to depart from New Orleans.

The days on the steamboat seemed endless to Daniel. He could not swing up on his friend Sandy's back to ride off and clear his head. The steamboat pulled into shore each night. Steamboat Captains had a hard time avoiding steamboat sinking snarls and obstacles in the daytime, let alone in the dark of night. He kept losing the battle each night in his quest to hold Cordelia. He could not sleep even when he threw his blanket down on the floor of his cabin and tried to lie down on it. During the day, Daniel walked along one side of the boat, coasting by the farms and cities. Then he would hurry to the other side, so he would not miss anything interesting, waving to the kids on the riverside. At the mouth of the Ohio River, the four travelers returning to Portland were dropped off with fifty-three other passengers and transferred to another steamboat: destination Louisville.

The four soldiers from Company 'G' in Louisville explored the city together. Daniel agreed with the arrangement. If left alone, the fear grew, afraid of what he could not describe. The next day the four veterans hiked around the falls, forsaking the coach. It felt a little like the Company marches of old, now seeming so long ago. On August 2nd, 1847, Daniel disembarked from the steamboat *A. N. Johnson* in Wheeling, Virginia. The stagecoach station on the National Road at Wheeling also housed the new electric telegraph office, completed and wired into the cities to the east the previous month. Daniel entered the office, walked up to the counter, and spoke to the telegraph operator on duty.

"Sir, could you tell me if a telegram can reach my wife in Portland, Maine?"

"Let me check for you."

The Operator scanned an extensive list of east coast cities, looking up and nodding.

"You are in luck, Mister. Portland came online one week ago. A telegram sent today will reach your wife in Portland by messenger no later than tomorrow."

With the operator's help, Daniel, his hand shaking, formulated his telegram.

Cordelia Martensen

Portland, Ward 2, Cumberland, Maine

Boarding the stagecoach Wheeling Virginia today -(STOP)- home in seven days -(STOP)- healthy -(STOP)- in one piece -(STOP)- desperate to hold you -(STOP)- love -(STOP)- Daniel -(STOP)-

When Daniel returned to the group and informed them that telegrams could be sent from Wheeling to Portland, the three other travelers followed suit with telegrams to their loved ones. The world had progressed in the short year they had all been away, at least here in the east.

Every day, every hour ground away, like watching molasses drip from a spoon. The four rolled into Baltimore in five days and boarded the next train for New York. No group members slept on the B&O to New York or the B&M train to Portland.

At ten o'clock on August 9th, 1847, the four remaining members of the 1st Infantry, Maine, Company 'G' stepped down from the train onto the station platform in Portland, Maine. Captain Wendell P. Smith called the group to attention and saluted.

"At ease, men. This is it. I would not be standing here if it weren't for you three. I owe you everything, including an adventure enough for ten lifetimes. Go home, love your families, and thank you from the bottom of my heart for helping to win this war. This country has grown stronger from your efforts."

Captain Smith shook the hand and gave additional support to each soldier. Captain Smith leaned close to Daniel so the others would not hear.

"Daniel, I would have you know what an exceptional soldier, scout, and leader you have been. If you get bored with fashioning hats, Portland could use you on the police force or perhaps as a constable."

"Perhaps, Captain, but I am through with enforcement for now. As you say, maybe someday."

"That's all I ask, Daniel; think about it."

Daniel began the long walk home, trying to get rid of the nightmare images the Captain had conjured up with his good intentions. When he neared his neighborhood that afternoon, he first went to his favorite barbershop. Barber Kyle did not recognize him. In fact, as Daniel set down his bed roll and leaned his M1841 rifle in a corner, Kyle looked almost apprehensive. Daniel let the shave and the haircut do his talking. Barber Kyle smiled at Daniel as he swept the shorn locks and whiskers into a dustpan.

"Daniel Martensen, I thought Daniel Boone had come into my shop. You look fit. Tell us what happened to you. We hear the war is getting close to being over. Mexico City might fall any day now, is what the paper says. How did you do? See any Indians?"

"It was what it was, Kyle. I'm just mighty glad to be home. Got to get along now and see if Cordelia will still have me. Here are your two bits."

"No, I don't charge veterans, Daniel. Come in anytime."

"Thank you, Kyle."

Home! Daniel held the stock of his rifle in his left hand, slippery with sweat. His bedroll slung across his back, tied with a length of rope. He could not stop clenching and unclenching his right hand, shaking with apprehension. Cordelia flung the door open and ran to him, stopping to look at him.

"Daniel, I've been watching for you all day. Is it you, really you?"

Then she wrapped her arms around him, burying her head against his buckskin coat and chest. Daniel remembered, now, Cordelia's strength.

"Let me set this gear down so I can get a proper welcome."

Cordelia slid to one side but did not let go of Daniel as they entered the house. Daniel set his rifle in a corner and his bedroll and gear nearby. Turning back toward Cordelia, Daniel reached out, and the couple hugged for minutes, rubbing each other's back, whispering, "I love you," repeatedly.

There came a cry from the bedroom. Tears streaming, Cordelia broke their embrace and left Daniel in the hallway as she picked up baby Lemuel. She came back holding Daniel's son. Cordelia smoothed Lemuel's tangled, sweating hair as he yawned, stretching his arms with closed fists and looking at the strange man.

"This is your daddy, Lemuel. Can you say, Daddy?"

Lemuel, at one year and three months old, answered Cordelia.

"Mummy."

"This is your Daddy, Lemuel."

As Daniel approached, Lemuel turned away and buried his head in Cordelia's neck.

"That's OK, Cordelia. We must get used to each other again."

"Let's go into the parlor. Lemuel's walking now. Maybe he'll show you."

Daniel sat close to Cordelia in the parlor, feeling her leg under her dress against his leg. When she put Lemuel down, Daniel put his arm around her shoulder. After she glanced down to ensure Lemuel's safety, Cordelia leaned into Daniel. They kissed until they were out of breath.

Lemuel had walked shakily over to the chair six feet from the settee. Cordelia called to Lemuel, and he waddled over close enough for Daniel to pick him up. Daniel kissed the boy on his ear, and Lemuel giggled, so Daniel tickled his ear again and bobbed the baby on his knee. Then he leaned over and kissed Cordelia again. The tension in his body, the many months-long tension in his body, built up trying to get back to Cordelia, drained away.

The first few weeks were rough on the Martensen family. Many nights Cordelia awoke to find Daniel tossing on the floor where he had decided to try to sleep. Cordelia became the caretaker for her husband. She reasoned he was fine physically. God only knew what he had seen and done in the desert. It must have been horrible because Daniel had never held anything back from her before. She shielded him from interviews with newspapermen, friends, and curious neighbors. From discussions with her mother, Cordelia knew how much internal pain her father had experienced when he returned from the War of 1812.

On Daniel's part, even though his dream of returning home had miraculously come true, he seemed left with skeletal men he had shot dead riding on his back, their bone arms and hands holding him by the shoulders, dragging him down; always a burden. If not for Cordelia's patience, her respect for him not wanting to talk about the West, and her willingness to cuddle him at night and make love to a broken man, Daniel may have never recovered. Months passed before Daniel returned to the hattery to work with his partner.

Little by little, Daniel re-emerged from behind his hollow eyes and frontier demeanor. He never let Lemuel out of sight except when he was sleeping. The cathartic little boy comforted Daniel. The closer they became, the more Daniel relaxed with Cordelia, their friends, family, and the city he had abandoned. Daniel remained in charge of the boy when Cordelia and Lemuel attended church at First Parish. The only stories he related to Cordelia and his son were about the great National Road, the mighty Ohio and Mississippi rivers, and the multi-culture of New Orleans. The stories never extended past the end of the road. Missouri, Mexico, or the Indian frontier never came up in conversation. Cordelia had to refer to the two letters that had made the trip back to her describing the country sides where Daniel had traveled.

She had entertained a visitor from Philadelphia last March, Mr. Jeremiah Capshaw, who indicated he had a close, but brief relationship with her husband out west. Mr. Capshaw helped Cordelia connect with her faraway husband, as tight-lipped about the encounter on the Santa Fe Trail as Daniel. Cordelia surmised mutual respect between Jeremiah and Daniel. She suspected there had been a tight spot that Daniel and Jeremiah had weathered. The elderly Mr. Capshaw talked about his successful son, a doctor in Philadelphia, and his three grandchildren, one of whom matched little Lemuel's age.

Many weeks after his return, Daniel traveled to his father-in-law's house to return the M1841 rifle. Lemuel Bryant took Daniel on a carriage ride to Lemuel's club for lunch. Mr. Bryant stayed as sensitive as Cordelia to a reluctance by Daniel to speak of the war.

"Son, I think of you as my own. Let me just say how proud your father, the Captain, would be of your endeavors on both fronts, here in Portland and out west."

"That means the world to me, Lemuel."

Daniel was quiet for a while. Lemuel sat with him, silent with his own thoughts. Finally, Daniel felt composed enough to continue.

"I've seen things, done things that I can no longer imagine doing. Someone is not supposed to kill someone's someone. I will leave it at that."

"That's decidedly so, Daniel. There are times when there is no other choice. Sometimes wrong must be done in war to get to the right."

"I suppose so. I'm finding it hard to see the right in all the wrong.

"You know the Missourians were outnumbered wherever we dug in, but our rifles, pistols, and artillery were always far superior. Our leaders weren't that much smarter, but our soldiers weren't dirt poor farmers more comfortable with a pitchfork than a rifle."

"I understand, Daniel, I do indeed. Let us talk about other things. Have a dessert cake. How is my little grandson?"

Lemuel gave the M1841 right back to Daniel as a gift. Daniel reluctantly took it home and put it in a locked trunk in the attic of his house.

The hauntings continued to subside. Cordelia announced in July that another child would be joining the family. Daniel and Cordelia were close in their love for each other now, more than ever. Daniel enjoyed sleeping in bed, cuddling his beloved wife, a joy Daniel hoped he would never be without again. His wife and his son. They expunged the war from Daniel, and Daniel felt whole again with another child on the way.

Cordelia's fervent work on abolition caught Daniel's attention, and he began actively participating in her endeavors. Daniel thought of the men and women dancing in the crawfish restaurant in New Orleans and the nearby slave market where Africans were auctioned.

Cordelia had argued against the war with Mexico from the start. Daniel had embraced the Manifest Destiny of his beloved country, reaching the Pacific Ocean. Then he went to war and discovered the cost of that belief. The Pawnee, the Apache, the Comanche, the Mexicans, and the Africans seemed to be just trying to move forward with their lives like he wanted to move forward with his family.

Daniel thought more and more about this need to balance what he had seen and done in the war with efforts to help pull others in need up by their bootstraps. Six months after his return, Daniel searched his desk and dug out his handbook of the Independent Order of Odd Fellows, a fraternity he had joined in '43. Daniel's father, the Captain, had been a founding member of the Portland, Maine, Fraternal Organization of Freemasonry. The Odd Fellows had appeared more inclusive to Daniel, but he had treated the organization as a social club.

Somehow, now, the symbol of the three rings of the Odd Fellows represented the balance Daniel sought. Friendship. Love. Truth. Each stood for what Daniel wanted to believe in and promote. One day, Daniel and Cordelia sat on the settee after dinner while Lemuel played with his wooden blocks on the floor. Daniel unfolded his handkerchief to show Cordelia a gold ring and a small, circular pin.

"I have never mentioned a man I met out west named Jeremiah Capshaw. I managed a mighty big favor for him out there, and he kindly offered me a bit of gold from his claim in California. A few weeks ago, I concluded that we could use that bit of gold to create symbols of my love for family and the less fortunate."

"These are beautiful, Daniel."

"This ring I will wear to remind me of the Odd Fellows tenets. These three interlocked oval rings engraved on the outside of the band represent Friendship, Love, and Truth. That is what I want in my life. I never want to be separated from you again. On the inside of the ring, the inscription reads D. F. Martensen, Maine Lodge, I.O.O.F. - 1843. My name, in case I ever accidentally lose the band, the lodge I belong to, an abbreviation of Independent Order of Odd Fellows, and the year I joined the fraternity, 1843, three years before I became lost in war.

"Your pin has an ivory carving attached to a quarter-size coin of gold. The carving is the Liberty Bell of Philadelphia, an abolitionist society symbol for the freedom of all men. On the back, the inscription reads Cordelia my love, 11-5-1844, Daniel. May We Never Part. If you wish, we'll donate the rest of the gold nuggets to the First Parish Church or the Abolitionists movement."

Daniel placed his half-inch wide ring on the middle finger of his left hand; his wedding band remained on his ring finger. He fastened Cordelia's pin to her sweater above her heart. Cordelia could not have been more pleased with this awakening in Daniel.

On February 2nd, 1848, the Treaty of Guadalupe Hidalgo signing prompted Daniel and Cordelia to attend church to pray and rejoice at the war's end. California, New Mexico, the Indian Territory, and the disputed Texas border were ceded to America for fifteen million dollars in reparations.

That March, news of gold discovered in northern California stirred citizens of Portland and across the United States. Three families from

First Parish Church suddenly disappeared from the congregation. They had abandoned Portland for the trip west in search of gold.

Daniel wished them luck. If the harshness of the trip did not kill them all, the Indians or the Yellow Fever probably would. The riches of gold might elude them.

Besides, Daniel thought, glancing at his wife and son at the breakfast table as he read the newspaper; *I already have all the California gold I will ever need.*

5 |

HANDLER

I saw two ants, one red, the other nearly half an inch long, and black, fiercely contending with one another.

From Chapter 12 of "Walden, or Life in the Woods"
(1854)

1863

The night was moonless, dark, calm, and cloudless. The grass where the boy lay warmed from the heat of the late June sun. He lay beside his father, Daniel, who took one hand away from pillowing his head to point skyward. The boy's legs were crossed and stretched like his father's. Like his father, he chewed on a tall weed he had pulled. Daniel, twice the length of his son, turned close enough to the boy to whisper.

"There, see those stars lined up in a gentle curve ending in those four stars? Looks sort of like a ladle. Like a dipper for a water bucket, maybe.

"I see it, Dadda."

"Ok, imagine a line from the two stars at the end of the dipper up to that brighter star? No, the stars at the other end of the box. Yes, that's right, now you have it. Let me take your hand. Up, up a little more. Yes, that star. That is the north star."

"It's not as bright as that star over there."

"No, but it is the star that the big dipper circles in the sky every night like a wagon train out west to keep out Indians. The points of light

|259|

appear to travel around one star like the center of a pinwheel. The tips turn in the wind. The north star would be the pin in the pinwheel.

"But none of the stars are moving."

"It's our planet Earth that is moving, just very slowly. Too slow to see. But if we came out and laid in the grass just before the sun, the big dipper would be upside down pouring water out instead of holding it like it is now."

"There's no water up there, Dadda."

"Son, the north star is always right there, no matter what time of night. Your grandfather could steer his ship toward that star and never be lost on his way to all the faraway places his ship sailed. To Germany, Sweden, Morocco, Brazil, and Ireland. You've heard your mother talk of Ireland, haven't you?"

"Yes, I will go to all those places when I'm older. Dadda, is that heaven up there? Is that where Ella Marie went?"

"Yes... You can't see her 'cause she's even farther away than all those stars, but she's there."

The boy curled into his father's side. He missed Ella. They had played together all day long until she got sick. Ella would have been eight last month, but she went away. The boy would be five next month. The family was off-kilter. Like a gurgling brook, Ella always giggled, always smiled. Lemuel and Cordelia, the boy's older brother, sister, and mother, rarely smiled. The boy kept looking at Ella's bed to see if she might be sleeping there. The stars seemed so far away, and Ella even farther. He wiped his eyes.

"Here now, let's get you up to bed. The Captain taught me all about the stars, and I've got to get busy and teach you. Perhaps we'll have time again tomorrow night if it is clear. How about it?"

"Yes, Dadda, I would like that."

"Tomorrow is Saturday, and I must patrol and inspect the docks, son. Want to come along?"

"Yes, Dadda."

The two entered the house, and the father swatted the boy to bed. As they breezed through the kitchen, Mother set down her knitting and stopped Father with a hand on his wrist.

"Everything all right? It is way past the boy's bedtime."

"Yes, Mother, I showed the boy the big dipper."

"Is that all? Is he OK?"

"He'll be fine; I'm taking him on my watch tour tomorrow morning. I'll drop him off here at ten and have a coffee before heading out again."

"I swear, since this Portland constable job, you're rarely home."

"I thought I'd take the boy with me tomorrow morning. I'm a year too old for the draft this time. They decided to throw me a bone when they hired me as a constable for Portland. Portland is about as far away from the war as Alaska.

The city needs protection, and you're the ablest for it. You know how I felt when you went off to war in 46, but this time it's about slavery, and by God, this country must get back on track once and for all. You've had your war, Daniel, and you're doing your duty in this one. If it helps the boy to get past Ella, take him with you, but stay safe, both of you."

"It helps me too, I guess."

Daniel drew up Cordelia from the chair for a long embrace. Ella Marie somehow between them. Daniel could feel the jump in Cordelia's chest, the beginning of a sob, and hugged her tighter to soothe it.

Daniel and the boy were checking doors and alleys down at the docks when Ben Jensen ran up to Daniel from further down the street.

"Sir, we've been looking for you. Something's going on down by the Chesapeake. Jedidiah Jewett wants you down at Customs; he thinks Lt. Davenport has deserted and stolen the *Caleb Cushing*. With the tide coming in, it's a slow sail, so we might catch her if we're quick."

"That makes no sense, man. I've met the Lieutenant. Since the captain died, the lieutenant is temporarily in charge of the *Cushing*. He's solid. There's another explanation."

The three jogged toward the wharf, the boy running to keep up. A block before reaching the empty dock where *Caleb Cushing* had berthed, the boy heard a scuffle and moan from the alley in the back of Gerber's bait shop. He tugged on Daniel's sleeve to stop. Daniel and Ben Jensen investigated with the boy in tow and found three men trussed up and gagged behind barrels. One of the men had a small gash on his forehead and caked blood across one eye, cheek, and chin. The three men were untied. The boy stood silently, eyes wide, as Ben attended to the gash with his handkerchief, and the shortest sailor answered to Daniel's badge.

"Name's Ezekiel Camden, sir; Zeke is how they call me. We're the crew of the Caleb Cushing. Rebel raiders led by Lieutenant Read boarded us at about 1:30 this morning while we were all asleep. Nothing we could do. Gagged before we could even raise the alarm. They worked over Lieutenant Davenport well and took him when they sailed.

"They knew about the *Agawam* and *Pontoosic* gunships we got here, and I think that's what they're after. I heard the first officer convince their lieutenant to take the *Cushing* out because the *Chesapeake* would take too long to fire its boiler. They intend to sneak back to blow the gunships."

Daniel cut off the explanation.

"Ben, you go rouse Mathew Stryker. You can see his house from here. It's green. See it? He's got a fast horse and rides in races at the fair each year. He needs to ride like the devil to Fort Preble and bring back soldiers, either by boat across the bay or fast march. We'll go to the customs office, gather some deputies and meet the soldiers at the Chesapeake."

Ben took off on the run. The others, including the boy, ran to the customs office. They joined a small group of men clustered around Mr. Jewett, the customs officer.

"We'll catch that deserter who took the *Caleb Cushing*. The *Forest City* is fired up and ready to go now, boys. Daniel, you coming?"

"Listen, Jedidiah, a Confederate raiding party attacked the *Caleb Cushing* ship. They captured Lieutenant Davenport, as his crew here can testify. I have sent for soldiers from Fort Preble. You men should follow the *Cushing*. These three men can stay and help fire the *Chesapeake*. We'll try to catch you with the Chesapeake when the soldiers arrive. The *Cushing's* no match for the *Chesapeake*, right boys?"

Ezekiel held up Daniel, grabbing his arm.

"Listen, these raiders were well informed. They tried to force Lt. Davenport to tell them where he hid our gunpowder cache. We've got 400 pounds on board, but we all played dumb on it."

"They must have come to port somehow. Jedidiah, have you seen any ships or boats you haven't registered?"

Jedediah looked down the line of boats at the wharf.

"Let's see, the *Jimmy Shot* here is registered, the blue sloop next to it, and then Kelman's trawler. You know that next boat, the fishing schooner? I don't recall that one. It's been so hectic this morning, but that boat, called The *Archer*, that one I don't recognize."

"All right," Daniel commanded, "We'll investigate the *Archer* while you men get going on the *Forest City*. Be ready; if the *Chesapeake* doesn't catch up, you must take on the rebels. I don't like your chances against Caleb Cushing's thirty-two-pounder pivot gun and 400 pounds of gunpowder. Be careful. These men here will fire up the *Chesapeake*. We'll look over the *Archer*, gather more men, and fill in whoever oversees the soldiers when they get here. All right, let's get to it."

The boy had picked a crate to sit on outside the gaggle of men but close enough to hear. Mouse-quiet, he kept still. He tried to make himself invisible, afraid his father would somehow send him home or make him go sit in the customs office. The man-talk fascinated the boy, especially his father's take-charge demeanor and steerage of the men.

His father always spoke softly, a gentleman at home as he put the boy to bed, read a book, or taught him about the stars. He never talked loudly to his mother or his brother and sister. The boy knew Father could be angry. He thought of the few times he had been spanked. It hurt like the dickens. Father rarely even spoke during it, and the spanking ended in seconds, stung for minutes, and the boy remembered the lesson learned hours later.

Eight men scampered around on the *Forest City,* casting off lines and loading the few muskets they had brought from home. Seconds later, the ship left the dock and headed after the *Caleb Cushing* ship.

Three men were asked to rouse more volunteers. Daniel clarified that they must awaken Samuel, his older brother, who lived four blocks from the dock. Samuel, a reputed shipmaster like the boy's grandfather, would pilot the *Chesapeake.* The legitimate captain was visiting relatives inland.

Daniel and two others walked over to the Archer while the boy followed behind about thirty feet. They boarded and began combing the fishing trawler for signs of life or evidence of the raiding party. Sure enough, two men were found down in the hold, gagged, and bound like the crew of the *Caleb Cushing.* The fishermen rubbed their wrists and worked their jaws to relieve the aches caused by the ropes.

They introduced themselves as Al Bibber and Elbridge Titcomb. Both were Falmouth fishermen who had been out hauling trawls. Yesterday, when they saw the schooner *Archer* approaching them, they assumed the crew consisted of drunk fishermen celebrating their day's haul. They had tried to wave off the *Archer,* but the ruffians boarded and captured Al and Elbridge. They hustled Elbridge down to the hold while the soldier in charge, Lieutenant Read, questioned Bibber.

At this point in their story, both fishermen looked at each other. Al Bibber, wringing his hands, continued.

"Well, sir, we ain't no soldiers. Elbridge's daughter was just born last month, and I, well, they wanted to know about Portland's armaments and the steamships in the harbor here. I told 'em about the *Agawam* and *Pontoosic* gunships, the *Caleb Cushing,* and *Chesapeake.* I didn't think they'd be foolish enough to mount a raid knowing we had Fort Preble soldiers and city constables patrolling. Wrong, I guess. They brought us up on deck at midnight, and we had to navigate them into the harbor.

We didn't know where they docked because we were blindfolded back in the cabin. Heard the rustle this morning and hoped for rescue."

Daniel had heard enough.

"Baby, family, soldier or not, you put many men's lives and this town in danger. One of you must go to the dock the soldiers might arrive on. The others should go around the bay to see if the soldiers are coming. Urge speed and signal us."

Within fifteen minutes, soldiers from Fort Preble arrived with a wagon full of muskets; sweat soaking their uniforms from the near-running march. They distributed the muskets to the fifty new volunteers that had gathered. The mayor, Jacob McLellan, an able seaman, and the boy's uncles, Samuel and Martin, were among the volunteers. The Mayor demanded to command the *Chesapeake* with Samuel to navigate. Daniel reminded them of the onboard cache of gunpowder hidden in the captain's quarters on the *Caleb Cushing's*. As the *Chesapeake* disembarked for the chase, the boy waved to Uncle Samuel. Fifty feet out from the dock, the *Chesapeake* lurched as the now full head of steam turned the propeller shaft.

The mayor assigned Daniel, the three other constables, five soldiers, and ten policemen on city protection duty. The boy stood out, noticed for the first time by Daniel as the confusion on the dock subsided.

"We've got to get you home, son; your mother is going to skin the both of us when she hears."

"I'll be quiet, Dadda; can't I stay with you?"

"Enough adventure for today. You are now a proper soldier," Daniel turned to the group awaiting his orders, "Men, we'll head for Franklin Wharf, where the *Agawam* and *Pontoosic* are berthed. I'll continue, drop off the boy at home, and return. Then we'll fan out across the coast of Portland and South Portland and await the result of the ship's chase. Don't fire your musket unless you are fired upon or can determine the advance of a Confederate soldier. The spies may or may not be in uniform. No sense in warning any Rebs. We won't start the city alarm siren either. With the Rebs retreating, a city-wide panic may be avoided."

The volunteers dispersed to take up positions at various intersections in the city. Daniel led the five soldiers to Franklin Wharf with the boy on his back. From a block away, Daniel could see that the crews of the two gunships were on alert. He started to walk down Union Street when the boy grabbed each side of Daniel's head and attempted to wrench it to the left. The boy pointed to a slight movement by a large shipping crate. He saw enough of a uniformed shoulder for Daniel to duck with the boy, signal the men to fan out, and proceed with silent caution. He set the boy down by a corner where two crates were angled and signaled him to silence. He checked his musket, ready to fire, and advanced at an angle to better determine the friend or foe that the boy had spotted.

"You there, throw down your weapons and put your hands up high where we can see them. Quick now, I'll fire and not ask twice."

Again, the strength of his father's voice astounded the boy as he peeked out from the protection of the crates. The first uniformed Confederate soldier stood and faced the Union regulars at Daniel's command. As Daniel advanced, a second Reb stood fifteen feet from the first, and then over on the far right, a third hidden Reb stood with hands held high.

Makeshift firebombs were found near the rebel hiding spots. The raiders had gotten close enough to throw them in the hope of hitting the gunships. No more raiders were located. The Captains of the gunships came forward, greeted the soldiers and Daniel, and ordered ten men from each crew to sweep the area for a five-block radius. No other raiders were discovered.

Daniel shook hands with both Captains.

"The boy spotted that one crouching, ready to light and throw. Knew enough not to cry out so we could surprise 'em."

Captain Tenbrink kneeled.

"That a boy. When this is all over, I'll give you a tour of our ship. How does that sound?"

The boy nodded. Daniel took the boy's hand.

"Let's get you home."

Daniel and the boy were walking side by side up the rise toward their home on Wilmot St. when an enormous explosion rattled their eardrums. Turning, they saw fire, smoke, and wood ascending high before falling back to the sea outside Portland Harbor. The blast's thunder reverberated through the city's hills and buildings. Daniel turned the boy toward home, and they marched double time the rest of the way.

Cordelia burst through the cheesecloth screen door and picked up the boy.

"That explosion, Daniel? It felt like an earthquake inside the house."

"Long story, Mother, but we are both safe, and I must get back to the docks. The short of it is that a Confederate raiding party landed in Portland last night and stole the *Caleb Cushing* ship. The *Forest City* and the *Chesapeake* gave chase, and we don't know yet what happened out to sea. I've got to get back to the docks."

"You stay right here and tell me what's going on? Are we in danger? Where was the boy during all this? Has anyone been injured? Are we going to evacuate the city? How close is the Confederate army?"

Daniel reluctantly gave a complete account of his and the boy's activities during the morning patrol and skirmish. An hour later, Daniel stood, retrieved his canvas-wrapped, percussion lock rifle from the closet, and started for the door. Just outside the door, he met his brothers, Samuel, Martin, and William, who had been late to the fray. Cordelia stepped outside as well. The boy heard the voices of his uncles and rushed silently to the cheesecloth door to listen.

Martin explained.

"You heard the gunpowder cache on the *Caleb Cushing* explode. Just about blasted me off the deck of the *Chesapeake*, Daniel. My ears are still ringing." He knocked the side of his head.

Samuel continued the narrative.

"We got 'em, Daniel. Picked them up in the *Cushing's* lifeboats after they set fire to her. The *Forest City* kept them tied up until we got there, skirting around, firing muskets, trying to stay beyond the range of the *Cushing's* 32-pounder pivot gun. Luckily, the Rebs weren't used to firing that big a gun. We just had the two six-pounders to work with on the *Chesapeake*. Samuel was a master at the wheel of the *Chesapeake*, Daniel. Mayor McLellan grew quiet after the first five minutes while Samuel cut off the *Cushing* and raised his arm when he wanted the six-pounders to fire. Something to see, all right."

"Ah, Daniel," Samuel shuffled his boots, "I know this harbor as well as the 'Captain' did. They were fighting the wind, and I had the steamer. The *Forest City* kept their pivot gun busy."

All the rebels had been rounded up and marched off to the fort. Lieutenant Davenport went to the hospital with one eye bruised shut and a broken jaw. Still, he had not disclosed to the Confederate soldier the whereabouts of the extra gunpowder on board the *Caleb Cushing*. When the Confederates ran out of ammunition and gunpowder, Lieutenant Read was forced to abandon *Caleb Cushing*, setting the ship on fire and jumping into the lifeboats.

Several soldiers from Fort Preble had stayed behind, and the Mayor had indicated to Samuel that Daniel, the other constables, and policemen should get a good night's sleep and take over from the soldiers in the morning. The crisis would be over if no other confederates were found in the city by Daniel and the other city officers or by the soldiers combing the countryside.

Cordelia heard a soft sigh of relief from the door, and when she went back into the house, she saw the heels of the small boy as he ran for the stairs. Daniel caught Cordelia by the elbow.

"I'll put the boy to bed, mother. He acted a lot bigger than his age today. Sleep will be slow."

Daniel went upstairs and sat on the end of the boy's bed. The boy turned toward his father, forgetting to feign sleep.

"Did you win the war tonight, Dadda? Is it over for good?"

"No, son. Portland and everyone who lives here were incredibly lucky tonight. No one died; only a few were injured, and we captured the rebel soldiers." Daniel looked at his wide-eyed son, trying to determine his tolerance for the realities of war.

"They blew up a valuable ship out there beyond the harbor tonight. So, who won? I'd say we both lost. The Rebs lost their freedom, and we lost a good size cutter. We won't talk about the war anymore, son. This Great Rebellion has been going on for years and likely will continue for years. Your mother, brother, and sister, and you are safe as can be here in Portland. Most of the war is way far away from here. It's my job to be sure you are safe. That's why I'm a hatter during the week and a constable on the weekends and at night. Now stay in bed and go to sleep, soldier."

The boy, exhausted, rolled over, tucking his head deep into his pillow, asleep before Daniel left the room.

1866

In 1866, the year after the war ended, Thomas Willow and his young wife Bethany boarded the train in Mechanic Falls, Maine, for what proved to be a two-hour trip to Portland. The six stops to Portland brought many passengers eager to get to the 4th of July celebration. Thomas had purchased tickets as soon as he read about the planned events in the Eastern Argus newspaper.

During the war, Willow had been an assistant surgeon at the camp hospital of the Army of the Potomac in Falmouth, Virginia. For the past year, since the end of the war, Thomas woke in the middle of the night sweating. He had visions of the arms and legs of amputees being carried off from the surgery in wicker baskets. Maybe the beautiful city of Portland and the touted grand fireworks display could refresh his soul and put the war behind him. Bethany hoped to see the hot air balloon exhibition. She also looked forward to the excitement of horse racing; and, of course, the fireworks.

The couple stepped off the Grand Trunk Railroad at the Portland station at eleven o'clock with plenty of time to walk the two miles to Deering's pasture, following signs to the hot air balloon exhibition. The day, hot and dry, lemonade stands along the parade route provided refreshments for one cent. The wind picked up and helped Bethany along the walk, billowing her dress and acting like a sail.

James Morris picnicked with his family on the wharf south of the parade's route. Thousands of Portland residents, out-of-town guests, and strangers established viewing spots for the spectacle. Setting out folding chairs or blankets, the people passed the time reading newspapers and books or playing cards. The excitement grew as the crowd multiplied, eager for the parade to begin.

James married the daughter of the majority stockholder in the Canfiss Brush Company of Portland. His wife, a daughter of Walter Canfiss, encouraged James to step up and manage the company when Walter retired. James drove his wife and three school-age children on a buggy ride in the country before establishing their picnic spot on the wharf, eight blocks east of the brush factory. Today he hoped not to have to hobnob with employees, customers, or anyone but the most important people in his life; his wife, his son, twelve, and his two daughters, seven and four.

The police department slimmed its ranks four months after the war ended as the nation settled into peace. Daniel returned to work at the hattery, no longer patrolling the city as a constable of Portland. Today, Daniel volunteered to help the department with crowd control as a mounted patrolman and to participate in the parade, which included members of the police force. Daniel did not mind.

As an avid abolitionist, Cordelia had demonstrated high spirits and smiles since the war ended. The dark time of Lincoln's assassination notwithstanding. The nation started anew, and Portland epitomized the heart of this new age of peace and reason. The city council had diverted war reserves to a promised firework display to rival the other great cities of America. Daniel proudly contributed to the momentous event. At the last celebration planning meeting, he handed out the custom powder blue bowler hats with red and white ribbon trim to each participating constable marching in the parade.

Daniel split his time between the baseball game crowd and the horse racing track. He stayed mounted, leading his horse between two men arguing and upsetting three older ladies trying to view the races. When the men saw the large baton holstered in Daniel's saddle, they dusted off and cooled down. Daniel, from his horse, asked another gentleman to fetch two lemonades for the men, and tensions lessened. Daniel provided buggy traffic control and parking at the baseball game.

Late in the day, Daniel put his horse into an easy trot to where the constables were to meet for the parade.

Cordelia had been baking since dawn, first at home and then at First Parish Church. Daughter Cordelia and her mother brought three rhubarb pies to the church. At least three boys had dogged Cordelia's seventeen-year-old daughter about the picnic. Cordelia picked Nels Peterson to walk her to the parade at the expense of William Grotten and Steven Lowver. She worked furiously next to her mother at the church, more than ready at five o'clock to escape baking duties and walk side by side with Nels to their favorite picnic spot in the park.

Cordelia and her daughter Cordelia made six dozen number cakes. The fast-to-bake and easy-to-mix cupcakes called for one cup of butter, two cups of sugar, three cups of flour, four eggs, one cup of milk, and one spoonful of soda. All the volunteers had brought their cup sets for these small individual cakes. Late in the afternoon, the last batch came out of the oven.

Lemuel, Daniel's eldest at twenty, attended the game between the Portland Eon baseball team and its rival, the Lowell Nine of Boston.

Cordelia's and Daniel's youngest boy played Cowboys and Indians at Timothy and Bradley Hammersmith's house on the north side of town. The boy would turn eight in a week. He had already invited Timothy, two years older than the boy, and twelve-year-old Bradley, to his birthday party. The three boys were good friends and First Parish Church Sunday school members. They considered themselves rugged cowboys. They were catching frogs while not roping fence posts or playing marbles. At 4:45pm, Mrs. Hammersmith directed Bradley and

Tim to walk the boy back to First Parish Church and hand him off to his mother.

This responsibility allowed all three boys to thread the gathering crowds and pick up other friends from school. They needed to travel southeast from the Hammersmith's house, an easy twenty blocks trip. They horsed around and made slow progress, excited for the parade and fireworks to start at dusk. They schemed ways of sneaking to where the circus animals might be housed. They bet whether the hippopotamus would be walking on a leash or housed in a circus car pulled by Clydesdales in the procession.

The boys had traveled south a few blocks, hoping to sight the hippo, when Timothy pinpointed smoke rising southwest of their position. They heard a church bell ring out, signaling a fire. The three lads headed toward the smoke, a new adventure. The boy figured his father would join the firemen in putting out the blaze.

The crowds the boys passed seemed more interested in the parade's start and a good viewing position than the smoke so far away. The boys broke away from the crowds and headed a few more blocks southwest, the wind blowing clouds of smoke overhead quickly. The boy pointed up at the tiny bits of burning debris floating overhead. The fire rained ash on them. The boys stopped. Timothy pointed to the three buildings seen in the distance, blazing away. The most significant fire any of them had ever seen by far. Bradley took control.

"That's it. We better head back. With this wind, that fire could come right at us? I say we get back to our house as fast as we can. Our house is three blocks from Back Cove. The closer I am to water during a fire, the better off I'll feel."

The boy made his own decision.

"I'll go with you and Tim. My parents both know I'm at your house today. They'll find me or my father might be too busy firefighting to bother with me. I can stay the night, right, if I need to?"

"Yeah, you bet. Let's go."

Heading north, the boys reencountered the parade crowd, women's faces masked in fear. The children gathered belongings to leave Portland or return home. The fire headed toward the people, and the wind blew with near-gale force. Many were heading home as rapidly as possible, thinking of their possessions. The obvious out-of-towners were hitching up and heading north, hoping they could get out of town to the west. They might be trapped against the Fore River or Back Cove if not. All thoughts of the parade and fireworks evaporated. The people, for the most part, packed up and moved along. Some little ones cried, with mothers trying to quiet them. The crowd became more challenging for the boys to push through. They reached a rise at around eight o'clock and looked back at the fire. The fire had tripled in size. Bradley said the largest building in the city, the sugar factory, now threw flames high into the sky. It looked like an eight-story square torch, lighting the dusk of the day, turning the glow in the sky orange. Luckily, the boys could not yet feel the heat.

Halfway back to First Parish Church after the ball game, Lemuel heard the church bell alarm, the game still on his mind. The Eons had lost to the Boston team, and he regretted quitting the team two years ago to pursue his career in the jewelry store. The clanging bell called for action. Lemuel turned around repeatedly to determine the direction of the sound of the alarm. He headed southwest, soon seeing smoke in the sky that urged his pace. When he arrived at the blazing warehouse on Commercial Street, the fire set a second and third adjacent building on fire. The wind gusting acted like giant bellows, hampering the scores of people trying to control the fire. As firefighting crews sprayed water on the east side of the buildings, three bucket brigades formed on the west side. Lemuel joined the end of one of the lines. He relieved an exhausted runner who traveled forty feet from the house, providing the water to the man at the back of the line, handing buckets from person to person. The fire was too large already for this slim help. Everyone kept at it as the fire chiefs from the various city stations conferred and organized around the new steam engines. More volunteers arrived, and the brigade lengthened, making unnecessary Lemuel's running. As more and more men and women came to help, building owners made themselves known and loudly cajoled the crowd into dousing faster and throwing water higher, pitching in frantically.

Mr. Morris had driven up with his buggy. The fire raged two buildings west of the brush factory.

"You men who just arrived, I have water in my building and tarps we could wet and tie down on the roof of the brush factory over there, preventing the spread of the fire; what do you say."

"Lead the way!"

Lemuel broke away from the brigade line to follow the ten men and two women led by James Morris. The group entered the building and climbed three floors of stairs and a ladder to the roof hatch, transferring the tarps through the opening. The tarps were heavy. The men struggled to spread them out in the strong wind. After a time, they succeeded, rigged a hose from the top floor, and produced buckets to wet the tarps. Mr. Morris thanked each man and woman for their efforts and used his coat to snuff any stray sparks from the burning warehouses. The fire raged two and then one building away from the brush factory. James worked faster and faster to catch and douse the sparks and burning debris traveling to his building.

A man standing at the roof's edge shouted at James, "Mr. Morris, Mr. Morris, someone on the ground is pointing to one of your corner windows."

"Alright, keep going while I investigate."

Lemuel followed James while the rest of the volunteer crew continued spraying the tarps with water, the roof well-wetted and safe for now. James ran along the hall toward the north side of the building. On the third floor, Lemuel searched in the opposite direction. Nothing to report. They knew there was trouble in the south corner when they reached the second floor. Sure enough, an open window in the corner room had let fire from the adjacent warehouse jump across to the office. The open office door gushed heat, preventing Lemuel from getting close enough to even think about working on the fire. James stepped through, however, and Lemuel reached for and grabbed hold of Mr. Morris's collar and dragged him back. The intense heat made breathing difficult and painful.

They both scurried upstairs to the roof. Mr. Morris yelled, "Everyone must drop what you are doing and leave the building. The second floor is on fire, and we must get past that floor to the street."

Lemuel ensured everyone heeded Mr. Morris's warning and was the last person off the roof. The heat in the stairwell when he reached the second floor intensified. He stuck close to the wall, able to make his way in the increasing smoke. Lemuel descended to the first floor and out of the building. The factory floor soon became engulfed by the blaze. The group that had helped wet the roof stood by in despair.

Choking a bit, James Morris addressed the bystanders.

"Thank you again for all your efforts, but you know what? We have to keep working and stop this fire somehow, somewhere. Come on."

Lemuel set off after Mr. Morris in the direction of the nearest fire engine for instructions on where next to assist. He glanced left at the Brown's Sugar Factory, now in full blaze. The eight-story building alone doubled the size of the fire, the heat from which kept volunteers and firemen back half a block.

Daniel's horse, Showdown, fire trained, held steady as could be expected in the face of the blaze. So far, the horse had not hesitated as Daniel pushed him to a gallop on a third trip over to the fire. He had been assigned communication duty between the City's west and east sides. He made stops at the City Hall, Custom House, and the fire command station, relaying the firefighting progress and the fire chief's directives and decisions to the Mayor's office. A mounted courier quickly became essential when two telegraph stations burned down and a third needed evacuating.

Daniel always chose Showdown, a chestnut 16-hand quarter horse on mounted duty. Every six months, he made sure to drill and reacquaint the horse with his riding habits whether or not he had been assigned mounted responsibility. A constable or policeman treated his horse as essential equipment for his job, like his baton, badge, and boots. As they galloped toward the fire Daniel, reins in his left hand, rubbed soft reassurance along Showdown's mane and neck with his right hand. Showdown stood two hands taller than Sandy, Daniel's horse in Mexico. Daniel had grown ten pounds heavier as well. He arrived back at the fire around nine-thirty. He handed Showdown to a volunteer for a quick towel rub down. Chief Tanley met him with yet another dispatch ready for transfer.

"Daniel, we've shifted crews further north along the west edge of the fire. It's getting bigger, not smaller. We've got two crews blowing up buildings we think might provide a break. If worse comes to worst, we'll make a last-ditch stand at Congress Street before it gets to City Hall. The beast is eating the business district now. I know residents are piling their belongings into City Hall, probably the most fireproof building in the city. Of course, I might have said that about Brown's Sugar Factory yesterday. Better get this new report back to Mayor Stevens."

"Yes. I've seen people heading for First Parish Church as well. My family needs checking. So, it's City Hall, the Custom-house, and First Parish Church. Then I'll be back."

Daniel nuzzled Showdown, thanked the man who toweled his mount off, mounted, and spun the horse around. Showdown jumped into a gallop.

Bethany Willow had changed her mind about the horse races. After the hot air balloon fiasco in Deering's pasture, she talked Thomas into seeing the hippopotamus and the elephants on the Western Promenade. The Australian circus promised a "gigantic show," according to the flyers posted all over Portland.

Thomas and Beth had waited patiently at the edge of the field while balloonists fired the burners and spread the balloon to allow the hot air to raise the envelope. However, the wind gusts proved too overpowering, a rip developed in the envelope, and the balloon shredded. The master balloonist apologized to the observers through his bull horn, shaking his head in grief, realizing that he should never have attempted a flight on such a windy, dry day.

The couple walked back to the Western Promenade, and both enjoyed the rest of the afternoon watching the carnies and animal trainers prepare the elephants for the procession. At six-thirty, the couple headed back toward Portland to catch the parade. Strangely, the further they walked, the more people they noticed heading toward them. They stopped a hurrying couple.

"Sir," they asked, "Isn't the parade and fireworks this direction?"

The man Thomas had stopped pointed to the east.

"There's a fire. You can see the smoke. It's bad, my man, and there will be no parade. If you want to see real fireworks keep going. We're heading for the train."

Thomas now saw the smoke in the east and flames reaching above the buildings in the distance. They were on the conflagration's west side and safe to proceed to the train station unless the wind changed direction. They arrived at the boarding platform along with throngs of others of a like mind, just as a train pulled out. The next train, the last train until morning, would depart as scheduled at ten-fifteen. A gentleman at the west end of the platform gave his seat to Bethany. Thomas, standing next to her, rested a hand on her shoulder. The wind, he surmised, would not change direction, and Bethany would be safely home by midnight. The aura in the sky to the east widened, brightening as the night darkened. The tips of the flames tried to lick the stars that emerged as the ever-larger crowd waited at the station.

Daughter Cordelia had returned to First Parish Church by eight o'clock with a nervous Nels Peterson, who addressed Cordelia's mother.

"I better get home, Ma'am. No telling what this fire's going to do. Oh, but of course, you'll be safe here. This church is built from granite and has weathered all of Portland's emergencies. My mother is alone, you understand, since my father passed, and I,,,"

Cordelia waved off his apology.

"We understand, Nels. You see how she's doing and bring her back if necessary. Looks like people are beginning to gather here. Our home is only five short blocks away on Wilmot Street, and Daniel's shop is two blocks further. Surely the fire will be extinguished before reaching this side of the city."

"I hope so, Ma'am. No, I'm sure. So long, Cordelia. What a strange day, I think, but thanks for the picnic basket and walk in the park. Goodbye, Ma'am."

Daughter Cordelia stopped sweeping and put the broom away in the utility closet.

"Mother, have you heard from Father or Lemuel? Weren't the Hammersmiths going to bring the boy back here an hour or two ago? Should I go fetch him, Mother?"

"We'll keep listening to these people coming to the church. Let us wait one hour for Daniel, Lemuel, and the boy to show up. We'll decide what to do next at that time. That will be at ten o'clock. In the meantime, we can help the people coming in to find a place for their wagons of belonging and feed them a cupcake. We'll stay busy until your father gets here."

They set to work, but Cordelia's glances at the clock became frequent. She anxiously anticipated the appearance of Daniel with news of Lemuel, the fire, and the boy.

Whenever Daniel turned north toward City Hall, he met the widening front of the fire, forcing him further east. The remaining citizens were in full panic now. Carts, wagons, and buggies piled high with belongings, pulled by men and women and pushed by children, scrambled to get out of the city. Women who carried family photos or bibles ran for the water away from the hot beast that hunted them.

One man driving a wagon at full speed rounded a corner a block ahead of Daniel, and his cart overturned: his possessions strewing across the street. The man jumped clear. Daniel continued.

Another large buggy crossed the intersection a half block before Daniel, belongings piled high. The driver did not realize that the rear of the carriage, hidden by his possessions, was engulfed in flames. He rushed out of sight before Daniel could hail him.

At the next turn north, a woman, still dressed in finery for the parade, saw Daniel and yelled.

"Officer, officer, stop that man. That box he is carrying is mine and valuable. If I lose it, I will be destitute. Please stop that man."

Without slowing, Daniel turned toward the man hurrying away south, carrying a box on his shoulder as he ran.

"Halt there, you. I said stop."

Daniel rode close enough to collar the man, but the man turned again and evaded capture, turning up an alley blocked by yet another overturned cart. Daniel dismounted, entering the back street, ready to run down the thief fifteen feet ahead. Grabbing his baton, Daniel boomeranged the stick at the thief's legs, hitting the man's left leg and tripping his right. The man went down with a crack of a knee, and the baton and box skidded away. The man got up, rubbing his knee, indignant.

"This is my property officer."

"I don't believe you; I have no time or use for you. The city is on fire, and you're going to jail now."

The lady who owned the box caught up to the constable and thief and thanked Daniel repeatedly. He did not have the time. He mounted Showdown and used his baton to urge the thief to speed the few remaining blocks to City Hall. He marched his prisoner inside and nodded to the duty clerk, who pointed down the hall.

"Take him to the north corner cell, Daniel, cell 15. He can cool his heels in the only cell with a window. We'll deal with him in the morning."

Daniel, glad to be rid of the idiot, reported to the Mayor, handing him Chief Tanley's dispatch.

"Daniel, unless the Chief gets a handle on this thing in the next half hour, we'll have to abandon City Hall, evacuate the prisoners and all the people who have found refuge here, and head for Munjoy Hill."

Daniel left Mayor Stevens' office with a set jaw, worried about any delay in reaching Cordelia and his family.

Thomas Willow had been known at the Virginia hospital for working long shifts without complaint during the war. He was regarded by the other surgeons as their equal, regardless of his lesser rank. Until Thomas met the daughter of Master Surgeon Kelsey Thurman at a social event in Falmouth, everyone thought him mechanical and obsessive. Bethany brought out a softer side of Thomas. He became childlike as he fell in love, and his reputation, even as a doctor, transformed into caring rather than strictly anatomical.

Now, Thomas viewed the fire raging away to the east. He wondered what resources Portland could muster to care for the victims caught too close to the fierce heat and smoke of the burning city. Cannon fire, often back-firing cannons, could cause injuries like this massive fire. Thomas squeezed Bethany's shoulder.

"Beth here is your ticket. I want you to go on home. I'm going to stay. We're starting to see people close to the fire joining this crowd. I am certain there are more and probably worse injuries out there."

"But the fire, Thomas. We've watched it for almost two hours, and it keeps getting bigger. You could be trapped. You don't know this city that well. How could you even help these people? Where would you go?"

"It's like the war, my darling. Injuries and need will find me. I must do what I can to help."

Bethany looked east at the swelling fire on the horizon. The fire stretched from as far as she could see north to an opposite point south. The wind was still strong. The fire sucked the air around the train station into its maw. Bethany shivered at the thought of Thomas heading in the same direction as the wind. Thomas could not be dissuaded. Releasing Bethany from a long embrace and after checking his luggage bag behind the ticket counter, he walked away, turning and waving to Beth from the end of the platform.

"Thomas," Beth cried out, "Wait. Please, Thomas, stop. I'm coming too."

Beth checked her bag with the ticket clerk and hurried to Thomas, intertwining and locking her arm with his.

"We do this together. I'll find some use cooking, cleaning, or sewing by your side."

"Bethany, my love, all right. We will do this together."

Silhouetted against the fire, they walked off. A man told the couple to ask along the way directions to City Hall or First Parish Church. The hospital no longer existed.

Mrs. Hammersmith laid an extra blanket on the floor between Timothy's and Bradley's beds. The only pillow available came from the parlor divan, hard and smelling musty. The boy voiced no complaints. Not doing well, his friend Timothy stayed in the parlor, crying. Although just as frightened as Tim, Cordelia's youngest son vowed to brave out the night. He focused on Bradley, the older brother, who remained calm and tried to reassure the boy.

"My dad said he'll check on the fire every fifteen minutes now. It's heading east, he says. The firemen tore down so many buildings on the north side of the fire's path that it shouldn't reach us."

The boy nodded, stuffing his hands into his pants pockets as he lay on the floor. Hang on. He listened for the sound of the front door opening and for his father to rush in. He kept thinking that would happen. The pandemonium outside made it hard for the boy to hear the conversation from the parlor or Timothy's sobs.

He thought about his mother and sister back at the church. He wished he had gone to the church that evening instead of looking for a stupid hippopotamus. *What were you thinking,* he could hear his mother admonish? *You weren't thinking, were you?*

He wondered about Lemuel and Sister Cordelia. *Were they safe? Were the four of them together? Without him? If only he could be doing something. Help in some way.*

As the minutes passed, the boy concentrated on staying quiet under the blanket. His hands were tight fists in his pockets. He would not cry but wanted Lemuel, Daughter Cordelia, or Father to come and get him.

Piling out through the front door of City Hall, the noise of the crackling fire, wind, and torrents of brick and tumbling structures deafened Daniel. For the first time, Showdown seemed nervous about the direction Daniel reined him. Daniel looked back at the wall of fire, and out of the smoke on his far right, a man hailed him, running and waving frantically. On fire? The man looked drenched in ash as he approached Daniel and Showdown. His pants and shirt offered little in the way of covering due to multiple fire burns. Red skin and blisters polka dotted the man through the holes. His hair was dark with soot; he had wisps of crispy eyebrows.

Lemuel!

Daniel shook as he recognized his son, usually a blond-haired, fair-skinned replica of himself. Instead, Daniel appraised the man, a broad-shouldered firefighter, carrying his weight and more on this fateful night.

"Are you heading home, Father?"

"I have a dispatch from the Mayor for Chief Tanley; then, yes, I intend to find Mother and your sister and brother."

"Father, I've been with a crew of sixty to seventy men using ropes and drag hooks to tear down all the wooden buildings just south of Cumberland Street. The explosions you're hearing now are from stone-faced buildings exploding; some of the crews have been hit by those flying chunks. Fire crews have blown up at least forty buildings to stop it. It keeps getting worse and growing. I came from Chief Tanley's new command post four blocks from here. It's a conflagration, he says. Don't know what that means exactly, but one three-story wooden building burned to the ground in less than ten minutes. It feeds itself in any way it can.

"I don't believe they will be able to stop it from moving through City Hall. The building may hold, but the heat of this thing can't be survived."

"You've been closer, seen more than I have, Lemuel. What are you saying?"

"I'm saying that it's down to every man for himself to survive the sweep of this thing. We only have twenty minutes to an hour before the fire reaches First Parish Church. City Hall is two more blocks east of the church."

"Yes, and our house is four blocks from the church. OK, it's time to get to the church. Maybe we can still save the shop or the house, or both. I'll go ahead. You'll be close behind. We'll decide what to do when you arrive."

"Father, you won't save the buildings. Got to save people, now. See you at the church."

Beth and Thomas walked east for two hours before catching up to the fire. The sizzling remnants of the fire-consumed city blocks reminded Thomas of the aftermath of the bombardment of Fredericksburg. Thomas had been assigned to patrol for the injured. The few people they met stared into space, unable to focus on the devastated surroundings. Thomas spoke softly to whoever they met, asking for directions and continuing. Bethany's feet blistered in her shoes, and Thomas began favoring his left knee, injured in a fall from a maple tree fourteen years ago. They headed south to the docks on the Fore River to avoid the fire.

Daniel strode into the heat of the hundred-degree church, crowded with people and piled possessions. Threading his way through the families, some who he knew as neighbors, he spotted Daughter Cordelia close by his wife. When she saw Daniel, Cordelia lost her color and sat down on a chair until Daniel picked her up, squeezing her with relief. Daughter Cordelia joined the family embrace. Cordelia freed herself with both hands and grabbed Daniel's cheeks to get his attention.

"The boy should have been here hours ago. Daniel, I'm so worried. The fire is getting so close. Have you seen Lemuel? He left for the baseball game late morning and hasn't returned."

"Lemuel is fighting the fire, but he will be here soon. I'm sure the boy is with the Hammersmiths. Doug Hammersmith can be trusted to keep him safe. Lemuel can tell us if the fire is headed toward their house."

"Daniel, that's not good enough. I need to see my boy. Go. I can't stand not knowing. He needs to be with us."

"We have other problems, Cordelia. Lemuel thinks the fire will be threatening the church in minutes now. These people must get out of here. City Hall is being evacuated as well. We've got to find someone to lead everyone north over to Back Bay if necessary. I'm apprehensive about the shop and our home. I have a plan, and when Lemuel arrives...."

"Daniel, I don't care about the house, but I've got to have my boy here with us."

Lemuel appeared, and Daniel thought Cordelia would be lost to a feint. He shook her hard by the shoulders.

"No time for that. We must get out of here. Alright, I'll speak to Frank Jefferson over there. He's single since his wife died last year. He can lead these people over to Munjoy Hill. The sight of Lemuel will get these people moving. They move their possessions at their own peril. I'll take Showdown, pick up the boy and meet you at the house. I need to stop by the shop and see what we can save. That could mean our livelihood. Lemuel, load up the wagon, and I'll hook up Showdown when I get there. We'll take what we can load up and carry down to your Uncle Samuel's ship, the *Creighton II*.

That's it. If Lemuel is correct, and by the noise of the fire out there, I bet he is, we may have only minutes to get over to the house."

Daniel spent two precious minutes explaining to Frank Jefferson his plea for evacuation. Lemuel got on a table and, by his looks, illustrated the inferno's power. People began moving at the urging of Mr. Jefferson. Cordelia, Lemuel, and Daughter Cordelia left the church, turned a corner down the block, and started running for home. Cordelia would not let go of her basket of cupcakes.

Daniel swung up on Showdown and headed northwest at a run. He cut close to the fire and heat, but Showdown did not break from his run, steadier again than before at City Hall, sensing Daniel's need for speed.

The boy sat up and scooched back against Timothy's bed, trying desperately not to break down. The boy stared intensely at a picture hung on the wall of a cowboy skidding his horse as the taut rope wrapped around the pummel reeled the long-horned steer's head high in the air, front legs, and hoofs off the ground. The cowboy's grit and the horse's power against the steer somehow helped the boy shut out the roar of the fire outside.

Suddenly he heard heavy steps rushing up the stairs two at a time, and the boy's father stopped in the doorway, his eyes adjusting to the room's dimness. The boy scrambled up and leaped into his father's arms, clinging tightly for a moment before pushing away to stand tall before him, composed.

"Your mother wants you home, boy. Got to hurry, now."

The boy ran out of the room and down the stairs, waving goodbye to Bradley. Outside, he eyed the fire blazing to the south but focused on Showdown. Daniel calmly walked right behind him. He mounted Showdown and, with one hand, grabbed the boy's wrist, pulling him up, seating him in front of him, just behind the pummel.

"Lean forward as far as you can and get a grip on Showdown's mane, boy. Hang on for dear life, boy, we'll fly."

Daniel heeled the horse into yet another run. He leaned forward over the boy, his head close, protecting him from a fall. He relaxed his hold on the reins, gently urging the horse to go as fast as he wanted.

Tears streamed from the boy's eyes from the horse's heat, wind, and swiftness. Part of his heart soared as he admired both his father's skill and Showdown's power. He had only seen Father walk his mount in parades. Never like the cowboys he heard stories about from the older boys.

Daniel slowed the horse when they approached *Martensen's Fine Hats and Accessories*. Relieved, he spotted Joshua Colter, Daniel's partner and Joshua's twelve-year-old son, loading a wagon led by a dappled grey. Daniel leaned over and shook Joshua's hand.

"Looks like you've got everything we'll need to start up again; thank you, Joshua. You too, Slim."

"Well," Joshua answered, "We aren't going to be able to bring the stove, but the felt's there, and the tools and the irons, and underneath those boxes are the work turntables. The templates are all there as well."

"Can you get this wagon to the *Creighton II* at Snider's dock? How about your house? Do you need a place for your belongings? There is plenty of space on the ship."

"We're far enough out that the fire is missing us."

"Thank goodness. We're off to save what we can from our house. Good luck."

Daniel backtracked toward the heat of the fire two blocks from his house on Wilmot Street. Lemuel, Daughter Cordelia, and Cordelia ran back and forth from their home to the wagon carrying heirloom furniture, photographs, silverware, and anything else that could not be replaced, piling the wagon high.

As Daniel dismounted and hitched Showdown to the wagon harness, he noticed the fire consuming City Hall. The smoke and heat of the conflagration reached them; the temperature rose by the minute. The whole family was drenched in sweat; still, they kept working. Cordelia breathed deeply. Lemuel looked exhausted. Daniel, an expert at hitching a horse, fumbled with the reins, his hands shaking. They had to get out of there.

The boy ran into the house after Lemuel and looked in his room for his box. It should be under his bed. He checked the closet, no, his dresser, no. When had he opened and seen it last? Ah, when he returned his tin star sheriff's badge, and yes, he had put the box back under his bed. Yesterday! He had put the box back yesterday. The carton should be in its place under the bed. He looked again. Lemuel yelled from the doorway, "Get out of here, you little fool, or be left behind."

There, the box behind his Sunday shoes. He had missed it the first time he had looked. The boy grabbed the box and followed Lemuel down the stairs.

As Lemuel and the boy passed by the parlor, the curtains in the window flashed on fire. Daniel sat in the wagon. He giddy-upped Showdown south toward the docks at a trot. The other family members ran along behind. Lemuel brought up the rear behind the boy, still carrying his box.

After ten blocks, the family was out of danger and beyond the fire. Behind them, they could see the fire continuing to move east. Smoldering buildings dominated the landscape to the west, smoke continuing to rise from the debris. At one o'clock, the family moved their belongings on the *Creighton II* and assisted Joshua and Slim with the tools of the hatter's trade from the shop. Staying the rest of the night on the ship seemed the logical choice. In minutes, Lemuel fell asleep on deck once Cordelia covered him with a blanket. Daughter Cordelia crawled into a bed in Samuel's cabin. The boy brooded over the heat of the fire and the excitement of the ride on Showdown. Thankful for the ship's safety and being with the family he admired and loved, he dropped into sleep, one hand on top of his precious box.

Thomas Willow had underestimated the walking distance they would travel to find people who might need medical attention. The extent of the destruction amazed the doctor. His pocket timepiece indicated one-forty in the morning, and the fire appeared running out of steam. Many people they passed were asleep on the dock or leaning up against cargo boxes, but none needed anything but sleep. They came upon the 'Creighton II.' Daniel hailed the two obvious out-of-towners.

"How are you. You look a little lost."

"We are from Mechanical Falls, here for the fireworks display, and decided to stay and help with the victims of this fire. I'm a doctor, and this is my wife. I couldn't convince her to take the train home, so here we are."

"You look like you could use a little medical attention and rest yourself. There's not much you'll accomplish tonight, but tomorrow will be another story. There is a second cabin down below. You'd be welcome for the night."

"We don't want to trouble you, sir. We'll go to the field hospital if you could direct us."

Cordelia also welcomed the couple.

"This is my husband, Daniel, acting constable for Portland today or yesterday, I guess. My name is Cordelia. We're certain a field hospital hasn't been set up yet. Please come aboard."

Thank you, Cordelia," Bethany said, "My name is Bethany Willow, and this is my 'always a doctor,' Thomas Willow. I hope to wear a more comfortable dress and shoes for work tomorrow."

"Yes, tomorrow will be another day of rolled-up sleeves. Welcome to our city. Did you know our city motto is 'Resurgam,' Latin for 'Rise Again?'"

The Willows were shown to their cabin, and Cordelia wished them a good night's sleep.

Daniel and Cordelia sat on the deck, his arm around her shoulder, surrounded by a blanket, smoke in their hair, clothes, and noses as the fire burned out to the east near Munjoy Hill. The broad pasture, at last, provided Portland with a natural firebreak. They could see no more fire in the distance by three o'clock in the morning. Only great clouds of smoke and steam.

"Delia, we made it. Worse for wear than many, better than some. Lucky. No house to go home to."

"A house is a house. A home is my family, Daniel, and I've been lucky to be with you and my family since you returned from Mexico. I love you. Thank you for all you do for us and for this city."

But Daniel did not hear her, already asleep on her shoulder.

On a sweltering day in the middle of August 1872, the fourteen-year-old boy sat down to a Sunday dinner celebration for his sister. Cordelia and Daniel took their traditional seats across the extra-leafed, dark maple table covered with Sunday's best lace tablecloth. Lemuel and his guest, Sarah Russell, were seated on one side, with Annie and Nathan opposite. The boy's chair hooked the corner between his father and Daughter Cordelia (who answered to Annie these days since becoming engaged to Nathan Fessenden.)

The boy had turned fourteen in July, and he knew as he spooned mashed potatoes that he would be queried yet again as to 'What his future may hold.'

He had given up telling his parents a year ago he wanted to go out west and be a cowboy. Whenever they asked now, he just shook his head, shrugged his shoulders, and thought: cowboy. Of course, he did not have a horse, had ridden one only a few times, and had never been west of the outskirts of Portland, but he still dreamed about it.

Wedding talk dominated the conversation at the table. Daniel veered the discussion to the newest hat style, and Lemuel suggested the couples walk the diagonal path to the bay through the park after dinner. Annie preferred the shadier, fresher walks along the wharf. But he listened to Cordelia and the same old song when they included the boy.

"Have you had any more thoughts? You can be the first in this family to continue your education. High school starts next month, and it's a brand-new school just for older students in upper grades. I understand they will have their own baseball team."

Daniel smiled, "What do you say, boy, school, a trade, or maybe law enforcement?"

Daniel's comment did not go over well with Cordelia.

"Daniel, the hours you keep as a watchman, middle of the night, all hours of the day and night, weekends, I don't think the boy should go in that direction."

"It's a good living," Daniel responded, "We've done well lately by it. Lemuel, please pass the potatoes."

Now Lemuel took a turn.

"I'm sure I can get you in at the store as a junior clerk in the stock room.

"Or you could apprentice with Uncle Martin. He's in his sixties but still the best carpenter in Portland. You could really help him out. His hands are often sore."

Having heard all the arguments, the boy waited a moment before giving his standard reply.

"I'm still trying to decide, father."

"I hope you figure it out soon, son."

Cordelia reinforced the need for a decision from the boy.

"Yes, we'll support your decision, whatever it is."

The boy refrained from bringing up his dream of the West.

Cordelia stood to begin clearing the table.

"We're visiting Papa Bryant today, don't forget. You're all welcome. The homestead is usually breezy due to the hill, trees, and pond."

"Mother," Lemuel said, "Sarah and I are heading back to church and then to a picnic with Sarah's family."

Nathan also bowed out.

"I apologize, Ma'am, but I've scheduled a portrait session in the park today with Brill's Photography. Perhaps we could walk over afterward."

A disappointed Cordelia, nevertheless, smiled.

"Oh, that's alright. We understand."

"Son," Daniel said, "I guess it's the three of us. How about taking our fishing poles, digging up some worms, and trying our luck with the pond?"

The boy hated fishing. Boring as hell. He would take along the book Grandpa Bryant gave him on his birthday, *The Count of Monte Cristo*. These days he felt as imprisoned as the "Count." Grandma Bryant had died a year ago, and Gramps was the oldest man the boy knew, approaching eighty years old. Ancient. Sometimes he made no sense, but the stories he told, most of which the boy thought untrue, were not dull. They were as exciting as the books Grandpa encouraged him to read.

The boy read by the pond, having made a gesture of fishing with his father that afternoon. His fishing pole leaned against the back of the bench, the hook safely buried in a cork and the line carefully wrapped around the rod to avoid the frustration of untangling. Grandpa Bryant, slow and quiet, surprised his grandson and sat close to him on the bench, leaning his cane near his elbow.

"Didn't catch anything today, I see. Is that the book I gave you last month?"

"It's great, Gramps, but I don't see how this man Dantès will ever escape prison."

"Maybe not! But maybe. It is a good book, I thought."

"Gramps, did you ever want to go west, maybe be a cowboy or mountain man?"

"Never heard of cowboys back then, but we all could have been called pioneers. The small town of Portland grew out of the ashes of the original town of Falmouth. Falmouth burned down during the bombardment by the British in the Revolutionary War."

"I know, Gramps; we learned about it in school after the 'Great Fire.'"

"We won our independence before my birth, but when I reached your age, just saying the word 'America' made me stand straighter, proud as can be. Why I must have been just a few years older than you when I fought in the 'Little York' battle up there across the big lake."

"What about that, Grandpa Bryant, a real adventure, I'll bet?"

"Yes, but no worse than what you went through with the burning of your home in the city. The years rebuilding the house, the shop, and Portland, including your school, were just as brutal as a war. You believe it.

"War is another workplace, son, a daily grind that may not end well. Rewarding a bit if it does. You don't want to run to it, but you can't shy away. Your father's father and I did our part because we were here. Your father did his part as well. I imagine when the time comes, you will be just as proud to be American and moving the world along, one way or another.

"We are done with war. Perhaps you will stretch this country out a bit. I heard some big dreams from you when you were younger."

"I don't talk about it, Gramps, but I still want to try cowboying someday."

"Ah ha! Are the folks steering you this way or that, huh?"

"They keep wanting me to decide, but when I do, they say it's no good."

"From what I read, ranching the Texas way is a quick way to die, son. Listen, I have a friend that has an estate east of here. The McMaster's place. You may have heard of it. He's a bit younger than I am, and his youngest son now runs the place. Seumas McMaster is about the same age as your mother. In fact, I'm sure they know each other, and your mother could perhaps put in a good word for you to the McMasters'."

"I know Seumas is trying to raise racehorses. Stable boy. Yes, that would get you a start, would it not? See what it is like, see if you like it at all. Lots of work, horses."

"Gramps, could you write a letter of introduction for me? That's a way to go about it, isn't it? I want to try this on my own."

"I can do that, shaky hands and all. I'll get to it now. Should have a letter ready before you leave. Now go fish with your father."

With Grandpa Bryant's letter in the inside pocket of his vest, the boy set off for the McMaster estate at six o'clock in the morning. Cordelia noticed the boy dressed in his 'Sunday Best' but did not want to spoil her son's initiative. He seemed to be pursuing his future.

The boy walked four miles across the length of Portland, and five more miles, crossing the turnpike. All the while climbing in elevation while the forest around the road thickened. The maples and birch were huge here, and the birds, crickets, and cicadas were twice as loud as in the city. Or perhaps the forest, so much quieter than the bustle of Portland, seemed peaceful. Either way, the boy could not get enough of it. The sky looked brighter, as well. Looking down and back at the city, the boy realized why. The sea breeze helped with the far east side of the town where the boy lived, but the factory smoke reached from the west end to the central area of Portland. If for no other reason than the smoke, the boy focused on the path ahead. He had experienced a lifetime of smoke during the 'Great Fire.'

The McMaster estate gate, located just off the road, could not be missed. The brick stanchions on either side of the tree-lined path held two eight-foot whitewashed wooden picket gates with wired turn-buckles for additional support. The gates were wide open even at this early hour. The boy had arrived at the gate at eight-thirty in the morning. He continued up the drive about the distance of two city blocks before seeing a large barn on the right and a long lower, one-story barn with lots of stalls for horses on his left. He continued another hundred yards to a colonial-style home with six pillars holding a ten-foot-deep porch stretching from one end to the other. The house, set at an angle to the approaching drive, allowed a visitor to see the house in three dimensions, catching the full effect of the size of the home. A circular turn of the dirt path around a ten-foot diameter fountain in front of the house completed 'the estate.' The deep green lawn was immaculate. The landscaping softened the edges of the house with large junipers and lower potentilla bushes in front of them. Yellow rose bushes dotted the grounds.

A branch in the packed dirt path led off to the side of the house. The boy assumed the footpath led to a service entry. He thought that entry was an appropriate approach for a soon-to-be 'stable boy.'

He knocked on the door, and in a moment, it opened. A girl blocked the opening who must have been somewhat close to his own age.

"Can I help you?"

"I hope so; I would like to apply for a position on the estate."

The girl leaned out the door, looking right and then left.

"Where did you leave your buggy? You didn't walk here, did you?"

"Uh, yes, I did, from my home on Wilmot St. In Portland."

"We have no jobs for a boy. I'm sorry."

"Perhaps if I could speak with the owners. Offer my services?"

"This is my house."

"Please, I'm a good worker. I have a letter of introduction from-"

"I am sorry. Goodbye."

The boy stared at the closed door but had no option but to turn and walk away. To ease his disappointment, the boy tried to remember if he had ever seen anyone with the color hair of that girl. Blond, he guessed, but kind of reddish orange. Lots of freckles, even on her neck and the opening in her shirt. He had concentrated on his smile and her eyes, but there were curves he did well to ignore.

No, he would not let this first attempt disturb his resolve. He had seen other estates along his walk. The idea of working on one of them still intrigued him. He would try them all, one by one. Many people knew the honorable Lemuel Bryant. His letter of introduction would help if he could get a chance to present it. From the shadow of the third stall, two men emerged: one tall, one short; the short man was only an inch or two taller than the boy. The tall man approached with an extended hand to shake the boy's hand.

"Whoa there, lad, are you a friend of Cynthia's? I hadn't heard that she expected anyone today. Glad to see you. She's been cooped up here for too long now. I'm Seumas McMaster, and this is Cory Hemlish, my trainer and rider."

"Pleased to meet you, sir, but I'm sure I just met your daughter back at the house. I came from Portland to offer my services as an extra hand on your beautiful property."

"Oh. Hey Cory, how about that. Weren't we saying just a couple of days ago how, with the two additional horses I just purchased, we would need more help as well?"

Cory Hemlish, not much taller than the boy, agreed with his boss.

"Yes, sir, Mr. McMaster. Well lad, what experience have you to offer."

"To be honest, sirs, I have little experience with horses. My house is on Wilmot Street in Portland, and we do not own or need a horse. I have ridden horses a few times, and once I rode with my father on a swift galloping quarter horse during the 'Great Fire.' I've never forgotten that day. I want to ride horses and learn about horses, and work with horses. That, and I want to work outdoors. Your country, here, is amazing."

"You were in the Portland fire?"

"Yes, sir. For a year afterward, I chipped grout off reclaimed brick every day for two hours after school. Then when I turned ten, and the city construction slowed, I helped my father finish the inside of our rebuilt house on Wilmot. My father had apprenticed under a ship's carpenter as a boy. With my brother Lemuel, we cleared and rebuilt our house on the old foundation. Then we finished the inside. Took us twenty-two months."

"Did you live in 'Tent City' on Munjoy Hill for those years?"

"There were thousands there, but no, sir. We stayed at my Uncle Martin's house. It hadn't burned, and he and his wife never had children, so they had plenty of room for us.

"I know I have no horse experience, sir, but I have a letter of introduction from my grandfather, Lemuel Bryant."

Seumas McMaster took the letter.

"Let me see it, lad."

> To Seumas McMaster,
>
> The operator of my dear friend Ira McMaster's estate on Croning Road, Maine.
>
> The young man before you, my Grandson, is the son of my daughter Cordelia and her husband, Daniel. You may recall they were both good friends of your older brother. I can personally vouch for this young man. He knows the value of hard work. He did well in school. He has great ambition to someday travel west, perhaps as far as Texas.
>
> Give the boy a chance, and he will prove his worth.
> Sincerely,
> Lemuel Bryant, Esquire

McMaster looked up from the letter.

"Yes, I remember Cordelia and your father, Daniel. My brother taught him how to ride. My father has developed and sold most of our former estate outside Portland. We bought these sixteen hundred acres, cleared what you see, and built the house and barns. My ambition is to raise the best thoroughbreds and quarter horses in Maine. Of course, I can't do that without good people like Cory here. We have four other ranch hands staying in the bunkhouse over the hill there."

"Would you consider me Mr. McMaster? Your daughter said there were no jobs for someone like me, but I'm sure I could learn and help you and Mr. Hemlish here."

"Cynthia has had a rough fourteen months, my boy. I fear she has retreated into her own world. She'll break free again soon. Cory, it is up to you."

Mr. McMaster nodded to Cory, who took over the interview.

"I'll put him through the paces, Mr. McMaster, and we'll see. No promises, boy."

Mr. McMaster shook the boy's hand again and returned to the house. Cory Hemlish motioned the boy to follow. They toured the barns and stables. Mr. Hemlish pointed to the hayloft high in the barn. They climbed the ladder and sat in the hay occupying one-half of the loft while Mr. Hemlish indicated the straw on the opposite side.

"You seem to have no trouble with the hay up here. If you did, you'd be sneezing a storm already. And the height doesn't seem to bother you. So far, so good."

They climbed down from the barn loft. The boy picked up two pails in front of one of the stalls, and Mr. Hemlish walked ahead of the boy, seventy-five feet, to the horse trough and well pump, where the boy filled both pails. Next, Mr. Hemlish told the boy to take the pails full of water to the furthest stall in the stable. The empty buckets were heavy oak with wrought iron bands and weighed much more when full of water. The wooden handles cut into his hands as he struggled to get the buckets to the furthest horses. He dared not set them down to rest either. He poured each bucket of water into each horse's water trough and returned the buckets to their place. The boy made sure he did not rub his sore hands together after the ordeal, attempting to show Mr. Hemlish the triviality of the task.

Next, Mr. Hemlish introduced the boy to each horse in the stable. He did not go into the stalls but stroked each horse from throat to muzzle and scratched them behind their ears. Only one of the horses, Black Lightning, shied away. The oats the boy held out tempted the horse to come forward, but at the last moment, Black Lightning reared in his stall and retreated. Cory Hemlish did not indicate if the boy performed satisfactorily on any tasks.

A shovel and a pitchfork were handed to the boy. Mr. Hemlish led Black Lightning to a holding pen from his stall, and the boy mucked the horse's stall. The shovel full the boy scooped at times dripped with manure, but the boy did not mind. He knew this would be his primary purpose as a stable boy. He climbed up a ladder to the loft and pitched fresh straw into Black Lightning's stall. When he thought he had enough straw, Daniel asked Mr. Hemlish if he should also give the horse a pitchfork or two of Hay. Cory Hemlish indicated the horse had been well-fed earlier.

Mr. Hemlish led the boy past the stable to the path leading away from the estate.

"Boy, you're as green as they come. We'll try you for two weeks. Be here at six-thirty tomorrow. Expect to work until five-thirty in the evening. I'll do the nine o'clock chores after you leave. You'll meet the other boys later. Any questions?"

"No, sir."

The boy formulated a plan to convince his father and mother that the farm on Croning Road offered an excellent opportunity for starting a career. He noted trainer Hemlish's balmoral boots, bowler, wool pants, and long-sleeve jacket. If paid, he would invest in that type of apparel. His biggest quandary was getting to the farm tomorrow by six-thirty. With such an exciting day ahead, he had no doubt he would be able to further prove himself worthy to Mr. Hemlish and Mr. McMaster.

Somehow, he must raise himself from bed at four in the morning. As he approached Portland, he veered off toward Grandpa Bryant's home. He knocked on the front door, Gramps emerged, and they both sat on the porch. Gramps in the rocking chair.

"So far, it's great, Gramps. The trainer, Mr. Hemlish, said I'm as green as they come, but thanks to your letter, he's giving me a chance. I met Mr. McMaster as well. He has a daughter about my age named Cynthia. I can do this, Gramps. I must tell Mother and Father about it next. I must get up at four o'clock and be at the farm by six-thirty. I'll do it if I must stay up all night."

"You are showing the initiative your father has been expecting; we have all been expecting. They'll approve. Say, I've got an idea. Wait here."

Lemuel Bryant entered the house and, returning, placed a box on the porch side table. The box contained his shelf clock from the mantle in the parlor. The clock stood about ten inches tall, four inches wide, and three inches deep. It had a beautiful mahogany cabinet, and the clock in the upper half of the cabinet had gold inlaid numerals. The winding mechanism and a brass gear extended beyond the face of the cabinet in the lower half.

"I imported this clock from Germany, my boy. This arrow on the front gear lets you set a time for this bell to clang on the top."

"I can't take this, Gramps; it must be expensive."

"You can borrow it, boy. Just be careful. I've read of Hutchen's clock that rings a bell at four o'clock, but with this German model, you can pick the time for the bell to ring. As you may suspect, I no longer need to look at clocks."

"Thank you, Grandpa Bryant. I'll take care of it."

He gingerly carried the box home, setting the clock on the table beside his bed. He decided not to tell his parents about the details of his job. After all, he was on trial. What if Mr. Hemlish believed he would not work out? What if he could not take the work or did not like it?

Over dinner that night, Cordelia and Daniel could hardly contain their curiosity about the boy's activities that day. They knew better than to query the boy. Their son tended to clam up when grilled. Instead, Daniel spoke of the minor incidents on his rounds as a watchman downtown.

Daniel sold his share of the hattery to Joshua Colter two years ago and returned to law enforcement. He never dwelled on the paths his life had taken. Looking back, Daniel felt fulfilled by them all. Mr. Colter had changed the name to Colter's Hattery, but the business struggled even with the reduction to one owner.

After the Great Fire, Joshua and Daniel worked weekends and nights rebuilding the shop. Lemuel and the boy worked on rebuilding Daniel and Cordelia's home under Daniel's direction. Since they had saved their tools, workstations, irons, and raw material from the fire, they could return to selling hats. With the purchase of a new, more modern stove, the company experienced only a momentary interruption.

But Daniel and Cordelia could see the writing on the wall. The bowler hat had grown tremendously popular during the civil war and afterward, fed by the expansion of the West. Daniel felt the bowler had little creative appeal. The bowler hat spurred the creation of new factories that could make them with machines instead of by a hatter at a workstation. Daniel and Joshua's shop did well for a few years as the factories worked out their processes. Most of the men in town wanted a bowler. The stylish bowler did not blow off when riding. Daniel and Joshua made them as fast as they could. They had a display in the window full of bowlers. When one sold, they brought out another from storage.

Boston, New York, and Portland factories made hats three times faster than Daniel could; therefore, they could price the bowler at one-third of what Daniel had to charge. An expert hatter like Daniel could tell the difference between a bowler he made and that made in a factory, but the man on the street could not.

Daniel had become a savvy businessman and judged the market correctly, selling to Joshua at the cusp of the downturn. Joshua could still make a living by ridding the store of accessory sales with low margins and concentrating on high-end custom top hats.

Daniel's reputation as a constable during the war, his heroics during the Portland Raid of sixty-three and again during the Great Fire of sixty-six, afforded him a choice of policeman and watchman positions. Not many in Portland knew of Daniel's Mexican/American War service. He became a member of the elite police force formed of civilians and marines after the fire. He had been invaluable as a watchman, preventing looting and catching opportunistic thieves in conjunction with soldiers assigned to enforce martial law. With what fifty-four-year-old Daniel and Cordelia had put away in savings over the years and the salary of a watchman, Daniel figured to live out their days well enough.

Cordelia had rebounded from the Great Fire as well. She had worked with Dr. Willow and Nurse Beth. The trio assisted in caring for those living in more than one thousand tents on Munjoy Hill, pitched to house residents whose houses had burned. The women of First Parish church were put to work supplying food and distributing the clothes and supplies donated from sympathetic Bostoners and New Yorkers and beyond.

The city was rebuilt at an incredible pace after the fire. The Great Fire destroyed a third of the town, but in a sense, it also leveled the social strata of Portland for a time as well. Everyone who valued the city worked together on whatever needed to be done. They got along. New relationships formed. The wealthy, insured businessman James Morris often visited Daniel's and Cordelia's house to reminisce about the fire and the city's progress. Daniel worked at the Canfiss Brush factory at a young age, so they had common ground. James had stopped in after the fire to thank Lemuel again for trying to save the brush factory. His family had rebuilt the brush factory bigger and better. Brick was used for the factories and business districts' rebuild. Wider streets that sparks could not blow across, stricter building codes, a city-wide alarm system, and a new water delivery system were just a few of the improvements after the fire. Portland soon became a great and beautiful city again.

To the boy who dreamed of the other side of the Appalachian Mountains, Portland became just where he came from. Buildings closed him in, and his parents were restrictive. Backed up to the sea to the east, to the west lay adventure and his future. The transcontinental railroad had been completed three years earlier. The railroad brought stories of cowboys and Indians, cattle, horses, and the heroes of Texas and the frontier into the homes of Portland, seemingly within the boy's reach.

He stood at the end of dinner, asking to be excused.

"I better get up to bed early tonight. I must be up early in the morning. I will be back for dinner tomorrow night."

Daniel, of course, could not help being curious.

"Oh, What's up, son? Mother said you went out early this morning as well."

"Father, mother, I have a possibility I'm working on. I'm trying not to get too excited. It may not pan out. I should know more in a few days."

"Let us know as soon as you can. We're excited for you as well. Do you need anything? Can we help at all?"

"Not that I can think of. Good night."

In his room, the boy practiced setting the gear and bell lever on the shelf clock to four o'clock. With the shelf clock set, the boy read on in *The Count of Monte Cristo* until he fell asleep.

In the morning, the bell rang out. He dressed in clean work pants, shirt, and jacket, tiptoed downstairs and began to push through the back door when he saw a sack on the table and a note:

Lunch if you need it. Good luck, Mother.

The moon, setting this morning to the west, cast a long shadow behind the boy as he hurried to leave the city. Since he carefully and softly closed the back door of his house, he had no idea about the time. He worried the clock may not have been accurate. He pressed on.

As dawn approached, the boy felt more confident of the timing of his arrival at the McMaster estate. As he came to the stable, Mr. Hemlish called out from within.

"Didn't know if you'd show, boy, but you're right on time. Let's get to work."

Mr. Hemlish opened the doors on the first and second stalls and encouraged the horses within to come forth. He guided the first horse to the aisle and then made the horse wait until the second horse approached on his opposite side. With Mr. Hemlish between the horses, he led them all the way out through the corral to a series of gates representing the four pastures where the horses would exercise for part of the morning.

Then he returned to the stable to gather the two horses and repeated the process.

"You want to provide discipline and regiment for the horses. Without it, they would break immediately for the nearest open gate. The horses are here to work for us. Run for us. They are allowed a small percentage of time to play with their herd. For the next two horses, walk close to me, and we'll see how the horses respond. Be relaxed but purposeful with your pace."

Due to the odd number of horses in the stables, eleven, the last horse, Black Lightning, walked alone to pasture with her escort. As the trainer feared, this horse displayed nervous and more skittish behavior than the rest. The boy wondered if he were the cause or if the horse always reacted this way. He felt it the wrong time to ask Mr. Hemlish in case his voice might spook the horse more. Mr. Hemlish had further instructions.

"Now muck out all the stalls down to the wood floors. I'll look in later to see if they are clean enough. After they are cleaned and scraped, mop them with hot water and soap and then rinse them. We designed the stable with these gutters and a slanted brick floor beneath the wood for drainage."

Two hours later, Mr. Hemlish returned to check the boy's progress. He still had three more stables to clean. Mr. Hemlish pointed out some corners in two of the stalls that needed further addressing, but the boy's work passed the review for the most part. Mr. Hemlish showed the boy how he wanted straw from the loft put down as a bed in the first stall. Also, how much hay to fill the manger, how to clean the water and feed buckets before filling them full of water, and the proper amount of feed.

"I'll be back when you finish all the stalls. If need be, busy yourself with the aisle here. Sweep it out and wash it down like the stalls."

At eleven-thirty, the boy finished mopping the brick-paved aisle. When he looked up, Mr. Hemlish, in the doorway at the other end of the stables, leaning against a barn post, watched him.

"Looks good, boy. Let's go over to the bunkhouse for lunch. I'll introduce you to the other men. I see you brought your own lunch. No need for that. We'll feed you. If you like Bessie's cooking, you'll be fine. If not, you'll get mighty hungry around here."

"Suits me. I could eat a horse."

The front door of the bunk house opened into a good-sized room with a dining table on the right and lounge chairs and two sofas on the left. The boy noted several bunk beds through a doorway to the left in the far wall and a second doorway on the right, presumably leading to the kitchen, where Bessie prepared the meal. She brought out three serving dishes cradled in the crook of her arm and a pitcher of water and set them in the middle of the table. Beans, cornbread, and roast beef chunks in dark gravy. After sitting for a noon meal of these proportions, the boy wondered what dinner would be like.

"Have at it, boys," Bessie said.

Four men appeared like steel to a magnet and pulled out chairs as soon as the serving dishes hit the table. Mr. Hemlish sat at the head of the table after bringing a chair from a corner of the room. He made space for the boy next to him.

"That's Jesse and then Carl. The redhead is Ben, and there at the end is Harvey. Men, this is our new stable boy. Treat him well, please; the last one only lasted a month. Bessie, you can plan on the boy for the noon meal for the next two weeks if he lasts."

The men nodded toward the boy and returned their concentration to their plates. Little of the talk at the table involved the boy. The boy assumed they believed he would not last, so why bother to get to know him. He did not mind. He ate the good food, took his turn visiting the outhouse, and followed Mr. Hemlish back to the corral. The trainer pointed to the cart the boy used in the morning to transfer the soiled straw from the stables to the manure spread.

"Take the cart out to the south pasture. I want all the dried piles picked and moved to the grinder. Ensure the piles are dry; otherwise, you have a mess in the grinder to clean."

For the next four hours, the boy systematically scoured the south pasture for horse shit, determining their state with the pitchfork and loading ready piles into the cart. When packed, he wheeled the wagon back from the field to the grinding machine and shoveled them in. The grinding crank chewed the piles into strawberry-sized chunks and deposited them into burlap sacks to be sold as fertilizer.

The boy could see the training track where Harvey and the other men exercised and groomed four horses. In the late afternoon, the men worked on training the four horses. These horses were still learning the basics, backing up, lunging, and saddle comfort.

The boy watched without interrupting his pitching. By the time Mr. Hemlish came out to get the boy at the end of the day, two blisters on the boy's left hand had bubbled.

"There's a pair of gloves in the tack house you can claim tomorrow if you return."

"I'll be back, Mr. Hemlish. I like it out here. The horses are beautiful, and I have a lot to learn."

"Help the men bring the horses in for the night. Same as this morning. Walk next to a man as he leads his horse in."

An excellent end to a tiring day. The boy could not tell if the horses adapted to his presence, but he followed directions, attempting to initiate small conversations with Ben and Carl as they led their horses into the stalls.

At six o'clock, the boy started for home, munching the sandwich his mother had prepared. When he reached the outskirts of Portland, his shins were throbbing. Fifty minutes later, he walked up his front porch stairs at home. He sat down on the front porch, exhausted. Fifteen minutes later, Mother shook his shoulder.

"Supper will be ready for you in a few minutes. Wash up. We had beef stew tonight. I made ice cream for dessert."

The ice cream perked the boy up just enough so that he could crawl into bed. Seven hours later, the bell on the clock on his side table sounded, and the boy dressed, ready to start off for the McMaster stables again.

The boy mostly shoveled shit for the next thirteen days. There were times when he helped walk the horses in and out of their stalls, and on one occasion, Mr. Hamlish demonstrated the proper steps for grooming a horse. He knew all the horses' names and some of their personality traits. Black Lightning continued to stand out as the unruliest and the most beautiful horse on the estate. On the Saturday before the two-week deadline, Ben walked Gabby, a chestnut with white stockings quarter horse, up the trailer ramp to be trucked away by Jesse. Ben ran his hand through Gabby's mane while talking to the boy.

"Didn't work out. The boss won't waste any more time on him. A foal from near Boston will arrive next week that Mr. McMaster has had his eye on."

The stable boy found that hard to believe.

"I didn't think Gabby was the fastest on the track, but he seemed like a great horse. Pretty young, wasn't he? Black Lightning is the horse that saps everyone's energy around here, and Gabby had to go?"

"Yeah, but kid, Black Lightning is the McMaster girl's horse. She trained him, such as he is. Do you want to someday be a handler? Take on that challenge. She won't go near him anymore."

"Oh?"

"The McMaster girl got bitched out by her mother one morning last April, according to Ben. He saw the girl storm off to the stables. She took it out on Black Lightning with her crop, all the way out to the track, round and back in a disgusting white lather. Never let up with the whip. I saw that nightmare display on one occasion myself. That girl won't even look at the rest of us, let alone take advice from a real handler. She only kinda listens to Cory. So, we leave her alone to ruin the horse."

"So, why doesn't she ride anymore. Is she being punished?"

"Because one day coming back to the barn, ole Black Lightning had enough. See that faded spot around that outline on the side of the barn over there? That was an iron and wood sign with the McMaster name and crest. Black Lightning paid no attention to that whip and slammed the girl into it, splintering the sign and tossing the girl high. She landed with her left leg pierced with that splinter. It took months for the surgeons to piece it together and for the infection to disappear. That's why she limps so bad."

"I've only seen her once; I didn't even notice a limp."

Cory Hemlish waited until the end of the fourteenth day to approach the lad. The boy's clothes hung like gunny sacks on his five-foot, four-inch frame. His neck looked stretched thin, and his eyes dark in contrast to the mop of long, sun-blond hair that made his hat such a tight fit.

"Well, my boy, what do you think about staying on. There is a lot more horse shit out there to shovel. You held up. The men think you can cut it around here, despite your size. The horses don't seem to mind you, and you're not jumpy around them like some men."

"I'd like to stay. Mr. Hemlish. The shit stink is nothing to me anymore; I'm so used to it. There is a lot to learn about horses from the fellas. The sky and the quiet out here away from Portland suit me, I guess

"I've got to be honest with you, sir, a few years from now, if I make good here and learn all I can, I'd be leaving for out west to start a place like this myself."

"Nothing wrong with that thinking, boy, if you keep your head in your work during your hours on the job. We can give you room and board and five a week. Every other Sunday after mucking out the stalls, you have the rest of the day off to visit your family or do what you want".

"I'll tell my folks I'm movin out here, Mr. Hemlish. Thanks."

"Alright, boy, we'll see you in the morning. By the way, I heard from Jesse you might be interested in trying to steer Black Lightning. Yes, he's unruly, very unruly, but he's got speed potential. Probably be one of the fastest here with the right attitude. He is a beautiful horse."

"I,,, I'll think about that, Mr. Hemlish. That horse is the only one that doesn't seem to care for me."

"He doesn't care for anyone, but I have yet to meet a horse that can't be turned. I can't get rid of the horse, and I don't have the time to spend on him."

The boy started walking home with a slight shake of his head, wondering if Jesse had done him a favor. If the boy failed to turn Black Lightning around, what would Mr. Hemlish say then? It could mean his job. His dream could be upended by a stubborn black horse.

The boy arrived at Wilmot St. in time for dinner. He washed up and even changed his clothes to hide his smell. The first family dinner he had attended in two weeks. Lemuel and Annie and Mother and Father did not seem to notice his presence as they recounted the events of their day.

Father asked the boy for news of his day at the end of dinner.

The boy put both hands on the table and explained.

"I have been working as a stable boy on a trial basis these two weeks. Today the head trainer offered me a permanent position, so I figure it's OK now to tell you."

Annie punched the boy playfully on his shoulder.

"You're always going on about horses around here. Congratulations."

"I knew it," commented Lemuel. "The smell from your room makes my eyes water."

Daniel beamed.

"Congratulations, son, you found a way to start. I'm proud of you. A ranch hand is a challenging, physical way.

The job description did not impress Cordelia.

"Wow, where is this job? Will you still have to get up way before dawn? What are you getting paid? So, you're not thinking of college at all? Did you accept this job? You lost at least ten pounds these two weeks. Two more weeks and there will be nothing left of you. This job must be hard for you to lose weight like this."

"Mother, I've had to get up early because I start work at six-thirty, and the stables are about nine miles away. I'll be OK. The job pays five dollars a week plus room and board. I'll be moving out tomorrow.

"What? Will you be gone tomorrow? We need to talk about this. Father, we need to sit down and talk through this. I want to make sure you've considered...."

"I've had two weeks to consider. The job is hard, I admit that, but I'm learning about horses. The owner is developing racehorses. My boss, Mr. Hemlish, is one of the best horse handlers in Maine. I'm lucky to be learning from the best.

Daniel's thoughts drifted to a vision of Sandy, his horse that had meant so much to him in Mexico. Not long ago, he had put down Showdown, his other good friend, after an ankle break.

"Sounds to me like the boy has thought this through, Cordelia. So, you're moving out. We'll miss you, son."

"I get every other Sunday afternoon off, so I can visit. Since you won't have to feed me, I should contribute two dollars a week to the family. That leaves three dollars a week for me. I need a good pair of balmoral boots, dungarees, a belt, a couple of shirts and probably a new hat, father. After that, I want to save my money."

"No doubt, son, a wide-brimmed fedora would be just the thing for out in the sun or a new bowler. I'll speak to Joshua and make you up one. I'm sure he'll let me use the shop for old times' sake. Mother, can you chop off some of the boy's hair, so I can get a measurement?"

Cordelia, more upset, raised her voice.

"I do not believe the boy is making a rational decision here. This horse thing has been a silly dream for four years. Son, you'll wake up in three weeks and wish you had listened to me."

"Maybe so, Mother, but I have made my decision. The McMaster estate is a beautiful place. You'll see when you come to visit. Then you'll understand why I...."

"What did you say? What estate?"

"It's an old friend of Gramps, Mother. Ira McMaster. His son, Seumas McMaster, buys and sells the horses. There are four huge pastures, a modern stable and barn, and a practice track, and the McMaster house is like a mansion with pillars and roses and...."

Mother rose from the table, slamming both fists on either side of her plate, catching and sending her fork flying toward Annie.

"You will not work for the McMasters. That is for sure."

Cordelia swished skirts into the kitchen and out the back door. No one spoke for minutes. Lemuel alone finished his potatoes. Father looked at the boy, and the boy looked back, closed his eyes, and then rose from the table.

"I might as well gather my things and head for Grandpa Bryant's house tonight, Father. I need to return his shelf clock. I don't understand why Mother is against me working with horses."

"The problem isn't the horses, son; it's the McMasters."

"Why Father, Mr. McMaster seems fine to me? He told me he remembered you and Mother."

"Yes, from a long, long time ago."

"I am not changing my mind. I'll stop in two weeks from now on my day off. The longer I work on the estate, the more Mother will come to understand this. I'm sure of it."

The boy packed up his belongings and left the house in less than fifteen minutes.

While walking down the block to calm her sorrow, Cordelia heard the door close. Turning, she saw her son heading down the street, waving back at her. After all these years, she had been shocked to hear the McMaster name again. With her son working for them, she worried the undertones of gossip would spread, and she would relive the drowning stories all over. She did not like horses and thought her son was far more capable of bigger and better things. And now he is gone. For the moment, Cordelia wondered if her son would ever return. She had mishandled things, she knew that, but the tension in her stomach at hearing the McMaster name would not go away.

The boy presented the shelf clock at Grandpa Bryant's house, undamaged. They talked on the front porch, Gramps swinging in his rocker, the boy filling in the details of the two-week trial by shovel the boy had endured under Mr. Hemlish. The boy wanted to know what his mother had against the McMasters. Nevertheless, Gramps, never one to shy away from long-ago reminiscences, hesitated at first.

"When your mother turned seventeen, maybe eighteen, she attended Westbrook Seminary. James McMaster, the brother of Seumas McMaster, also attended. That is how she knows the McMasters."

"Gramps, that doesn't explain why she is so upset.

"I should have told you before I sent you out there. Cordelia is my dear daughter, who has shut out that name since the accident and the funeral. After that, it took a while for her to even want to be with her friends. So, your father and I never bring it up either."

"What accident. What happened, Gramps."

"All right, I'll tell you, but it's ancient history. No one likely associates your mother with the McMaster name anymore."

"You see, your mother became engaged to James McMaster. The three of them, James, Cordelia, and your father were good friends. Your father melted with despair when James proposed to Cordelia, and Cordelia accepted that engagement ring she always wears. Truthfully, she loved your father even then, but your father swallowed his feeling, shy about such things. Women need security to get on with their lives. Let that be a lesson to you, boy. If you find the right girl, don't hesitate for anything or anyone."

"Yes, but what happened?"

Grandpa Bryant told the boy the events of that January day to the best of his aging mind's capability. For once, he thought it best to stick to the facts he remembered without his usual embellishments when telling a story to his grandson.

The boy sat entranced by what he heard and the seriousness with which Grandpa Bryant spoke.

"Thanks for telling me, Grandpa. I don't think Lemuel or Annie know about this. But then, why does she still wear that ring if it's not from Father?"

"Just because you don't talk about a thing doesn't mean you can't respect forever what happened. That terrible event affected the whole city. Your father paid his respects through that ring. It told me a lot about your father's character at the time. Regarding my daughter and your father, I can't tell you how happy I have been that they moved past that day, married, and provided me with wonderful grandchildren, you included."

"That must have been something, though, don't you think, going underneath the ice like that? Makes me shiver, now, thinking about it."

"There are all kinds of bravery, lad, believe me. Your father didn't even think about it that day. It may not seem equal, but you are acquiring a job and proving yourself to men twice your age. To me, it's the same. You come from good stock. Remember that."

The boy used the Bryant shelf clock one last time to awaken at four o'clock and head out to the McMaster estate.

Wintertime at the stables brought different chores and some easing of others. To some extent, shoveling snow replaced shoveling shit. Picking horse shit in the pasture would be left to the spring. Lanterns and stoves need to be kept lit or extinguished in the evening. The horses still needed to be exercised and groomed twice a day.

The boy had time to spend with Black Lightning and was encouraged to do so. He also took charge of the Clydesdales Mr. McMaster had purchased as part of the deal to acquire the foal from down in Boston. All the men guided the boy in his skills as a horse handler. Black Lightning ever so gradually responded to the stable boy.

When he took on Black Lightning, the boy decided to stay as close to the horse as possible, attempting to force the horse's acceptance of a friendly human. In that regard, the boy made a bed of hay in one corner of Black Lightning's stall, protected from horse hooves by a large branch the boy dragged in. He slept there almost every night, even into the winter months.

The boy mirrored the other trainers and their manner toward their horse charges. The boy scratched Black Lightning behind the ear, pulling his hand down the horse's neck and patting him on his shoulder, the boy's signature hello to the horse. He repeated it the same way dozens of times a day. The horse knew and trusted him. The boy had not ridden Black Lightning during all this getting acquainted time. He really did not mind caring for the horse. The more the boy groomed Black Lightning, the more her beauty affected him, and the more he cared for the horse.

The Maine winter wound down, and the roads cleared. Mr. McMaster's requested the boy polish and hitch up the buggy on Sunday morning, so the McMaster family could again attend church in town. He held the horse at the hitching post when Cynthia McMaster came out of the house, attempting not to call attention to her leg, limping to the buggy.

The boy took her elbow to assist with the step up, but the girl violently shook his hand away. She climbed in by herself and looked straight ahead, ignoring the boy, who could not resist his sense of politeness.

"Good morning Miss Cynthia."

Cynthia turned her head slightly in the boy's direction, forgetting her stalwart aloofness for just a second before glaring angrily at the boy and snapping her head back.

Mr. and Mrs. McMaster came out of the house. Mr. McMaster took the reins from the boy, patted his shoulder in thanks, and the family departed. At the designated time, the boy stood at the hitching post, waiting for their return to take care of the horse and buggy.

Two weeks later, the boy again prepared the McMaster's buggy for church. Same thing. The boy wished Miss Cynthia a good morning, and she again ignored him.

The boy decided to forge ahead on the third Sunday he prepared the buggy.

"Good morning Miss Cynthia. Isn't it a beautiful day? The Cardinals are singing this morning, and the breeze has died overnight. You should have a pleasant ride to church this.... "

"You are not to speak to me," Cynthia mumbled.

"Alright then, I'll enjoy this pleasant morning. I hear the cardinals, one of my favorite birds, because of their song. It is nice that the breeze died overnight. I bet the ride will be pleasant.... "

"You are not to speak at all."

"I beg pardon. Miss Cynthia, I've not been instructed to be mute while preparing your carriage ride. Ah, here comes your father and mother. Good morning Mr. McMaster and Mrs. McMaster. I hope you have a pleasant ride to church."

"Thank you, lad. Nicely polished buggy this morning. Thanks again."

The boy spat in disgust as the buggy pulled out of the driveway. *He did not like that girl.*

Spring turned to summer, and the boy rode Black Lightning now, and they were getting along as well as the other trainers did with their horses. The pastures needed picking, and the manure from the winter pile needed to be spread. His twelve-hour workdays had returned. He still spent most of his meager free time with the horse. The real trainers (trainers that scratched Black Lightning's ear with the boy's signature hello) could groom and exercise the horse without complaint.

One day, as the boy practiced lunging Black Lightning in the small coral beside the barn, he noticed Miss Cynthia watching him from the second-story window on the west side of the house, presumably her bedroom. She did not know that he knew she watched him. Over the next few days, as the boy exercised Black Lightning, he noted Miss Cynthia always stood watching from her window. Eventually, he did not look up, but he knew she stalked him.

When Miss Cynthia approached the buggy that Sunday, the boy tried again. The boy hailed the girl.

"I understand Black Lightning is really your horse Miss Cynthia. Why don't you ride him? He's a beautiful horse. Or not, your choice, of course, but you should at least come to the stable and say hi to him occasionally. He is your horse, right?"

"Yes, he is my horse, and I will do what I want with my horse."

"Yes, but what about what Black Lightning wants. I'd saddle him and help you up if you come over."

"I do not need help riding my own horse, boy."

"Then I will have Black Lightning at the hitching post at ten o'clock tomorrow."

For the next four days, the boy brought Black Lightning to the house hitching post and went away, returning in a half hour to lead Black Lightning back to the stables. After removing the tack, he shooed the horse off to pasture.

On the fifth day, just as he walked away from tying Black Lightning to the hitching post, Miss Cynthia came out the service door dressed in a riding habit. Her brown skirt and black boot covered her leg, and her limp was less evident in her determination. She went straight to the mounting block next to Black Lightning and turned around, preparing to sit side saddle. The boy advanced out of nowhere and prevented Cynthia from mounting.

"Wait, Miss Cynthia."

"What do you mean, wait? I'm going to ride my horse. Get back."

"You cannot, Miss Cynthia. Listen to me. I've been training this horse for eight months and must show you what he has learned."

The boy stepped between the girl and the horse.

"Get out of the way."

"Not until you listen."

"Why should I listen to you. This is my horse ranch."

"Are you going to listen to me or not? I don't care whose horse this is, but I trained him, and no one gets near him without learning how to handle him first. You listen to me, or you get the hell away from both of us and go back inside your big white prison box."

Miss Cynthia nearly fell as she scrambled down from the mounting platform and huffed into the house.

For the next three days, the boy brought the horse to the hitching post ready for riding, but he stayed with Black Lightning, giving the girl fifteen minutes to come out and ride before returning the horse to the stables.

On the fourth day, the service door opened, and Miss Cynthia came out, approaching the horse and the boy.

"All right, what must I know before I ride my horse."

"Certainly, Miss Cynthia. Black Lightning has been working for months on his manners."

The boy calmly grasped the girl's right wrist in his left hand and, with his right hand, took hold of the riding crop the girl clutched, tugging a couple of times until she relaxed her iron grip and released it to the boy. He hid the crop behind his back, tucking it into his pants belt, out of sight."

"Scratch his ear like this. Rub your hand down his neck and pat him on his shoulder. See that? See his head bob up. Watch one more time. OK, you try it. That's good; a little firmer pat at the end, and maybe a circular rub and another pat. That's it; see his head bob? Black Lightning says you're OK."

"That's it, that's all?"

"Spend the next fifteen minutes saying 'Hi' like that. Here's Black Lightning's brush. He likes that too, of course. Go ahead. I'll go over to the shade while you two get reacquainted."

Five minutes into the brushing and scratching, the stiffness in the girl's movements began to dissolve. After ten minutes, the boy caught the girl smiling. Suddenly, dimples appeared at the edges of her cheeks, smothering freckles. Cute when she smiled. The boy decided the girl and the horse were ready for the next step.

"He's ready to ride, Miss Cynthia if you're of a mind. Otherwise, he seems to be enjoying what you're doing."

"What will he do when I mount up? I need my crop in case he tries to bolt."

"You pick up that crop, and he will bolt, Miss Cynthia. Maybe groom him today. When you have the confidence to get on a horse without holding that crop, Black Lightning will also be ready.

The girl decided to continue grooming. The boy fetched Black Lightning's other brushes and combs, and together they groomed the horse for another half-hour. Afterward, the girl set the curry comb down on the mounting block and returned to the house. Nary a thank you nor a smile of appreciation was shown toward the horse handler. He thought *I do not like that girl.*

The boy continued to learn the ways of a horse ranch. He worked hard, awfully hard, but he ate well, growing taller and more muscular. His mother had long since recovered from the McMaster connection. The women's circle at church never connected her son's position to that long-ago accident. The boy visited his family and Grandpa Bryant on his days off. He would tell them about his new skills and accomplishments with Black Lightning. The money he saved contributed to the family's welfare, and the boy spent frugally on clothes and equipment needed for his work.

As the weather turned colder and the snow returned, the boy stayed on the estate, but in December, the boy trudged through the snow for Annie's wedding celebration.

The First Parish church pews held nearly two hundred fifty friends and relatives that day. The boy wore his new boots and purchased a suit coat matching his vest. He ushered the ladies to their seats.

To his surprise, Mr. And Mrs. Seumas McMaster and their daughter Cynthia stepped down from their sleigh as it pulled up to the church vestibule. The boy held out an arm for Miss Cynthia. She had dressed in pink finery, and as she took off her bonnet, her reddish blond hair framed a face still freckled but rosy-cheeked from the cold. For his part, his suit startled Miss Cynthia. She was surprised that he now stood two inches taller than she remembered. His arm bulged the suit coat as she slipped her gloved hand around.

On December 9th, 1873, Cordelia Ann and Nathan Fessenden were happily wed.

The boy never approached Miss Cynthia at the reception, and she ignored him as well. At one point, his mother and father conversed with the McMasters. Grandpa Bryant caned over to the McMasters and shook their hands. Seeing these efforts at socializing among the people in his life pleased the boy.

The years on the McMaster estate began to blur for the boy. Mr. Hemlish assigned more horse-handling tasks and expected him to handle harder and more strenuous farm chores.

In the spring of seventy-four with his workhorse, Molly, he plowed, mulched, floated, and planted ten acres of alfalfa in addition to his mucking duties. That September, beginning two weeks before his brother Lemuel's wedding to Sarah Russell, the boy worked with the crew on the third cut of the field. After the wedding and the wheat field baled, he moved the hay to the loft.

As the boy grew taller, the estate expanded as well. More horses were purchased, and another five acres were cleared of maple trees beyond the west pasture for an additional track. The clearing had been back-breaking winter work in seventy-five. The boy struggled to lift his axe at the end of the first day of chopping. Twenty-three trees later, with shoulders as broad as the maples he chopped down, it swung like a hammer. When spring broke, the boy and two workhorses used the stump puller to finish clearing the site.

In seventy-six, around his eighteenth birthday, he accompanied Cory Hemlish and Ben on a trip to the Lancaster Races in Massachusetts. They were scouting horse heritage, trying to determine which stable raised and trained the most competitive horses among the various horses shown. The techniques on the training track were examined, down to crop use and design of the saddle stirrups.

Cory Hemlish gave his notice to leave the McMaster's estate for another horse ranch in Massachusetts a few weeks later. Ben also called it quits, acquiring a new position at the same stable as Cory Hemlish. The boy could not believe his friend Ben.

"Ben, I thought we'd leave together one day. Start our own ranch in Kansas or Nebraska."

"Yeah, we talked about that kid, but this is a good opportunity and a pay raise for me. I've worked for other trainers over the years, and Cory Hemlish is worth following."

"We'll miss you two around here, that's sure. Maybe I'll look you up in a few years, and we can still give a try out west together."

"I'd be okay with that. Can't hardly call you a boy anymore by the look of you.

"I'll be seeing you."

The boy said goodbye to Cory Hemlish.

"I want to thank you for giving me a chance to work here, Mr. Hemlish. I'd still be trying to figure out things if it weren't for you. I've learned from you, sure."

"The name's Cory, son. No more Mr. Hemlish. A good hand will always be a friend of mine no matter where I'm at; believe me, you're a good hand. Thanks for all the work you accomplished here. The estate has your mark on it as well."

"Thanks, Mr. Cory. I'll miss you and Ben both."

Mr. McMaster ran the crew for the next month, so the boy worked under his management until he hired a new head trainer, Joseph Conklin. In the boy's opinion, Conklin, younger than Cory Hemlish, did not manage as well as Mr. Hemlish. His horse skills were evident. Perhaps because of his age, he tried to be harsher and more particular about the length of time tasks needed, as well as start and stop time for breaks and meals. Conklin, a man in his late twenties, established his authority, but all the hands found it difficult to adjust. Grumbling increased.

For whatever reason, Conklin's crosshairs focused on the boy, perhaps to set an example. The more the boy excelled in meeting Mr. Conklin's expectations, the gruffer the man became toward the boy. The boy began to plan his departure from the estate in earnest for the first time.

That summer, Cynthia McMaster, home from finishing school, showed up wherever the boy worked to ask a question about Black Lightning or the progress of the new track. Civil to the boy these days; it irked him. When she approached, he would stop, lean on the pitchfork, in the middle of a good sweat, to answer her questions. Invariably, Mr. Conklin would appear around the corner of the barn and yell at him to get to work.

At the end of the summer, Mr. McMaster hired a new stable boy, elevating the boy to the status of head horse handler.

In the spring of seventy-seven, three men and the boy gathered around Mr. McMaster and Mr. Conklin. Mrs. McMaster had hired a garden designer to draw plans for a pond to be built east of the great house beyond the fountain. A natural spring about one hundred and fifty feet up the slope behind the house could provide water. The crew would need to dig out an area fifty feet by thirty feet in the shape of a kidney bean. The basin must be packed with clay and lined with stones and boulders found and gathered during the track clearing. The dammed spring would fill the pond. The runoff after the dam would allow the water to continue to the creek. Benches and a picnic table were planned at the pond's edge. A winding path, edged with additional yellow rose bushes, leading to the big house would complete the project.

The crew dug the basin. The boy hitched his workhorse to the big wagon to haul the dirt away. A contractor brought the clay in from the foothills north of Portland; to be tamped by the boy. Two inches of gravel covered the compacted clay. By summer, the reduced pond crew consisted of the boy and Molly for hauling the rocks and the boulders to the pond's edge.

Curiously, Cynthia McMaster, home again from school, appeared daily to sit on the wood and iron bench Mrs. McMaster had ordered built by a blacksmith in Portland. After a week, she brought a pitcher of cold water or lemonade and a couple of cups. The boy would come over to the bench, take a cup full, drink it, and return to work. The two were so close that the boy felt obliged to comment on Cynthia's attire or her bonnet to be polite. The conversation was kept to a minimum. Cynthia's questions or comments about the pond, while he tried to concentrate on lifting or maneuvering a large rock drove the boy crazy. On this summer day, Cynthia didn't have a question; she stated, "Black Lightning seems to have forgotten his manners again. Tomorrow I want to take him to the track while you ride with me to observe."

"Miss Cynthia, you've been away for the winter. Black Lightning needs some time and patience, and he'll be fine. I really have too much to do. I have the new yearling to exercise and groom, and this pond is a priority with your mother. Her garden club has been invited to the unveiling next month. It must be done by then, and the seeding and planting are scheduled for Thursday, and these rocks have to be in place by then.

"I've already spoken to Mr. Conklin, and he has agreed to my plan."

"Really, he hasn't mentioned anything to me."

"He seems to want to do anything he can for me. He helps me every day with Black Lightning. He has him saddled and helps me up at the mounting block for my morning ride like you used to."

"He's head trainer. You should really ask him to help you with Black Lightning."

"Oh, he admitted you knew the horse better than anyone. He is fine with you taking the time."

"I guess that's it then. I'll check with Mr. Conklin and bring the horses around at eight o'clock tomorrow. We'll have the track to ourselves for a couple of hours. That way, we can isolate Black Lightning's behavior. Now I must get on with levering this boulder next to the big one over there."

The boy stared at her, willing her back into the house, but she continued to sit quietly. Over the past year, Cynthia McMaster had filled out; the prettiest girl he had ever seen. He really had no friends on the estate since Ben had departed. One year older than the handler, Cynthia seemed to want to befriend him. He noticed her speaking with Joseph Conklin on many occasions, assuming, as a McMaster, she required something. She still treated the rest of the crew like dirt. At least she no longer mistreated Black Lightning.

Her freckles had thinned, but her hair still held that reddish-orange tinge amongst the blond. Full in bust and bustle and thin at the waist, the boy could not imagine how she breathed in the corset she wore.

On the other hand, he would extend his reach when offered a cup of water so he would not drip sweat on her. He knew he reeked like a working hand; OK with him. He wondered how many boys followed her around at school like puppy dogs. Then again, no one ever came to the house calling for her. Girl or boy. Surely her limp could no longer be a barrier in her social circle. She was beautiful.

The boy checked in with Mr. Conklin.

"I guess Miss Cynthia spoke to you about me riding with her on Black Lightning to see how he's doing."

"That's right. Go ahead. It's hard for me to say no to that woman. I must admit, she's got me wrapped around her finger. Has she mentioned me at all? One of these days, I'm going to say something to Seumas. She could do worse. A top trainer is not a bad match, do you think?"

"I don't think the leg would bother me," exclaimed Conklin, "Have you ever seen it?"

"No, I have not. More power to you, Mr. Conklin. I'll get the horses ready."

Black Lightning performed well on the uneventful ride that morning, as the boy suspected he would. The boy sat on the fence while the girl rode around the track. Miss Cynthia and the boy traded horses for a while. He helped Cynthia up on his horse without using a mounting block. Her leg was stiff and gnarled underneath the riding skirt. He did not say a word about it, but she looked down at him with a curious, questioning look. He blanked back at her as if to say nothing abnormal had occurred. After the boy rode around the track a few comforting turns on Black Lightning, the boy and the girl switched mounts again.

The sky had darkened, threatening rain, so the boy indicated he needed to get to work on the pond, and they had better get back to the stables. The girl looked to the western sky and kept riding, ignoring the boy's warning. Five minutes later, the light rain became a downpour. Setting the horses into a gallop, they headed to the closest building, the tack shed at the other end of the track. Black Lightning outdistanced the boy's mount by two lengths, but the girl waited for him to skid to a stop, so he could help her down. They rushed into the shed. She took her top hat off and shook her hair loose. She removed her jacket, hung it on one of the saddle pegs, turned to the boy, hugged him close, and rubbed his back.

"I'm freezing; rub my back to warm me up."

The boy was caught off guard. He kept his arms and hands away from her, not about to rub her in any way. However, she locked on to him, and he could not decide how to get away in such close quarters.

Next, the girl, her face burrowed into the boy's chest, looked up at him, raised herself on her tiptoes, and kissed him hard.

The boy's head snapped back, out of balance. The girl pushed him against a post and kissed him hard again.

Finally getting over his surprise and shock, he took her by both shoulders and pushed her back and away.

"Miss Cynthia, we must get out of here."

"Cynthia, call me Cynthia."

Astonished, the boy watched the girl unbutton her shirt, soaking wet from hugging him.

"I'm getting out of these wet things. You should too."

The boy had never seen the girl move so fast. She had somehow gotten her boots off. Now she removed the riding skirt, quick as a blink. She spread it on the hard floor, presumably to dry. Cynthia stood before him in her combination camisole and bloomers. As she bent over to smooth out the skirt, the low scoop of her camisole revealed a lush breast and dark extended nipple.

"What are you doing, Miss Cynthia?"

"My name is Cynthia, just Cynthia. Come over here and kiss me."

"I can't do that, Miss Cynthia, you know it."

She paused, cocked her head, and looked at the boy with lowered eyelids, "I'm not pretty enough, is that it?"

"You are beautiful, Cynthia, you must realize. You're lovely. Your hair, your eyes, and those freckles? I'm no saint, girl. Put something on, and let's get out of here."

Cynthia's cheeks crimsoned, and her wet eyes glistened.

"It's the leg, isn't it? You can't stand my ugly twisted leg, can you?"

This was too much for the boy. Standing before him, this girl, overpowering him with her beauty, was causing an excruciating dilemma. *Truth be told, he did not even like her that much.*

He withered.

"What leg!!! Come here."

Cynthia crossed three steps to the boy, hugged the breath out of him, and at the same time, pulled his head down and kissed him as hard as before. She tried to eat away years of despair over her leg and limp, the rejection by all who watched her walk, forcing the boy to want her and take her.

For his part, the girl had brought forth a shiver of needles in the boy's chest, groin, and lips that now could not be upended. The girl kept trying to squeeze the boy's biceps and dig into his back as they kissed, amazed at the strength of the boy and the width of his back and shoulders.

Cynthia pulled the boy's shirt up until it swaddled above his chest. He unbuttoned the top button and drew it off, Cynthia being too short of reach to pull it off by herself. While he discarded his shirt, Cynthia wriggled out of the combination top, baring breasts wet from rain and sweat and moving to kiss him again.

Her breasts and nipples squashed against the boy as she hugged and kissed him, pulling him back toward the splayed skirt on the floor. As they kissed, the fever in his head and the coolness of the girl's hands gently holding his cheeks paralyzed the boy. He tried to think through the ecstasy of the moment, to remember the campfire stories of the older men. At the same time, he remained respectfully gentle with the creature he held, so easily crushed.

Cynthia broke from him and, with both hands, tried desperately to unbutton the wool pants that kept scratching her. Failing that, she reached inside the boy's pants to handle his cock. Her hand seemed ice cold. She eased the fire there, yet her touch urged him to want more. He stepped back again and unbuttoned the first button of his pants.

The door to the tack shed opened with a swing in the wind. Joseph Conklin, water dripping from his broad-brimmed hat and the hem of his mackintosh, stared, eyes widening. Then he cocked his head in disbelief. A second mackintosh hung over his arm, folded carefully to prevent the inside from getting wet, presumably to help Miss Cynthia get home in the rain.

"Miss Cynthia, I brought this...."

While the boy looked first to Conklin and then to Cynthia in a blinking display of indecision, Conklin shook his head, clearing his thoughts.

"I'll close this door, and you two get dressed. I'll give you one minute. Then we're heading for the house. Mr. McMaster will tan both your hides. You can bet on that. Here's a Mac for you, Miss Cynthia. You, boy, deserve a soaking."

Conklin closed the door, and the boy scrambled into his shirt, tucking it in and arranging himself. Halfway through putting on her skirt, tears began to run down the girl's cheeks. Her breath caught on every sob, but she refused to display fear, rejection, or outright despair. Perplexed by the girl over the years, the boy, for the first time, respected the girl.

She just barely managed to look put together when the door opened again.

She did not put on the Mackintosh; the rain had let up some. Instead, she breezed past Conklin without a word, mounted Black Lightning using the mounting block attached to the shed, and surged with a gallop back toward her house with a kick of her right heel.

Conklin and the boy trotted back to the stables in silence. They hitched both horses in the stable aisle and headed toward the house. Before Conklin could knock on the door, Mr. McMaster opened it, stiff with anger.

"Come into the office, both of you."

Once in the office, Mr. McMaster went to his desk chair but did not sit. The boy stood in front of the desk, hands at his side. Conklin sidled to a corner, leaning against the wall, his arms folded. McMaster placed both fists down on the blotter on his desk. He looked down at his desk, then at the boy, looking up and leaning over the desk. Then he changed his mind and motioned Conklin to follow him into the adjoining room. A minute later, they both emerged and resumed their previous positions in the corner and behind the desk. McMaster again leaned over his desk, staring at the boy. The boy did not flinch. McMaster, tense, spoke with spit.

"There is only one reason you are not swinging from a tree, boy. My daughter told me what happened. She says that she was at fault. I can't describe my disgust for you. The years you have been here. The opportunities I have given you. My, God, the trust that I have shown you. You touched my daughter and on my own property. I don't care what she says; you disgust me."

"I don't know what hap-"

"Shut up. I can't take hearing your voice. Conklin says your fucking pants were still buttoned when he arrived, thank God. If you had soiled my daughter with your slimy worm, you'd be looking down my shotgun barrel now."

The boy found a fountain pen on the front of McMaster's desk to stare at. McMaster changed his mind yet again and left the room. The boy heard raised voices from deep in the house. He thought one of them was Cynthia's.

Suddenly the office door opened, slamming the wall, and McMaster stormed through, rushing around the desk. The boy now saw the riding crop McMaster had hidden at his side. He raised it high and swung down as the boy instinctively ducked. The boy's shoulder stung after the full-force blow. McMaster raised the crop and swung again, hitting the opposite shoulder near the boy's neck. The leather popper flicked a cut to his cheek. The pain settled into the boy's shoulders and face. He bent forward and grabbed the edge of the desk with both hands, bowing his head between his shoulders. He clenched his teeth, prepared.

McMaster swung five more times across the boys back; settling on a line across the shoulder blades; each swing intensifying the pain, deepening and widening the bleeding welts. Then came a blow across the boy's lower back that broke the crop. McMaster looked at the crop remaining in his hand and threw it in the corner of the room, spent.

"Get out of here. I want you off my property within five minutes. I'll hunt and kill you if I hear rumors about you and my daughter. Go on. You better move faster than that. The same goes for your silence, Joseph. This matter stays in this room."

"Yes, sir, Mr. McMaster. I'll see to it."

The boy, unbending from the desk, found strength in the relief from the blows. The pain spread across his back with each step. He turned, straightening to his full height and without looking at either McMaster or Conklin, retrieved the broken riding crop, walked through the hall, and out the front door. Not to be hurried. Upon reaching the stables, he glanced back and up, finding Cynthia watching from her bedroom window. As he passed the stable aisle, he glanced at Black Lightning among the horses tied to the hitching rail. The horse bobbed his head, turning to watch the boy walk away.

He stopped at the bunk house, sacked his meager personals, including the picture of his mother and father, and headed down the drive. The pain eased somewhat. He looked ahead down the road and up at the sky. Only one thought pierced the relief of the fresh rain, the brightness of the sunshine in the rain's aftermath, the sway of tree branches, and the songs of birds flitting by.

I do not like that girl.

Turn the page for an excerpt from:
RADIOMAN
In Book II of the Martensen chronicles, Charles' son Harry continues the dream of building and working on Charles' farm on the Saskatchewan prairie. World War I, the Spanish Flu, and extreme weather provide additional tests to the hardship of living a rural lifestyle.

The Gardener grows tall in the final section of Book II and must navigate the challenges of the Great Depression and World War II.

HOMESTEADER

Ants, like most small insects, are rather potent. They can lift three times their body weight and dangle while holding one hundred times their weight.

1883

Shifting from one job to the next, the drifter became known by his name, **Charles Martensen.** No ranches or farms in Cumberland County would hire Charles. Seumas McMaster somehow saw to that, his reach wide and influential. Charles found work after the estate at a sawmill north of Portland. He worked for six months, swinging an axe and floating logs. Then a load of trees came into the mill from the McMaster estate directed by Joseph Conklin, who saw to his dismissal. Charles drifted from lumber camp to lumber camp. Sometimes he lasted four months. At the Kendrake Sawmill, he lasted eight months before McMaster heard he lumbered there.

Charles did not mind the drift. The high pay in the camps allowed him to save money. The axe turned his arms, wrists, and hands to stone. Mindful of the imminent dangers of logging work, not where he pictured himself in the long run.

After five years, Charles had exhausted the opportunities in most of the logging camps in the territory. He found a job as a laborer on a farm just over the border in Massachusetts. The widow Sellars appreciated the quiet man with the strong back who never took his shirt off. The farm was so remote Charles had no fear of McMaster's reach. He learned more farming techniques from the widow and her two sons in their late teens. The widow had a great crop year and then a rotten, too rainy, too cold second year, and she had to let Charles go.

In 1883, upon turning twenty-four, he had saved enough money for a stake and fare to head west on the train. Since the age of eleven, Charles had reveled in the stories about the transcontinental railroad's completion and the striking of the golden spike. He planned to stop in Chicago, a thousand miles west, for advice from Uncle George, by then a prominent businessman in Chicago. His goal: Nebraska farmland or perhaps California.

Reaching Indiana on the last leg of his train trip, kidneys jostled and bladder full, Charles turned in his seat, looking for directions to the toilet. He became distracted by the eyes and hat of a woman just tall enough to peer over the headrest at Charles. Charles moved over in his seat toward the window. Able now to discreetly glance around, he caught more than a glimpse of the petite woman watching towns rush by out the window.

Charles noted a pleasant profile, a nose just a little long but balanced by a delicate chin and forehead. Her clothes were prim, and her hat was not outrageously ribboned. As if sensing his stare, the woman turned in his direction, garnering further approval. The woman sat straight-backed on the wooden train bench. The rolling and bumping of the train bothered the woman not a whit, further impressing Charles.

After disembarking at Great Central Station, Charles emerged at the new cable car pavilion on Michigan Avenue. He searched for the carriage and driver supplied by his Uncle's company and prearranged by telegraph from South Bend. By chance, he saw the woman from the train, dress blowing in the chilled Chicago wind, rain dripping from the small, clutched parasol. Charles walked up to the woman, set down his satchel, and dug out his dress wool shirt, snapping it in the wind and draping it over the shoulders of the woman.

The woman, startled and purple-lipped, turned to Charles, smelling the shirt on her shoulder. The smell was not unlike the scent of a hug from her father coming in from fieldwork back on the farm. She did not hesitate, slipping her right arm into the shirt sleeve. She did the same with the left arm, Charles helping to overcome the puffed sleeves of her blouse. She fastened the faded brown shirt button at her midriff, paying no heed to the frayed hole in the shirt at her right elbow. Charles, eyes focused on the buttoning, shivered and raised his eyes to her face. Julia, one eyebrow raised, smiled.

"Thanks."

"My name is Charles Martensen."

"Mine is Julia Swart. You were on the train, weren't you?"

Charles's heart fluttered; she had noticed him.

"Yes. Are you waiting for the cable car?"

"Yes, I'm heading to my Cousin's house in Oak Park."

Charles knew little about Chicago, but his Uncle resided in Oak Park. A carriage pulled up, and the driver held up a sign. Charles, intently peering down at the woman at his side, did not notice the sign.

Julia did notice, however, and waved to the driver, placing a hand on Charles' shoulder.

"This is Charles Martensen, driver; he is new to the city."

Charles looked up.

"Yes, sir, we are headed for Oak Park; we'll give the lady a ride and get her out of this wind."

Charles gently took her elbow and helped Julia into the carriage. She handed a card to Charles. The card contained the names and addresses of her aunt and cousin. Charles, in turn, handed the card up to the driver.

The driver, Winslow, chatted with both riders as he snicked the reins occasionally to turn the carriage. Upon arriving at her aunt's home, Charles helped Julia and said goodbye. He watched her turn and walk toward the house, skirts still billowing, her bustle swaying to the measure of her walk. She stopped after twenty feet and turned back to Charles.

"Let me return your shirt."

Charles held up the address card, waving it so she would see his intention.

"I will return for it on a warmer day."

Julia smiled and turned back toward the house. Winslow waited until she had entered before turning his horse and trotting off.

www.ingramcontent.com/pod-product-compliance
Lightning Source LLC
Chambersburg PA
CBHW060516220726
48290CB00015B/1566